The Chenille Ultimatum

Ann Anastasio

and

Lani Longshore

A Russian Hill Press Book
United States • United Kingdom • Australia

 Russian Hill Press

Cover image courtesy of © Gelpi and Can Stock Photo
Cover Art: Joleene Naylor
Cover Design: Christine McCall

LCCN: 2017961815

ISBN: 978-0-9995162-2-5

Dedication

Ann dedicates this book to Michael, Alison and Robbie, and Alexandra for their continued support, despite their incredulity about the genre that we have invented.

Lani dedicates this book to Stewart, Meredith, and Alexander for laughing at my jokes.

Also by Ann Anastasio and Lani Longshore

Death By Chenille

When Chenille Is Not Enough

Acknowledgments

The Chenille Ultimatum is the third book in the Chenille series. We are grateful to our friends and family for continuing to encourage us.

Lani's two critique groups have gently pushed us to become better writers. Thanks to Jordan Bernal, P.C. Chinick, Marlene Dotterer, Neva Hodges, Edward Miracle, Violet Carr Moore, J.K. Royce, and Elaine Schmitz for your comments, instructions and patience. We are very grateful to Linda Todd, our editor, for her sharp eye and gentle manner.

Ann's quilting friends, especially Gale Oppenheim-Pietrzak (co-producer of Art Quilt Santa Fe), have been generous in their support of our novels and the first ones to ask when the next book will be out.

We also wish to thank Evelyn and Richard Judson who gave us a title for a fourth book, *The Captain and Chenille*. Don't say we didn't warn you.

The Chenille
Ultimatum

ONE

Susan and Gary heard the ship land ten seconds before the egg-shaped transport pod appeared between the garden shed and the pear tree. They watched the ship reveal itself as they drank margaritas on the patio. The pod's silvery top reflected dancing lights on the tin roof of the shed, like tiny auroras. The leaves of the tree curled in the heat, and the faint smoke smelled of roasted pear. A whisper of warmth swirled about them as the evening breeze rose. The scent of flowers and grilling food from neighborhood backyards surfed along the air currents. "So this is summer in the suburbs," he said, squeezing her shoulders.

"Same as every year," she said. "Except for the alien spaceship."

He tilted his head and considered the craft. "It's smaller than I expected."

Susan tugged on a lock of her blonde hair and bit her lower lip. "Cecily said it was cozy inside, but I hoped for something bigger than a delivery van."

"Don't disparage delivery vans. I used to make my living driving something that size."

"How could I forget?" Susan said, smiling into his dark brown eyes. "I only met you because my quilt shop was on your route."

They strolled toward the ship, looking like weekend gardeners inspecting new plants at the nursery. Susan tapped the hull with her fingernail.

"No one is inside," Gary said. "They're parked on the dark side of the moon in the mother ship."

Susan stroked the cooling metal. "I wish Cecily had come back with the pod."

"And run the risk of being sent off to the farm with her sisters?" Gary asked. His eyes twinkled.

"Cecily loves my brother's place. She always talks about the summer she spent there."

"She's your daughter, and Edna's granddaughter. Given a choice between two months in Northern California watching heirloom tomatoes grow or stopping a civil war on an alien planet, what did you expect she would do?"

Susan grimaced. "She'd stay on the big ship and practice target shooting. I'm just glad Olivia and Eleanor are young enough to do as they're told. They'll have a wonderful time on the farm. And they'll be safe, with their cousins."

They turned their heads toward the crescent

moon. A frog croaked in the distance. The communication device that Cecily had left with her mother before heading to the stars with her grandmother and a shape-shifting alien glowed on the patio table.

"Are you going to get that or should I?" he asked.

She rotated her shoulders down and back, stiffening her backbone. "I can do this." She reached the table in two strides. Except for a pulsing orange square on the screen, the device was unobtrusive—black, close enough to plastic for a casual glance, and small enough to be mistaken for a computer tablet. "Hi, sweetie," she said, "the pod is here."

"Great," Cecily said. The image of her face broke apart into pixels, coalesced again and came into focus. Her tousled hair, with dark brown roots giving way to fading purple curls, formed a halo around her face. "It didn't attract any attention when it materialized, did it?"

"No, the one neighbor's trees block that view, and the others aren't home yet." Susan picked up the device and spoke as she walked into the kitchen. "Just in case anyone is listening at the back fence, I'm taking you inside."

"Grab some paper while you're at it," Cecily said. "I want to go over the procedures one more time. The communication device will open the door once you've entered the correct code, but the security protocols limit the number of tries you get."

"Sweetie, I think I can type in a few numbers."

Cecily pressed her fingertips against her temples. "It's more complicated than that, Mom, and I know how you hate computers."

Gary rested his hands on Susan's shoulders for a moment then eased her into a chair. He slid the device from her hands. "While your mother decides how to answer your insult to her technical skills, bring us up to date. Have you heard anything more about Edna and Scott?"

"Yes. Maybe. We're not sure." Cecily turned toward a gurgling sound somewhere between a growl and a whine. "Bozidar, hush. We've got plenty of time before they need to take off."

"Hi, Bozidar," Gary said. "Say, do you still look like a human, or were they able to reverse that once you got home?"

Cecily held up her hand to the screen and shook her finger. "Let's not talk about that now. The reversal procedure didn't work. He's a little sensitive." She turned to the side again. "Stay where you are. You don't need to talk to them. Relax, I've got this." She faced the screen and clasped her hands at her chest. "Okay, here's what we know. Grandma Edna is in hiding. The beige clan still wants her to be the queen and lead the army against the blue clan. Scott was captured, but we expect him to be treated well. First off, he's Edna's husband, so that makes him royalty as well as a hostage. Second, the beiges have figured out that Scott's the only one who can come close to making Edna behave so it's in their best interest to keep him happy."

"How do they expect to do that if he's a prisoner?" Susan asked.

"I have no idea," Cecily said. "It wasn't clear to me how he was captured. I'm thinking maybe he surrendered and is trying to negotiate a deal for them both to be sent back to Earth."

"If that's true," Susan said, "maybe you should come home and let Scott take care of things on Schtatik."

"We considered that option," Cecily said. "Bozidar thinks we should prepare for the worst."

"And what do you think?" Susan felt a fluttering in her stomach, and her skin tingled.

Cecily compressed her lips. "I'm not sure, but it feels like we missed something."

"Missed something? Like a clue to a puzzle?" Gary asked.

"No," Cecily said. She grabbed her hair below her ear. "It feels like we missed a weapon."

The tingling feeling on Susan's skin spread inward toward her gut. The image of her family heirloom, the crazy quilt her great-grandmother Agnes had made, flashed through her mind. "We need the crazy quilt," she said.

"We need the crazy quilt," Cecily said at the same time.

Gary sucked in air with a force that made him sputter and cough. "Are you having visions of Agnes again?" he asked, his voice raspy and worried.

"No. Maybe. I don't know," Susan said.

"But you feel it, Mom, right?" Cecily asked. "That sense you can't explain or deny that all three of us have to be together, on Schtatik."

Susan nodded. "Yes."

"Good. Let me give you the codes to open the hatch and initiate the return trip."

"No."

A wailing screech from somewhere off-screen filtered through the speakers of the communications device. Cecily's head drooped, and she covered her ears with her hands. The tinny cry rose, and Bozidar shoved Cecily out of the picture. His mouth was open, showing beautiful white teeth. His features softened, and his skin glistened like hot caramel sauce.

"Do not torment me! You are needed here. You have promised to come. Get in the transport, now! You may argue with your offspring later," Bozidar yelled.

Cecily patted his shoulder. "Get some rest, Bozidar. You know what the doctor said about stress." When he wandered away, muttering, she said, "I have to agree with him, Mom. Why wait?"

"First, I want to know more about the plan. Second, I need to tell you some important news."

Cecily rubbed her eyes and said, "Fine, we'll do it your way. What's the important news?"

"Gary is coming with me."

"No! Not one more human than is absolutely

necessary!" Bozidar shrieked.

"Let me handle this," Cecily said over her shoulder. "Gary, you were a huge help when the aliens came to Earth, I can't wait to see you marry my mother, but I've got to go with Bozidar on this. The situation changes minute by minute, and there are already too many people involved."

"I'm not leaving my husband behind," Susan said.

Silence was Cecily's only response for several breaths. She opened and closed her mouth twice before words emerged. "You had the wedding already? But Grandma Edna and I had so many plans."

Susan arched an eyebrow. "Did you hear yourself?"

Gary leaned over Susan's shoulder. "We wanted a quiet ceremony, although we're open to having a party when the whole family is back together."

"Are you saying I get to plan the party?" Cecily asked.

"You can be involved," Susan said.

"And Grandma Edna?"

Susan glanced at Gary, the beginning of panic in her eyes. He grimaced, but nodded. She stared; he shrugged. She closed her eyes and sighed.

"If we can survive a civil war on an alien planet, I guess I can survive you and your grandmother planning the reception," Susan said. "Now, tell me how we're going to stop that war."

"I don't know. Both clans are … well, the blues are ridiculous, and the beiges are just as silly."

"We are not silly," Bozidar said. "The beige clan is noble and wise."

"Your cousins transformed themselves into bolts of beige fabric and tried to invade the Earth. You transformed yourself into a human and tried to kill my mother for revenge," Cecily said. "The whole lot of you are bonkers."

"Sweetie, let's stick to the problem of rescuing your grandmother. I think Bozidar has proven that he regrets taking the assignment to kill me, and he's kept you safe."

A muted ringing filtered into the kitchen. "Hold on, there's the phone," Susan said. She glanced at the empty receiver on the wall. "And I've left it someplace."

"I'll get it, love," Gary said. He patted her arm and left the kitchen. His broad shoulders filled the doorway, and his footsteps kept time with the tune he whistled.

Cecily shook her finger at her mother. "You landed a good one, Mom, so I'll give you a pass on eloping. But we're having a huge party when we get home. No one cares that you're older than Gary."

"We took the opportunity to have a quiet wedding," Susan said. "Your grandmother helped with the planning when I married your father, and it felt like a circus."

As if waiting for an invitation, the memory of

Susan's first wedding melted into the first vision she received from her great-grandmother, Agnes. The room lost its solidity around her, and the walls seemed to stretch into the distance like polka dots on a balloon as it expands with air. She felt the presence of a child, then a young woman, then a matriarch. *Help me keep my promise*, she heard echoing in her mind. An image of a spaceship crashing in the harbor flashed before her, and flour sacks being stacked on a horse-drawn delivery cart. Susan's head fell forward, and the words *help* and *promise* faded as she became aware of Gary catching her as she slid from the chair.

Gary knelt beside her, calling her name. A shrill voice sounded from the phone on the floor where he dropped it. Cecily and Bozidar shouted from the communications device. Susan opened her eyes and grimaced.

"Enough with the yelling," she said, her voice soft but steady. "I'm fine."

"What happened?" Gary asked.

"Agnes," Susan said in a husky whisper. She coughed. "I had another vision. Could I have some water, please?"

Gary helped her to a seated position before he brought her a glass of water. The liquid sloshed over the edge as his hands trembled.

Susan put her hands around Gary's and eased the glass from his grip. "You'd better sit down too. We don't want both of us keeling over."

Before sitting next to her, he picked up the

phone and took the communications device from the table. "She's okay," he said into the phone and at the screen. "She had another vision."

"What did you see, Mom?" Cecily asked. She leaned into the camera, while at the same time pushing Bozidar away.

"Agnes gave me a message," Susan said. She sipped more water and closed her eyes. "She wants us to go to Schtatik, with her quilt."

TWO

Susan opened her eyes, patted Gary's hand, and sat straighter. "I'm okay. Either I'm getting better at understanding the visions, or the ghost of Agnes is getting better at giving them. She wants me to help her keep a promise."

"Which promise?" Cecily asked. "The one to help the aliens who crashed in the San Francisco Bay when she was a child or the one to introduce humanity to a new civilization?"

Susan closed her eyes again, grasping at threads of memory. "I think she wants us to help the beige clan. Maybe she bonded too closely with the leader of the expedition and is channeling whatever remains of that consciousness, or maybe she feels some responsibility toward the clan. I can't tell. I only know that she wants me to go to Schtatik, with the quilt."

"Her timing couldn't be better," Gary said.

"Louise is the one who called."

Susan held out her hand for the phone. "Agnes apparently can tap phone lines, Louise. I'm fine, really. I had a vision about the crazy quilt. You wouldn't be anywhere near Quilting Parade, would you? Wonderful, we'll see you soon."

She put down the phone and adjusted the communications device. "Sorry, honey, but there'll be another delay. Louise will bring Agnes' crazy quilt to the house. Kyle is with her too."

A tiny smile brightened Cecily's face. "He's back from college now? I keep forgetting we're traveling faster than light. It's only been a few weeks for me, but months have passed for you."

Gary shifted next to Susan. "Your mother has marked off all the days on the calendar."

Cecily shook her head and laughed. "Of course she has."

"I'm not the only one," Susan said. "Louise told me Kyle asked about you every time he called home."

"Really?" Cecily bit her lower lip. "Well, it will be nice to see him."

Gary cleared his throat. "We should move to the family room," he said to Susan.

"Yes," Susan said. "I don't want Louise to find me on the floor."

Gary helped her to her feet. He took the communications device into the family room while Susan started a pot of coffee and put cookies on a serving plate. The doorbell rang as she placed the cookies on the coffee table.

"I'll let them in," Gary said.

Susan nodded and settled on the couch. She heard Louise in the foyer, then Gary's calm voice.

"You'll see," he said as he returned to the family room. "She fainted with the vision, that's all."

Louise lingered at the end of the hall. She held a folded quilt fragment in her arms as if she were carrying a grandchild.

Susan patted the couch. "Come sit by me so Cecily can see you."

Louise perched on the edge of the cushion, examining Susan's face. Kyle leaned against the wall, and Gary settled into an easy chair next to the couch.

"The quilt is here," Susan said as she unfolded it. "Can you see everyone? Kyle, come a little closer and say hello. I promise your mother and I won't make you hold up the quilt."

Kyle moved behind the couch, leaned over and waved at Cecily's image on the screen. "Good to see you again? Where are you?" A faint rosy tint showed under his mocha skin.

"Far side of the moon," Cecily said. "How was school?"

Bozidar's face appeared on the screen. "We have no time for pleasantries. Please, let me see the quilt again."

Susan gave the quilt back to Louise, who smoothed it across both of their laps. Using the communications device like a video camera, Susan scanned every inch of the quilt in smooth, even passes.

What remained of Agnes' quilt seemed to come alive with everyone's attention. The satins in the ten small blocks and partial border glowed, and the embroidery appeared to vibrate as if begging to tell a great secret.

Susan set the device on the coffee table and stroked a soft, pastel velvet patch. "I still can't believe Agnes used piecing and embroidery to tell the story of the first time aliens came to this planet. I wish we had the whole thing."

"It's amazing anything remains of it at all," Louise said. "Not much survived the great earthquake in 1906. Think how often it was packed as your family moved from San Francisco around the bay. And wasn't it divided between your grandmother and her sisters?"

Susan nodded. "They didn't know what they had. None of us did until last year, when Bozidar showed us the foundation wasn't really a flour sack, but part of the transformed skin of the alien captain." She traced a ring of embroidered daisies with her finger. "It's time she went home."

Louise pressed her hand against her chest and clutched at her beaded necklace. She closed her eyes, blew a quick breath of air between her lips, and released her fingers. Tugging her coral sweater, she said, "I had hoped you would change your mind about going to Schtatik."

Susan shook her head. "No. The vision from Agnes was clear. I need to be there, with the quilt. I've got to rescue my mother and stop a war."

"What can you do?" Louise asked. "The problems between the blue clan and the beige clan are political. You remember what Bozidar said. The splits between them have been growing. It seems to me they don't want to get along anymore. No magical quilt is going to stop a war. And there's something more—the factions within the beiges. The aliens we battled a couple of years ago, the subset of the taupes, came here on their own. They planned to infiltrate the area by disguising themselves as bolts of beige fabric."

"Which didn't work," Kyle said.

"Bozidar also said the taupes aren't very smart," Susan said. "I know it seems foolish to think I can solve the problems of an alien race on another planet, but I have to try."

"Could I come too?" Kyle asked. "Gary and I thought of making chenille shields like the one I brought from Africa. Cecily and I work well together. Having another person on the team might be a help."

Louise trembled, staring at her son. She tried to speak, without success.

Susan's heart ached at the panic in Louise's dark brown eyes. "The transport pod is going to be cramped enough. Besides, sending an expeditionary force will only make things worse. The blues will say Earth is invading Schtatik in revenge for the beige's aggression."

"Oh, please. Three humans is hardly an

expeditionary force, Mom," Cecily said.

"The pod is too small," Susan said.

"If you want to get into med school, you need to take that internship at the clinic," Louise said. She crossed her arms, and her long, brown fingers drummed along her bicep.

Kyle scowled. "I can't argue with that, but I'm going on the next trip."

"The next trip!" Susan threw her hands in the air. "Please, one exercise in madness at a time. Cecily, how do we get into the ship?"

Cecily's face disappeared from the screen as Bozidar shoved her aside once again. His skin no longer glowed like hot syrup, but his eye color rolled from brown to green to brown. A curl of green smoke drifted around his nostrils.

"I know this is stressful for you, Bozidar," Susan said. "Parts of you are transforming into your native shape. Take a deep breath."

He exhaled green-tinged breath. "The pod was programmed for one passenger. The entrance codes will need to be changed, as will the fuel-consumption programs for the return trip. When those tasks are completed, I will give you the sequence that will allow you to enter the pod."

Susan nodded. "Tell me about your plan. There may be something else we should bring. Better to discuss the possibilities now than discover after we arrive that we should have packed more of Agnes' things, for example."

"How about lavender?" Kyle asked.

Cecily joined Bozidar on the screen. "That's a good idea, and lemon and rosemary too."

"They like those scents?" Susan asked.

"More like they prefer it to our scent," Cecily said. "It might be useful for dealing with the taupes."

"Are we likely to run into them?"

Cecily and Bozidar looked away from the camera and each other. His skin glistened. She chewed her lips.

"This is why I want to discuss the plan," Susan said. "Cecily, what other surprises are in store for us?"

Cecily glanced at Bozidar and squared her shoulders. "We have taupe allies. Sort of. They aren't with us now. I don't think they'd step foot on the *Snapping Shellfish* if we paid them."

"Focus, Daughter."

"Right. Well, a taupe agent helped us to escape the palace. Zenoa. She was disguised as a servant, but Salia said she was pretty important, and Salia would know, being a taupe and all."

"Cecily, you're rambling." Susan tapped the screen at Cecily's forehead.

"This behavior is chronic for her," Bozidar said.

"You're not helping," Cecily said. "It's complicated, Mom. Maybe we should wait until you and Gary are on board the *Snapping Shellfish.*"

"Fine." Susan twisted a lock of blonde hair.

Gary patted her arm. "Let's try this from another angle, honey. What would be useful when we get to

Schtatik? There's the crazy quilt, lavender, lemon, rosemary, and more of Agnes' things. What else?"

Louise cleared her throat. "At the risk of sounding like the voice of doom, what about chenille? We know chenille can kill Schtatikians. Not that you would want to do that, but if you have to."

"That isn't a bad idea," Cecily said. "Scott sneaked some along last time, and it came in handy."

"How would you feel about that, Bozidar?" Susan asked.

A crashing sound accompanied by squeaks and squeals came from a corner of the bridge. One voice rose above the din. "Bring the shields, bring the shields!"

"Marsel!" Bozidar said, rosy smoke puffing from his ears. "We will not use weapons of mass destruction on our own people."

"Marsel is with you too?" Susan asked. "I thought he had enough of us when he was helping Bozidar last time."

"The beiges are big on guilt by association," Cecily said. "He sort of had no choice but to throw in with us again."

Cecily glanced to her left and stepped away as a pinky-beige creature muscled past her. Marsel's eyestalks shimmied and wriggled, and green smoke rings drifted over his head.

"The blues are not our people," Marsel said. "They are slow-witted, vengeful, reprehensible."

"Boys, please," Cecily said from off-screen, her

hand visible on Bozidar's shoulder. "Plans now, politics later."

Susan said, "You know, I think we can figure out what to pack on our own. Contact us again when you finish the calculations." She touched an icon on the device and the screen went dark. She smiled at Gary. "Are you sure you want to come along?"

He hugged her. "Wouldn't miss it."

"Just remember that you volunteered," Susan said. "Now, about that expanded packing list."

"I have one thing to offer," Louise said. She reached into the main pocket of her handbag and gave Susan a small metal box with a hinged lid. "It was Kyle's idea."

Susan stroked the brushed aluminum lid. The box was the size and shape of a well-loved paperback novel, with rounded corners and a tiny latch on one side. She opened the lid to find a stack of folded fabric squares, embroidery floss, three small containers of beads, a packet of needles, and a tiny pair of scissors.

"A handwork project," Susan said. "What do you have in here?"

Kyle took the box and unfolded a square of pale gray shirting fabric with narrow silver stripes. "If Agnes could make a quilt to commemorate her encounter with aliens, why not you?"

"I haven't done any beading or embroidery in ages," Susan said as she examined the beads. "These are beautiful mixtures. Tell Li-Ming to stock them.

They will fly off the shelves."

Louise choked back a laugh. "And that's why you don't have projects of your own. You're too busy running a quilt shop to enjoy the merchandise."

Susan held up a skein of soft green embroidery floss to one of the bead containers, making the square peridot beads, round forest green seed beads and emerald bugle beads pop against the rest of the mixture of browns, golds, and coppers. She noted with approval the variety pack of needles and embroidery scissors.

"Thank you," she said. "I don't know what I'll do with it, but I love it."

"You taught a series of embroidered flower blocks, remember?" Louise asked. "When you opened the shop. Margaret and I took that class."

"You framed one of those blocks," Kyle said. "It's in the guest room."

Louise put her hand to her throat. "You noticed what's in the guest room?"

"Men pay attention to decor," Gary said, his eyes twinkling.

Her head drooped like a chocolate lab caught stealing the cat's food. "It's always a surprise when your children are aware of what you do." Her chin jerked, and her eyes widened. "And now I've made it worse. Moving on," Louise said. "Maybe you could embroider Earth flowers on some squares and Shtatik flowers on others."

"That's a splendid idea," Susan said, patting

Louise's arm. She glanced at the communications device. "We should get busy. Bozidar could call back anytime with the new codes. Louise, could you get some lavender from my studio? You remember where the chenille things are, don't you, Kyle?"

"After you find them," Gary said, "come help me in the kitchen with the lemon and rosemary."

Susan headed for the hallway. "I'll go see what other treasures Agnes wants me to bring."

She climbed the stairs to her bedroom, willing Agnes to speak to her again. *It's your promise*, she thought, *and I expect some guidance on how to keep it.* As she opened the door, a cool sea breeze flowed over her. *The window is closed and we're forty miles from the ocean. I'm taking this as a sign.*

The small chest with Agnes' embroidery and sewing supplies creaked as she opened the lid. She set the narrow top tray on the bed. A brass chatelaine occupied most of the tray, glittering against the rose velvet lining. The brooch was pinned to a thick damask ribbon, to be worn around the neck. The top of the piece was a floral filigree the size of a silver dollar, with three metal loops at the bottom. Two graceful chains extended from each loop, with hooks at the end to attach scissors, keys, even a pencil from a special holder. Susan held the chatelaine in her palm and stroked the delicate metalwork. Her eyes flitted from one corner of the room to another. *My choice, I guess.* She slipped the chatelaine in her pocket and examined the bottom of the chest.

A stack of embroidered blocks, remnants of other projects or one-time experiments, nestled against a collection of thimbles. Packets of needles, brass hand-sewing tools that reminded Susan of weapons for miniature medieval warriors, and random buttons caught her attention briefly. A ruby sparkle attracted her hand.

"Where have you been hiding all these years?" she asked as she lifted a silver ring with a single oval gem mounted in a thick collar. She slid the ring on the fourth finger of her right hand, and the sea breeze returned. Its salt scent gave way to a whiff of lavender. Susan smiled, snatched the top three embroidered squares, and repacked the chest.

She descended the stairs and heard laughter in the kitchen. She hovered at the edge of the hallway, watching the others arrange their treasures on the kitchen table. Gary lifted a hand, as if calling for attention from an unruly class, then glanced in her direction.

"There you are," he said. "I just remembered the last item we absolutely need to bring." He opened the bread box and pulled out a package of miniature red velvet cupcakes. "Cecily's favorites, right?"

Susan nodded. "She might even forgive us for eloping when she sees them. Tell me about the rest of all this."

Louise indicated two tall bottles. "One is lavender lotion. The other is lavender essence. I tried to think of all the situations you might encounter, and this seemed like the most comprehensive solution."

"I put some cuttings in containers," Gary said. "One rosemary, one lavender." He pointed to a paper bag. "There are four lemons and a bottle of lemon juice."

"Last but not least, five chenille bean bags, two hoods, and a pillow," Kyle said. "I suggested taking a shield, too, but Gary said that might be too much trouble to cart around."

"Good work," Susan said. "I think I've got a tote bag that will hold all of this."

"Of course you do," Louise said, and she picked up a large denim bag with padded handles and pockets on the outside. "I put a pad of graph paper and some sketching pencils in there too."

"You are a gem," Susan said. "Has Bozidar called yet?"

"I'll check," Gary said and headed for the family room.

"Kyle, go with him," Louise said. "You're good with computers. If there's a problem, you can help."

Kyle rolled his eyes but followed Gary.

"You raised a smart boy, dear, but can he really understand alien programming?" Susan asked.

"I doubt it, but he'll get a chance to talk with Cecily," Louise said. "Thank you for keeping him on this planet. You're much stronger than I am. You let Cecily go."

"If I had my way, she wouldn't have, but it wasn't my decision to make." Susan shoveled the chenille items into the bag. She squirted some lavender lotion in her palm. "I have Agnes, too, and you don't."

Louise put the lemons in the tote. "How does that work? Does she talk to you?"

"Not really." Susan leaned against the counter. "The first vision was concrete, specific. The one today was like an art film. Just images and impressions. Then upstairs, when I was going through her things, I sensed she was with me, but that was it." She extended her hand to show Louise the silver ring.

"How beautiful," Louise whispered. She turned Susan's hand to the light.

"I've been through that box dozens of times, but I've never seen this before," Susan said. "And I know Edna didn't see it, or she would have kept it. My mother is generous, but she does have an eye for pretty jewelry. As soon as I touched it, I knew Agnes wanted me to bring it. No voices, no visions, I just knew. And that's how I could let Cecily go into space. Somehow, I knew she would come home."

"How about now?" Louise asked. "Do you have that same feeling?"

Susan focused on the denim tote and mini cupcakes. She held her breath a moment then met Louise's gaze. "Not exactly." She smiled. "But isn't that what adventures are all about?"

The air shimmered around her. Agnes' voice echoed in her head. *Try again. You can sense it. You're part of it. Part of the coming war.*

THREE

Susan and Gary stood at the base of the landing pod. Susan held the black communications device as if taking a picture. She tapped a whirling orange square twice with her right thumb and two flashing red triangles once each with her left thumb.

The pod's hatch rolled open like a garage door, and a platform extruded from the hull. It extended to its limit and locked in place with a metallic clang. Linked metal panels unfolded from its lower surface. The first silvery metal panel touched the ground and stopped. It rose on its edge and dug into the earth like a shovel. This panel became a riser, and the rest settled into place to make a stairway.

Gary tested the first tread with his foot. "It seems sturdy," he said.

Susan turned to Louise, who stood behind her with the crazy quilt. "We'll leave the device with you.

I'm not sure how often we'll be able to call, but I'll try to keep you updated."

Louise traded the quilt for the black tablet. "Will your staff need help at Quilting Parade? I can drop by if they need me."

"I think they'll be fine," Susan said as she tucked the quilt under one arm and picked up the grocery sack with the lemons and herbs. "Of course, they'd love to see you whenever you can get away from Queen of the Needles."

Gary took the sack from Susan and climbed the short stairway to the hatch. He hesitated on the platform, scanning the interior of the pod. "It's smaller inside than I expected," he said. "Maybe we should stow the luggage in the storage compartment."

Susan sighed. "I'm a quilter, dear, I'll make it fit." She leaned toward Louise and whispered, "All those years at UPS, he thinks there's only one way to stack boxes. Keeps talking about the reality of finite space."

Louise chuckled. "My husband's the same. And I can always fit in more." She motioned to Kyle. "Bring him the suitcase, sweetie. We'll be up in a minute to help."

"No, I'd better go now," Susan said.

She led the way up the stairs, glancing over the fences as she went. "Keep an eye out for the neighbors," she said to Kyle.

Gary and Kyle brought the rest of the supplies while Susan stacked and stuffed them around the pod. As she found a spot for the last item, she turned to

Gary with a victorious smile. "I told you it would fit."

"And you almost have space to walk around," Kyle said under his breath.

"I heard that," Susan said.

"So did I," Louise said from the platform. She edged past her son and handed the communication tablet to Susan. "It's buzzing."

Susan touched the purple icon, and Cecily's face appeared on the screen.

"Are you ready, Mom?" Cecily asked.

"All packed," Susan said. "We were just about to say good bye. Oh, and I'm leaving the tablet with Louise if that's okay."

"Fine with me. Does she know how it works?" Cecily said, pushing Bozidar away.

"No more delays!" Bozidar shoved back.

"I know," Kyle said. He motioned for Susan to give him the tablet. "I push the purple and two orange to answer a call, the red and turquoise to initiate. No problem."

"See, Bozidar, no delays," Cecily said. "He'll teach her how to use the device."

"I won't have to," Kyle said. "I'll be living at home this summer."

"Enough!" Bozidar shrieked. "We must initiate the launch sequence now, or the pod will be in the wrong position!"

Susan hugged Louise, then Kyle, and shepherded them out the hatch. "See you soon," she shouted as the hatch closed. She sat next to Gary on the bench.

The stairway and platform retracting filled the pod with metallic clicks and pings, a symphony of metal sliding against metal, then silence.

"We're off," she said, squeezing his hand.

He put his arm around her and settled against the wall. "How long is the ride?"

"A few hours."

He looked from side to side. Bright light from a glowing ring at the top of the pod splashed the curved walls. Cool air tinged with a hint of lemon swirled around the interior, although there was no obvious vent or fan. He stretched and scanned the console in the center of the room. "Do we have to push any of those buttons?"

"No, it's all automatic." Susan leaned against him. "There's nothing to do but sit and relax. Take advantage of it. This may be the only quiet moment we have."

He squeezed her shoulder. "I'm supposed to tell you to relax. Are you really calm, or so overloaded with worry that you only appear at ease?"

"I'm not sure." She closed her eyes. "It's remarkable. I don't feel any acceleration, any turning, nothing. We're just sitting on a couch."

"Your couch is a lot more comfortable." He shifted. "I wonder who won the golf match."

Susan laughed so hard she sputtered. "Since when do you care about golf?"

"Since my agent told the director of the pilot I shot last spring that I play."

"And do you?" she asked. Her expression bounced between amusement and incredulity.

He nodded. "As a matter of fact, I do. My dad taught me when I was a kid. I remember just enough to not embarrass myself on the links."

"My late husband played with his boss. He made sure he never won."

"He was a wise man," Gary said. "Did you play together?"

"God, no." She shuddered. "I tried it once and decided I could find better things to do with my time. I took up quilting."

"I thought that was part of your heritage, passed down the generations."

"Not really. Agnes taught my mother, but her own daughter, my grandmother, had no interest in it. Mom tried to teach me." Her voice trailed to silence.

"Yeah, I can imagine how that went. What made you take it up again?"

"Mom brought over a sewing kit for Cecily. She couldn't have been more than five years old, but she was a quick learner. She finished the little nine-patch that Mom cut out for her and wanted to do another. I took her to the quilt store to get more fabric, and the rest is history."

He frowned. "You say 'the' quilt store, but there are half a dozen in the area."

"Back then there was only one, Queen of the Needles."

"That's Carolyn's shop. Where Louise works."

He shuddered. "Where I picked up the box of the renegade Schtatikians when they first invaded."

"That's the place." Susan patted his leg. "If the aliens hadn't attacked you we wouldn't be together now."

"Seeing those monsters come out of their box and rush me from the back of the UPS van is not my favorite memory. Or the green smoke they make when they attack. My eyes water just thinking about it." He wiped his face as if clearing the memory from his mind, like wiping steam from a bathroom mirror. "Carolyn's always been your competition, right?"

"Yes, I guess so. Why?"

"How did you manage to stay friends? I mean, Louise works for Carolyn, and yet she helps you whenever you ask."

"Carolyn always said there was business enough for all of us if we cooperated rather than competed, and she was right."

"Maybe we should have brought Carolyn along with us," he said. "We need someone to get the beige clan and the blue clan cooperating rather than clobbering each other."

Susan tugged on a lock of hair, twisting it around her finger. "You're right, that's exactly what we need. Maybe Agnes will send me another vision when we get to the planet, give me the words that will grab their attention." *And please let them be words to bring peace, not escalate the violence.*

They sat in silence for a time. The ship was quiet,

the ride smooth. A whiff of lavender infused the air, now warmer than when the journey began. The lights in the pod gradually dimmed, until it seemed they were surrounded by candlelight.

A purple square appeared on the console. As it began to whirl, two orange triangles glowed beneath it. Susan lurched toward the screen and pressed the icons.

"Hi, Mom," Cecily said. "You're going to dock with the mother ship soon. I thought you'd like to know what will happen." She squinted. "Did I wake you guys?"

"I think so." Susan blinked when the lights grew brighter. "You didn't tell me this thing has a nap mode."

Cecily laughed and turned her head. "I told you that was a good upgrade." Returning her attention to Susan, she said, "I explained to one of the crew about energy savers in computers on Earth, and she developed a program to detect motion and heart rates in the transport pod. With autopilot, it doesn't matter if the passengers are awake or asleep."

Gary rose from the bench, steadied himself against the wall, and picked his way along the narrow path to join Susan. "Tell me you have a pick-up truck for all the stuff we brought."

Bozidar came to Cecily's side, jostling her as he bent toward the screen. "Stuff? What does that word mean?"

"Valuable possessions that must be protected,"

Cecily murmured as she shifted him behind her. "They've got anti-grav sleds that can move a herd of elephants."

"We brought two," Gary said.

"Two? Two herds? Of elephants?" Bozidar's features glistened and his hands trembled.

"He's joking," Cecily said. "Go sit by Marsel. You'll be happier."

Susan scowled at Gary, but with a twinkle in her eyes. "You shouldn't tease him, dear."

"I'll apologize later," he said. "Makes you wonder why they chose him to be your assassin if he falls apart so easily."

"This is one of his better days," Cecily said. "You'll understand when you get here." She glanced to a panel below the screen. "Which is, like, now. The guys with the anti-grav sleds will bring all your things to your quarters. I'll meet you in the docking bay."

The screen went dark. Susan and Gary returned to the bench, backs straight, feet braced against the luggage. The air stilled, and an icy metallic scent drifted around them like blowing snow. The sound of metal clamping metal accompanied a small jerk. The hatch glowed pink, rolling up from the bottom to reveal a large open space filled with harsh green light.

Susan walked to the edge of the hatch, her hands on the opening as if she were preparing to parachute to the floor. She heard a rumbling as a large, rolling platform approached. Squat beige creatures that looked like walking rectangles followed the platform.

Two toddled side by side on stumpy, wheat-colored legs. Short red scarves covered their shoulders. A third creature lagged behind, pulling a wheeled cart. Its bulbous head knob drooped, as did the two eyestalks flanking the head.

Gary put his hand on her shoulder. "I thought our distribution center was big. We could fit two or three of those warehouses in here and still have room."

The docking bay contained two other transport pods of similar design and a third ship that resembled an origami crane. Machines around these ships rolled along tracks in the floor, stopping at intervals and beeping, buzzing, or clanking as probes jutted out and connected with the hulls.

The tracks crossed in patterns reminiscent of Celtic knotwork. They converged at the walls, where metal tubes ran from floor to ceiling like the ribs of a star-roaming whale. Between these tubes lay rectangular panels, some opaque and colored, some clear. A strong lemon-rosemary smell permeated the bay.

The rolling platform locked into place against their pod. Susan and Gary descended the steps while the three beige creatures huddled at the bottom, chittering to themselves. The tallest of the three bowed to Susan when she reached the floor.

She bent her head forward, more than a nod but less than a bow, and said, "I'm pleased to meet you. My name is Susan, and this is my husband, Gary."

The creatures shuffled back, bowing and chittering.

"Maybe we shouldn't talk to them?" Gary asked. "Cecily said something about needing to disinfect around humans."

"They've seen Edna. I'm certain they're used to our kind by now."

"Assuming this is the same crew," Gary said.

"Oh," Susan said, pushing a lock of hair from her eyes. "I never thought of that." She scanned the edges of the bay. "Cecily said she'd meet us. I should have asked her how long it takes to get down here."

The creature that had bowed approached, its tiny, stiff arms waggling. The one with the cart edged close as well.

"I think they want us to move aside so they can unload the pod," Gary said. "I recognize the universal gesture of the warehouse worker."

Susan backed away, and her heel caught in one of the rivers of track. She jerked her foot upward, pulling her knee higher than her waist. The movement unbalanced her, and she stumbled along a neighboring track into the path of a machine the size of a shopping cart. Her arms shot out to break her fall, elbows rigid and wrists flexed. She spread her fingers as her palms hit the top of the machine, and pushed four small glowing rectangles simultaneously.

The machine convulsed as if it had hit a concrete barrier. Panels on either side popped open, spilling wires and hoses on the floor. A high-pitched whistling blasted through the space, alternating with a sound like a lost calf in a far-off meadow. The green light pulsed harsher, yellower, then went out.

"Mom, what did you touch?" Cecily's voice echoed in the darkness.

FOUR

Darkness and panic competed with Susan's intention to remain calm. She lurched sideways, away from the metal box, and stubbed her toe. Pain settled her mind. She inhaled, blew the breath out softly while counting to five and said, "I'm fine, thank you for asking."

The opaque tubes along the walls glowed a pale blue. Pinpoints of green light appeared in the ceiling, growing in intensity. Motors whirred, machines rolled along the tracks again. The metal box in front of Susan beeped three times and inched away from her, dragging hoses and wires like a tired child.

Cecily and Gary converged on Susan, followed by Bozidar.

"Mayhem," Bozidar said, his voice trembling. "That's what you bring. All of you. Mayhem. It would have been better if She Who Found Us had left my ancestors to die."

"Bozidar!" Cecily said. "Don't talk about my great-great-grandmother like that. Agnes was a brave little girl."

Susan shook her head. "No, dear," she said, "I know exactly how he feels. If Agnes hadn't saved the beige clan when they crashed in San Francisco, the taupes wouldn't have heard stories about Earth. If they hadn't heard the stories, they wouldn't have returned two years ago, and I wouldn't be standing in an alien spaceship, battered and bruised."

Gary took her hands and inspected them. "Oh, you did get bunged up. They're small cuts, but I bet they hurt."

"I stubbed my toe and wrenched my knee too." Susan lifted her chin. "And I didn't touch anything. That metal box rolled into me."

"Can you walk?" Cecily asked. "The medical bay isn't far."

Susan tested her knee. "I guess so. What about our luggage?"

"Your belongings are in your quarters," Bozidar said. "The crew has instructions not to touch anything. Unless you have brought something that will explode of its own accord, we should be leaving your moon for Schtatik after the pod is unpacked."

Gary glanced at Susan. "We didn't bring any bombs, but I've got to ask, why did the lights go out?"

"The ship detected a solar flare," Bozidar said. "Power was suspended for all non-essential activities until it passed."

"I told you I didn't touch anything," Susan narrowed her eyes. "Unless you're blaming me for the solar flare."

"The sensors detected the flare the moment the transport pod left Earth." Bozidar dropped his head and muttered, "I have come to distrust coincidences."

Cecily patted Bozidar's shoulder. "The women in my family are strong, but we don't actually run the universe. Let's get Mom to the medical bay. We can discuss our next steps during the treatment."

She motioned to Susan and Gary, then led the way from the hanger as three crew members approached Bozidar. He chittered instructions to them and followed the humans as if marching to his own hanging.

Soft light with a pinkish tinge bathed the corridor outside the hanger. Cecily touched a green triangle on the wall and said, "Medical bay." Two rows of green rectangles flashed, one halfway up the wall and one along the floor.

"Marsel installed a ship-wide information system," Cecily said. "Touch any of the green triangles and ask a question or name a destination. The ship will tell you what you need to know."

"Clever," Susan said. "So we follow the lights?"

"Yep," Cecily said. "Marsel was going to use yellow, but I kept singing 'Follow the Yellow Brick

Road' so he changed it to green."

"The singing was acceptable," Bozidar said. "The dancing was not. It frightened the crew."

"You didn't," Susan said.

"I did."

"Did what?" Gary asked.

Cecily blushed. "I did the dance from *The Wizard of Oz*. You try not skipping when you've got that song in your head."

"Please, stop," Bozidar said.

"Don't worry," Susan said. "I'm in no mood to dance. Tell me what happened on Schtatik. Start from the time you landed and don't leave anything out."

"As soon as I get you hooked up in the medical bay," Cecily said. "We're almost there."

As they rounded a bend in the corridor, the green rectangles flashed faster. Cecily stopped at a closed door and pressed a panel with three purple squiggly lines. The green rectangles stopped flashing when the door opened.

The medical bay held three couches and two platforms that resembled padded camping cots on sawhorses. Monitors and racks of equipment sat in shallow niches on the wall beside each of the platforms, while the couches sported hoods that could have been used in high school chemistry labs. The floor was soft, almost spongy. The entire ceiling glowed with a subdued, yellowish light.

Cecily motioned Susan to one of the platforms, then tapped a panel on a nearby counter. The light altered, becoming bluer, more Earth-like. A faint scent of lemon and rosemary filled the space, drifting down from vents near the ceiling. An arm from the equipment rack swung out a few inches, and the monitor activated.

Susan put her hands on the edge of the platform. As soon as she touched it, the legs retracted. The platform adjusted to her height and locked in place with a metallic clunk. She poked it but did not sit.

"This is another of Marsel's upgrades," Cecily said. "Don't worry, it's safe."

Susan settled onto the platform, her hands positioned to push her off in an instant. "They've made a lot of modifications for us, haven't they?"

"Your daughter insisted," Bozidar said. "She worked the engineers and fabricators to the brink of exhaustion."

"You know that isn't true," Cecily said. "I made some suggestions, and Marsel ran with them. He'd make a great diplomat, if the Schtatikians had a diplomatic corps. He persuaded the crew to accept him as captain, and he's kept them busy enough to take their minds off the situation."

"What situation?" Gary helped Susan swing her feet onto the pad.

"Their treason," Bozidar said.

"Treason?" Susan grabbed Cecily's hand. "What's going on?"

Cecily wriggled from her mother's grasp and pulled the arm of the equipment rack to its full length.

She chose three attachments and positioned one on Susan's thumb, one on her knee, and one on her shoulder. The monitor displayed four lines, each a different color, each wriggling from top to bottom with a different pattern.

"Treason is too strong a word," Cecily said, keeping her eyes on the monitor. "I admit we stole the ship. And outran the pursuit ship the beiges sent after us."

"And shot at it," Bozidar said.

"Near it," Cecily said. "A warning shot, that's all. But we had no choice." She sat next to Susan, hands in her lap. "Here's what happened. We went to Schtatik to stop the beige clan from sending any more expeditionary forces after us."

"I was at the planning meeting," Susan said.

"Let me tell this in my own way, Mom," Cecily said. "On the trip there, Grandma Edna and I did everything we could to prepare. She had her grandmother's thimble that would prove we were descendants of the little girl who saved the beige clan when they first landed in San Francisco before the 1906 earthquake. I had the movie I made about the renegade taupes invading a few years ago by disguising themselves as bolts of beige fabric, which we expected would prove we didn't start the fight. Finally, I had the footage we shot of all of us eating ice cream with Bozidar and the four taupes who escaped. We thought that would show that we had forgiven the taupes for invading and the council for sending Bozidar to avenge the taupes we killed, since they didn't know that they owed us a life debt."

Cecily ran her hands through her hair, faded purple curls against her pale fingers. She jiggled her foot, bright blue toe-nail polish peeking from the straps of her sandal.

"But the plan fell apart," Susan prompted.

"From the moment we boarded the ship for homeworld," Bozidar said. He slid his hands into the pockets of his brown-striped trousers. "I should have known it would be a disaster. The conflict between the blue clan and my own has been building for generations. I should have anticipated that news of the taupe invasion would spread. The council has never been good at keeping secrets."

"Is that why there was a blue representative at your trial?" Cecily asked.

"I suspect so."

"Wait," Gary said. "I thought the trial was just a formality. Didn't Marsel arrange that the taupes would be returned to the clan and Bozidar acquitted of failing to complete his mission? I mean, the elders didn't want Susan harmed after they found out who she was. Right?"

The monitor beeped a shrill note that caused Cecily to leap from the bed. She adjusted the device on Susan's thumb, and watched the lines on the monitor scroll by.

Gary embraced Susan. "What's wrong?"

"Nothing," Susan said. She squeezed his arm

gently, but compressed her lips into a scowl. "My blood pressure always skyrockets when I remember I was the target of an assassination attempt."

"That must be it," Cecily said, still studying the monitor. "Your knee should be okay now. The cuts on your hands will take a little more time. About five minutes."

Susan inspected her hands. She flexed her fingers and prodded her knee. "You're right. I feel much better."

Gary sat beside her, his hand on her shoulder. "Good. Just stay that way, please?"

Susan relaxed against him. "I'll do my best. Continue with your story, Cecily."

"Like Bozidar said, the tension between the blue clan and the beige clan had escalated before we arrived. We had no idea what was going on, because no one would translate for us. I don't think Bozidar and Marsel knew what was happening, either, until the two clans declared war."

"And that's when the beiges made Edna their queen?" Susan asked.

Bozidar nodded. "The memory of She Who Saved Us is still potent. The council hoped to rally the entire clan under her leadership."

"Except that she's more of a figurehead," Cecily said. "Of all the beige subsets, the taupes are the best soldiers, and they wouldn't take orders from Edna, even if she is Agnes' granddaughter. And the losers have to surrender their ruler."

"Surrender? They'll put Edna in prison?" Gary asked.

Cecily shook her head. "They'll kill her."

FIVE

"War reparations," Bozidar said, a hollow echo bouncing off the medical bay walls. "I believe it is an ancient custom on your planet as well."

"It was," Susan said, her voice shaking as much as her hands. She caught the attachment on her thumb as it slipped. "We stopped killing the leaders of the losing side a long time ago." She concentrated on the clip, but could not reposition it.

"Let me help," Gary held Susan's hands until they stopped trembling. "What would the blues get out of killing a human?"

"For any other human, or any other species, nothing," Bozidar said. "However, killing a descendant of someone to whom the beige clan owes a debt, that would be a humiliation from which we would never recover."

"If it's any consolation, Mom, we were kept in

isolation most of the time. Grandma Edna didn't have a chance to, um, show her true nature, so the elders are still willing to do whatever it takes to save her."

Susan stared at her daughter. The lines on the monitor lost their squiggles. Susan's breath came short and shallow, and her skin turned ashen. Her mouth opened, and a noise like the death throes of a much-abused motor scooter filled the room.

Cecily glanced at Gary and Bozidar. "That's a good sound, guys," she said.

Susan collapsed in Gary's arms, and her laughter modulated to relief and amusement. "Thank heavens for small favors. With any luck, someone will disable all the translating devices around her. If they don't know what she's saying, she can't offend them. At least not as easily."

Marsel skidded into the room, eyestalks whipping about. He bounced off Bozidar into a wall, where his footpad caught in an equipment niche. His rubbery, rectangular body crumpled to the floor, resembling a Naugahyde ottoman after a flood. One arm flailed at the air, while his eyestalks drooped over his body like dying poppies.

Cecily knelt by his side, slipped a hand beneath him, and propped him against the wall. "I told you the cleaning crew used too much wax on the floor." She turned to Gary and Susan. "It's the third time he's fallen this week."

"I wanted everything to sparkle for your

mother," Marsel murmured.

"That's very kind of you, Marsel," Susan said. "Are you injured?"

Marsel shimmied up the wall, rested a moment, and toddled toward Susan. "Only bruised. But what of you? I heard you squeal in pain. Are the medical settings not appropriate?"

"That was the sound of joy that Her Majesty has not put her own head on the executioner's block," Bozidar said.

Marsel gasped. "Blasphemy, blasphemy! I beg of you, Bozidar, do not make my position more difficult than it already is. The others will find it impossible to believe we are acting for the greater good if you speak of the descendant of She Who Found Us so disparagingly."

"Her name is Edna," Susan said. "And as her daughter, I give you permission to use it."

Cecily patted Marsel's head. "I kept telling them that, but they insist on using titles for us."

"Well, I insist that they stop," Susan said. She tucked her soft blonde hair behind her ear, curled her fingers, then flexed her leg at the knee. "I'm feeling great. Unhook me and let's get to work."

Cecily checked the monitor. "Yup, everything normal." She removed the clips and tucked all the equipment back into its niche. "Your quarters are next to mine in a suite with a large shared space. I thought we could use that for a conference room."

"Sounds good." Susan slid off the examining

table and tested her balance. "Lead on."

Cecily ushered Bozidar and Marsel out the door.

Gary touched Susan's elbow. "When were you going to tell me about that laugh?" he asked. "And is it genetic?"

* * *

Susan stood in the doorway between her quarters and the common area. The viewscreen behind the large table showed the dark side of the moon, and beyond it, Earth. The planet seemed to shrink to the size of dinnerware before Susan realized the ship was leaving orbit prior to engaging the stitch-runner engines.

She sensed she was moving toward the viewscreen, then through it, accelerating toward a pinpoint of light to the left of the moon. Her hand clutched the edge of the doorway, but the sensation of spinning through space persisted.

This is what I imagined space was like, a voice echoed in her mind.

She closed her eyes, willing the vision to ebb and reality to return.

Please don't, the voice said. *I've waited three lifetimes to fly in the celestial ether. And you're going to need me.*

Susan opened her eyes and, in the moment before they entirely focused, saw a young girl in a Victorian pinafore cartwheeling in space. She wiped her eyes and the image faded.

"Hey, Mom," Cecily said as she entered. She walked to the screen and pressed her nose against it. "I love this view, especially when we're traveling faster than light."

"Yes," Susan said.

Cecily turned. "Mom? Are you space-sick? You look a little green."

"No."

Cecily sprinted to Susan's side and guided her to an upholstered bench built into the wall. She propped her against the pillows and grabbed a green throw at the end of the bench.

"I'm not cold," Susan said, "but I would like some water."

Cecily tapped a code onto a pad on the wall. A panel slid to one side, revealing a tiny alcove with a small pink glass filled with a glittering clear liquid.

"Here." Cecily handed her the glass and knelt beside the bench.

Susan drank in sips, taking time to breathe between each one. She smiled at Cecily. "Relax, I'm not sick. Just another visitation."

"Agnes?"

Susan nodded. "I saw her. As a little girl. Out there." She pointed toward the viewscreen.

"In space? What was she doing?"

"Playing." Susan handed the glass to Cecily. "She said this was just what she imagined space would be like."

Cecily put the glass back in the alcove and closed the panel. "So, my love of science fiction is genetic. My great-great-grandmother dreamed of spinning around in a space suit before it was fashionable."

"No space suit," Susan said. "It looked like she was turning cartwheels in her play clothes, except she had stars under her feet instead of grass."

"Cool." Cecily edged to the screen, watching the squiggly lines of light the stars emitted as the ship pleated space around it to travel between the planets. "Did she say anything else?"

"That we would need her."

"Who will we need?" Gary entered the common room from the hall with Bozidar and Marsel in tow.

"Agnes," Susan said, her voice even and sweet.

"We left a team member behind?" Spikes of green smoke circled Marsel's head.

"She Who Found Us," Bozidar said. "Her spirit has appeared to Susan of late."

"Yes, I remember," Marsel said. "Her first visitation saved your life, and revealed the path to our redemption."

Bozidar tossed his head, and vibrant, swirling streamers of orange smoke curled out of his ears. "You have been around humans too much, Marsel. You have become as melodramatic as they are."

Gary patted Bozidar's shoulder. "Don't be so sure, buddy. I was ready to break your neck for kidnapping Cecily, and Edna had a gun trained on you. If Susan hadn't had a vision from Agnes about your people crashing in San Francisco Bay years ago, you wouldn't be here to enjoy our company."

"Precisely!" Marsel said. "What exciting times we live in."

Susan narrowed her eyes and frowned at Marsel. "Have you taken any medication recently? You're a lot more cheerful than I expected."

Marsel sat on a stool designed for Schtatikians. His beige body bent in a neat line, with his legs folded precisely at 90 degrees. "Other species have visions as well as you humans. While preparing for this meeting, I experienced a revelation of my own."

"Not the tea leaves again," Bozidar said.

"Yes, the leaves." Marsel quivered. "You may not believe, but those raised in traditional familial groupings have more respect for the wisdom of our elders."

"You drink tea?" Cecily asked. "You've never offered me any."

"It is not the beverage you imagine," Bozidar said. "Most blobblings find it a punishment rather than a treat. Similar to your cod liver oil or medicinal herbs steeped in hot liquid. An old tale promises that while any worthy blobbling may attain honor through service, the exceptional ones will see their destiny in the tea leaves. The story is usually told during the frozen times, when the very young are susceptible to infection."

"And are forced to drink the tea to keep healthy?" Cecily asked. "Thanks for sharing the information, not the tea."

"I'll probably regret asking," Gary said, rubbing his temples, "but what did you see in the leaves?"

Marsel wriggled on his stool. "It was not so much seeing as sensing. I felt an uplifting calm, much as I experienced when I helped commandeer this ship."

"That was the logical result of panic," Bozidar said. "Your emotional system was overloaded."

"I will not argue with you," Marsel said. "I will only say that hidden at the center of that peace was the knowledge that we would succeed. Schtatik will be spared another round of conflict. We will rescue The Descendant, um, Edna, and our exploits will be sung for generations."

"Yeah, I knew I would regret asking," Gary said. He sat with Susan and held her hand. "Are you okay? What did Agnes show you?"

"That she's happy," Susan said. "Maybe Marsel is right to be optimistic."

"We need more than optimism," Bozidar said. "We need a plan. A better one than we had before."

Susan nodded. "I agree."

Cecily sat at the table and tapped a panel embedded in its surface. "The only thing wrong with our last plan was that we didn't know the situation on Schtatik. Now we do."

A computer screen emerged from a slot. Cecily tapped again, and the image on the screen was projected in the air above the table. The hologram showed a ringed planet with three moons. The planet was shimmery and lilac-colored. The three moons varied in color, reflecting shades of purple and shadow.

"It's beautiful," Susan said.

"You'll love the flowers, Mom," Cecily said as she tapped commands. She highlighted one of the continents. "We think Grandma is hiding here."

The image rearranged itself, zooming in on a large mountain range as if the viewer were flying in a helicopter. It skimmed through a rocky pass and descended into the valley beyond, giving an aerial view of a large stone fortress. It swirled around turreted towers, rushed down the walls to the rock base supporting the structure, and focused on a glittering pink river far below and inaccessible except by parachute.

"It looks like Machu Picchu," Gary said. "Not the fortress, the land. That sheer rock face with the river below and mountains above."

Cecily nodded. "That's where they got the idea. Before they crashed in the San Francisco Bay, the first beige expedition sent back images of Earth, mostly from the Pacific side of the Americas. Machu Picchu was one they really liked."

"The yellow clan was fond of the statues on what you call Easter Island," Marsel said.

"I thought you said the yellow clan was extinct," Susan said.

"More like over-dyed," Cecily said. "Intermarriage

with other clans. Yellow is a recessive gene, apparently."

"They are as weak-willed as they are weak-hued," Marsel said.

Green smoke trickled from Bozidar's ears. "Let us not waste time with colorist gossip. We have issues enough in our own clan, and rescue missions do not plan themselves."

"You got that right," Cecily muttered as her fingers danced on the panel. The image shifted again, zooming to the pink river and a section of the river bank that widened to a flat, smooth beach. "This is the only open space anywhere near the fortress," she said.

"Can the beach be seen?" Gary asked. "It isn't much use as a staging ground if they know we're there."

"Agreed," Cecily said, "but it is perfect for a diversion. We'll drop some building material there and make a platform. When that's done we'll drop furnishings. Chairs, tables, whatever we can think of to make it look like we're setting up a place to negotiate."

"Won't that be dangerous?" Susan asked. She shivered as chilled air flooded the room. The scent of lemon and rosemary drifted on the breeze. "Did the air conditioner just kick in? It's freezing in here."

"Yes, and yes," Bozidar said. "The crew constructing the platform could be fired upon at any time by those guarding the fortress. However, our last attempt to rescue Edna was conducted with subterfuge and force. Those guarding her now will expect us to try diplomacy."

"Why?" Susan asked.

Marsel's shoulders jerked. "That is the procedure among the beiges." His tone was clipped, sharp. "Does your species not have rules governing conflict?"

"Yes, but we break them all the time." Gary shook his head. "Cecily, what have you been telling these guys?"

"They don't listen," she said as she went to the food dispenser. "Like this arctic wind. I keep telling them it's too cold, but they won't reset the thermostat." She returned to the table with a tray of cups filled with steaming liquid. "This will help."

Susan sniffed the liquid and inspected its color. She raised one perfectly plucked eyebrow. "It's clear, pink, and smells of cinnamon. Tell me what I win."

"Good nose, Mom," Cecily said. "This is water from the stream below the fortress. Well, a replicated version. Think of it like the coca leaves Peruvians chew in the Andes, but without the narcotic side effects."

Susan sipped. She closed her eyes and relaxed her shoulders. "Not bad. I feel warmer already. What's sweetening it?"

"That's what the water tastes like," Cecily said. "Sort of a cross between chai and wassail."

"I had hoped to retrieve Edna in my lifetime,"

Bozidar said. "Shall we continue with the plan?"

Gary drummed his fingers on the table. "I hate to be the voice of doom, but we're in over our heads. We're not soldiers. I can fall on stage without breaking my bones, but parachuting into a fortress? Shooting people? We don't have the training for that."

Marsel wriggled on his seat, and deep green smoke puffed from his skin. "You killed my clan members with relative ease, or don't they count as people?"

"They were attacking us," Gary said. He lowered his gaze. "And we didn't shoot them. We threw pillows at them."

"Dead is dead!" Marsel said.

"Yes, dead is dead." Susan set her cup on the table and leaned toward Marsel. "So let's not repeat past mistakes and get more people killed. You said they're expecting a diplomatic effort to free Edna. Why don't we try that?"

"We have nothing to offer them," Bozidar said.

"We have us," Cecily said. She pointed at Susan. "Remember the color experiments you let me do at the shop? You'd give me some fabric and let me do whatever I wanted."

"I hoped that would turn you into a quilter," Susan said.

"Not yet, but I do remember one thing. All blues fight."

"How does that apply here?" Gary asked.

"It suddenly hit me. The blues are cantankerous beyond belief." Cecily looked at the blank faces surrounding the table. "Guys, let's persuade the beiges that we're their best hope of stopping the blues from declaring war."

Susan opened her mouth, snapped it shut, and grabbed her cup. She did not drink. Her eyes might have been focused on a spot on the table, except there were no spots.

Gary cleared his throat. "Cecily, in the best of all possible worlds …" The sentence remained stillborn in his mouth as his voice faded into silence.

Marsel slid from his seat and toddled to the viewing port. His wheat-colored skin looked like buttery suede in the starlight. His stubby legs flexed in the middle as if he were doing knee bends.

"Do not even consider the possibility," Bozidar said.

Marsel twirled about. "But it could work!"

"Not with Edna as queen." Bozidar bent forward and rapped his head gently on the table as he repeated, "Not with Edna, not with Edna."

Marsel's skin glistened, and a riot of brilliant yellow and purple smoke swirled around him. "Yes, yes. Especially with Edna. I know some of those who have studied the legends and prophecies. Not all of them are entirely sane after spending their lives stuck in the library vaults, but that could work to our advantage." He rocked on his footpads, lurching from side to side like a wind-up toy.

Susan went to Marsel and pressed her hands on his shoulders, restricting his bouncing dance. "What legends?"

Bozidar lifted his head. His skin sagged like cheese about to melt, and his human-looking hair appeared to be made from plastic. His brown striped suit shrank against his body.

"Bozidar, breathe," Cecily said. "You're starting to morph back to your Schtatikian form, and you know how depressed you get when you snap back to the human shape."

Susan released Marsel and whirled toward Bozidar. "I thought you couldn't revert back to your normal form."

"He phases in and out when he's stressed," Cecily said.

Marsel skipped in circles around Susan, wreathing them both in yellow and purple smoke ribbons. "You will be healed, cousin, I promise. The prophecy will be fulfilled by the descendants of She Who Found Us."

Susan massaged her temples. "Marsel, please, you're not helping. Stop spewing smoke all over, and tell us what you know."

Marsel jiggled like gelatin, but the smoke dissipated. As the yellow and purple faded like morning mist, he toddled to his seat. Once at the table, he extended his arms and tapped at the panel in front of him. The image of the river fractured, replaced with scrolling, wavy lines that resembled the embroidery on Susan's crazy quilt.

"These are some of my favorite stories," he said. "The old legends about past glories and a peaceful empire when all Schtatik was harmonious. Then an argument ruined the balance between the clans. Each strove for dominance, which brought chaos and suffering to the people."

"A tragedy, I'm sure," Susan said. She slid into her seat and sipped from her cup. "Get to the part about rescuing my mother."

"The universe itself wept at the misery of our people," Marsel said. "A young beige blobbling, born in the ashes of our last city, with her very first words spoke a prophecy that promised redemption."

"And when is that supposed to happen?" Cecily asked.

"When the beige clan is purged of its pride." Marsel prodded Bozidar. "Is it not obvious? We were brought to our knees by the foolishness of the taupes, and their ill-fated invasion of Earth. You did not find yourselves fighting them by accident. The universe itself brought them to your door. Your easy defeat of them is proof that we were meant to meet. Again."

Cecily rubbed her hands together. "This would make a great movie."

"Sweetie, let's stop the war first. We can think about your next film later," Susan said.

"Come on, Mom. You've got to admit this has all the makings of an epic."

Marsel leaped from his seat and bounced around

the table. "I know this word! It is a magnificent word. *Epic. Epic, epic, epic.* Oh, I will write the story of She Who Found Us, your ancestor Agnes, and her courage. She saved our first expedition, keeping the knowledge of their existence secret. Then comes Edna, who could not keep a secret upon pain of death and whose mere presence causes chaos and trembling."

"That's actually a spot-on character analysis," Gary whispered to Susan.

Marsel did not notice. He swayed as if to music only he could hear. His rubbery skin glowed like polished brass. "Her arrival on Schtatik, her elevation to queen, it was part of the fabric of reality. When the stars were born, the universe itself planned that she would come, show us the error of false pride, and let the beige clan fulfill its destiny to save our world."

Bozidar inhaled and lifted his head from the table. He exhaled, and the edges of his face firmed, his clothes and hair returning to their human condition. "Every clan has the same story, you idiot. Even the yellows tell their mixed-hue young that somehow true yellows will appear to reclaim Schtatikian values."

Susan rested her elbows on the table and leaned toward Bozidar. "How seriously do the clans take these legends?"

Bozidar froze, as did Cecily and Gary. Marsel continued swaying.

Susan laughed. "Pick up your jaws and relax. I'm

not suggesting we try to prove the beige clan's prophecy, only that we use elements of it to convince the factions to work together."

"We reframe the story," Gary said. He leaned back in his chair, crossed his arms, and fixed his gaze on the scrolling lines of the hologram. After a moment, he nodded. "It's a better idea than trying to storm a castle."

SIX

"T RYING TO STORM A CASTLE?" B OZIDAR SHUDDERED. "I do not understand that phrase. Do you mean you would create a storm around the structure, or within it?"

"No, it means to attack a fortified position," Gary said. "I meant that persuading the beiges to work with us is better than fighting them."

"We've got a week or so before we reach Schtatik," Cecily said. "I can help Marsel research the old legends."

"Gary, why don't you help too?" Susan suggested.

"Why? I'm not a politician, or a historian." Gary grimaced. "You don't want to know my grades from college."

"True, but you are an actor. Look at the legends

as back story for the characters we need to be when we start negotiations." Susan pursed her lips. "If I'm going to rescue my mother, I have to be more of a queen than she is. I need to present myself as the most powerful person in the universe."

"Yes!" Marsel said. He dropped to his knees and bowed to the floor. "The Descendants of She Who Found Us have truly returned."

Cecily scooped Marsel from the floor and propelled him out of the room. "Come along, my little acolyte. Show us the files." She turned her head and motioned with her chin for Gary to follow.

He tilted his head toward Susan and narrowed his eyes. "You so owe me for this."

"I know," she whispered.

The door closed behind him. Silence filled the room. Flashes of light from the stars swirled against the walls.

Bozidar inhaled. "Please tell me that one of the meanings of acolyte is he who will be sacrificed to the gods at the earliest opportunity."

Susan kept her voice light and sweet. "I'm sorry."

Bozidar tapped his fingers together. "He was not like this before he met Edna. He was cautious, especially around off-worlders."

"Oh, I don't know," Susan said. "He always seemed a little excitable to me."

"He will not survive what is to come."

Susan jumped at the note of doom in Bozidar's voice. "Don't think like that. We're going to get through this. All of us. We'll find a way."

Bozidar smiled but kept his gaze fixed on the view from the port. "You misunderstand. I have promised myself he will not survive. I will throttle him before the end."

"He doesn't have a neck."

His smile grew wider. "I will find a way."

* * *

Gary and Cecily sat at a long table in a narrow room. Shelves lining the walls held rolled mats made from small sticks bound by bright cords woven in a herringbone pattern. Four screens rose from slots in the table, and holographic keyboards appeared on the surface in front of Gary and Cecily, responding to the movements of their fingers.

The lighting also adapted to their movements. When Gary moved from the table to the shelves, the shelf glowed around the scrolls he examined. As he returned to his seat, the glow faded, and the walls were left in shadow.

Marsel entered, pulling a cart behind him that squeezed between the table and the shelves. He parked the cart, pressed the top, and stepped back as the cover opened and a silvery metal rack of plated food rose from the interior.

"Our work has occupied several days, and I suspect we will continue our research until the last moment before reaching our destination," Marsel said. "We need to fortify ourselves to be as productive as possible in the remaining time."

He took the top plate and set it on the table. The rim of the pink plate sparkled with a painted silver vine twisting in loops and swirls around and over the edge. Three small dumplings nestled in the center, glowing golden atop a bright green leaf that could have come from a gigantic rose bush. Surrounding the dumplings was a ring of sparkling, bite-sized bits that resembled candied cherries dipped in silver glitter.

Cecily leaned across the table and inhaled. "That smells really good," she whispered. "Amazingly good. You've been holding out on me, Marsel. Most Schtatik cuisine smells like wet grass."

"I have tried to explain to the blessed granddaughter that I programmed our food production units to provide optimal nutrition," Marsel said to Gary. "Based on the air quality analysis, the computer has determined that the crew requires more simple vegetable matter."

"Thus, the wet grass smell." Cecily reached for the plate.

Gary pushed it toward her. "Eat. He's right about needing a break. Lunch was a long time ago." He accepted a plate from Marsel. "Did you bring us something to drink?" He popped a dumpling in his mouth.

"Yes, a very special beverage." Marsel pulled the rack higher to reveal three glasses filled with a thick, ruby red liquid—a milkshake in jewel tones. "My clan has guarded the secret of this recipe for many cycles. I swore an oath to protect it until the time of prophecy had arrived." He lifted a glass to the ceiling, and a shaft of light flashed down to illuminate the liquid. "That time is here." Marsel offered the glass to Cecily.

She raised her eyebrows at Gary, but took the glass and sipped. "Omigod, it's delicious. It's like the ripest strawberry you've ever tasted."

Gary dipped his finger in the glass Marsel placed in front of him, scooped a tiny mound and tasted it. "What is the secret you vowed to protect?"

Marsel hunched forward. "Luck and wisdom," he whispered.

"I beg your pardon?" Gary whispered. He shook his head and in a normal voice said, "What do you mean by luck and wisdom?"

Marsel's eyestalks rotated, scanning the room. "Drink, and whatever secrets you require will reveal themselves."

"Seriously?" Cecily asked. "I could have used this for my physics class. Cheers."

As she touched glasses with Gary, Marsel yipped. "Do not spill!"

"Relax," Cecily said. "This is an old Earth custom. Come on, join us. Just touch the rim against ours."

Marsel wrapped his hands around the last glass on the rack. He inhaled and lifted the glass toward Cecily and Gary. As they clinked, the tiniest ringing chime hovered above the three.

"That's the spirit," Cecily said.

"Down the hatch." Gary gulped his drink.

"Should I say something as well?" Marsel asked.

Wiping his mouth, Gary said, "To luck and wisdom."

"To luck and wisdom," Marsel repeated. He tugged on the rack again, bringing up a tray of rubber domes with straws sticking out the top. Pressing one on the top of his glass, he brought the contraption to his mouth and pushed a blue circle on the side of the dome. When his mouth sealed around the tube, the liquid was vacuumed up to the last drop. He placed the glass in front of him, hummed five tuneless notes and drummed the top of the table. "Yes, to luck and wisdom. I feel the forces of the universe clipping the edges of misfortune away from our endeavors."

He propelled himself from his stool and paced along the shelves. He slowed, scanned one shelf from bottom to top, and squealed, "There is the scroll." His knees bent into a sort of crouch. He shot into the air, his arms stretched like thick rubber bands. They snapped back, fingers clutching the scroll, as he landed. He toddled to his stool and unrolled it.

Cecily dragged her chair around the table. She slid next to Marsel on one side as Gary shifted closer on the other. The three stared at the sticks and cords. Cecily ran her fingertip along the edge.

"Okay, I give up," she said. "I thought I understood your language, but I can't decipher any of these symbols. Tell me what it says."

"The language is very old. We do not speak it except in temple," Marsel said. "Only a priestess trained in the ancient forms could read it easily. My mother learned as a young acolyte, and she taught me. I am teaching Bozidar, but he is a difficult pupil."

He brought his hands to the sides of the scroll, hovering above the sticks. Again he hummed the five tuneless notes and chanted.

In the time of despair, in the age of uncertainty, the clans will quarrel. One clan, two clans,

will seek to set the bonfires alight, bringing grief to all the world.

Gary erupted in laughter. "You're kidding. That's worse than the script for the first movie I ever did."

"I didn't realize you were doing a sci-fi movie last winter," Cecily said.

"I wasn't. Years ago, in college, a bunch of us made a film. Sort of for a class. It was so awful."

Marsel smacked the table. "Do not disparage the gift we have received. With luck, I found the scroll. Where is your wisdom to understand it?"

"You're right, I apologize," Gary said. "Please continue."

One clan, one only, will bend to the will of life. This clan will lead the rest,

not as a despot but as a cousin, neither older nor younger. The moons will rise

in harmony, and the young will rejoice.

"The will of life. That's Grandma Edna," Cecily

said. "You were right about luck and wisdom, Marsel. This is exactly what we need." She swung herself around and pressed a panel near the door. "Mom? Get Bozidar and meet us in the common room. It took days, but we found something."

Marsel's skin glowed. He rolled the scroll into a tight bundle. He tapped Gary on the shoulder. "You have not added your rejoicing. Are you not pleased?"

Gary nodded. "No. I mean, yes, I am pleased. I'm just trying to get my head around the words."

Marsel pressed the scroll to Gary's temple. "The words are on the sticks. The scroll is longer than the distance from your mouth to the back of your skull. Also, I recall your alimentary canal extends downward, not upward. So how will your head go around the words?"

Gary batted Marsel's hand away from his eye. "We really have to write a dictionary of idioms for you. I meant I was trying to imagine how your people would interpret the prophecy. I think we could use it to co-opt the taupes as well as stop a war with the blues."

"How so?" Cecily asked.

Gary held up his finger. "Remember the line about cousins. The taupes are still angry over their defeat on Earth. They'll probably oppose anything that lets us get away. Isn't that right, Marsel?"

"Yes, I am afraid they will insist on punishment."

Gary nodded. "The rest of the beiges are angry with the taupes for launching an invasion without permission, and for getting their butts kicked."

"I see your point," Cecily said. "Even if we can persuade the blues to let us go, splits in the beige clan could be as much a problem for us."

"Exactly." Gary smiled. "But this prophecy might give the taupes a graceful exit strategy if we emphasize the part about cousins acting as equals. By working together everyone saves face, and we get to go home alive."

Marsel leaped off his stool and pushed past Cecily. "Hurry! We must tell the others about my luck finding the scroll and your wisdom interpreting it."

Gary and Cecily raced after Marsel the entire way to the common room. When they burst in the door, Bozidar and Susan were sitting at the table. The viewing port behind them was filled with light from the swirling stars as the ship swam pleated space ahead of it.

Marsel bounded across the room, untying the scroll as he went. He spread the bundle on the table, sticks clattering as they unrolled. "Here, read as I taught you."

Bozidar bent over the scroll, tracing the symbols with his finger. "I owe you thanks, Marsel. If I understand the words here correctly, this could work for us. The blues might agree to negotiate peace if we present the prophecy to the right people in the clan first."

"What about the taupes?" Gary asked.

"The taupes are not threatening war," Bozidar

said, but as the words left his mouth, he sat straighter. "I see your point. They need a way to hide their shame."

"Gary called it a graceful exit strategy," Cecily said.

Bozidar nodded. "Yes, let us focus on positive messages. We will need to use every advantage."

A rattling buzz echoed through the room as a holographic image of a planet appeared above the table. A small orange blip winked on and off near the planet.

"What's that?" Susan asked.

"That is Schtatik," Marsel said. "We are approaching orbiting distance. The bridge requires my presence." He bowed and dashed from the room.

"I keep forgetting he's the captain," Susan said.

"I know." Bozidar closed his eyes and sighed. "I wish I could forget." He shook his head, brown curls bouncing, and examined the scroll again. "No matter. We have a glimmer of hope with this prophecy. Let us transform that hope into a plan, and quickly. We have mere hours before we land."

SEVEN

"If we're that close, won't someone see us?" Susan asked. "Don't you have radar or sensors or something?"

"Yes," Bozidar held the scroll in one hand, tapping it against his thigh as he paced. He stopped in front of the viewing port.

The swirling starlight slowed. Darkness filled the screen as the stars re-emerged like glittering drops hanging in the fabric of space.

"If all goes as planned, the bribes we made before leaving will keep those monitoring the sensors from reporting our arrival." Bozidar glanced at the others. "Of course, nothing has gone as I planned for a very long time."

Susan snapped her fingers. "Bribes! I completely forgot. Do we have enough time to thaw some cupcakes?"

Bozidar's mouth opened and closed, his jaw tensing. "Your language is difficult enough to interpret without adding the leaps in logic of which you humans are capable."

"Cupcakes, Mother?" Cecily asked. "Are you holding out on me again?"

"No, it's my fault," Gary said. "We brought some red velvet cupcakes as a surprise for you. Your mother was going to bring them out at dinner the first night we were on board. That didn't happen, so I put them in the freezer."

Bozidar threw the scroll on the table and clenched his hands. Green smoke puffed from his ears. "It is no wonder Marsel has become impossible. You humans are incapable of completing a single thread, following a single thought. I understand the word cup, and the word cake, and neither can be reasonably associated with bribes." He waved the smoke from his face. "At least I am not afflicted with smoke disorder. Marsel will need to spend a great deal of time in meditation once we are finished with you."

Cecily picked up the scroll and tied it with a neat bow. "A cupcake," she said, her voice as sweet and sing-song as a preschool teacher's, "is a small cake. It might have been baked in a cup a long time ago, but not anymore. It's a treat parents often use as a bribe to get their children to behave."

"Thank you," Bozidar said.

"My turn," Cecily said. "What is smoke disorder?"

Bozidar dropped his head. "I should not have mentioned that," he mumbled.

"Well, you did, so tell us what you mean."

Cecily sat at the table, drumming her fingers. Susan and Gary also sat, watching Bozidar. He turned to the viewing port, inhaled, and spun on his heel.

"The multicolored smoke." He lifted his chin and glared.

Cecily motioned for him to continue. Gary passed his hand across his lips, not quite hiding a smile.

Bozidar shifted from one foot to the other. He cleared his throat. "My species gives non-verbal clues to our emotional state, as does yours. Smoke is one of them. Green is anger. Red is confusion or embarrassment. As blobblings, we learn to control ourselves. Marsel is forgetting those lessons. His excitement over the prophecy has … " His shoulders sagged, and his head drooped.

"I see," Gary said. "So that's why you've been so hard on him."

"It is humiliating to watch," Bozidar said.

"I thought it was cute," Cecily said.

"But we won't mention it to anyone," Susan said.

Gary sat straight. "Why not? Marsel's mother was a priestess, right? In our culture, priests and shamans get to behave in ways most people never would, or should." He pointed to the scroll. "Here we are in space, surrounded by machines and computers, and Marsel has us reading painted sticks. Why would you even have them here?"

Bozidar sat next to Gary. "I would not. Marsel insists on creating a small sanctuary wherever he is. The ancient texts are available in the data banks, but he prefers to study them in the traditional ways."

"Is he part of a religious order, like his mother?" Susan asked.

Bozidar shook his head. "Our roles change as we do. Our aptitudes and skills are monitored so that we can be moved into the positions most required by the clan and most likely to suit our abilities. Perhaps after this, if we survive, he will be requisitioned by the temple. They will regret their decision, but it will benefit me."

Cecily snorted. "That's not remotely true. You and Marsel are friends. He's done everything you've asked him to do, and rescued both of us back on Schtatik."

"Yes, he did." Bozidar sank his head onto his hands. "I am most vexed. There is no order left in the universe."

Gary patted Bozidar on the back. "I thought you figured that out when you met Edna." He smiled at Susan. "Yes, she's your mother, but you know I'm speaking the truth."

"Did I hear someone say we have cupcakes?" Cecily asked.

"Yes, we do," Susan said as she rose from her seat. She scowled at Gary, but her eyes twinkled, and the flat line of her lips arched into a grin. "Cheer up,

Bozidar. My mother gets into the worst kind of trouble, but everything works out in the end. And life is always interesting. So why don't you get a crew member to bring the cupcakes here while I get another surprise from my quarters."

Susan retrieved the ruby ring and slipped it on her right index finger. The silver band felt tight, so she put it on the ring finger instead. Once again, the scent of sea breezes filled the air around her. She scanned the corners of the room for traces of a ghostly child turning cartwheels.

Finding herself alone, Susan rejoined the others just as the hatch to the hallway slid open. A crew member toddled in with the red velvet cupcakes on a gleaming bronze tray. Marsel followed.

Susan checked the stars visible in the viewing port. "Have we arrived?"

"Almost." Marsel wriggled onto a chair. "We successfully eluded the monitoring array, and those holding Edna made no threats when we entered the stronghold's airspace. It appears the bribes were sufficient. I am pleased you expected good news."

"What do you mean?" Cecily asked.

"The crew member is bringing the special treat your mother brought. Is this not part of the celebration of our success?"

Susan popped open the top of the container. "Not quite. I had forgotten all about the cupcakes. Now seemed as good a time as any to enjoy them."

Marsel leaned over the table, stretching his whole

body toward the container. "What do you call these?"

"Red velvet," Susan said. "They smell good, don't they? Even after being frozen and thawed in alien contraptions." She plucked a cake and offered it to him.

Marsel reached for the treat, then snapped his hands to his body and flicked one eyestalk toward Susan's ruby ring. The other coiled around her hand and examined the ring from the bottom.

Susan dropped the cupcake. "What are you doing?" she said as she slid her wrist from the appendage.

"Bozidar, did you notice her ring?" Marsel asked, settling back on his chair. "You did not. I can see it in your face. Surrounded by clues, and oblivious to their meaning."

"Clues?" Bozidar asked. "In off-world food and off-world ornaments?"

Cecily motioned her mother to give her the ring. "Huh, how about that. When did you get this, Mom?"

"I must have had it for years. It was in a case of things that belonged to Agnes. How Mother missed it I'll never know, but I remember her giving me those mementos."

"It was waiting for the proper moment to reveal itself," Marsel said. "The captain who led that first expedition to your planet left it there, as She Who Found Us left it for you."

Gary examined the ring. "We read about rings in one of those scrolls. And a red biscuit."

"That is a very crude translation," Marsel said.

"Hey, don't complain to me," Gary said as he handed the ring to Bozidar. "That's how the translation came up. Biscuit."

Bozidar fell silent as he stroked the ruby. He ran his finger around the setting and placed the jewel next to the cupcake Susan had dropped. "Red and white."

"What about red and white?" Susan asked, retrieving her jewelry.

Bozidar sat, angling the chair to look out the viewing port without turning his back on the others. "The captain of that expedition, the one whose transformed remains is in the quilt your great-grandmother made, had many talents. Not only could she hold together the transformation of her entire crew and communicate with an alien species, she could also manipulate stones for healing. The old stories tell of her using a red stone and a white metal."

Susan twisted the ring around her finger. "Silver could be considered a white metal. You think she showed Agnes a ring like this in a vision?"

Bozidar shook his head. "I think she gave Agnes that ring."

Marsel jumped from his chair and danced. "Blindness has been wiped from your eyes, cousin."

Gary rapped on the table. "Excuse me. What about the cupcakes?"

Marsel stopped in mid-step, one foot hovering above the floor. "They are red and white. They are small and baked. These symbols from our legends will clear the way for us. Our plan will be embraced." He dropped his foot pad and bounced like a pogo stick.

"Marsel, please. Save the joyous dancing for a true victory." Bozidar rubbed his eyes. "I agree we have a better chance now with artifacts as well as prophecy."

"A better chance? We will succeed brilliantly," Marsel said. "You will see."

"Yes, we will," Bozidar said. "We have arrived."

The scene in the viewing port had changed from stars in a black field to the lilac, ringed planet of Schtatik. A spikey ridge extended from the top of the screen to the bottom, split through the middle by a thin pink line.

"That's the mountain range, isn't it?" Gary asked. "And the river. Unless there's more than one pink river on your planet."

"No, that is the only one. We will land here tomorrow, before dawn." Bozidar pointed to a small disk-shaped region. "We arrived later than I expected, but perhaps that is just as well. I need to consider the precise language I will use at our first meeting. Since we do not know who will greet us, it would be best to craft several versions of the speech." He gathered the cupcakes on the tray. "I would like to take these with me, and your ring. Please."

Susan placed it in his hand. "Will we all be going?"

Before Bozidar could speak, Gary said, "If you're

going, I am too. Cecily and Marsel should stay here, in reserve."

Bozidar nodded. "An excellent suggestion."

"I'd protest, but I'm pretty sure I'll be outvoted," Cecily said. She folded her arms. "Don't think I'll be this pleasant about being left behind next time."

"The plan is mine," Marsel said. "I should be there."

Susan patted his head. "Not this time. Gary's right about keeping some ammunition in reserve. Let's talk more over dinner."

* * *

The lights in Susan and Gary's room brightened to a dim glow. A pitiless, mechanical female voice announced, "Time to awaken. Time to awaken. Time to awaken."

Gary groaned and covered his head with a pillow.

Susan shook his shoulder. "You volunteered to come with us." She sat on the edge of the bed and rotated her ankles. When the clicking in her joints stopped, she stretched one arm to the ceiling. Yawning, she switched arms.

Gary groaned again. "Why are you so serene this morning? I didn't sleep at all."

"Single mom. Three kids. Business to run. I'm used to not sleeping."

"Right." He threw off the covers and ambled toward the bathroom.

Susan entered the common room and nodded to

Bozidar, who sat at the table. She straightened her bathrobe and tapped the food unit. A cup of steaming liquid appeared that smelled something like fresh-brewed coffee. "Do we have time for breakfast?"

"Since no one is expecting us, our schedule is open." He stared at the viewing port.

"You don't seem as upbeat as you did last night."

"I have had the entire sleep period to consider the many flaws in our plan." He pointed to the landing area. "The first flaw is assuming someone will monitor that precise location."

Gary entered, tucking his shirt into his jeans. He ordered toast and orange juice from the food unit. He sat near the viewing port and watched the mountain tops flash with reflected light as the night receded. "It's already dawn in the valley."

"Not quite." Bozidar rose from his chair and stood in front of the screen. "The valley is quite deep. We have time yet before the sun is high enough."

"I'd better get dressed," Susan said.

As she returned, clad in jeans and a blue sweater, Marsel entered the room. He carried a small box made from a dark wood and trimmed with brass fittings. "The cupcakes are in here." He placed the box on the table in front of Gary. "Where is the ring?"

Bozidar retrieved it from his pocket. "I think you should wear it, Susan."

She slipped the ring on her finger and picked up the box. "If we're going to go, we should go."

"Aren't you going to say goodbye to Cecily?" Gary asked.

"She was never a morning person," Susan said as she headed toward the corridor.

The landing pod stood in the hangar, its skin glinting green from the lights glowing in the ceiling. Crew members monitored the retractable staircase as it unfolded from the pod and worked its way to the floor. When all the supports had clicked in place, Bozidar climbed the steps, his feet thumping on each tread. Gary took the box from Susan and followed Bozidar.

Susan rested her hand on the railing. She looked at the ruby ring, sighed, and scanned the hangar. She squared her shoulders and took a step.

"Mom," Cecily said. Her hair clung to her scalp like crimped pie crust. One purple-tipped curl wavered above her eyebrow. She wore dark, stretchy pants and an oversized green tunic. Her feet were bare. "You were just going to leave?"

"I didn't want to wake you." Susan hugged her. She buried her face on Cecily's shoulder and pressed her lips together. *If you cry now, she'll insist on coming along.* She raised her head, willing herself to smile as she drank in one last look at her daughter. "You don't have slippers?"

"The floors are heated. Schtatikians don't wear shoes." Cecily held her mother at arm's length. "Good luck. Be careful."

Susan chuckled. "That's my line, sweetie. We left

one of the cupcakes for you."

Her voice dried in her throat like grass under an August sun. She hugged Cecily until she heard Bozidar call her. She released her grip, spun around and ran up the steps.

The hatch closed behind her. The console glowed under Bozidar's fingers. Squares, triangles, rectangles, and circles swirled in their turn, flashed, and disappeared. Susan sat on a bench next to Gary. The pod shuddered, and a low roar whirled around the compartment. The lights modulated from a harsh blue-white through green-tinged and settled into a soothing amber glow. The ship strained as if it were a racing sloop tacking into the wind for an instant, then silence and stillness prevailed.

"How long will it take?" Gary asked, his voice barely above a whisper.

"Minutes," Bozidar said. "The engines are most efficient, now that we are flying in the atmosphere for which the ship was designed."

Bozidar stayed at the console, tapping codes. As the ship approached the ground, the lights reverted to a harsh blue-white. The low roar was followed by a shudder. Bozidar pressed a flashing rectangle. The hatch opened onto a shadow-shrouded vista.

Susan shivered in her sweater as the three descended. The sun cleared the peaks of the mountains as her foot touched the ground. She inhaled the cool, floral-scented air.

A series of soft clicks sounded around them like

hundreds of tiny mouse traps springing at the same time. As the sun rose higher, Susan could make out a dozen squat Schtatikians, all the color of wet sand on an overcast morning, and all pointing weapons at them.

"Ah," Bozidar said. "It appears I was wrong. They did know we were coming."

EIGHT

Susan closed her eyes. *I'm going to wake up now and make breakfast for Olivia and Eleanor. I'll get them to school and go to the quilt shop. Cecily will call about her film. My mother ....*

A vision of Edna's snarky gaze flitted across Susan's imagination. She opened her eyes to see the pink river, the glowing sun warming the landscape with green-tinged light, and the arc of Schtatik's rings like a permanent rainbow in the sky. She raised her hands and scrunched her lips into what she hoped looked like a smile. "We mean you no harm," she said in a voice so soft she barely heard herself.

"They have the weapons," Bozidar said. "Any sentient being with a moderately evolved logic function can see that we are harmless."

Agnes' face flickered in Susan's brain. *Tell them

what you want, Agnes said. Susan lowered her hands. The air shimmered behind one beige creature. It wore the same scarf and held the same weapon as the others, but a flash of Agnes in her pinafore flickered above his head.

Susan addressed that creature. "I'm here to speak with my mother, Edna."

The creature trembled. Its scarf slipped to the ground as it lowered the gun, beige skin rippling around the edges of its squat body. The creature squeaked once as if clearing its throat. It grunted a series of sharp syllables.

Another soldier squawked in return and left the circle. The others remained, weapons aimed at Susan. The one who gave the order retrieved its scarf but left its weapon pointing toward the ground.

Gary took a step toward Susan, stopping in mid-stride as half of the Schtatikians aimed at him. He clutched the box of cupcakes to his chest. "Sweetheart, should we let Bozidar speak for us?"

Bozidar said, "No, you should not. She is doing extremely well."

"The guns are still pointed at us." Gary edged closer to Susan.

"But the leader has lowered his."

"How do you know he's the leader?" Gary asked.

"I recognize him. The question that concerns me is how *she* knew he is the leader," Bozidar said.

"Shush," Susan said. She nodded to the creature in front of her. "I am grateful for your work caring for Edna, granddaughter of She Who Found You."

"Can he understand you?" Gary asked, his lips moving only enough for the words to escape.

"Does it matter?" Bozidar said. "They are not killing us yet."

"Stay calm," Susan said. "It will all work out because it has to. I have two daughters back on Earth who need me."

The sun crept higher. Mist from the river evaporated in the warming air. A buzz settled over the banks as winged things, small and large, darted between rocks and plants. Some dived into the water, emerging with breakfast. Others skimmed the surface as if washing their undercarriages.

A whisper of a breeze floated over the riverbank. Underneath that whisper was the sound of pounding feet. The buzz dissipated as the winged creatures fled. The Schtatikians guarding Bozidar, Gary, and Susan tightened their circle. Susan raised her hands again.

The pounding intensified. Susan could visualize her mother racing from the castle followed by bouncing beige creatures.

"Susan!" Edna burst through the ring, shoving aside Schtatkians. She grabbed her daughter in the biggest hug her smaller frame could manage. She shifted to hold more of Susan, and the two fell on the ground in the tangle of her robes.

Edna's pursuers skidded into the guards she had pushed aside. The ring smacked into each other like billiard balls. Bozidar pulled Gary from the path of churning legs, scarves, and eyestalks. The weapon of the last guard to fall sailed overhead, bounced off the landing pod hull and discharged an energy bolt across the river.

Susan rolled to her knees, smoothed back her hair, and smiled. "Hello, Mother. We've come to bring you home."

"Good luck with that." Edna spit out sand. "These critters won't let me get more than two feet from the castle. I only escaped now because someone left the door open. I may be old, but I'm wiry. And faster than they are."

A guard leaped to his feet. "We are protecting you, Your Highness."

Edna glared at him. "I knew you could understand me. No one made a peep the entire time I've been here. Just chitters and squeaks. I could have gone crazy talking to myself. You call that protecting me?"

Bozidar stepped over the tangle of guards and lifted Edna from the ground. "Actually, it is. A mere guard would not presume to speak to the queen."

Gary helped Susan to her feet. "You just know she's going to use that line when we get her home."

"You said that out loud," Susan whispered.

"I wouldn't. I couldn't. Edna would punch me." He handed her the box.

"Who would I punch?" Edna snatched the box and removed the lid. "Oooh, cupcakes. Not my favorite, but after all these weeks of healthy eating I'm not picky." She removed one of the treats.

The beige creatures chittered and bowed. The leader of the guards trembled, then emitted a string of howling syllables that sounded like wolves on Halloween.

"Oh, for Pete's sake, it's a cupcake," Edna said. "And a miniature one at that. There aren't enough carcinogens in this to kill a goldfish."

Bozidar took the cupcake and returned it to the box. "They are not reacting to the fat and sugar. They are awestruck in the face of prophecy." He gave the box to Gary. "I do so hate it when Marsel is right."

* * *

"The castle looked a whole lot closer to the river in the picture," Susan said as they trudged up a rise that grew steeper with each step.

"Maps do that," Gary said. "Leave out vital information like elevation changes. Or road closures."

"Jeez, you're in the middle of paradise and still you complain." Edna muscled her way along the path to a wider spot. She waited for Susan to catch up. "I'm still cheesed that you eloped, but thanks for coming."

"You're welcome." Susan paused, panting. "I thought I was in better shape."

"You probably are." Edna pointed to the mountains. "We're pretty high up. I've had time to acclimate."

"There are other differences between the planets," Bozidar said. "The oxygen content in the atmosphere, for example. I am surprised no one thought to offer you a *turgan*."

"They did. It looked like a floating guillotine and I told them to keep it." Edna said.

"What's a *turgan*?" Gary asked.

"A transportation device similar to your scooters, but with anti-gravity capability," Bozidar said.

Susan blocked the path. "Bring me one. Now."

Edna folded her arms. "This is new, Daughter."

"Mother, we are on an alien planet on the brink of war. I'm having visions. I think I'm entitled to a little assistance getting up this bloody mountain." Susan mimicked Edna's stance from the planted feet to the extended chin.

"Who's complaining?" Edna said. "I like it."

"Of course you do," Bozidar muttered.

The guards trained their weapons on Bozidar. A creature resembling a dragonfly but twice the size and with pulsing lights rimming its wings hovered over Bozidar's head before zipping toward the river. It squealed like a pack of children running from the neighborhood bully.

"Oh, for crying out loud," Edna said. "Put those damn things down. We're all the good guys here, understand?"

The beige soldiers trembled, eyestalks shaking in the breeze. The leader chirped twice, and they lowered their weapons. Bozidar stepped toward Edna, and the guards tightened the circle.

Edna rolled her eyes and shoved through the soldiers. She glowered at them, and grabbed Bozidar's elbow. "Space boy is under my protection, understand? If anybody's going to break his neck, it'll be me. Until that happens, lay off."

"Mother, what on earth makes you think they'll obey you?" Susan asked.

"We're not on Earth, child of mine," Edna said, dragging Bozidar along as she headed up the path. "On this planet, I am queen of the universe, and my word is law."

"Not queen of the universe, just the clan," Bozidar said.

"Don't ruin it, space boy." Edna spun around and pointed her finger at the guards. "Has someone called the castle for a cart for my daughter? *Turgan!*"

The leader pressed a jewel on the end of his scarf. After a series of chirps, the creature approached Edna, bowing so low its eyestalks brushed the ground. "The *turgan* will arrive in a moment, Your Majesty. Regret upon regret, ma'am, that we did not fulfill your will more quickly."

Susan leaned against a boulder. "What have you been telling these guys, Mom?"

"Nothing. Well, I told them to let me out, but I didn't think they were listening because I'm still here." Edna joined Susan at the rock, with Bozidar right behind. "I sure as hell wasn't spouting dialog from *Hamlet.*"

A low thrumming vibrated dust that danced around Susan's shoes. "Is that the *turgan*?" She leaned toward the noise but shrank back with a gasp as the machine came into view.

The contraption hovered above the ground and towered over the humans. A platform the size of a wading pool rested on a thick ring of glowing silver metal. Six slender rods of the same metal rose up around the perimeter of the platform. Delicate ivy-like plants grew at their bases. Tendrils from the plants wove themselves around and between the rods to make a living railing. A fabric canopy stretched across the top of the rods and a large metal plate hung from the center. The plate was thin and angled, with a razor-sharp edge.

"I told you it was a floating guillotine," Edna said.

"The blade thingy looks scary," Susan said.

"It is an energy collector," Bozidar said. "The plants and the metal have a symbiotic relationship. The interaction between them creates the anti-gravitation field."

The *turgan* stopped in front of Susan. She touched the ivy tendrils, which parted while she stepped on the platform, then rewove themselves when she gripped one of the rods. "There's room for more."

Gary clapped Bozidar on the shoulder. "Come on, space boy. You'll be safer with us." The tendrils parted for them, also.

The guards motioned for Edna to join the group. She scowled at the leader, snapped her fingers, and pointed to the ground behind her. One by one, some with drooping eyestalks, the little beige soldiers formed a line. Edna nodded and set a steady march along the path. The guards followed like ducklings, their rectangular bodies rocking from side to side on stubby legs.

The *turgan* whooshed a foot higher and floated behind the last guard. "Does anyone else think my mother looks like the mayor of the Munchkins leading her people to the Emerald City?" Susan asked.

Gary's shoulders heaved as he swallowed a laugh. A tiny snort escaped. "I won't tell Edna what you said if you don't tell her I laughed."

Susan nodded. "We're lucky this contraption is noisy."

"I do not understand you," Bozidar said. "There is no city near the castle, which is pink, not emerald."

"Just another one of those cultural references," Gary said.

"You spoke of creating a dictionary of idioms. I do not remember a conversation about cultural references." Bozidar twisted a leaf until it whimpered. "Forgive me," he whispered to the plant.

Susan edged away from the railing. "The plants can feel?"

"All living beings feel," Bozidar said. "Some are better than others at expressing those feelings." He grabbed a metal rod as the *turgan* jigged to avoid a rocky outcropping. "Perhaps your suggestion for a dictionary is more important than you intended. I have lost too much information. For example, I have yet to understand the significance of *red* velvet cupcakes. Why is that color of velvet edible, but others are not?"

Susan patted his arm. "I can't think of a way to explain that wouldn't confuse you more."

"The success of my mission to Earth depended on knowing such small details," Bozidar said.

"I guess I should be grateful your intelligence agency screwed up," Susan said.

Gary grabbed a metal rod as he rolled to his feet. "We screwed up too. When Cecily, Edna, and Scott came here to settle the beige clan feud with us, we didn't know about the problems between the beiges and the blues. The film Cecily made to show your family connection to the beiges backfired and made the blues think we were going to help the beiges wipe them out. We can't stop the war until we understand what really started it."

"There is not enough time left in the universe to understand the blues," Bozidar said.

"Yes, there is," Susan said. "What's lacking is the will to try. Maybe that's what Agnes has been trying to tell me."

* * *

The stone fortress glowed a rosy pink against the

lavender sky and swirling blue clouds. Susan descended from the *turgan* and stared at the stark, blank walls rising above her. Rectangular slabs the size of dining room tables interlocked, row by row. Some of the slabs glittered in the sun, while others absorbed whatever light touched their surface. There were no openings of any kind. Susan remembered wide balconies from the holographic image Bozidar showed her, but none of them were visible from the ground.

"Don't lean too far back, you'll land on your butt," Edna said. "Ask me how I know."

"I saw a picture of the fortress before we landed," Susan said. "It looked big, but not this big."

"It's a monster all right," Edna said. "It takes an army to clean it. Come on in and let me give you a tour."

She hooked Susan's arm, motioning Gary and Bozidar to follow. They stepped onto a semi-circle of flat stones fanning out from two larger, dark rose slabs at the base of the center wall. Music flowed toward them down the walls, sounding like a cross between a trumpet blast and violins tuning.

"Apparently, that's my theme music," Edna said. "Now watch the doors."

The dark rose stones opened outward. A rush of chilled, lemon-scented air poured out from a polished malachite hallway.

"After me," Edna said as she entered the fortress.

Susan discovered her eyes did not have to adjust to being inside. "Where is all this light coming from?"

"Poke your head around the corner," Edna said.

Susan turned left into a wood-paneled room filled with furniture she couldn't quite identify. It also possessed a view of the outside. She threaded her way through the groupings of what could be seating areas to the exterior wall. The window matched the dimensions of the stone slabs.

"Figure it out yet?" Edna followed her.

"Some of the stones are transparent, at least from one side," Susan said. "Like a two-way mirror."

"That's what I think," Edna said. "Not that anyone will tell me."

Bozidar entered and sat on an upholstered piece. "As I mentioned before, a mere guard would never presume to instruct someone of your rank."

Susan held up her hand. "Shush. We've got more important things to argue about." The sentence trailed away as Susan remembered the ruby ring. "Mom, was this yours?"

Edna joined her at the window. "I don't think so. Where'd you get it?"

"You must have given it to me. I found it in a box with other mementos from Agnes."

Edna arched her eyebrow. "I love you dearly, Daughter, but no way I would have parted with a ring this pretty. Is the ruby real?"

"I think so."

Bozidar cleared his throat. "There are more

pressing matters to discuss."

"How about you fill me in first," Edna said. "I've been cooped up here for ages. No explanations, no news, nothing."

"How long has it been, Mom? Since the trial, I mean." Susan perched on a wooden structure that combined a bench and a stepstool.

"I honestly don't know. Three weeks? Five? Hard to keep track of the days without a newspaper."

"Don't worry about the timeline." Gary stood in the entrance. "Tell us what happened."

Edna settled onto a large upholstered seat that resembled a throne. "I swear it wasn't my fault. I just wanted to be in space, see the stars, walk on another planet. Not that we did much walking. As soon as we landed, we were herded around like diseased cattle."

Bozidar cringed. "I am ashamed that you, Cecily, and Scott were treated so disgracefully."

"It's only one incident on a long list," Susan said. "Starting when part of your clan decided to invade Earth."

"Enough with the score-keeping," Edna said. "It's what got us into this mess. The blue and the beige clans feud, so the taupe sub-clan tries to grab power by invading Earth. We kick their butts, so the beige clan elders send Bozidar to avenge their honor. By trying to end the violence, we end up causing more. A Greek tragedy by any other name. You want to hear the rest of the story or not?"

Gary sat next to Susan. "Please, continue."

Edna leaned forward. "So, we get here and the welcoming committee isn't exactly friendly. I'm guessing the taupe renegades who came back with us had a worse time. The council of elders was determined to get rid of us. Cecily played the documentary she made, showing how my grandmother Agnes helped the beige clan when their first attempt to explore Earth ended with them crashing in San Francisco Bay. They hated it. They especially hated the part with the ice cream."

Bozidar sank lower into his seat. "I thought seeing the similarity between human ice cream and *stotlet* would bind our two species in harmony."

"It didn't. Get over it." Edna smoothed her robes. "The elders thought I was crowning myself queen of the clan. There was a blue critter, supposed to be an observer, but he made a big deal about the ice cream and about our giving Bozidar a thimble that belonged to Agnes. He got huffy. The beiges got huffier. Next thing you know the clans declare war on each other."

"But no one's started shooting, right?" Gary asked.

"Not yet," Edna said. "I don't understand why, but I'm not complaining. If the beige clan loses, I get executed as a spoil of war."

"Yes, we heard about that." Susan glared at Bozidar. "I'm still not clear on how you got away."

"One of the taupe critters, Salia, suggested bribing our way out of the palace," Edna said. "It almost worked, but we got separated. Scott and I ended up with the taupes, who took us from one safe house to another. Seemed like we were running for days. Then the one in charge, Zenoa, decided to pack me off here."

"And Scott was okay with that?" Susan shook her head. Her eyebrows arched to her hairline.

"He didn't have a choice."

The light from outside flickered, casting mottled shadows around the room. A strong wind danced along the windows, throwing raindrops at random. A gong sounded in the hall.

"Ah, that must be the afternoon squall and snacks," Edna said. "Every day around this time we get a bit of rain, and I get a snack."

"What do you mean, Scott didn't have a choice? He's your husband, doesn't that count for something?" Susan asked.

"Not as much as the critters finding his stash of chenille." Edna motioned to Gary. "Poke your head out in the hall. They should have brought food by now. Anyway, they found the chenille. Got real excited about it. They made Scott put it in a hazmat box. At least I'm guessing that's what it was."

"Was it a large crate? With flashing orange lights at the edges, and a swirling pattern of various shades of red glowing on the sides?" Bozidar asked.

Edna nodded.

"If I am correct, Scott was taken to a research facility. Our scientists are still working on an antidote to *machute* poisoning. Since your chenille has the same effect as the *machute* plant, I suspect they were delighted to investigate its properties."

"But why bring Scott along?" Susan asked. "Why would your people expect him to be useful? He's not a scientist."

"No, but he can touch it without turning to dust," Gary said. "The hall is empty, by the way. No sign of food."

"Dang," Edna said. "I'm hungry." She scratched her wrist. "So you think my husband is a lab lackey, space boy?"

Bozidar closed his eyes. "If you mean that he is handling the substances which can do him no harm but which are deadly to my people, yes. It also means he is being treated well, since he can provide protection for the researchers."

Edna grinned. "That's the best news I've heard since I arrived. I thought they'd hurt him if I got out of line. Do you know how hard it is to be a goody two-shoes? For weeks?" She jumped from the throne and ran to the hall, shouting, "Where's my afternoon snack?"

Susan rubbed her temples, then moved her fingertips into her ears. She could still hear Edna shouting.

Edna returned, her footfalls heavy against the stone floor. She smiled at Bozidar like a crocodile grinning at a wildebeest. "You wouldn't happen to know where the call button is."

Bozidar crossed to the doorway and pressed an incised marking on the wooden paneling. He stepped into the hall. "I believe someone is bringing refreshments now." He whirled around at the sound of a voice and dashed down the hall, screeching.

Edna crossed her arms. "Is it just me, or is he twitchier than ever?"

Susan grabbed Gary's hand. "We should follow him."

Gary shook his head. "I'll go. He doesn't sound angry, and he isn't one to run toward danger. This may be a good sign."

Before Gary could rise from the bench, Bozidar returned. He dragged a quivering Schtatikian, who pulled a small wheeled serving cart. "Look who it is!" Bozidar announced as he pushed the creature toward Edna.

Edna raised an eyebrow. "I can't tell you apart."

Bozidar caught his breath. "It is Salia."

The little beige soldier bowed low to Edna before throwing herself into Bozidar's arms. "Blessed be all that is holy and soothing, you are here. I told the others that you would not fail the clan."

Bozidar patted her shoulders and inched away from her embrace. "I am honored by your trust. I am also amazed—your normal appearance has been restored. When did that happen? How did that happen?"

"You can talk and serve at the same time," Edna said. "Cart. Goodies. Now."

Susan trotted to the cart and pushed it toward Edna. "Knock yourself out, Mom." Cooing soft syllables of nonsense words, she settled Salia on an upholstered bench.

Salia's eyestalks craned toward Bozidar, trembling. She stuttered, chittered, and fell silent.

Bozidar stared at Susan. He inhaled with a sound like a hiccup crossed with grinding gears. "How do you know that song?"

Susan and Edna turned their heads toward each other. Susan raised one eyebrow, an entire unspoken conversation conveyed in the lift. Edna shrugged, a lifetime of replies in the movement.

"That wasn't a song," Susan said.

Edna swallowed the cookie she had been chewing and took a tray from the cart. "My mother cooed to me the same way when she wanted me to calm down. Anyone want a snack?" She scooped another item from the tray.

Gary took a small round fruit that looked like an emerald strawberry as Edna passed. "Did your mother ever tell you where she learned the song?"

"No," Edna said between bites of a custardy tart. "Mom wasn't creative … oh." She finished her tart. "My grandmother sang that song."

"Agnes?" Bozidar asked. "Are you certain?"

"I ought to be. She hummed those notes to me, to the cat, to the teakettle."

"But the words, were they the same words?" Bozidar said.

"They must have been," Susan said. "I didn't make them up."

"Then that's another gift from Agnes," Gary said. "Those syllables sound a lot like Schtatikian."

Edna snorted. "When did you learn the critters' language?"

"I have a good ear," Gary said. "I can mimic almost anything I hear. I don't know what the words mean, but I recognize the sounds."

Salia slid from her seat and knelt, touching her head to the floor but keeping her eyestalks focused on Bozidar. "The days of prophecy have arrived. Blessed be the holy and soothing."

Green smoke puffed from Bozidar's ears. "At least Marsel did not hear her," he muttered.

Susan pulled Salia from the floor and shifted her onto the bench. "Tell me about the song."

"It is a lullaby," Salia said. She bounced her rubbery beige hand pad against Susan's arm with a patting motion. "I remember my mother singing it when I was a blobbling and frightened by a storm. It comes from the dawn of the beige clan, sung by the Sky Queen herself."

"Sky Queen?" Susan turned to Bozidar. "A goddess?"

"A legend." Bozidar crossed his arms. "Every clan has a creation story. How we became the color that we are."

"Save the bedtime stories," Edna said. "Agnes learned a song from the beige critters. She taught it to us. Big deal. I want to know why Salia ignored me all this time."

"I have only been here a short while." Salia covered her mouth. "Forgive me. I meant no disrespect." Her eyestalks bent toward her midsection, and she hummed a long note that hovered around A-flat. She straightened and said, "As punishment for my part in the expedition to your planet, I was not allowed to accompany you to this castle and fulfill my pledge to protect the family of She Who Found Us. After days of weeping, and with the assistance of an elder affiliated with my family, I was transferred to another assignment. I traded my documents to a junior cook, who had been posted here but was reluctant to leave her home, and arrived two days ago."

"What news do you have of Scott?" Bozidar said.

"The queen's consort is at a research facility not far from here," Salia said. "The elder who helped me change assignments knows the researchers in charge."

"Free Scott and you can name your reward," Edna said.

Salia trembled. "Free him? He is not a prisoner."

Edna growled and lunged toward the bench. Susan shielded Salia.

"Mother, let her explain." Susan's voice softened. "Is Scott free to leave whenever he likes?"

"Why would he leave before his work is finished?" Salia said. "He is helping to cure *machute* poisoning."

"Let's try this again," Edna said. "I want Scott with me. Bring him here, or bring me there. Now."

"Does anyone else hear footsteps?" Gary asked.

Four guards marched into the room. The leader carried a black box, small and rectangular. He stood as straight and tall as a yard-high blob of rubbery beige flesh could.

"Once again, the failure of our leaders becomes obvious to all, Bozidar," he said. "Have you spent so much time surrounded by power that you thought your bribes could tempt the faithful and honest? Were it not for the presence of the Descendant of She Who Found Us, and my dedication to duty, I would execute you without hesitation." He lifted his arm, pointing the box at Bozidar.

Susan leaped to Bozidar's side. She reached her hands toward the guard. "Everything we did was with the clan's best interest in mind. Put down the weapon, and let us explain."

"This is not a weapon," he said. "Did you not listen? I said it would please me to execute him, but duty prevents me. This is a communications device. The council would speak with you."

"Well, that's splendid," Susan said as she edged toward the wall. "Carry on."

Bozidar took the box and touched a flashing icon. A holographic image of the council of elders seated in a row beamed from the top of the box. Bozidar bowed.

"I am honored," he said.

"Of course you are," the creature in the center said. "But the honor bestowed upon you by us does not include you speaking. Gather the Earth beings and listen."

"Jeez Louise, do you critters even hear yourselves? No wonder you're on the brink of war," Edna said. "How did you survive this long with that attitude?"

The guards in the room and the council in the image made a sound like gas escaping a leaky oxygen tank. "My deepest regrets, council. There is a disturbance," Bozidar said as he flicked the icon and the image disappeared. He held the box at his chest and nodded to the leader of the guards.

"I regret that the transmission suffered … interference." Bozidar smiled as he spoke, but his lips curled and froze in place. His eyes showed more misery than mirth. "Perhaps the reception will be better outside." He addressed Susan. "You should continue your tour of the castle. Without me." He nodded at the leader as he dashed from the room.

Susan took Gary's hand and motioned for Salia to follow her. "You heard the man, Mother. Show us your favorite rooms."

Edna snatched another tray from the cart as she stomped into the hall. "Favorite rooms, bah. You try spending weeks in a cold stone castle with only your own voice bouncing off the walls for entertainment. There's no favorite place in a prison."

She whirled around and saw the guards trudging

behind Salia. Edna threw a cookie at the leader. "Scat!"

Susan turned to the leader of the guards. "We're fine on our own."

The guards backed into the room.

Salia toddled to Edna's side. Susan watched her whisper toward Edna's ear, Salia's eyestalks flicking from side to side.

Gary put his arm around Susan's waist. "Everything will be okay."

She arched her eyebrow. "You think so? Our track record isn't that great, in case you haven't noticed."

"We're still alive. More important, Scott is still alive." Gary gave her a little squeeze. "And by some miracle, your mother behaved herself. If she can do it for him, she'll do it for you and the girls."

"Stop dawdling," Edna said. "You want the fifty-cent tour, get a move on."

She led them down the hall. Along the way, she pointed out a particular slab of rock on the wall. "I'm pretty sure they have a bug there. One day I said 'nuts' out loud. I was just ticked off, can't even remember what about now, but that day there was a bowl of nuts at lunch."

Susan scanned the space. The unadorned walls were a combination of wood and stone which extended far above her head. The floor was polished stone. Spots of color glowed at random intervals. The light and warmth reminded her of her quilting shop although Susan couldn't see any windows, vents, or lamps.

"Mom, where does the light come from?"

"Do I look like an architect?" Edna stopped in front of a spot of coral-colored light. She tapped the glowing circle twice with her toe. A hidden door in the wall slid open to reveal a small wood-paneled room with an upholstered bench along the back. Edna stepped inside, followed by Salia.

"Is this an elevator?" Susan asked as she leaned away from the opening.

"No, it's a washing machine. We're taking a ride on the spin cycle." Edna shook her head and snorted. "Of course it's an elevator. My elevator, apparently. I've never seen anyone else use it, and none of the other circles work for me."

Gary gently pushed Susan into the room. He scanned the paneling, pressing parts of the grain.

"That's just the wood," Edna said. She squared her shoulders and pronounced, "Mezzanine."

The door slid back in place.

Susan braced for a movement that never came. She noticed that the elevator was as bright and warm as the hall, again without benefit of fixtures. The sound of her breathing seemed to be absorbed by the room, and her pulse eased into a calmer rhythm.

"We aren't moving," Gary said.

"Not now," Edna said. "We're here."

The door opened, and she walked out on a large balcony overlooking an empty courtyard. The faint outlines of the Schtatikian moons shimmered in the sky. Light glinted on the stone walls and reflected from the surface of a fountain in the sunniest corner of the yard.

"This is beautiful," Susan said. She sank onto a chaise longue, stretching her legs along its entire length.

Gary leaned on the railing, scanning the ground below. "Where is everyone?"

"Not a clue," Edna said as she perched on a stool next to a table. She studied a tray of brightly-colored snacks, selected a brilliant red-orange square that looked like distilled fire, and popped it in her mouth. "These are really good. If you want some, get 'em now before I eat every last one."

Salia bowed to Gary. "I believe the gardeners have withdrawn. This is the queen's private balcony."

"How did they know we're here?" Gary asked.

"They were alerted the moment we engaged the elevator," Salia said. She shuffled her foot against the rough stone floor, took a step toward Edna, then rocked from side to side.

"Spit it out," Edna said. "My grandkids do the same dance when they want something their mother won't give them."

"Thank you so much for reminding me," Susan said without lifting her head.

"It is ... I mean to say ... " Salia voiced a few more syllables before she fell silent.

Gary patted her head. "Take your time."

"If you're going to apologize for not being here, forget it," Edna said. "All I want is Scott. Bring him here, and we're even."

Salia wriggled where she stood, her rubbery flesh pulsing and her eyestalks shaking. She stuttered, held her breath, and spoke. "I have a plan."

Susan heard Salia speaking but could only decipher part of one sentence.

" ... succeed as soon as Marsel and Cecily arrive."

Susan's fingernails pricked her palms. Her skin turned to ice. In her mind, the courtyard below filled with soldiers, some beige, some blue. They all held weapons, metal tubes shooting arcs of searing light. The energy cut through stone easily. Flesh incinerated just being near it. Cecily appeared in the scene, running. She zigged and zagged across the yard, heading for an opening in the ruined walls. She jumped over dying soldiers, almost safe, then stumbled head first into the fountain. A swirl of red surrounded her, spreading across the surface of the water.

Susan fell to her knees, screaming.

NINE

Susan felt hands lifting her to her feet, settling her on the chaise. She recognized syllables but no words. A distant clanging silenced the voices. She heard a squishing sound, like suction cups straining against wet tile. The noise grew louder, now accompanied by voices, some harsh, some frightened.

"Enough already," Edna bellowed. "Shut your traps and we'll get some answers."

Susan blinked. "Answers?"

Gary was holding her. Edna paced in front of four guards. Salia cowered at the foot of the chaise.

Susan noted the fear in their eyes. *What do they want with me? Why don't they go away?*

Bozidar ran onto the balcony, breathing hard and waving away the guards. "I heard the attack alarm. We must evacuate to the bomb shelter."

"The only bombs are going off in her head." Edna pointed at Susan. "From the way she's shaking, I'm guessing another vision. Not a happy one."

"A battle," Susan said. Her voice quivered, and her whole body trembled.

Salia crept toward Bozidar. "She must have seen a great catastrophe."

"Then we should keep quiet until the meaning is revealed." Bozidar helped Salia to her feet and nudged her toward the guards. "All of you will return to your duties. Do not speak of this until I direct you."

"You have no authority here," one guard said.

"My rank is still intact," Bozidar said. "No one has rescinded my guardianship of the Descendants of She Who Found Us. In this matter, I and only I, have any authority. You will follow my orders."

Salia bowed. "I will obey." She motioned to the guards and led them into the hall.

Edna sidled up to Bozidar. "How much of that speech was bull crap?"

"There are advantages to strict chains of command," Bozidar said.

"Will they keep quiet?" Gary asked. "And what will happen if they don't?"

"I have no idea," Bozidar said. He took Susan's hands. "You still suffer from the vision. Please tell us what you saw as soon as you are able."

After-images of the battle scene filled the balcony with ghosts. Susan shook her head, willing the pale soldiers to evaporate like mist. She swallowed the last bit of moisture. "I'm thirsty."

"Good luck getting someone to bring us something." Edna nodded at Bozidar. "He sent everyone away."

Salia chirped from the entrance. "Forgive me for returning, but I thought refreshments would be needed." She pushed a cart toward Bozidar and poured a pink liquid into a small cup. "And I wish to be of service," she whispered as she passed the cup to Bozidar.

Bozidar placed it in Susan's hands. "This will calm you."

She drained it in two gulps. The warm liquid quenched the taste of burning bodies in her mouth. She let her eyes close. The vision did not reappear, and her breath came easier. "There were blue soldiers in the courtyard. They were fighting beige soldiers. There was a break in the wall, like a bomb hit it. Cecily was running toward the break. She didn't make it. I saw her die."

Bozidar refilled her cup. "Drink. Then describe the battle."

"Leave her alone," Gary said.

"If this vision is a prophecy, we need to know more." Bozidar retreated a step. "Before she forgets."

Gary glared at Bozidar. Salia moved the cart closer, almost between them. "I have sweetened baked goods, if anyone is hungry."

"It's okay," Susan said. "Bozidar is right. The more I remember the better." She pulled Gary's arms tighter around her. "I don't know who was winning. If anyone was winning. There weren't any aircraft or tanks, just soldiers. The weapons emitted bursts of energy. Like a power line arcing."

"Did you see us?" Edna asked.

"No," Susan said. "I only saw Cecily."

"And our kinsmen?" Salia said as she offered a plate of food. Her eyestalks arced toward Susan's face, and a lavender droplet fell from the left eyeball.

Susan met Salia's mournful look. "Your kinsmen died too. I'm sorry."

Salia straightened. A final tear rolled down her eyestalk. "The biscuit is similar to your fudge brownie. The other is more like a cinnamon confection we saw in one of your drive-through restaurants. I think it was called a *charno*."

Susan took a bite of the fragile pastry tube. "Churro. You had a churro." She smiled at Salia. "I always wondered what you and your friends ate that year you were hiding on our planet."

Bozidar cleared his throat. "Do you remember anything else?"

"I said leave her alone." Gary rose from the chaise.

"I'm okay." Susan tugged on his arm. "That's all I remember."

Edna grabbed a biscuit from the cart. "So what do we do now?"

"I do not know." Bozidar paced, head down. "Salia's plan seemed sound. But your vision indicates it will not work. It could never work."

"I did hear one thing," Susan said. "Someone mentioned bringing Marsel and Cecily here. That won't happen. I forbid it."

Edna swallowed her biscuit. "Don't assume what you saw is set in stone. Or that keeping Cecily off the planet will keep her safe. The rest of the plan could work, the part about showing the quilt around."

"How will that help?" Susan asked.

Salia trembled, but spoke. "I have been told the clan would recognize the … remnant … of our ancient captain." Her skin glistened and rippled as she fell silent.

Susan said, "You mean the transformed remains of the beige captain who crashed in the San Francisco Bay? The one my great-grandmother found but couldn't save?" The air glimmered above Salia, and the image of Agnes in her play clothes appeared for a moment. "It's all right to tell the story. We know it, anyway. The captain transformed the survivors of that crash into flour sacks to hide them until they could escape with Agnes' help. Agnes made a crazy quilt to tell the story, and hid the flour sack that was really the captain's skin inside it."

Salia nodded. "If the elders could see that quilt, could touch it, they would know that everything the Queen said at the trial was true."

"Who cares what the elders believe?" Edna munched the last brownie. "You've still got the blues pointing guns at you."

Bozidar studied Salia. "I believe this little taupe speaks with more wisdom than she knows. The captain sacrificed herself to let her crew escape. Taupes are especially fond of stories of sacrifice. They believe they are the noblest subset of the beige clan. Sorry, Salia, but you know it is true."

Salia nodded. "The Descendants of She Who Found Us sacrificed, also, to come here and offer forgiveness to the clan."

"For all the good that did," Edna said. "You got locked up, and I became a scapegoat waiting for the ax to fall."

Bozidar held up his hands. "You overlook the symbolism. We can use the theme of sacrifice to unite the clan, not for a war with the blues but to find a way to prevent the war. For the good of all."

"You know, space boy, I'm up to my ears in sacrifice." Edna advanced on Bozidar, waving her finger at his nose. "Let me tell you about the next sacrifice. That's going to be you and every little critter I can get my hands on if Scott isn't brought here immediately."

"Mother, please." Susan rubbed her temples.

"No, in this case I agree," Bozidar said. He took Edna's hand and shook it as if sealing a bargain. "Thank you so much for presenting me with the solution. We will request that the entire laboratory be transferred to this castle. It is much more secure, and when all three Descendants of She Who Found Us are planet-side, the spiritual blessings will undoubtedly overflow into the research on *machute* poisoning."

"Absolutely not," Susan said. "I forbid you to use Cecily as a bargaining chip. She returns to Earth at the first sign of danger. Bring the quilt down if you must, but she stays on the ship."

Bozidar pressed his lips together. He folded his arms. "Very well. The ship is in synchronous orbit over the castle. When we offer the triple blessing of the three descendants, we will simply not mention that Cecily is hovering above you and the Queen rather than standing in the same room."

"I don't like this plan," Gary said. He cupped Susan's face and turned her to him. "You've brought the quilt here. Let them figure out how to stop the war on their own."

Susan felt the air grow cold around her, and a pleading voice echoed in her head. *Stay.* She curled into Gary's chest. *Stay.*

"I can't leave," she whispered. She pushed away. "I have to stay. Cecily doesn't."

"What about me?" Edna said. "Since you're making plans for everyone, what are my marching orders?"

Susan snorted. "Since when have you taken orders from anyone?"

"Since I was three," Edna said, "but I stopped when I was four."

Gary shook his head, defeat mixed with determination in his eyes. "Then you need an escape plan." He turned to Bozidar. "Give me your word that you'll get Susan off the planet before things go bad."

Bozidar ground his teeth. "I cannot promise what I do not have."

Salia wiggled where she stood. "The elders may be persuaded to provide a shuttle." She cowered as all eyes riveted on her. "I know people to ask," she whispered.

Susan nudged Gary. "Salia is very attentive. And she did pledge herself to protect you."

"What are you suggesting?" Gary asked.

"Maybe Salia could be assigned to us?" Susan shifted in the chaise. "Would you like that, Salia? I hate using the word servant, but … "

Salia threw herself at Susan, hugging her knees. "It is an honor. For you to request my service is more than I could have asked."

Susan patted Salia's head, sat straighter, and turned to Bozidar. "Salia could be our mole."

"I don't want to transform again," Salia said, horror in her voice. "The process of reverting to my original form after a year in disguise caused me great pain."

Bozidar shook his head. "No need to fear. I understand this reference. You will not be turned into a small rodent. You will, however, report to us should other members of the clan make plans that could interfere with ours."

Salia nodded. "I will obey."

"Good," Bozidar said. "Let us hope that others

will be equally as cooperative." He offered his hand to Edna. "Shall we contact the elders together and present our demands for the relocation of your husband?"

* * *

"This can't be good," Edna said in a low growl as she watched Bozidar pace the length of the small room.

"Don't look for trouble, Mom." Susan examined a solitary tapestry on the otherwise bare wall, tracing lines of embroidery on the rough, linen-like fabric. "Come look at this instead. Do you know what it is?"

"It could be an old Babylonian liver omen for all I care. Ask the native," Edna said. "He doesn't have anything else to do."

Bozidar continued pacing. "Marsel can translate when he arrives."

"Let me try," Gary said. "I learned a few things when we were looking for the prophecy."

"Hush," Susan whispered as Gary joined her.

Gary leaned close. "I thought the reason we came down was to use the prophecy to spring Edna."

"Bozidar hasn't mentioned it, so let's not bring it up first. Besides, it will be easier to handle my mother with Scott here." Susan raised her voice. "So, dear, do you recognize anything?"

Gary studied the tapestry. "That." He pointed to a row of lavender chevrons followed by three green chain stitches. "Marsel nearly fell off his perch when he saw similar markings on the scrolls."

Bozidar inclined his head. His pacing slowed as he looped around to the tapestry. "Are you certain?"

"I wouldn't bet the rent money, but yeah, I'm certain. I don't remember what it means. He may not have told us."

Bozidar nodded, his lips compressed into a stern line. "Marsel can be remarkably lax in his reports." He studied the tapestry. Wrinkles on his forehead shifted in and out of phase as his body glistened with a green, plastic sheen. He held his breath and ran his hand over the embroidery. As he exhaled, his skin settled into its human aspect. "I do so hate it when Marsel is right."

The view screen flashed to a fanfare played on something that might have been a dying accordion. A soft blue glow resolved, pixel by pixel, into the face of a beige Schtatikian wearing brilliant scarlet robes and a tall, cylindrical hat.

"Minister," Bozidar said, bowing as he rushed to the screen. "We are honored."

"You will not feel honored," the minister said. "The laboratory will be relocated, but not to the castle."

Edna pushed Bozidar aside. "Move the blasted lab wherever you want, but bring my husband here, now."

The minister removed his hat. "Greetings. I regret that you are displeased with our decision, your majesty."

Gary steadied Bozidar while Susan pulled Edna from the screen. Edna locked her knees and braced her feet, but Susan slid her mother aside like a curling stone on ice. Smoothing his jacket, Bozidar resumed his position. The minister, hat back on his head, waited.

"My apologies, minister," Bozidar said.

"The actions of the queen do not require apology or explanation."

"No, sir, I would never dare," Bozidar said. He pressed his hands together and bowed. "My apology is for allowing the council to deliberate without all the facts."

Susan came to Bozidar's side and placed her hand on his arm. "I must interrupt here," she said to the minister. "We discovered a prophecy on our journey here. Bozidar wouldn't have mentioned it at all, except we have two pieces of evidence that corroborate your religious records."

The screen flashed a brilliant green as the connection ended.

TEN

Susan pushed a lock of blonde hair from her face. "Did not see that coming."

Edna pounced on Bozidar. She knocked him to the ground and sat on his chest. "Bring him back."

Gary lifted Edna off Bozidar. "We need him alive. He's the one who knows the right phone numbers."

"Would that I did," Bozidar said. He remained on the floor, hugging his knees and rocking. "Terminating a discussion that way is not a good sign. I do not know how to proceed."

Susan knelt next to him. "Maybe there were technical problems."

"I've got your technical problems right here," Edna growled, swinging her arms.

"Mother, please," Susan said. "I know you're

scared, but for once in your life don't respond to fear with anger. It won't help us, and it won't help Scott."

"Let her rage," Bozidar said. "I do not have a better plan."

"Salia might," Gary said, still struggling with Edna. "She used her connections to get here. Maybe she knows someone who can help." He shook Edna. "You're heavier than you look, but I'm not letting you down until you behave."

Edna snorted but stopped flailing. "Fine. I promise not to punch anyone."

"No biting, kicking, or tackling," Gary said.

"Whatever, just put me down," Edna barked. She adjusted her robes. "Who knew you'd have a backbone. I promise I won't even think 'off with his head.' Unless he deserves it."

Susan opened her mouth, but Gary spoke first. "That's as good as we're going to get, sweetheart. Your mother is a handful, but she keeps her promises."

"Standing right here, listening to every word." Edna pointed at Susan. "I'm still ticked with you for eloping, but he's a keeper."

Gary bowed with a flourish. "You do me honor, your majesty."

"Don't push it, kid." Edna folded her arms and glared at Bozidar. "So what do we do now?"

"Do you never listen?" Bozidar said. "I did not have a plan when you attacked me, nor has one revealed itself in the last few moments."

"Yes, it has," Susan said. "Gary suggested Salia. Maybe the elder who helped her can help us."

Bozidar rose and pressed a panel near the view screen. Within minutes, Salia appeared at the door. She curtsied before entering.

"Our petition was refused," Bozidar said. "No explanation was given. We need the elders to reconsider."

Salia stood silent, motionless. Her taupe skin shimmered, turning to the color of skim milk.

Susan spoke in a low, quiet voice. "We were hoping you could contact the elder who helped you."

Salia shivered, and her hand moved to an inner pocket of her robes. She retrieved a small black device and offered it to Bozidar.

"I recognize that," Edna said. "It's like the little box you left Susan when we came out here." She turned on Salia. "So who's he supposed to call?"

"My cousin."

The stone walls seemed to absorb all sound, even Edna's huffing breaths. Bozidar's finger moved across the box, hitting glowing icons, in silence. The colorful images faded, and the viewing screen remained dark.

Edna's shoe squeaked against the floor.

Bozidar inhaled, and faced Edna. "The call didn't go through, as you would say. This new information explains a great deal, however, and is most useful. Please do not complicate matters by murdering us where we stand."

"Salia has some explaining to do." Edna kept her

fists at her sides, but her elbows were bent and her stance resembled a terrier about to pounce on a disobedient squeaky toy.

Susan went to Salia and patted her shoulder. "I think I understand. You were trying to protect us and your family at the same time, weren't you?"

Salia nodded. "If it became known that my cousin sat on the council, she would have been punished for the invasion. She had nothing to do with it, but she is a taupe, and she has been helping me."

Gary held up his hand. "Question. You called her your cousin. Bozidar called the taupes we defeated cousins. Does the word mean the same thing to you as it does to us, or are you all just inbred beyond belief?"

"In many cases, the term is an honorific. In this case, it denotes a close blood tie." Bozidar returned the black box to Salia. "I should have realized who you are, but you were still transformed into a bolt of beige fabric the last time I saw you."

"Our doctors found a way to restore us to our normal appearance," Salia said. "It was a priority since our clan members were horrified by our presence. You had already escaped, or they would have found a way to restore you as well."

The squishy sound of footpads echoed in the hall before two armed guards burst into the room.

"Traitors! We have you now!"

Edna launched herself at the guards, bellowing. "You think you have something? I'll show you what you've got. A pissed off queen, that's what you've got."

She pounded on the first guard's shoulders. As he fell to the floor, his weapon sailed across the room, crashed against the wall, and discharged. An energy bolt ricocheted off the stone perimeter, setting Bozidar's sleeve on fire. Gary helped him slap the flames out. Susan rushed to Edna, who sat on one guard while yanking on the eyestalks of the other. Susan broke Edna's hold on the second guard, but not before Edna kicked him in the midsection. The first guard rolled toward the door when Edna's feet left the ground. Her heel caught on his arm. He skidded in a circle, knocking down his companion before crashing into Salia.

"Mother, stop fighting," Susan said as she wrestled with Edna. She looked to the tangle of guard and Salia. "Are you two okay?"

Salia whimpered, and the guard groaned. Gary and Bozidar helped the two to sit upright. Susan sniffed the air and pointed to the burn marks on Bozidar's coat.

"I am uninjured," Bozidar said before she could speak. "Gary's hands are burned."

"It's nothing," Gary said. "A little ice and I'll be fine."

As Susan inspected his hands, she noticed the ruby in her ring glowing. The air in front of her shimmered, and she saw Agnes as a child, watching the leader of the expedition point a red rock at her crew. *Think of healing* she heard the leader explain. She thought of a cooling balm and repairing cells. All evidence of the burns faded from Gary's hands.

"Did you do that?" Gary asked. "Because if you did, thanks, but it's kind of scaring me."

"Me too." Susan went to Salia and took her arm. "Tell me where it hurts." Salia pointed to her foot. Susan closed her eyes and thought of balance, strength, and flexibility.

Salia gasped. "There is no more pain." She bowed, then tugged at the guard. "Now him. Show him we are here on a mission from the gods."

The guard recoiled. Edna shook her fist at him, and he extended his hand to Susan. "You saw what the queen did to me."

Susan nodded. Touching his shoulder with one hand, she visualized bruises healing, muscles relaxing and repairing. As she worked, the other guard crept closer. When she released the first guard's hand, the second draped his eyestalks across her arm.

Susan smiled and let her fingertips brush the soft, mangled appendages. The ring glowed. The guard sighed, retreated a step, and bowed. Susan nodded.

Bozidar retrieved the weapon and handed it to the guard. "We are not here to harm the queen or the clan. Allow us to complete our mission, and we will bring peace."

The guards chittered together. They snatched glances at Susan and her ring. They nodded as if they had reached consensus, stood side by side, and backed themselves in front of the doorway.

The guard with the gun held it at his chest, not pointing at anyone. "We are grateful for the healing but must ask where this magic came from."

Words spilled from Susan before she realized she knew the answer. "Your leader. The first one to visit our planet. The one who taught my great-grandmother, She Who Found You."

The guards trembled, stumbled back, and dashed from the room.

"Is that a good sign?" Edna asked. "I've given up trying to figure out why you critters do what you do."

"I suspect the feeling is mutual," Bozidar said. "As to your question, they may be running in fear. They may be calling for reinforcements. They may be regrouping to ask for instructions. We will know when they return."

* * *

The view screen glowed. Bozidar and Susan gathered in front of it, watching the entire council of elders come into focus. "We agree to inspect the artifacts. Have them available for our arrival."

"What about my husband?" Edna said as Gary and Salia blocked her from approaching the screen.

The council whispered among themselves. "He will travel with us. The laboratory will move to the castle over the next few days."

"We appreciate your kindness," Bozidar said.

"The guards informed us of their miraculous healing. The clan reveres the memory of She Who Found Us and honors her descendants."

The connection ended. Gary released Edna, and Salia scampered to the doorway.

"That answers one question," Edna said. "We know what those critters did when they ran away."

"And we know that the council is willing to listen now," Gary said. "I sure hope you can repeat that performance for them, my love."

Susan twisted the ring. "I hope I won't have to. Salia, what are you doing?"

"I await the sound of running feet."

"Why does everyone speak in poetry?" Edna threw up her hands. "Space boy, translate."

Bozidar folded his arms and wrinkled his brow. After a pause, he said, "Unless the taupe sub-clan has grown so used to their own deceptions that they expect it from all, I am at a loss."

Salia faced Susan but kept one eyestalk trained on the hall. "The council would not tell us one thing and the staff another. They would instruct the staff to be more accommodating to the queen, her daughter, and guests."

Salia leaped back as a dozen servants entered at a trot. They bowed twice, then separated into groups of three. One group surrounded Bozidar and propelled him from the room. Two more approached Gary and

Susan, formed a square around them, and urged them to follow Bozidar. The last group bowed before Edna. They motioned for her to accompany them.

"I guess it's good to be the queen," Edna said. She grabbed Salia and marched from the room.

* * *

Edna stood on her balcony, examining goodies arranged on a table. Salia, holding two pillows—one purple, one midnight blue—darted to Edna's side.

"Please choose the color," Salia said.

Edna fingered them. "I like both colors. But I prefer the fabric of the purple one. It feels like silk. The blue one feels like linen. Too many years ironing linen blouses will put you right off the stuff."

Salia toddled away with the pillows, but turned on her heel and announced, "Your daughter and her husband approach." She backed away as Susan and Gary entered.

"Call us by our names," Susan said.

"You can give them permission every hour on the hour for all the good it will do," Edna said. "Have a cookie."

Gary accepted the jam-filled cookie. He scanned the table and took a chilled glass of pink liquid. "They are going all out to please. You should see the suite they gave us."

"Mine's not too shabby, either." Edna waved her hand to the view. "This balcony is even better than the last one."

"Has anyone seen Bozidar?" Susan asked before taking a bite of a brownie-like treat.

"Haven't seen a curl on his head since they hustled us out of that little conference room. Maybe Salia knows." Edna took a sip of hot tea and bellowed Salia's name.

The little taupe creature scurried to the balcony. "How may I serve you?"

"Do you know what happened to Bozidar?" Susan asked. "We would like him to join us."

Salia squeaked once but made no move, and no other sound.

"They didn't put him in the dungeon, did they?" Susan asked.

"Maybe you should tell the guard to be nice to Bozidar, Edna," Gary said. "We're going to need his help."

"Fine." Edna pointed at Salia. "Go tell someone who outranks you to fetch the warden."

"Warden?" Salia asked.

"Whoever is in charge," Susan said.

When Salia left, Susan said, "We should have a plan."

"We've been winging it so far," Gary said, "and it's worked."

"If by worked you mean we're still alive, yeah. If you mean getting us back home, think again." Edna ate a candy-coated berry. "Not that the plans we made there panned out."

Susan shrugged. "We could set our conditions."

"Like not having Cecily involved?" Gary asked.

"And that she gets safe passage to Earth. That's non-negotiable." Susan crossed her arms. "I don't care what happens to me, but my daughter gets out of this."

Edna said. "You're my kid. I could make the same demand for you."

"Please do," Gary said. "I would prefer to have my wife alive when I get back. And trust me, I intend to see Earth again."

"That is my fervent wish," Bozidar said as he entered. He carried a stack of folded robes. Salia trailed him with more robes. "Salia informed me of your concern, but I have been treated well. The guards wished to consult me regarding the ceremonial clothes you will wear when the council arrives."

"Are those the same ones we got on the ship out here? The ones we were supposed to wear at the trial but never got a chance?" Edna asked.

"No," Bozidar said. "These are much more elaborate, reflecting your new status as queen."

"Be still my beating heart," Edna said. She wandered back to the snack table.

"Before we get sidetracked with clothes, we need to agree on certain demands." Susan waved Salia aside. "I want Cecily kept safe. Marsel can bring Agnes' crazy quilt down with any of the scrolls we need to show the elders."

"I anticipated your request," Bozidar said. "While waiting for the robes, I sent a message to Marsel. I ordered him to collect the scrolls and the quilt in secret. I also instructed him to teleport to the balcony while Cecily was distracted or otherwise engaged. I considered it likely that she would discover he was leaving and convince him to bring her along if he came in the landing pod."

Susan closed her eyes and exhaled. "Thank you, Bozidar. You have no idea how relieved I am."

The air at the opposite end of the balcony shimmered, glinting turquoise and emerald. Cecily and Marsel materialized, surrounded by crates. Cecily held the quilt.

"Hi, Mom. How are you doing?"

ELEVEN

Susan's hands shook. "Get out of here. Now."

Cecily arched one eyebrow. "Good to see you too, Mom." She strolled to Edna, hugged her, and placed the quilt in her arms. "Here's your heritage, Grandma, all safe and sound."

"Ix-nay on the okes-jay," Edna said, standing between Cecily and Susan. "You were supposed to stay on the ship."

"Yeah, like that's going to happen." Cecily folded her arms. "Did you honestly think Marsel could keep a secret from me? Why did you even try?"

Edna shuffled Cecily toward the hall. "You know, darlin', if you had answered that question yourself before you came down, your mother would not be trying to kill you now."

Marsel threw himself in front of Susan. "Forgive

me! You have no idea how powerful your daughter is."

Bozidar yanked Marsel to his feet. "Of course she does. We all do. They are of the line of She Who Found Us."

"And he scares easily," Cecily said. She stepped around Edna. "Mom, all three of us are supposed to be here. It was part of the vision, remember?"

"Your mother had another vision," Bozidar said. "You died."

"Way to break the news gently," Edna said.

"Time is a limited resource," Bozidar said. "When the elders contact us, we must present our evidence succinctly. Cecily is here, so we should use her insight."

Susan pressed her hands against her temples. She whirled around, saw a small vase on a table and smashed it at her feet. "Stop talking. Nothing matters. The war, the elders, nothing. So everyone just shut up."

A brisk gust of wind scattered small pieces of the vase across the balcony. The shards tinkled as they rolled over the stone slabs. One fell off the edge. The icy ping it made as it shattered on the courtyard pavers was the final sound for many moments.

Edna cleared her throat. "My, isn't it chilly out here when the breeze picks up. Cecily, find a sweater for your grandmother. The rest of you, go help her."

Gary reached for Susan, but Edna held up her hand. "You too. Susan and I need to talk."

"Grandma, that may not be a great idea," Cecily said.

Edna rolled her eyes. "I'm not going to yammer at her. We're going to catch our breath. Making the right decision is more important than making a quick one. Go along. That's a good girl." She waved them toward the hall, flicking her fingers.

When the others disappeared into the next room, Edna tucked the crazy quilt fragment under one arm and linked her other arm through Susan's. She led her to the railing, where they stood in silence.

"Oh, just say what's on your mind, Mother," Susan said. "You're not this quiet even when you're asleep."

Edna cackled. "I'd say I won, but this isn't the time for us to spar. There are bigger battles to fight." She edged closer to Susan. "The clouds are pretty today. I like the yellow tinge at the bottom of that blue fluffy one."

Susan said nothing. Her fingers clenched around the lip of the railing.

"The pink river reflects the sky nicely. Of course, you can't see it on this side of the castle, but it does." Edna put her hand over Susan's. "I can talk about the weather all day, or you can tell me what's really eating you."

"Olivia and Eleanor are waiting for me to bring their sister home." Susan blinked and bit her lip. "If Cecily dies here, how will they ever trust me?"

"And how will you ever forgive yourself?" Edna

said. "The answer is they will trust you because you love them, and you *won't* forgive yourself because you think you can control fate. All mothers do. We'd go barking mad if we didn't."

"What was I thinking when I said yes to … to everything."

"What is anyone thinking? We do what makes sense at the time. If it works, great. If not, we say life would have been better if we'd said no. That's a lie. Life would have been different."

"And different isn't always better." Susan clutched at the quilt. "One of these days I have to embroider a pillow with that saying."

"This family has too many sayings for a pillow. Make a tapestry." Edna pushed the quilt into Susan's hands. "You're scared, and with reason. We could all die out here."

"You're not helping."

"Face reality, Daughter. It's what you do best." Edna patted the quilt. "The taupe captain whose remains are part of this probably had a family she wanted to keep safe. She probably didn't want to die. But her crew needed her to be strong, so she was. Agnes didn't want to be treated like a nut her whole life, but that's what happened when she talked about space creatures crashing into San Francisco Bay."

"I wish I had known her," Susan said.

"Probably not. You're too much like my mother. Agnes would have scared you."

Susan chuckled. "Maybe. You would have been

there to take the edge off."

"I'm here now."

"So you are." Susan peered at Edna from the corner of her eye. "You're falling down on the job, Mom. There's a whole lot of edge hanging over us."

"And me without my sandpaper." Edna leaned her elbow against the railing, twisting to look at Susan. "So what are we going to do? Throw more vases on the floor, or figure out how to get through this in one piece?"

"I don't know what to do, Mom. All I can see is Cecily getting shot."

Edna rocked on her heels. "How do you know that vision is true? Was Agnes there?"

Susan closed her eyes. "No." She opened her eyes and shook her head. "The beige leader wasn't there either."

"Who sent the vision?"

"I don't know."

Edna pushed her face toward Susan's. "So how do you know it's going to happen?"

Susan blinked. "I don't." She edged away from the railing, clutching the quilt. She walked around the balcony until she came to a bench. Sitting with the quilt in her lap, she gazed at the sky. "You're right. The clouds are pretty."

"Well, you listened to one thing I said. Did you hear the rest of the speech, or was I exercising my vocal chords for nothing?"

"I heard the part about facing reality." Susan

stood. "Let's go inside. I'm cold, and there's bound to be some disaster brewing."

As they made their way to Edna's suite, Susan listened for voices. "I don't hear anyone talking. Didn't Bozidar want to discuss what to tell the elders?"

"Maybe they went back to the communications room." Edna poked Susan. "Or they could be watching the windows, waiting for you to throw me off the balcony."

"I thought about it." Susan kept her tone light, and her smile relaxed.

They found the others in a small sitting room. Gary and Cecily sat on overstuffed chairs. Marsel and Salia cowered in a corner, and Bozidar paced by the window.

"I told you they'd be waiting to see me hurtling to the ground," Edna said.

Gary jumped to his feet. "Are you okay?"

"I'm fine," Susan said.

"I'm fine too," Edna said, "in case anyone cares."

Bozidar stood, back to the window, arms folded. "Please tell me there will be no more broken vases. We have work to do."

"Don't count on the calm, space boy," Edna said. "The one thing you can rely on is a meltdown coming at the wrong time."

Susan took Gary's hand. "I'm sorry. I don't know what got into me."

"War, no chocolate, and me showing up when I wasn't supposed to," Cecily said. "Bozidar told me more about your vision. I'll go back to the ship if you want."

Edna opened her mouth, closed it, then smiled. "It's a mother's job to keep her children safe. Of course she wants you back on the ship." She eyed Susan. "But sometimes, we can't play it safe."

Susan stared at Cecily for a cold minute, spared a quick glance at Gary, then turned to Edna. "Right. All three of Agnes' descendants are needed to end the war. We've got the quilt, the Schtatikian prophecies, and the ring Agnes left."

"Are you sure, Mom?" Cecily asked.

Susan sat next to her. "What if I was shown what would happen if I sent you back? If we fail, you'd come down to find us."

"You know I would," Cecily said.

Susan nodded. "And you would be alone. That's how I saw you die—alone." She focused on Bozidar. "Panic is always an option. Consider yourself warned. So, how are we going to convince the elders to listen to us?"

Marsel pushed Salia to the center of the room. "Tell them your good news."

With all eyes watching her, Salia shivered and shrank into herself. Her skin rippled, and her legs and eyestalks retracted until she resembled a block of old wax. Marsel prodded her. Her head popped out. "My cousin will speak on your behalf."

"That's wonderful," Gary said. He patted the top of Salia's head. "You've done very well."

"There is a condition," Salia whispered. Her legs extended enough for her to kneel before Gary. "When the war is over, the taupes must have their honor restored."

Bozidar shook his finger at Salia. "You are not in a position to make demands."

Salia's hands reformed. She clasped them and entreated Gary. "I ask nothing but to serve you, as requested by the Descendants of She Who Found Us."

Gary coughed. "And you're doing a splendid job."

"What can we do to restore your honor?" Susan asked.

Salia curled her back and whispered, "We don't know. My cousin expects a miracle."

"Ye gods and little prairie dogs," Edna said. "We're going to use up our share of miracles getting off this planet with our skins intact."

Cecily took Susan's hand and motioned to Edna to join them. "Let's ask Agnes for help."

Edna arched her eyebrow. "My grandmother never came when she was called. She pretty much did what she pleased when she pleased."

"Let's hope she's in the mood to help," Susan said.

Cecily scooted closer to Susan and draped her free arm over Edna's shoulder. "Come on, you two.

Now is as good a time as any to explore our powers."

"I'm not chanting," Susan said.

"Hush," Cecily said. She closed her eyes and lifted her face to the ceiling.

Edna watched Cecily, then shrugged and closed her eyes. Susan scanned the room, shook her head, and closed her eyes as well. They sat in silence.

Marsel crept toward them, his breath quick and shallow. "Do you see anything yet?"

"The back of my eyelids," Susan growled.

"I told you not to expect Agnes to do our bidding," Edna said.

"Hush." Cecily sat straight and inhaled deeply. "Agnes, we need you."

Bozidar tapped his foot. "This is not working."

"No, it isn't." Susan opened her eyes and stood.

The room shimmered. Tinkling laughter echoed around her as if hundreds of tiny silver bells were bouncing off the walls. The smell of seaweed pulsed through the room, followed by the scent of lavender. The image of Agnes as a young girl appeared near the ceiling.

"You can't solve anything with magic tricks." The child disappeared as soon as the words faded.

"Said the ghost who hitched a ride to a different planet," Susan said.

Cecily leaped to her feet. "Can you see her? What's she saying?"

The air glowed so bright Susan closed her eyes. Agnes' voice enveloped her. *She's clever, your Cecily. Tell the little taupe servant she'll get her miracle. She won't ask how, and you shouldn't either. Tell Edna she'll get her fondest desire very soon. And tell her I'm proud of her.*

The voice faded.

"How is this not a magic trick?" Susan whirled around, looking for the image of Agnes.

Edna crossed her arms. "So the old girl came."

"Young girl." Susan rubbed her temples. "And she was not helpful."

"What did she say?" Cecily asked, grabbing Susan's arms.

"Salia will get her miracle, Edna will get … something, and you're clever."

"Blessings upon She Who Found Us!" Salia tottered to her feet, her normal appearance restored. "I will inform my cousin." She bowed to Gary, then to Bozidar. "With permission."

Bozidar dismissed her with a wave. Gary nodded.

Salia scampered from the room and closed the door behind her.

Marsel danced. "What a momentous day. I must record the events."

"Do as you wish," Bozidar said. His voice sounded as weary as his sagging shoulders looked.

Marsel toddled to him and tugged on Bozidar's elbow. "You still have no faith. Prophecy, visions, the fortuitous appearance of all that we need just when we need it—none of this gives you hope. I will make a special chant for you after my meditation."

Bozidar peered down into Marsel's globe-like

eyes. "In my experience, joy is often followed by terror."

Footsteps sounded in the hall, both the squishy thump of Schtakian footpads and the distinctive click of hard-soled shoes. The procession stopped, and the door shuddered under the rapping of a heavy, blunt object.

"Prepare," said the voice of the head guard. "The elders have decided your fate."

TWELVE

Bozidar clenched his jaw and took one step toward the door. He stopped in midstride as a burst of chittering came from the hall.

Salia rushed into the room. She slid across the floor and crashed into Bozidar. "They said it wrong. They said it wrong."

Bozidar helped Salia to her feet. "There is no right way to announce a death sentence."

"No one's getting executed today." Scott entered the room. His skin was pale, and his clothes were loose, but his eyes twinkled. "The elders decided to send me here directly rather than wait for their arrival. Our fate is still under discussion."

Edna leaped into Scott's arms and grabbed him fiercely around the waist. "You're alive."

"Alive and reasonably well," Scott said. "Being the husband of the queen has some perks." He smoothed her hair, lifted her chin, and kissed her.

Susan, Gary, and Cecily rushed to Scott and Edna as the guards in the hall pushed their way into the room. Marsel danced through the merging groups, singing.

Bozidar pulled Salia to the wall. "We should be safe enough here, out of the way."

One guard held a thick, heavy staff topped with a round copper finial. Beige ribbons curled from the edge of the finial and looped around the dark, smooth wood of the staff. She thumped the end on the floor.

Scott held up his hands. "Quiet down. There are speeches coming, and it will just take longer if we try to avoid them."

Three other guards stepped beside their leader, each followed by a trembling taupe creature. The leader chittered, and the guards turned to glare at their prisoners until they stood straight, eyestalks peering ahead.

"Rupon?" Susan approached, but his guard stepped between them.

"Behold the taupe renegades Dajdar, Mercon, and Rupon." The leader pointed toward the three. "The elders, as a token of kindness, return them with the consort of the esteemed queen, Edna of Earth."

"How is this a kindness to us?" Edna said.

"Shush," Scott whispered. "Let her say her piece."

"The elders wish calm and prosperity upon this place and all who labor here for the good of the beige clan. Food and drink will be provided in abundance, and the work of Scott, defender of the clan, will continue."

The leader rapped her staff against the floor twice. The other guards took one step back from their prisoners. The squad turned as sharply as four rubbery blobs on spindly legs and squishy footpads possibly could and exited the room.

Marsel toddled to Salia, grabbed her by the arm, and led her in a circle dance. As they passed Cecily, Salia took her hand.

"Dance with us," Salia said. "My comrades are safe, and we must celebrate."

Cecily mouthed *help* to her mother, but Susan only shrugged. Edna pulled both Susan and Scott to the center of the room. Cecily reached out and took Susan's free hand as Marsel snaked his way in an intricate pattern across the floor.

"I haven't had this much fun in donkey's years," Edna said. She skipped as if doing a jig and wiggled her wrists to-and-fro, making the line of dancers sway.

Scott fixed his attention on Gary and offered his hand. "Come along, my boy. When Edna dances, everyone dances."

Green smoke wafted above their heads.

Bozidar stepped in Marsel's path and knocked him to the ground. "I have no vase to throw, but I will toss all of you out of the window if you do not pay attention."

Marsel and Salia scurried to the corner, joining the other taupes cowering against the wall. Gary and Scott turned to each other, eyes as wide as their smiles had been a moment before.

"Bozidar, you've lost your temper," Susan said.

"The elders still have power over us. Without their consent, we have no hope of stopping the war. No hope of surviving. I believe my anger is justified." Bozidar's face sagged like butter melting over pancakes.

"You're right," Susan said. She shook off Edna's clasp and went to Bozidar's side, waving away the puffs of green smoke that streamed from his ears and nostrils. "Close your eyes. Take a deep breath." She motioned the others to join her. "We're ready."

Bozidar's face absorbed the extra folds of flesh, settling into its human aspect again. The green smoke drifted out to the balcony. He opened his eyes. "We must convince the elders to believe us. A logical, detailed summary of the prophecies regarding a great queen should be persuasive."

Gary choked back a sharp bark of laughter. "I don't think so. Humans talk a good game about sensible decision-making but in the end, we're all just a bunch of random impulses. Your people seem to be the same."

"I have to agree," Scott said. "The beige scientists and soldiers I've worked with for the past weeks are intelligent and loyal, but prone to the same voids in thinking as anyone on Earth."

"Then we are doomed." Bozidar sat on a small, velvet-covered bench.

"Not necessarily." Susan glanced around the room. "Let's spread the quilt out on that low table. Bring some of the chairs over. Marsel, fetch the scrolls, please."

Salia stepped forward. "What shall I do?"

Susan tugged on a lock of hair. "Help Marsel with the scrolls and any tapestries he remembers seeing." Her expression softened, as did her voice. "Rupon, Dajdar, and Mercon can help too. After that, you four can catch up. I imagine you have a lot to talk about."

Salia bowed, as did the other taupes. They followed Marsel, chittering.

"That's how we're going to convince the council," Susan said.

"I do not understand," Bozidar said.

"Gary gave me the idea." Susan patted Bozidar's shoulder. "You don't persuade people with logic. You appeal to whatever motivates them the most. Give them something they want in exchange for something you want."

"We have nothing they value." Bozidar's head drooped.

"That's not entirely true," Scott said. He placed two chairs next to the table. "Come over here, and let me tell you what I've been doing at the lab."

The others scooted chairs or benches around the table. Bozidar rose from his bench as if the entire weight of the castle pressed upon his head. He shuffled to the chair next to Scott and lowered himself like a bucket on a frayed rope.

Marsel returned, cradling his scrolls. The renegade taupes trailed him, laden with tapestries, which they stacked on a corner of the table. Marsel sat on a bench next to Cecily, still clutching his treasures.

Scott crossed his legs and rested his hands on the chair arms. "I had a scrap of chenille with me when I was captured. I planned on using it on a suicide run to take out as many soldiers as I could before they killed me. Didn't happen."

"Clearly, or you would not be recounting the story," Bozidar said.

Edna hissed at him. "Hush, space boy."

"What I mean," Scott said, "is that it wasn't necessary. Once they saw the chenille, they backed off. One of them sent a message up the chain of command, and pretty soon a delegation from the council arrived. They promised they wouldn't harm me if I helped with research on the *machute* plant. Luckily, I remembered that word."

"And it never occurred to you to ask for me?" Edna said.

Susan nudged Edna's foot. "Hush, Mother."

"Of course I asked for you, my dear," Scott said. "I was assured you were in no danger. They showed me security footage of you every day. They promised to bring me here when the work was done. I had no choice but to accept their terms."

"How did you help the research?" Gary asked. "You aren't a scientist."

"No, but I learn fast, ask questions, and don't keel over dead when I touch *machute*." Scott leaned forward. "That made me valuable, and acceptable. The scientists included me in their review sessions."

"That's more than I got." Edna scowled. "Here I am, queen of the whole frickin' clan, and no one says a word to me the entire time."

Marsel shifted on his bench. "I have already explained that. It would be disrespectful to speak to one of your rank."

Bozidar, Susan, and Edna replied in unison. "Hush."

Scott chuckled. "So far, the results are promising, at least for an antidote to the poison. Weaponizing the plant isn't going as well. There were some interesting possibilities, but we've hit a dead-end with all of them."

"Weaponizing?" Bozidar sat straight. He clenched his hands, and his face grew pale.

"Yes," Scott said. "Making a gas or a bomb from the plant would give the beige clan a huge tactical advantage in the war."

"Scott, we came to stop the war," Susan said. "Are you saying we're too late?"

"I have no idea." Scott examined Bozidar. "You're mighty quiet."

Bozidar shuddered. "The *machute* plant is the last

of the great hazards. Knowing we were all susceptible to annihilation afforded a measure of balance to politics. If the elders plan to disrupt that balance, the consequences could be horrific."

Scott nodded. "I expect so."

Edna cocked her head. "You had your finger on the button at a nuclear silo, didn't you?"

"Even a queen isn't cleared for that information." Scott nodded at Susan. "To return to your question, until someone starts shooting, we still have a chance. The elders might be more responsive to your idea of negotiating a truce if it gives them time to develop a weapon of mass destruction."

Marsel dropped his scrolls, and his eye stalks writhed. "You would leave, knowing we might destroy ourselves?"

Scott shrugged. "My first loyalty is to my wife, her daughter, and her granddaughters."

The air around Susan shimmered and the sound of voices faded. She saw a young Agnes, holding hands with a beige creature she knew must be the leader of the doomed first expedition to Earth.

"Right you are," Agnes said. "This is my friend. Her name is Pala."

Agnes' mouth moved. Susan knew the voice came from across the room, not from inside her head. "Are you real now? Can everyone see you?"

"No, only you. We thought it might be easier for you to have a real conversation."

"I'm getting used to the visions," Susan said.

"Splendid," Agnes said. "But this is too important. We need you to be very clear. Family loyalty, clan loyalty, all that love. Sometimes it leads to joy, sometimes to ferocity. You must remember that when you talk with the elders."

Susan blinked. Agnes and Pala vanished.

"That's a fierce love, Scott," she said. *Did I mean to say that, or is Agnes speaking through me?* "Maybe that's how the taupes felt when they invaded my quilt shop. Maybe that's how the blues feel now."

Gary leaned against the chair arm, turning toward Susan. "If that really is their motivation, we have common ground."

Susan nodded. "What do you think, Bozidar? Can you help us find common ground?"

Bozidar clasped his hands and tucked them under his chin. He scanned the circle, ending with Marsel. He pointed at the scrolls.

"Can you find a prophecy that will appeal to the elders without offending every other clan on the planet?"

Marsel slid from the bench, gathered the twine-bound sticks, and spread them across the quilt. His hands hovered above the surface, tracing the designs without touching them. He whispered to himself, a soft chant that rose and fell in a hypnotic rhythm.

Bozidar's eyelids drifted toward closing, and his shoulders folded. He shook his head and sat upright. "Even if he finds what we need, the elders can be stubborn."

Susan arched one eyebrow. "You want stubborn? Look at my daughter. I have two more at home just like her."

"Gee, thanks, Mom," Cecily said, but she smiled as she spoke.

"Don't forget me," Edna said.

"The stars will grow cold before anyone forgets you, my dear," Scott said.

"All we have to do is pique their curiosity," Susan said. "Present one idea, let them digest it, hear what they say."

Bozidar scrunched his face. "Time is our enemy. We should be concise and complete."

"If we are, they'll say no without considering the proposal. I've seen it before." Susan rose and stood behind her chair. "There are five other quilt shops within driving distance of mine. Most businesses couldn't survive that kind of competition, but ours does. I got to know the other shop owners and convinced them there was plenty of trade for everyone. We just needed to share. It took time, but we figured out how to do that."

"That isn't the way government works," Scott said.

"You're right, it isn't," Susan said. "But non-profits thrive on cooperation. I've never run for office, but I've raised a boatload of money for the community. Some of the people I worked with on those committees did run for office, and they've changed local politics for the better."

"Change is not a word the elders appreciate," Bozidar said.

"That's why we have to be subversive," Cecily said. She stood and approached Salia. "We offered you a choice. Stop hurting us and we'll stop hurting you. Do you remember how you felt?"

"I did not believe you. None of us believed you."

"Exactly." Susan crossed her arms. "What we're offering is the beginning of a process. At the end, maybe there's a chance for all the clans to have a peaceful life with choices and hope. There's no guarantee our idea will work. Everyone will have to sacrifice something, especially the notion that they've got all the answers."

"That sounds scary," Gary said.

"There's nothing scarier." Susan leaned on the back of the chair. "Welcome to my world."

"What about spoilers?" Scott asked. "The ones who would rather see everyone dead if they can't have their own way?"

"I don't know," Susan said. "That's why finding common ground is important."

Marsel stopped chanting. He lifted a scroll and pointed to a passage. "This may be what we need."

"Hurrah, some good news for a change," Edna said.

"Read it to us," Susan said.

Marsel returned to his bench. He hunched over the scroll, and his legs retracted until his feet swung in the empty air.

"Stop that," Edna said. "You look like a peanut on a string. With legs."

Bozidar held up his hand. "Something is troubling him. I recognize this behavior."

"Oh, just spit it out," Edna said.

Marsel squirmed. "Well, the language is inclusive enough. It refers to a golden age when all the clans lived in harmony. The prophecy specifies the spirit of generosity and courage that will exist before a new golden age will begin."

"That sounds spot on," Cecily said. "What's the problem?"

"The prophecy requires certain actions to prove the agent using it is, in fact, the right one."

Edna twirled her finger. "Cut to the chase. What do we have to do and when?"

Marsel slid off the bench and ran to Cecily. Hiding behind her, he said, "The queen must perform a miracle."

THIRTEEN

The wind whistled in from the balcony. Marsel stretched one eyestalk around Cecily's knee and pointed it in Edna's direction.

Bozidar held out his hand. "Show us the passage, Marsel."

"Perhaps it would be better to read it to us," Cecily said, pushing Marsel squarely behind her. "Gary and I were starting to get the hang of the metaphors. Maybe there's another interpretation."

"I don't care what the passage says or how many interpretations you can fit on the head of a pin, what do you mean I have to perform a miracle?" Edna did not move from her chair, but her eyes glinted, and a rage-red flush rose in her cheeks.

"Save the shouting for later, please," Cecily said. "Let's hear the passage first."

Marsel's knees wobbled as he unrolled the scroll. The bundle of tied sticks rattled, and he emitted three short squeaks.

"If that's the Schtatikian version of clearing your throat, stop it," Edna said.

Marsel nodded. "This is the verse. *Behold, and see a wonder. The blood of the unfortunate will flow, but the chosen will not flinch. The squeal of the wounded will sound as a slaughtered beast, but the chosen will sing. She will cause pain to ebb and fear to flee.*"

Scott coughed, but the rumble of a laugh slipped out as well. "Edna, I love you beyond words, but we are so screwed."

"What do you mean?" Marsel asked.

Bozidar closed his eyes and shook his head. "Oh, my poor friend. Even the blind can see that pain and fear are the unseen guests accompanying Edna wherever she goes."

Salia gasped and huddled closer to her quivering friends. Cecily put her arm around Marsel.

Edna shrugged. "You know he's right. I'm not the healing type."

Marsel spoke, his voice almost a whisper, "But you have to heal someone. The prophecy says so."

"It would be a true miracle," Scott said. "But I think we can reframe the prophecy to suit Edna's skill set."

"What do you mean?" Edna asked. "And be careful with the next words out of your mouth."

"Our first impression is that this prophecy refers

to healing. However, we could say the first two events, blood spilling and wounded crying, represent what happens in war. The chosen is a reference to Edna. She doesn't flinch. In fact, she sings. We'll say this refers to the actions of a victorious queen. The last line, bringing the end of pain and fear, refers to the end of the war."

Edna crossed her arms, raised her chin and studied Scott through narrowed eyes. "You were a traveling preacher in a past life."

"No." Scott patted Edna's knee. "That would be my Uncle Thaddeus. I learned a lot from him but not always what he intended."

Gary thrummed his fingers against his knee. "I think we could pull it off. Edna could bluff the horn off a rhinoceros. She could easily convince the elders that the prophecy refers to her if we all stick to the script."

Bozidar leaned toward Scott. He clasped his hands, lacing his fingers as if in supplication. "Is this a common human trait? To invent whatever one wishes to be true? And does it end well?"

"If you work at it," Scott said. "And you're lucky."

Marsel clutched the scrolls. "Truth does not need to be invented. The prophecy is written on the sticks. The words are clear."

"The words, yes," Susan said. "The interpretation, no."

Marsel's eyestalks glistened. A film of milky

liquid rimmed the knobs holding his eyes. "Prophecy should not be used this way."

Cecily turned around and knelt by Marsel. "Are you crying?"

"And why not? You have taken my work and twisted it. You lied about your intentions."

Edna threw her hands in the air. "Of course they lied. Everyone lies. How do you think the current unpleasantness started? That rat-faced weasel the blues sent to our trial heard what he wanted to hear, and fibbed about what we really did."

"I do not lie." Marsel's voice was barely audible. The milky liquid around his eyes flowed down to his shoulders and dripped on the floor.

Cecily put her hands over his. "Marsel, I will tell you one true thing. We are creating a story to fit the prophecy because we have to. If we fail, the clans go to war."

"Would you do the same to your own sacred texts?" Bozidar asked.

"Yes," Cecily said. "Our religions are full of prophecy, and no one really knows what it means. We do the best we can."

"How can you do your best when you do not begin with truth?" Marsel asked.

Cecily gulped and turned to Susan. "Mom?"

Susan glanced at Gary and Scott. "Any words of wisdom? You two both deal in motivation."

"Stop," Edna said. "Marsel, when the war is over and we're out of here then you'll know our version of prophecy was correct. If your gods don't like it then they should be more specific."

"The gods will not like it, and we will be punished," Marsel said.

"We have not been rewarded regardless of what we have done," Bozidar said. "It is my decision. We will do as Scott suggests."

Scott nodded. "When the elders arrive, they'll make us sit in silence while they study the scrolls, the quilt, and the other artifacts. Then they'll question us. If we all speak, the end will be like the trial. One person should speak for us, and that person needs to keep on script. It doesn't matter what the elders want. We keep telling them the same thing."

Salia and the renegade taupes whispered together. They motioned Marsel to join them. He gave Cecily the scrolls and toddled to the group. They huddled so close they looked like a wall of putty.

"Salia says the taupe leadership repeated warnings of disaster if the expedition to Earth did not proceed and promises of glory if it did," Marsel said. "You know the result."

"So your leader was a false prophet," Scott said. "On Earth, we kill the false prophets. Since we're likely to die if we do nothing, what do you have to lose?"

Marsel quivered. His lips wobbled, and his hands twitched. "Scrolls." He ran to Cecily and snatched the stick bundles. Pressing them against his rubbery midsection, he wiggled on the bench and chanted.

The syllables grew louder, and the amplitude of his wiggle increased until he leaped off the bench with a shout. He hopped from one footpad to the other, waving the scrolls like maracas.

The renegade taupes grabbed each other, eyestalks twining together. Cecily reached toward Marsel, then retreated as his jig brought him perilously close to her feet. Bozidar buried his face in his hands.

"Marsel, sweetie," Susan said, "are you dancing for joy?"

Edna shook her head. "He's gone crackers."

"No, no, all is splendid." Marsel bounced in a circle. "I understand your strategy. Your people have a saying about a leap of faith. You offer the opportunity to soar like fine, strong birds. How could the gods refuse such a glorious gift?"

"You want that alphabetically or by the size of the explosion?" Edna asked.

"Quiet, dear," Scott said. "So you'll cooperate?"

"Yes, with great pleasure. We will do all that you ask, without question." Marsel spun around and beckoned to the ball of interlaced taupes. "Unravel yourselves, my friends. We stand on the edge of a great adventure."

* * *

The morning sky looked like a strawberry parfait.

The breeze came in small bursts that could ease to gentle wafts as the sun rose or roar like solar flares if the mood struck. Froth swirled on the pink river below like ice cubes melting in a punch bowl.

Susan paced on the balcony, ignoring the view. She whispered to herself, counting on her fingers, shaking her head. Reaching the railing again, she gripped the edge until her knuckles turned white.

Gary waited at the archway. He cleared his throat. "I can feel you fretting from here."

Susan relaxed her hands, shook out her fingers, and counted to five before she turned. "Who's fretting? I'm just enjoying the peace."

"I'd accept that at sunset, but this is sunrise, and you are not a morning person."

"I used to be."

"No, you never were. You get up early when you have to, but it's painful to watch." He crossed the stone tiles. "Still, it is a beautiful sight."

"In California, it would be a beautiful sight." She scanned the clouds, the shadows on the mountains, and the rollicking river. "Who knows what that sky means here. It could be their tornado sky for all we know."

"A-n-nd there's that sunny morning personality we all love." He embraced her. "It will all work out because it has to. You've got two more kids and a quilt store waiting for you."

Susan closed her eyes. "If I could just keep my mind from racing. My brain cells are competing with my heart to see which will explode first."

He held her at arm's length. "You haven't had a needle in your hands for weeks. Where's that project box you brought? A little time with your embroidery would calm you down."

"I left it on the ship." She snuggled back into his arms again. "I'll ask Bozidar to have someone send it down."

"Send what down?" Bozidar asked. "Have we forgotten something the elders should see?" He scurried across the balcony, grabbed Susan and Gary by their elbows, and pulled them toward the archway. "The council could be here at any time. We must be dressed and waiting when they arrive. Where are your robes? Are your shoes clean?"

Susan skipped on her toes to keep up. "The robes are where you instructed the staff to put them. They took our shoes, so I'm assuming they're clean. Salia told you last night that her cousin would send a message as soon as the council embarked so we wouldn't be caught by surprise."

"Good," Bozidar said, increasing his pace.

Gary dragged his feet against the stone. "Slow down. Breathe. Susan is nervous enough without you falling to pieces."

"I have performed three calming ceremonies since I arose," Bozidar said. "They have not helped."

"Have you tried whiskey?" Edna blocked their path. A glittering silk scarf the color of new copper covered her hair. She wore a bronze satin caftan trimmed with ribbons the same color as her scarf.

"Mom, don't you look regal." Susan circled her mother. "But getting Bozidar liquored up won't help."

"Maybe not, but it could be amusing." She frowned at her daughter. "You look like you could use a drink too."

"It will have to wait until I change." Susan took Gary's hand and smiled at Bozidar. "Where do you want us to gather once we're dressed?"

"Downstairs, in the large hall." Bozidar bit his lower lip. "I should check on the others." He dashed from the room.

"He already did," Edna said. "Am I the only one who isn't flat out crazy this morning?"

Susan hugged her mother. "You're the only one who isn't nervous, so you're either the only sane one or the craziest person in the room. Either way is fine with me. I'm going to change."

Susan replayed alternate scenarios for the day. The tiniest bud of hope poked through the layers of imagined disasters. She could almost envision a quick and peaceful resolution by the time she opened the door and saw her outfit.

The stack of garments glistened in the pink light. On top was a simple, straight gown that shimmered between a pale rose and champagne. It slid over her skin, falling almost to her ankles. She wound a variegated rose scarf around her head. The thick weave reminded her of jacquard. She tucked the ends to make a turban, allowing a few blonde tendrils to curl along her neck. The jacket seemed more like satin, patches of antique silver and scarlet assembled in panels that reached to her knees. The shawl collar rolled effortlessly into place.

She stood in the center of the room, facing the window. The reddish sky grew pale. The breeze rustled her hem, carrying a hint of cinnamon and basil. *Is this a good sign? Bad? There's never a vision when you need one.*

She made her way to the great hall through empty corridors. The silence fit a haunted house rather than a fortress filled with soldiers and staff. The aroma of cinnamon faded, and the scent of lemon swirled around her.

Upholstered benches and long tables covered with glittering runners replaced the furniture in the wood-paneled room. Marsel's scrolls occupied a table by themselves, the artifacts Susan brought lay on another, and a third table held stacks of bound books. The renegade taupes sat on one of the benches. Edna and Cecily sat together, Scott and Gary stood by the window. Bozidar paced beside the table with the artifacts.

Susan joined Bozidar. She ran her hands over the quilt. Her fingertips tingled when she touched the edges, but the room did not shimmer, and Agnes did not appear.

"Do you feel her energy?" Bozidar asked.

"Whose? Agnes or Pala, the captain?"

"Either. Both." He thrust his hands into his green robes. The hem skimmed the surface of the malachite floor, and seemed to merge with it. "I am not comforted by the colors assigned to us."

"Why?" Susan smoothed her dress. "I usually wear beige, or tan, but somehow this crimson outfit seems right. I might have to expand my wardrobe when I get back."

Bozidar pointed to the ring. "It matches your ring."

"So? They know I've used it to heal."

"What if they ask for a demonstration?" He shook his head. "My robe is meant to remind me that I have little status. It blends into the floor."

Susan bit her lip but said nothing. She pointed at the red velvet cupcakes arranged on a wide pewter-colored platter resting on a granite block. "Those need to be eaten soon. They're going to go stale."

"Your mother and daughter said the same thing."

Susan considered the two on the bench. "They're conspiring to eat them, aren't they?"

Bozidar nodded. "I told Edna that the elders would need to see the entire collection."

"And she told you she was the queen and could do whatever she pleased."

Bozidar grimaced. "Her words were not as pleasant. Cecily led her away. I was grateful."

"I'll talk to her." Susan patted his arm.

Marsel dashed into the room as the sound of drums and flutes echoed from the hall. "The elders are here." He slid onto the bench next to Salia.

Bozidar maneuvered Susan toward Edna and Cecily. He motioned to Scott and Gary to join them.

In cadence with a brassy fanfare, two columns of soldiers entered. The first six were musicians, followed by a pair carrying banners on slender wood poles. They wore tabards of beige and gray linen, and gold bangles on their legs above their footpads.

Four elders followed. Three wore long, elegant coats made from velvet panels. Large beige beads resembling antique pearls encrusted the panels. The fourth wore a similar coat of taupe with silvery-gray bugle beads strung in long, vertical lines, and an emerald broach at the collar.

"Stand up, Mother," Susan whispered.

"I'm their queen." Edna remained rooted on the bench.

Cecily pulled Edna to her feet. "Consider it noblesse-oblige."

"I feel silly standing for someone that barely comes up to my shoulders. You don't stand for me when I'm the shortest person in the room."

"You told us never to mention your height," Susan said.

The musicians lined the walls and ended their fanfare. The flag bearers stood in front of the window. Rosy light filtered through the banners. The long streams of off-white silk now flashed as if LED lights were embedded in the fibers.

The elders formed a semi-circle in front of the

table with the artifacts. The one in taupe stepped forward.

"We represent the noble beige clan. Please address me as Neela. Our meeting is being transmitted to the rest of the council, and will be preserved in the annals."

She gestured to the others. "My worthy colleagues may speak if they choose. Until then, direct your responses to me. For the sake of your weak senses, we each wear a jewel. Thus may you tell one of us from the other without embarrassment."

Edna's jaw clenched. Susan poked her in the ribs before the muscles relaxed, then bowed.

"We appreciate your kindness, Neela. I am Susan. Will you permit me to show you the items we brought from Earth to demonstrate our good intentions?"

Neela nodded and motioned to the flag bearers to approach. "These are our transmission devices," she said, pointing to the banners. "Speak clearly, so your words may be captured accurately."

Susan pressed her palms together at her chest. *This isn't yoga class*, she admonished herself, as she dropped her hands to her side. She picked up the quilt and draped it over her arm. Tracing a line of embroidery with one finger, she said, "This is a fragment of the quilt my great-grandmother Agnes made to honor those of your clan who first came to our planet. Agnes was only a child, but your captain was able to communicate with her, after a fashion.

Agnes recreated your symbols as best she could, and she preserved the remains of Pala."

Neela touched the flour sack between the top and lining. "I feel her essence. Her power to transform into another substance has never been equaled."

Susan placed the quilt on the table and took the ring from a velvet-lined box. "The captain's powers to teach, and to heal, were also considerable. The ruby stone came from your planet, the silver setting from ours. Agnes kept this safe."

She slipped the ring on her finger and held it for Neela to examine. An unexpected breeze swirled around the two, and the scent of lavender filled the space.

Neela took a step back. "The stone accepts you."

"It is our hope that you, also, will accept us," Susan said. *Now, where did that come from,* she thought. *If you're speaking through me, Agnes, at least let me make sense.*

Susan thought she heard a deep laughing voice coming from outside the window, but the rattling panels convinced her that it was thunder. She shuddered, remembering the morning sky, and moved to the cupcakes. "Marsel has found references in the scrolls that our coming here was foretold. As evidence, we brought a human treat. Red and white, baked. Marsel will show you the passage. As you can see, the colors of the cupcake echo the colors of my ring."

She offered the platter to Neela. The other elders drew near, and Susan offered each of them a treat.

They examined the paper wrapper and the frosting. They held the cupcakes as if they were made of porcelain.

Edna grabbed Cecily's hand. "It's about time we ate those things." She snatched two cupcakes.

"Mom, hold on," Susan said. "You know there's going to be a ceremony before we get to peel the paper off, much less lick the frosting."

"Too late." Edna winked and took a huge bite.

The elders gasped, green smoke pouring out from all of them. Marsel dived under the bench, followed by the other taupes.

Susan slid the platter on the table and rushed to Bozidar. "What did we do?"

"What you always do," he said with a low growl. "You bring chaos and mayhem."

Thunder boomed again, and the window slabs rattled. The noise grew louder and deeper, and the entire wall rippled. The floor shook.

"Everyone out," Scott shouted. He and Gary grabbed the musicians and propelled them toward the door.

Susan heard a loud snapping like a case of glassware falling from shelves. She pushed Bozidar underneath the table. Rose-colored shards shot through the air as the window splintered and wind-driven rain flooded the room.

FOURTEEN

Green lightning spread tendrils around the walls. The splatter of bullet-sized raindrops sounded like side-drums, and the wind whined like bagpipes. The concussion of thunderclaps rolled through the room as if a line of bass drums pounded on the downbeat.

Susan felt hands tugging at her. She felt the drenched tiles scrape against her legs, and remembered hauling a canoe to shore and the way the river bottom scraped against the hull. She wiped the water from her face and discovered that Bozidar was pulling her into the hall.

"Stay here," he said as they rounded a corner. He propped Susan on a sheltering wall and stumbled against the wind back to the great hall.

Susan tried to protest, but only a groan escaped

her mouth. She rolled to her knees and continued rolling until she fell on the cold stone floor. The icy surface jolted her enough that she curled her knees under her and pushed herself to all fours. She crawled back to the wall.

Bozidar returned carrying Cecily. Her eyes were open. Blood covered her face, and she cradled one arm against her stomach. He settled her next to Susan.

"Thank you," Cecily said. She rubbed her eyes. "Mom? Are you okay?"

Susan nodded. "I think so. You aren't."

"Cuts. Shoulder hurts. My arm may be broken." She blinked. "You are too calm to be okay."

"I'm fine."

"When Olivia broke her toe, you had a melt-down. You should be screaming now."

Scott and Gary arrived, supporting Edna between them. She winced each time her left foot touched the floor.

"Gary," Cecily said, "check Mom for a concussion."

Edna jerked forward. "Did you hit your head?"

"Not that I remember," Susan said.

Gary knelt by her and studied her eyes. "Your pupils look okay." He felt her head. "I don't feel any lumps, and there's no bleeding."

"It's shock, that's all," Susan said.

Marsel limped into view. Leaning against the wall, he shouted down the corridor. "The humans are here." He bowed to Edna. "Healers will arrive soon."

Susan's hand grew warm. She raised it and saw the ruby stone glowing. She ran her hand over her forehead and down her face. The sluggishness in her brain subsided as aches she hadn't noticed earlier faded. She edged along the wall and stroked Cecily's cheek.

"Whoa," Cecily said, sitting straighter and breathing easier. "I'm not seeing double anymore. Do my arm."

Susan rested her fingertips on Cecily's wrist for a moment. She inhaled, and moved her hand up and down the arm, hovering above the skin.

Cecily flexed and stretched her fingers. "That's amazing." She leaned her head against the wall and observed Edna, balancing on one foot. "Grandma, are you next?"

"Don't waste your strength on me," Edna said. "Some of those critters took a bigger hit. I can wait for the medics."

"Are they badly injured, Marsel?" Susan asked.

Marsel slid to the floor. "Yes, and so am I."

He kicked one footpad and wiggled his hands, as if slapping the air would propel him up from the floor. His eyestalks twined together, then relaxed and drooped over his shoulders.

"Marsel?" Cecily asked, fear in her voice. "Mom, help him."

Susan's skin grew cold, and her heartbeat slowed. The air shimmered, and she felt the presence of

Agnes and Pala. *The captain can help you.* The voice in her head was that of a child, calm and yet expectant.

Susan stared at the ruby ring. The stone glowed, warming the silver setting around her finger. The heat spread across her icy hands, up her arms, and across her chest. The blood in her veins whooshed through her body, and her heart beat stronger, faster. I can do this, but not alone, she thought.

Then let us help you. This time the voice in her head was older, alien, but comforting.

Susan reached toward Cecily and Edna. "Agnes and Pala are here. I can feel them."

Cecily pulled Susan toward Marsel. Edna waved at Scott, who moved her closer to Marsel while Gary helped Susan.

"Now what?" Edna asked. "If you tell me we have to hold hands and chant, I'm out of here."

Tell them to think kind thoughts for Marsel, the older voice whispered in Susan's head. *We'll guide that energy. Watch and learn.*

Susan touched Marsel's midsection above a slash that oozed a milky, custard-like liquid. She rested her fingertips on his skin. "Just wish him well. Pala will do the rest."

"Seriously? She grants wishes?" Edna said.

"Hush, Grandma," Cecily said. "We need positive energy now. Save snarky for later."

Susan watched the wound, but out of the corner of her eye, she saw tendrils of light twist toward her. The air sparkled as if filled with flecks of silver glitter and tiny lilac crystals. The tendrils twined together like branches. The tips prodded the edges of the cut, pushing them together. In time with Susan's heartbeat, the wound shrank. Only a crust of liquid remained, like old pudding in a bowl. Warmth and peace filled her with energy, and she willed that energy to join the light.

Marsel shuddered. His arm grew warmer under Susan's fingertips. His eyestalks plumped and perked up. He patted the now-healed cut. "My pain is gone. I am no longer injured." He rolled to his feet and bowed, first to Susan, then Cecily, then Edna. "I am grateful beyond words."

The elders came into the alcove, accompanied by red-robed Schtatikians. "The healers are here," Neela said. "Show them your injuries."

Marsel twirled in place. "I was hurt but now am healed. The Descendants of She Who Found Us have used the ancient art."

"Is this true, my queen?" Neela asked Edna.

Edna shrugged. "Maybe." She pointed to Susan. "Ask the heir to the throne. She's the one getting lessons from Agnes and your captain." She rotated her foot. "Looks like they healed my ankle in the bargain."

"Make sure your own people are treated first," Susan said. "It took two ghosts and the three of us to help Marsel. Don't wait for a miracle from us."

"Indeed not," Neela said. "Your own impetuous behavior caused this disaster. The gods are swift to punish blasphemers."

"But they did not," Marsel said with a gasp. "This is the miracle that was promised." He danced in place as if he were a child waiting for an ice cream cone. "The more I am with these humans, the more gifts from the universe I receive."

Edna opened her mouth, but Susan and Cecily both shushed her before she spoke.

Neela raised her hands, and a green mist spread over her body. "Marsel, contain yourself. Under what sky is a storm considered a miracle, much less a blessing?"

"There was no mention of a blessing in the prophecy," Bozidar said. He threaded his way between the healers, Salia at his side. Bozidar examined Marsel, then addressed Neela. "My experience with the gods, any gods, has always been one of unexpected pain. It makes as much sense that our gods would send a disaster to show their approval as it does to elect a human queen of our clan. Since we have already done the one, I can readily believe the other."

"And you call me cranky," Edna said.

"Yes, we do. Hush." Susan held the ring, still warm and glowing, for Neela to see. "The ghosts of your captain and my great-grandmother channeled our energy through this device to heal. I understand that talent has been lost. Wouldn't rediscovering how to use rock and metal to repair serious injury count as a miracle?"

"What do you mean *our* energy?" Neela said.

"The three of us," Susan said, pointing to Cecily and Edna. She shifted on the floor. "Hang on. I almost missed that. I'm the only one Agnes talks to, and I've done a little healing, but for something really big it took all of us."

"Epic, epic," Marsel said, adding a shuffle step to his jig. "The very first prophecy I found spoke of one clan uniting the rest. The three of you are united as one. We will follow your example, and all be as one on our lovely, lilac world. It will be the beginning of a new age, and we will attend the birth."

Neela leaned toward Bozidar. "Did this one actually advance through the ranks in such a damaged condition?"

Bozidar shook his head. "I attribute his behavior to excessive contact with the Descendants of She Who Found Us."

Susan's skin tingled. *That's my girls*, she heard in Agnes' voice. The air shimmered, and once again Susan's mind stretched out of time. An adult version of Agnes stood before her.

"It might help if you would talk to everyone," Susan said. "They interrupt me when I repeat our conversations. Vital information gets lost."

That is the way of life. Pala's voice echoed around the room.

"You may be right, but we'll have a better chance of saving some of those now living if we could be more efficient," Susan said.

"The problem with efficiency is that only the ones in charge learn," Agnes said. "When plans go smoothly, the people at the edges don't see how much work is involved. That's one reason the blues and the beiges are at each other's throats. They've forgotten how hard it is to compromise enough to live in peace and still keep your pride."

"How do I tell them?"

"You don't," Agnes said. "You show them. And before you ask, that's something you'll have to work out for yourself. I'm a ghost, not a magician."

"Neither am I," Susan said, clenching her jaw. "I don't have the experience for this."

"Yes, you do. You've raised a family and run a business. All you have to do is scale up."

A burst of cold air surged into the alcove. Susan heard the staccato drumming of rain on the floor of the great hall. She blinked, and Agnes disappeared.

"We may have been a bad influence on Marsel, but he's right about the prophecy," Susan said, shaking off the last shreds of her vision. "You need to open a dialog with the blues, as well as address the differences among members of your own clan."

"That is not a trivial problem," Neela said.

"It never is, so use every weapon you have." Susan folded her hands in her lap. "Use the prophecies, and us."

"Listen to her," the taupe elder said.

All eyes focused on the elder, who pushed her way to Marsel's side. Salia trotted two paces behind.

The elder scanned Marsel, one eyestalk glancing up and down his body, the other peeking at the back of his head. She rested her hands on his shoulders briefly. She turned on her heel, slow and deliberate. Bowing, she offered her hat to Salia.

Salia bowed and cradled the hat. "I am grateful, cousin."

"Grateful for what?" Susan asked.

"My cousin has relinquished her place on the council to me," Salia said.

"That is impossible," Neela said. "The other members have not approved."

"The taupes do not care what the council approves," Salia said. "We follow our own leaders. That leader now is me." She toddled to Susan and placed the hat on her head. "And I give my unconditional allegiance to her."

Bozidar crossed his arms. "It appears we have our miracle."

"But she did not perform this act," Neela said, pointing at Edna. "The prophecy specified the queen would perform a miracle."

Cecily coughed. "May I speak? What if we expanded the concept of queen? Agnes was my ancestor, as well as my mother's, and my grandmother's. You could tell the clan that because we're from another planet, it takes three of us to do what one of you could do."

"Clever girl," Scott said. "It makes the healing fit the prophecy and flatters the locals at the same time."

Neela turned to Bozidar. "You understand these creatures better than anyone. Can they help?"

"The evidence is before you, elder," Bozidar said. "They already helped us when they had no reason to wish us well."

Neela stood a moment, silent and still as a concrete plinth. "In our desperation, we must trust these aliens. We will go to the capital, and ask the blues to discuss peace."

* * *

An afternoon breeze swept the remaining shreds of clouds to the horizon and pushed them over the edge. Susan sat on the balcony, sketchbook in hand. She drew a line, erased it, drew another. She inhaled the cool, moist air as her eyes drank in the delicate, lilac-tinted light.

"I'm glad to see you doing something with your hands." Gary joined her on the padded bench. "Feeling better?"

"Only when I don't think about how crappy my drawing skills are. First thing when we get home, I'm signing up for art classes." She closed the book and stuck her pencil behind her ear. "Marsel promised to bring my embroidery supplies back on the next supply run. I had hoped to have some landscape sketches to work on, but maybe I should stick to plants. I have better luck drawing leaves and flowers."

"It's taking so long to get ready to leave for the capital, you can sketch every plant around the castle. How can such little creatures need so much stuff?"

"You've clearly forgotten packing for Olivia and Eleanor. They took three suitcases each. And they shared another one for their shoes."

"Oh, that's right," Gary said. He stopped speaking when noise from the hall blasted onto the balcony, bouncing off the slate and amplifying laughter and chittering.

Salia entered first, followed by Edna and Scott. Behind them came Rupon, Marcon, and Dajdar, each pushing a trolley.

"We bring refreshments." Salia motioned to the others to display the snacks on the trolleys.

"This is very nice," Susan said. "Mother, did you threaten them if they didn't bring us food?"

"No," Edna said as she settled into an oversized chair. "I apologized, and Salia did the threatening."

Susan and Gary both stepped back, mouths open.

"You … apologized?" Gary asked.

"I know the theory," Edna said. "I just avoid the practice whenever I can." She laced and unlaced her fingers. "But I figured it was time. I've been a little testier than usual. You may have noticed."

"You think?" Susan said.

Edna narrowed her eyes and pointed a finger at Susan. "Yeah, well, next time you have to win a war or die, not to mention coming up with a miracle that no one tells you about, you can be Miss Sweetness and Light."

Susan raised her hands. "Point made, Mother. Stress rarely brings out the best in people."

"I've been told that nothing brings out the best in me." Edna slid out of the chair and examined the trolleys. "So, I apologized to Salia. And Marsel. The poor critter fell on the floor in some kind of fit."

"He said it was another miracle," Salia said. "A special gift, just for him."

Gary patted Salia's shoulder. "You are full of surprises. There's one thing that puzzles me, though. Why did your cousin give her position on the council to you?"

"I've been wondering that," Susan said. "Not that I'm complaining, but I am curious."

Salia took a glass of pink liquid and sipped. "I am not certain you will understand, but I will attempt to explain. We taupes are a small group in the beige clan, but we have provided more leaders than any other. Our pride, while understandable, made the other groups angry. They envied our talent and wisdom. We found our brightest blobblings refused entry to the best training centers, and employment that had been given to taupes for generations went elsewhere."

She placed the glass on a small table and toddled to the railing. Her eyestalks drooped.

"Was that why you went to Earth?" Susan asked.

"Yes." Salia's voice was a pained whisper. She whirled around. "I was *proud* to take part in the invasion. Until we failed. Until we met you. Until I saw that our role was a tiny part in a much larger destiny."

She waved her hand at the view. "This was my entire concern. The land of the beige clan, and the position of the taupes within it. I have learned so much more. That is what I told my cousin, what I discovered on your planet. Your kindness, a quality the taupes dismiss, but which gives you such strength. Your ability to forgive, a quality our leaders despise. Most of all, I told her how we failed."

"That still doesn't explain why you're on the council," Gary said. "Your cousin took one look at Marsel and handed you her hat. What did she see?"

"She saw us working together to save an enemy," Edna said.

"More important, you are not afraid of what is new." Salia bowed to Edna and Susan in turn. "She Who Found Us accepted the great gift Pala offered without question. Now her descendants accept the invitation to see our world, without question. You are not of Schtatik, and you are not taupes, but you are worthy."

"Well, it's just raining miracles," Cecily said from the doorway. She joined the group, choosing a pastry and beverage on her way. "Grandma apologized, Marsel is vindicated, the taupes accept an outsider as worthy. Someone is going to make saints out of us."

"Don't get cocky," Susan said. "We've still got a war to stop."

FIFTEEN

A hint of lemon-basil wafted through the corridor of *Cold Fire*, not quite masked by the scent of fresh-baked bread. Susan ran her finger around the panel on the wall outside her quarters. She let the edge of her fingernail hover over one symbol after another but did not press any of the flashing icons.

"Do you want information?" Cecily asked. "Or did you lock yourself out of your cabin?"

Susan whirled around. Her cheeks flushed. "I can't remember what the icons mean. How will the blues take me seriously when they see how little I know about their planet?"

"That's what aides are for, Mom." Cecily pressed the panel. The door opened, and with a flourish of her hand, she motioned for Susan to enter first. "And there's always the protocol manual."

"Assuming I could make any sense of it." Susan settled on a low couch near a long table. A large, ruby red notebook lay open on the edge.

The door opened again, and Edna marched through. "Do you smell that? I've got a bad feeling about this trip."

"I smell bread," Susan said. "I'm guessing a really good sourdough. Hope that's what we're having for lunch."

"No such luck," Edna said as she sat next to Susan. "But that's not the smell that bothers me. It's the lemony scent. The captain flooded the ship with disinfectant. She still hates us."

"How did you come to that conclusion, Mother? We haven't even met the captain." Susan picked up the notebook and laid it on her lap.

"Actually, we have," Cecily said. "I checked with Marsel. We're on the *Cold Fire*, the same ship that brought Grandma, Scott, and me to the planet before. It's under the command of the same taupe, and she really did hate us."

Susan glared at Edna. "What did you do?"

"I existed."

Cecily nodded. "She's telling the truth, Mom. The captain is a taupe. She disdains anyone who isn't."

"I hate politics." Susan opened the notebook and added a few lines to a sketch of a flower. "Have Bozidar and Salia discuss the captain. Scott might have some useful ideas. We don't dare leave any loose ends for the blues to pull."

Cecily saluted. "Yes, ma'am." She marched to the door, then turned. "You say you hate politics, but you're pretty good at it."

Susan flicked her fingers at Cecily. "Go."

"She's right," Edna said. "You are good at this. I'd be looking for some heads to knock together right about now."

"I'll leave that to Bozidar," Susan said. "It's easier to hear bad news from one of your own." She continued sketching. "You know, I have an idea for an embroidery project." She turned the notebook and handed it to Edna. "If we were at home, I'd try one of Betty Busby's techniques, maybe paint the flower on some Evolon and appliqué it to a piece of hand-painted silk."

Edna pointed to a leaf in the sketch. "This would be a good leaf for thread painting. If you had a machine. And thread."

"Which I don't. But I do have embroidery floss. I can make a small piece to test the design." She went to her bedroom and returned with her work box. "Here. This square of blue velvet will work for a base. I have some silk ribbon as well."

"Knock yourself out," Edna said. "I'm going to find Marsel and see if he can get us some snacks. Why does the disinfectant have to smell so good? I did nothing but eat on the trip here."

* * *

Cecily returned to Susan's quarters with Bozidar, Salia, and Scott. They sat in silence. Susan finished a silk ribbon rose and placed the blue square in the work box. The only sound in the room was the clink of scissors against a steel thimble.

Susan drummed her fingertips on the table. "How bad is it?"

"Could be worse," Cecily said.

"I do not see how it could be worse, nor do I wish to," Bozidar said. "Salia did not succeed."

"She didn't fail, either," Scott said. "The captain wasn't impressed that Salia is on the council. She doesn't like foreigners, and she doesn't like using a warship as a taxi."

"This is a warship?" Susan asked. "Like a battle cruiser?"

"I don't know." Scott rotated his head and stretched his back. "The point is, the clan isn't united. Not yet."

Susan compressed her lips. "How serious is the split? Will the taupes try to sabotage negotiations with the blues?"

"It is possible," Bozidar said.

Susan turned to Salia. "What do you suggest we do?"

"I do not know," Salia said. Her voice quavered, and her skin rippled. "I could never imagine disobeying the council."

"That is a false statement," Bozidar said. "The invasion of Earth was not sanctioned by the council. We would not be facing this crisis if you had been obedient."

"Let's not waste time on old arguments." Susan held up her hand. "Or maybe we should. These two feuds, how long have they been going on?"

"Forever." Bozidar crossed his arms and scowled.

"That is a false statement," Salia said, her words almost a whisper.

Susan shook her head. "It doesn't matter. You answered my question. The clans have been fighting so long they've forgotten what started it. Let's come up with some reconciliation ceremonies."

"That didn't work out the last time, Mom," Cecily said.

"The ice cream ceremony did," Susan said.

"Yes, but we stumbled on that one. And Kyle and I nearly wrecked it all when we brought back the spumoni."

Bozidar rose and paced in front of the window. He turned as if to speak, shook his head, and resumed pacing. When he paused again, Susan snapped, "Oh, just spit it out."

"I understand that command," he said. "Your idea has merit. Reconciliation rituals have often been used in our history. Perhaps our mistake was in creating something entirely new rather than adapting something more ancient and revered. Marsel will assist me. He has become quite adept at stumbling onto the correct path."

"I will assist too, if you wish," Salia said.

"Count me in," Cecily said. "Gary and I helped find those prophecies, after all."

"Great," Susan said. "Have at it."

Scott rose with the others. "There might be something I can contribute. A stick to your carrot."

* * *

Edna arrived in Susan's quarters carrying a tray of rolls. "They're not sourdough, but they're tasty."

Susan took a final stitch in a daisy chain. "Is there any butter?"

"Not that I could find. What do you suppose a Schtakian cow would look like?"

Susan considered the question. "I have no idea. Maybe it's a good thing you couldn't find butter." She bit into a roll. "Oh, this is good. I'd love to bring some of their flour back home with us."

"You're in a good mood. You should have started your embroidery sooner."

"I do find it calming, but that's not why I'm cheerful. We made a breakthrough, I think."

Edna sniffed the air. "I still smell lemon."

"Fine, a tiny breakthrough. Salia will work on the captain. In the meantime, I've got the whole group looking for an ancient reconciliation ceremony we could use."

"For the blues or the taupes?"

"Both, I hope. If not, they'll have to find two. But they can do it. I have a good feeling about this."

Edna leaped to her feet, grabbed a roll, and stuffed it in Susan's mouth. "Never say that out loud. The universe hates it when we're content."

Susan removed the roll. "When did you get so superstitious?"

"Since I got kidnapped and put on the firing line as a scapegoat."

Susan took her mother's hand and squeezed. "This time will be different."

"Is that a promise?"

A frown replaced Susan's smile, and she dropped her gaze. "No."

Edna sat next to her. "I don't want to be the rain cloud chasing your parade, honey. Really I don't. But I'm still scared, and that hasn't happened since I was a kid."

"What do you suggest we do?"

Edna leaned against the back of the couch. "Keep our eyes peeled for an escape route."

* * *

The clouds in the lavender sky grew thin and wispy. Sunlight faded, turning the sky gray, then black. Stars twinkled with cold brilliance.

Susan watched the change from the couch. She

started a row of buttonhole stitches but set it aside and went to the window. *Did we go this far out in space on our way here?*

Gary and Cecily entered, followed by Bozidar. They joined Susan at the window.

"What are you looking at, Mom?"

"The stars. Should we be out this far? I thought it was a short hop to the capital."

Bozidar squeezed to the center of the viewing screen, peering at the darkness. "Excuse me. I must consult with the navigator. We do not appear to be on course."

Scott and Edna arrived as Bozidar left. "I just heard dinner will be delayed," Edna said.

"My good feeling is evaporating," Susan said.

"Over a late dinner? You had a snack."

"Look." Susan pointed to the window.

The light from the stars whirled in a rainbow of colors. The darkness behind them deepened and softened until the window looked like a piece of black velvet dotted with jewels.

Scott cleared his throat. "Susan, that stick I mentioned? I brought some *machute* from the lab. We haven't weaponized it yet, but it's still lethal to them."

"Unless there's enough to kill everyone on board, it's of no use." Susan put her hand on Scott's arm. "Do you really want to kill them all?"

"I'd rather not wait until they kill us." Scott's face was calm, his eyes hard.

Edna slipped her arm around Scott's waist. "As

much as I would love a good fight to the death, I'm with Susan. Besides, if we kill the pilot who's going to land this sucker?"

"There's something out there," Gary said, pointing to a blur in the lower corner.

The blur grew larger, more defined. The space in front of it looked as if it were made of cellophane being wrinkled by an invisible hand.

"It's another ship," Marsel said. He and Salia stood just inside the room as the door closed behind them. "A blue ship."

"It looks silver to me," Cecily said, "but I'm pretty sure we all know what you mean."

"Are we under attack?" Scott asked.

"I do not know." Marsel toddled toward the window. His eyestalks skimmed the entire surface as if working a grid.

"Salia, can you tell us anything?" Susan asked.

Salia's body shook. "No, but I fear the worst. I am sorry to have failed you." She collapsed, folding into a tight bundle on the floor.

The other ship looked huge and menacing as it pulled close to *Cold Fire*. Panels opened along its hull, and long metal tubes extended from inside. The ship looked like a giant, metal lemon with massive straws stuck into the rind.

"I believe those are cannons," Scott said.

SIXTEEN

SPACE RETURNED TO BLACKNESS WITH PINPRICKS OF white light. The ships remained in their same relative position. The light in the cabin dimmed, and Susan held her breath.

Energy pulses popped from the blue ship's cannons as if they were gumballs spilling out of a broken machine. The pulses burst halfway between the two ships and arced, enclosing *Cold Fire* in a sparkling bubble.

Bozidar dashed into the cabin. "The situation may not be as dire as it appears."

"It looks like we're rabbits in a trap waiting to become the main course for someone's dinner," Edna said.

Bozidar halted in mid-stride. "We do not eat sentient beings."

Edna shook her head. "Fine, whatever, but we're still trapped."

"Do you actually believe we are capable of eating you?" Bozidar's hands clenched. "Not even yellows committed such atrocities in the worst of their wars."

Marsel crept to Salia's side. He crouched next to her as if shielding her. "We are not monsters."

"Why should they believe us?" Salia wailed. "Is it such a long way from betrayal to butchery?"

"Uh, yes, it is," Edna said. "Geez, every time I turn around I've got to apologize. I was just using an old Earth comparison. I didn't mean to insult you."

"Bozidar," Scott said, "you were going to give us some good news?"

"It is not bad news," Bozidar said. "*Cold Fire* has mutinied."

"How is that not bad news?" Susan said.

"The blue ship will not destroy us." Bozidar pointed to the window. "Their force field constrains us, but only to provide our captain an excuse to enter negotiations with the blues. It appears her intention all along has been to sabotage the beige plan."

"Why?" Susan clutched her hands over her stomach.

"She is a taupe," Salia said.

Scott nodded. "I was afraid of that as soon as I knew we were on the *Cold Fire*. We'll need a strategy. Bozidar, do you think we'll be handed over to the blues?"

"Very likely."

Marsel rose. Pulling Salia with him, he approached Susan. "I have an idea. You do not trust the prophecies, but I do. Wherever we are taken, bring your embroidery with you."

"Why? I've only made a few squares, and they're just experiments."

"The gods are slow to reveal their plans," Marsel said. He patted Susan's arm. "I have faith enough for all of us. We are where we should be. In time, you will understand."

"Is that promise just for Susan, or will all of us become enlightened?" Edna asked. "Because I have to tell you, right now I'm pretty confused."

"You have a saying, it is always darkest before the dawn." Marsel toddled to the table and picked up the embroidered fabric. "This symbol, what is it?"

"That's a buttonhole stitch," Susan said.

"In the ancient texts, that symbol is used for courage against the elements." Marsel stroked the threads. "Such a tiny thing, these two connected lines. The symbol must be repeated many times before it is even noticed. Yet I noticed it, as I grieved with Salia over the events that have befallen us. Now I am calm. Our cause is just. Our aims are noble. All will be well."

The door opened, and four guards from the blue clan entered. Their skin shimmered an intense blue the color of a high mountain lake on a cloudless summer day. They wore royal blue tunics edged with indigo piping and held their weapons at the ready.

Susan snatched her embroidery from Marsel and picked up the sewing kit from the table. She motioned the others to stand next to her.

Bozidar held his hands out in front of him, palms up. "We are a protected committee under the rules of conflict."

The guards did not speak. They aimed their weapons and advanced. Two guards circled around the group. Two of them positioned themselves on either side.

Susan tugged on Bozidar's elbow. "Step back, and let me lead. If Marsel is right, I'm our best hope. Or my artwork, at any rate." She inhaled, lifted her spine the way she learned in yoga class, and nodded to the two guards on either side of her as she stepped toward the door.

One of the guards scurried ahead of her and led the party out of the cabin. Once in the corridor, they were joined by a detachment of beige guards. The entire group marched in uneasy silence. Even the sound of shoe and footpad on the carpeted floor seemed muffled.

The captain of *Cold Fire* met them in the dining hall. The beige guards separated Bozidar, Marsel, and Salia from the humans and boxed them against the wall.

Salia broke ranks and rushed toward the captain. "I am a member of the council of elders, and bound by oath to protect the visitors from Earth. I protest this treatment, and demand that we be kept together."

A beige guard raised his weapon and fired. Salia convulsed in the center of an energy ball that wrapped itself around her. The speed of the swirling energy created its own sound waves, a tinny whine that almost masked Salia's scream. Her limbs twisted as if an unseen hand were making balloon animals from them. She fell to the floor as the sparkling light and whine faded. Her scream ended with a hollow, rattling wheeze.

Cecily reached toward Salia, but Susan restrained her. "Mom, we have to help her."

"There's nothing we can do," Susan said. "Don't give them an excuse to shoot us as well. Or Bozidar and Marsel."

Two beige guards dragged Salia from the room. The rest of the detachment forced Bozidar and Marsel to follow. The captain stared at Susan, green smoke puffing around her.

"Please don't hurt them," Susan said.

The captain spun around and followed her crew. When all the beiges were gone, the blue guards pointed their weapons at the hostages, then at the floor.

"I think they're giving us instructions. Sit down carefully," Scott said. "No sudden movements."

He settled Edna beside him and motioned for Cecily to join them. Susan knelt next to Cecily. Gary kept his eyes on the blues as he lowered himself to the floor by Susan. The blues lined up, facing the group, their weapons pointing at the floor.

The moments flowed into minutes in silence. Susan checked her heart rate on her wrist, controlling her breathing until her pulse slowed. As her heartbeat returned to normal, her knees began to ache. She shifted to a cross-legged position. She put her embroidery squares on one knee, and the sewing kit on the floor next to Cecily.

"How are you holding up, sweetie?" Susan whispered to Cecily.

The guards twitched at the sound but did not raise their weapons.

"Not great," Cecily said. Her voice was high and strained, almost a squeak. "What are they going to do with us?"

Shoot us. Fricassee us. Space us. As images of gruesome deaths raced through her imagination, Susan forced herself to breathe rhythmically. When she could trust her voice, she said, "I think we're fine for the moment. Scott is right. We should do as they demand, and no sudden movements."

Cecily's hands trembled. "I wish I could be as calm as you are."

"Try to keep your mind occupied." Susan stroked the fabric on her knee. She reached for the sewing box. "Excuse me," she said to the guards, holding the box out to them. "Would you mind if we did some embroidery? You can inspect my supplies."

The guards stepped back as one. They chittered together. Two approached Susan. She opened the box and slid it across the floor as far as her fingers would reach. The guards stared at the contents but touched nothing. The other guards joined them.

"They aren't saying no," Gary said.

"They aren't saying anything," Edna said. "Give me the square you were working on, the one with the needle and floss. If they don't shoot me, it's safe for you."

"Edna, keep your voice low and sweet," Scott said. "Don't reach for the square. Let Susan give it to Cecily, who will hand it to you."

"Good idea," Susan said. Keeping her eyes on the guards, she pulled the square with the needle from the stack and let her hand creep over to Cecily's arm. Cecily took the fabric, put it in the palm of her right hand, and held it out to the blue creatures. Keeping her palm open, she moved her hand across her body. Edna took the square, removed the needle, and started on the line of buttonhole stitches Susan had begun.

The blues remained silent and still. Susan took yellow floss from the box, threaded a needle and started a new block. Her eyes flitted from the line of blues to the line of stitching until she had completed a daisy. The blues did not react as she passed the block to Cecily.

"What do you want me to do, Mom?" Cecily fingered the soft blue fabric. "I can almost remember how to make a chain."

"That's why I put the daisy on the square. Make more flowers, make a squiggle, whatever comes through your fingers. Since Marsel isn't here to instruct us with his scrolls, we'll have to trust that prophecy will attend to itself." Susan threaded two more needles.

"Please tell me you don't expect me to embroider flowers," Gary said.

"You know your way around a needle. Do a spiral with a simple running stitch." Susan handed him a square. "And you, Scott."

Scott held the needle and studied Edna's work. "My grandfather learned to crochet after he was injured in a mining accident. I can learn to embroider."

Edna jerked as the needle pricked her finger. "Don't bleed on the fabric. That's my specialty." She put her finger in her mouth, then rubbed saliva on the tiny drop of blood on the square.

One of the guards inched toward Edna. It stretched its eyestalks down to her finger. When the bloodstain disappeared, the creature hopped back. It squeaked, waved its arms, and dashed into the corridor.

"Who knew they were squeamish," Edna said.

Another guard moved in front of her, observing her sew. It glanced at Scott's square, then stepped over to Cecily.

"It's making me nervous," Cecily said. She continued stitching, but her hands shook.

"Take a deep breath, honey," Susan said. "If you need to calm yourself, hold the square for it to see."

Cecily took a deep breath, smiled, and held the square up to the guard. The creature squealed, dropped its gun, and ran behind the other two. The three spoke over each other, squeaking and squawking. The one who had dropped its gun began to leap in place. The others joined in until all three were jumping. One of them shrieked, and all three fled the room.

"Is this a good sign or a bad sign?" Gary asked.

Edna reached for the weapon. "We can make it a good sign if we can figure out how to use this thing."

"Wait, Mom," Susan said. She closed her eyes. *Agnes, we could use some help.* She opened her eyes, but the air did not shimmer, and no spirit appeared.

Scott took the gun from Edna and put it back on the floor. "We're outnumbered, we can't fly the ship, and we don't know what would happen to our friends if we start a fight."

"So we just wait to be slaughtered?" Edna said as she stared at the gun. She folded her hands in her lap. "Or is this strategy? Show we're no threat?"

"Maybe it shows we trust their prophecies." Susan tugged on a lock of hair. "Something about this embroidery spooked them, but they didn't harm us. That's got to mean something."

Cecily reached for the sewing box and retrieved a length of pale green embroidery floss. "I think you're right, Mom, and I just had an idea for a leaf to add to these flowers. That's got to mean something too, because I don't know what I'm doing."

Susan passed the sewing box to Gary. "I have a very strong impression that Cecily is right."

Gary took a length of red floss. "So do I."

Time scrunched and stretched as they continued to embroider. Organic motifs, geometric shapes, and artfully arranged lines flowed from the needles to the fabric. Cecily and Edna gathered around Susan with Gary and Scott anchoring the sides. The men sought advice for their work. The women created designs that seemed to extend beyond the boundaries of the squares taking up in one square what began in another.

"I am impressed," Susan said as she arranged the squares on the floor in front of her. "The colors, the motifs, the workmanship, it all fits. I couldn't be happier if I had planned everything from the start."

"You've never been this pleased with my work," Cecily said.

"That's not true." Susan switched the corners of her arrangement. "I've always liked your, your … "

"You can't finish that sentence, can you?" Edna patted Susan's hand. "You always did set the bar high."

Susan drummed her fingers on her knee. "Have I really been that exacting?"

"Well, duh, it's sort of your trademark." Cecily hugged her knees. "I don't resent you for it, if you're worried. Your cracking the whip was the only reason my GPA was good enough to get into my first choice college."

"Your high standards made your quilt store successful," Edna said. "And it gave us all something to argue about at holiday dinners."

"A-n-nd that's enough sharing for today," Gary said. "My question is, who's going to read this? Cecily and I can translate a few symbols, but we can't make sense of it. We don't want to insult the blues by putting the squares in the wrong order."

Scott leaned toward the arrangement. "I don't suppose Agnes has any suggestions?"

"She hasn't been in contact." Susan stacked the squares and closed the sewing box. "Maybe it isn't time for prophecies."

"Do you think it might be time for dinner soon?" Edna glanced around the dining hall. "I'm hungry enough to start pushing buttons. There's got to be something we can eat." She hauled herself to her knees and wobbled to her feet. "I'm getting too old to sit on the floor."

"Cecily, help your grandmother find some food," Susan said. "Try to keep her from opening things that will explode."

"That's your party trick, Mom." Cecily rolled upright in one fluid movement. "Hang on, Grandma. I'm supposed to make sure you don't find the booby trap."

"It's a mess hall not an arsenal." Edna probed the panels on a cabinet attached to the wall. She pressed the top corners of one panel simultaneously.

A faint chime rang as the panel slid down into a

slot in the frame. The recess hidden behind the door looked like stainless steel, gleaming and smooth.

"What did you find?" Cecily stood at Edna's side and peered into the recess. "It's empty."

"Really? I hadn't noticed." Edna put her hand inside, running her fingers along all the edges.

The chiming grew louder, and flashing lights created a multicolored display within the recess. Cecily yanked Edna out of the way as a burst of energy shot across the room.

Bozidar entered the dining hall as the burst dissipated into small sparkles that crackled as they popped and disappeared. "I should have expected as much. Wherever you go, you bring chaos."

Susan stumbled as she raced to Bozidar. "You're alive! Where is Marsel? What's going to happen to us?"

"Yes, he is resting, and I do not know." Bozidar shook his head. "I had planned to prepare you for the worst. Seeing you here, unharmed … perhaps Marsel is justified in his optimism. The gods may set things to right to chastise me for my disbelief."

Susan grabbed his shoulders and shook him. "You're making less sense than Marsel. What's going on?"

"We are in the midst of another mutiny. Two, if you count the blues."

SEVENTEEN

"All I did was open a cabinet! On what planet does that start a mutiny?" Edna waved the remaining sparkles from her path. She fist-bumped Bozidar's arm when she reached his side. "Glad you're not dead."

"I am pleased," Bozidar said. "And I beg your forgiveness. You are correct. Even on Schtatik, it takes more to incite a violent response than opening a cabinet. Although too often not much more."

Susan shook him again. "History can wait. What's happening now?"

"The blue guards are convinced you performed a miracle." Bozidar eased Susan aside. He tapped panels, opened drawers, and retrieved packets of food. "If you will assist me, I can prepare a dinner for you while we discuss our options."

Cecily trotted to his side. "Show me what to do."

"We can eat later," Susan said.

"I'm hungry now." Edna pushed her to a chair by the counter where Cecily and Bozidar were working. "Sit. Ask questions. We'll cook."

Bozidar pushed two platters toward Cecily. "Arrange the food on those. I will show you the heating device. Under no circumstances allow your grandmother near the controls." He brushed his hands against his trousers. "Where shall I begin?"

Edna sat next to Susan. "From the moment they hauled you out with Marsel." She leaned toward Susan and whispered, "He does better if he goes from start to finish in a straight line."

He scowled at Edna. "We were brought to a detention cell. No one spoke to us."

"Marsel must have been scared out of his mind," Gary said as he and Scott gathered at the counter.

"Marsel collapsed on the floor. His whines were painful to hear. The guards retreated when Marsel lost control and emitted a rainbow of smoke." Bozidar blinked. "At that moment, I would have been grateful if they had tortured us. At least there would have been a reason for Marsel's distress."

"Salia was killed in front of us. Isn't that reason enough?" Cecily said.

"Oh, but she was not killed," Bozidar said. "That is the reason the taupes have mutinied."

"I don't understand," Susan said. "We saw her die."

"No, you saw her wounded. Gravely, yes, but she

survived." Bozidar placed a platter in a small metal box and tapped a panel next to it. The device hummed, and a red circle flashed on the panel. "The taupes believe she survived as a sign from the gods that the elders are following the correct path. They locked their captain in her quarters and released us."

"Did they have to fire on the blues?" Susan asked. "We'll never pull this off if there was fighting."

Bozidar switched platters when the device stopped humming. "A battle was not required. The blues guarding you fled to their commander. They were nearly as distressing to watch as Marsel."

"You said we performed a miracle," Edna said. "Mind telling us what we did so we can add it to our bag of tricks? Unless this counts as the miracle I'm supposed to pull off, in which case I say we all go home."

"You will have to consult with Marsel regarding the prophecy. I am not certain what frightened the blues. I am grateful to be released from the cell." Bozidar paused. "The blues will not forget their shame. If Salia dies after all, our fate will be unpleasant."

Cecily drummed her finger on the countertop. "They ran out of here when Grandma pricked her finger. We thought they didn't like the blood."

Scott held up his hand. "That isn't exactly what happened. They noticed when Edna jabbed herself, but they didn't run until she spit on the fabric to make the blood dissolve."

"Let me see," Bozidar said. He held out his hand.

"I'm not sticking myself with a needle again," Edna said before she stuffed something that resembled a corn fritter in her mouth.

"No, the fabric."

Susan rifled through the stack of squares. "This is the one. See the little damp spot?"

Bozidar sniffed the square, brought it close to his eyes, then held it at arm's length. "This is not unusual for you?"

Susan laughed. "No. Even experienced quilters stick themselves now and again."

"I think he's talking about the stain, Mom," Cecily said. "There's nothing miraculous about it. Human saliva contains enzymes that break down food. That aids in digestion and protects tooth enamel. It also helps careless quilters rescue their work from tiny drops of blood." She smiled at Susan. "See, Mom, I paid attention in school."

Bozidar gave the square back to Susan. "On our planet, embroidery is a sacred art. Practitioners are not allowed to make mistakes, or desecrate the work. The blues are particularly superstitious about these things. I suspect they have a prophecy that mentions outsiders, ruined work, miracles, and destruction. Marsel would know."

"Then let's fetch him," Edna said. "He might be hungry." She piled food on a plate and headed for the door.

Bozidar rubbed his temples. "I have no better

plan, and who knows what will happen if we do not follow her."

Susan gave him a gentle shove. "She doesn't know where she's going. Get ahead of her and lead the way."

Bozidar reached the door in time to press the panel release and slip into the hallway ahead of Edna. The rest followed, with Cecily and Gary carrying food.

They walked in silence, alone in the corridors. The lights brightened where they moved, dimming when they passed. The smell of rosemary and lemon faded.

"This is creepy," Cecily said. She let Edna scoop some fritters onto her empty plate. "Shouldn't there be someone around? Where's the crew?"

"I do not know. Perhaps they are hiding." Bozidar increased his pace. "I would be happy to hide, but that is not my destiny."

As they passed a transport, its panel flashed. Bozidar stopped, alert. Edna backed toward the wall, motioning the others to join her.

The transport door opened, and Marsel bounded from the car. "There you are. I went to the main bridge first, then the auxiliary. You were not to be found."

"Why would I go there?" Bozidar asked. "I wanted to ensure the safety of the humans."

"Yes, of course," Marsel said. He bowed to Edna. "But the taupe captain is under arrest, so naturally I assumed the queen would take command."

Susan cleared her throat. "How sweet, Marsel, but Edna doesn't know how to fly a spaceship, or where we're supposed to go. Wouldn't it be better if Bozidar took over?"

Edna muscled her way through the group, grabbed Marsel's eyestalks and pulled them toward her face. "Let me make this easy. Don't put me in charge anymore. I don't want to do it. I'm not trained for it, and you critters are driving me crazy."

She released her grip, and Marsel tottered backwards. He massaged his eyestalks and bowed. "As you command."

Edna smacked her forehead.

"Never mind, Mother." Susan shepherded Edna toward Scott. "You'll take care of this, won't you, Bozidar?"

"With pleasure," he said. "Who is the leader of the loyal taupes, Marsel? Is the ship secure? What is the status of the blue ship? Are they friends or foe? And what of Salia?"

Marsel trembled. "Forgive me. In my joy at seeing prophecy revealed, I rushed to find you."

Susan grimaced. "You mean you've just been running around by yourself? Without a weapon? Without a plan?"

Gary glanced up and down the empty corridors. "We all know the answer to those questions. Yes, yes, and yes. Now, let's go. Someplace safe." He leaned toward Bozidar. "Got any idea where that might be?"

Before Bozidar could answer, footsteps echoed in the corridors all around them. Gary and Scott herded Cecily, Susan, and Edna toward the wall with Marsel. Bozidar joined the men, making a shield for the women.

Edna shoved herself between Scott and Bozidar and wriggled out of the barrier. "Husband of mine, I love that you want to protect me but if the folks coming aren't friendlies, we're all toast. I keep telling you I'm the queen. I'm the best chance you've got."

Blue and beige critters appeared in opposite corridors. All carried long tubes resembling shotguns, but with buttons on the end where a trigger should be.

Edna crossed her arms. She stared at the blue soldiers approaching on her right. They stopped and lowered their weapons. She glowered at the beige soldiers slowing to a halt on her left. They backed up a step and lowered their own weapons.

"That's better," Edna said. "Let's get a few things straight. No running at us. No shooting at anyone. No delaying dinner."

"You have not fed your queen?" Marsel said. His voice squeaked, and he quivered.

Cecily put her hands on his shoulders. "Hush now," she whispered. "Let Grandma do the talking."

One of the beige soldiers bowed to Edna while at the same time attempting a salute. "We are at your command."

One of the blue soldiers stepped forward. His

eyestalks bristling. "We are at the command of the beige queen. The honor of the blue clan demands this."

"Good. You're both at my command," Edna said.

The blue soldier took another step forward. "No. They report to us. We report to you. Give your orders to us, and we will relay them down the ranks."

"No." The beige soldier faced his counterpart and planted his feet. He pointed his gun at a spot on the floor in front of the blue.

The two squads shuffled and grumbled. Gun barrels twitched but remained aimed at the floor.

"You guys will argue about anything." Edna marched between the opposing commanders and knocked the weapons from their hands. She grabbed them above the wrists and mashed their palms together. "Shake hands and play nice."

They separated their hands. Slowly, they lifted their other hands and wiggled their fingers at each other.

"Did we shake long enough? We are not familiar with this custom." The beige leader lowered his hands. "Also, I do not understand how a soldier could play with the enemy at all, much less play nice."

Edna snorted. "I don't know whether to laugh or swear." She tapped her foot. "Fine, here are my orders. Everything goes through Bozidar. You want to know what to do, you ask him. You got a question, he brings it to me. I am off limits to anyone outside of him, my family, and Marsel. And Salia, when she's able. So someone better make sure she recovers real fast." She pointed at Bozidar. "Okay, space boy, it's your show now."

Bozidar smoothed his jacket. "Inform your captain of the queen's command. I expect the captain to drop the force field around *Cold Fire* and report to me immediately. An honor guard is acceptable, but weapons will be ceremonial. Negotiations between our two ships will begin as soon as your captain arrives. You are dismissed."

The blue squad came to attention and bowed as one unit. The leader squeaked a command into a communications device, and they were transported off *Cold Fire* in a sparkling energy beam.

Marsel rocked on his footpads. "Is it not delightful to live in the time of prophecy?"

"Splendid, dear." Susan patted his shoulder. "Bozidar, what do you intend to negotiate?"

"Our return to the capital. That is the primary goal. If possible, I would like to lay the groundwork for better cooperation between the clans."

Susan nodded. "My thoughts as well. Who will you have represent this ship? The captain is in the brig."

Scott said, "We need the taupes' cooperation before we can hope to get the blues and beiges to work together."

"I agree." Bozidar tapped his chin with his finger. "I do not have an answer to your question, Susan."

"Salia will help," Gary said. "She's pledged to us. She'll do whatever we want."

"If she lives." Susan took Bozidar's arm. "Lead us to the medical bay. Maybe the queen and her entourage will encourage the doctors to work miracles."

* * *

The walls of the medical bay glowed a warm peach. A soft, pinky light shone through translucent panels. Spotlights highlighted equipment and gauges by the bed. Gentle whiffs of lavender circulated through the air. A brilliant green fluid flowed into Salia from tubing attached to her arms and legs. A dark purple fluid flowed from another tube anchored in her shoulder into a metallic case on the floor.

Susan and Bozidar consulted with the doctors while the others gathered around Salia. Marsel patted her head between her eyestalks.

"Does that help?" Cecily asked. She stroked Salia's hand.

"It helps me," Marsel said. "The healing staff on board has excellent training. There is no task left for me except to let her know I am here."

"Ease up a bit," Edna said. "You don't want her waking up with a headache."

Susan joined the group. "They say she's not doing well. She isn't responding to treatment."

"Does anyone know why?" Gary curled his

finger around one of Salia's.

"No." Susan rubbed her eyes. "One of them thinks she doesn't want to live with her failure."

"She didn't fail. The idiot taupe captain turned traitor and ambushed us," Edna said.

Cecily leaned toward Marsel. "On Earth, we sometimes talk to patients in comas. They can hear, and it can help."

Marsel patted Salia more vigorously. He snatched his hand away when her limbs moved from the impact. "I am sorry. I do not mean to injure you."

"I'm guessing he thinks your idea will work," Edna said to Cecily. "I've got this."

Edna moved Marsel aside. "Now listen to me, Salia. You've got a job to do, so open your eyes and get cracking. The captain is under arrest, the blues are terrified of me, and Susan's got a plan. She needs everyone to help, and that includes you."

Gary squeezed Salia's hand. "Remember your promise to protect us. We're counting on you."

Salia shuddered. The purple fluid streaming through the tube at her shoulder lightened to a pale lilac. She coughed and sat bolt upright on the bed. "I live to serve."

EIGHTEEN

Marsel prostrated himself and chanted. Salia swayed, babbling about duty. Edna planted her palm on Salia's shoulder and pushed her back on the pillow.

Gary patted Salia's arm. "Lie back and rest. We don't want you falling out of bed."

Cecily took Marsel's feet and dragged him out of the traffic path. He continued chanting. Susan edged to the other side of the bed, motioning Bozidar to follow her.

"Marsel," Bozidar said, "praise the gods quietly. They can always hear you. We do not need to at this moment."

Salia flopped on the pillow like a hooked trout on a riverbank. She inhaled, and the twitching stopped. Exhaling, she looked at Edna. "I am prepared, and will obey. What is your wish?"

"Choose your words with care," Bozidar told Edna. "My people interpret your pronouncements literally when it is least convenient."

Edna pressed her lips together. She cleared her throat. "My wish is for you to help Susan." She twisted away from the bed and covered her mouth. "My brain is full of wisecracks, and you make me behave."

"We're all very proud of you," Cecily said. She thumped Marsel—still chanting—on the leg. "Hush."

"Get him off the floor," Susan said. "I need his knowledge of the prophecies. Salia, while we were separated, I brought out my embroidery to pass the time. You remember the squares I had at the castle? Edna was working on a square when she pricked her finger. A speck of blood dripped on the fabric."

"May the gods forgive," Salia whispered. Her hands trembled, and her eyestalks twitched.

"It's fine, dear," Susan said, patting her head. "We know how to fix those little accidents. The thing is, we frightened the blue soldiers guarding us. We have a chance to regain control of the ship and our mission, but only if we can use the disappearing blood to our advantage."

Marsel rolled to his feet. "There is a prophecy. It is obscure, but appropriate to our situation."

"Obscure is good," Scott said. "The well-known passages have too much commentary. What does the prophecy say?"

"The exact words escape me, but I recall a reference to sins disappearing, and the unworthy pointing the way to salvation." Marsel rocked on his footpads. "Oh, and something more. An omen of disaster turning to a sign for prosperity, and peace among the clans." He rubbed his hands together, curling his shoulders until he resembled a ball of bread dough waiting to be kneaded. "And strangers. Something about trusting strangers. Or perhaps that was another word for the unworthy. It is a prophecy from the blue clan, after all."

Susan scanned the faces turned toward her. "That's good enough for me. We're certainly strangers."

"The blues think everyone else in the universe is unworthy," Bozidar said. He bit his lower lip. "I did not intend to say that aloud."

"It's okay, space boy," Edna said. "I've had my fill of the blues too."

Gary leaned toward Susan. "Even if no one on the blue ship has a different interpretation of that prophecy, we still can't guarantee they'll listen to us."

"Or that the captain has the authority to make an alliance with us," Scott said.

Susan held up her hand. "One threat at a time." She helped Salia sit. "We need the taupe captain to join us."

"She is imprisoned," Bozidar said.

"Not good enough," Susan said, shaking her head. "If some of the crew are still loyal to her, they could sabotage our plans. You know I'm right. We wouldn't be in this mess if the taupes had been loyal."

Salia whimpered. "My cousins have brought shame upon me."

"Which makes you the unworthy," Cecily said. "From the prophecy. Marsel said the unworthy points to salvation."

Gary squeezed Salia's hand again. "You were born to play this role. What do you say?"

"I hear and I obey." She bowed her head. "I will atone for the taupes who have become traitors. I will make amends for my past sins and theirs, even at the cost of my life."

"You already took a bullet for us," Edna said. "Get the taupe captain on our side, and we'll call it even."

Bozidar squared his shoulders and strode to the communication panel. He tapped the surface, brushing the twirling icons with his fingertips as if they were burning hot. "I am Bozidar, agent of our most gracious queen, Edna of Earth. The gods have favored us with a sign so powerful even the forces of the blue clan cannot deny it. A member of the council of elders will explain all, first to your captain, then to the rest of the crew. That is all."

Cecily covered her mouth, and her eyes sparkled with the giggles she kept from escaping. Gary and Susan glanced at each other. Gary bit hard on his lower lip while Susan bowed her head. Her shoulders shook.

Edna leaned against the bed, arms crossed. "You better make sure that thing is turned off, space boy, because these guys aren't going to hold it for long."

Her last words were obscured by the others laughing so hard it sounded like barking.

* * *

The taupe captain stood in her cell. Her slate gray scarf clung to her shoulder, a drab oil slick of color on her skin, which looked like sand on a cloudy day. She nodded as Bozidar and Salia chittered at her. She bowed, saluted, and sat on her cot, letting the scarf fall to the floor.

"Is she in or out?" Edna asked when Bozidar and Salia left the cell.

"She will not assist us," Bozidar said. "She will not oppose us either."

"We had the interview streamed to the rest of the command staff. They will inform the crew," Salia said. "Her second-in-command will bring us to the capital. Marsel will sit in the captain's chair to assure the orders are given correctly."

"Excellent." Susan matched her mother's pace as they left the brig. "Let's hope Marsel's research goes well. We need an airtight argument to persuade the blues to cooperate."

"I'm not so sure," Edna said. "All we had for the taupes was 'work with us, or we'll tell on you.' That's not much of a threat."

"The way we presented ourselves conveyed the measure of our power," Salia said. "The blue soldiers fled to their ship. You showed them prophecy in action. I am still alive. Since she had no response to our persistent success, the captain was forced to surrender. Honor demanded it."

Edna arched her eyebrow. "You are the strangest critters."

"You have a saying about gift horses and mouths," Bozidar said. "It was written for such times as these."

They took a transport tube to the conference room. Crew members of the *Cold Fire* saluted as they passed. Two guards at the entrance to the conference room bowed low and opened the doors.

Marsel, Gary, and Cecily sat at the conference table. Two holographic images of sacred scrolls hung in the air before them, rotating as they were scanned. Scott sat at a desk along the wall examining documents on a computer screen.

"What's the good news?" Edna asked. She pointed at the holograms. "More prophecies?"

"Commentary," Cecily said. "From every blue philosopher, theologian or crack-pot that ever lived. We've found a few things we can use. Scott is going through treaties between the blues and the beiges, just in case there's already an agreement in place we can exploit."

Susan felt the air around her turn cold as each molecule sparkled like a diamond. *You heard the answer, but you didn't listen.* Agnes's voice inside her head was old and wise. *Salia told you everything.*

"She's right," Susan said. She realized her eyes were closed and her hands were clasped at her chest as if in prayer. "Sorry, Agnes just gave me one of her cryptic messages."

"Which was?" Edna asked.

"That it is the way we present the message, not the message itself, that will win over the blues. Just as Salia and Bozidar won over the captain. We heard, but we didn't listen."

"Yeah, that sounds like my grandmother. Crazy old bat." Edna eased herself onto a chair. "Is there anything to eat in here?"

Bozidar tapped a screen near the door. When a guard stepped inside, he whispered an order and pointed at Edna. The guard bowed and retreated. "Food will arrive soon. Could you explain the strategy She Who Found Us suggested to you?"

Susan tugged on a lock of hair. "I think Agnes wants us to just get on with it. We can search your sacred scrolls for days, but nothing we find will be as convincing as our own resolve. Salia said it—we're still here, and mostly getting our way. If that doesn't persuade the blues that the gods are on our side, nothing will."

Gary sat on the edge of the table. "The only thing we know for sure about this clan is that they're stubborn."

"And ornery." Cecily typed a command on the

device controlling the holograms. One image disappeared, while the other expanded.

"Exactly," Gary said. "We need to have an answer to any question they could possibly ask, and we should expect them to argue each and every point."

Scott swiped his hand across the screen, shutting down the program. "While I agree we should be prepared, these treaties suggest we won't persuade them with logic alone. I've never seen such nit-picky legalese, and I sat in on union negotiations. I had a sergeant who used to say there's always one more son-of-a-bitch than you counted on. I think we're going to encounter that with the blues, no matter how prepared we are." He nodded at Susan. "We might as well call for a conference now. The longer we wait, the more time we give the spoilers to wreck everything."

"There's one thing we haven't decided," Edna said. "Who's going to be on this negotiation team?"

Susan watched the others turn toward her, waiting. She put her forefinger to her lips, tapping gently.

"If that's Morse Code you're using, I can't read the message," Edna said. "Let me make this easier. I'm not in favor of sending a big party. Bozidar and Salia did just fine with the taupe captain. Let them parlay with the blues."

"Bozidar, yes." Susan paced from the door to a small cabinet along the wall. "Salia should stay here.

Marsel too. We need him on the bridge. I'll go with Bozidar."

"And me," Gary said.

Susan smiled but shook her head. "I need you here. You and Scott need to keep Cecily and Edna safe. If there's a problem, take off for home."

"Home?" Cecily asked. "You mean Earth?"

"Earth is not my home," Marsel said. "Nor is it the home of the crew."

"You don't have to stay there," Susan said. "Drop my family off and you can do whatever you think is best." She raised her hand as Cecily opened her mouth. "This isn't a debate. Your grandmother already delegated most of her power to Bozidar. I'm the one with the visions, so I'm the logical choice to accompany him. Also, my embroidery got us this far with the blues."

"Your mother is right," Edna said. "Close your mouth and sit this one out with me like a good girl." Edna winked. "I'll make sure you've got a seat on the next mission."

The door opened, and a beige crew member pushed in a wheeled cart. Aromatic steam rose from plates and bowls filled with golden brown rolls, tarts that resembled small quiches, and ruby red fruit compotes. Edna leaped from her chair and pulled the cart to the table.

The group planned as they ate. Marcel and Cecily drilled Bozidar and Susan in passages from sacred texts. Scott quoted sections from recent treaties. Gary ran them through role-playing exercises, with him acting the part of an obstreperous blue captain. When the last roll was devoured and the bowls of compote scraped of all syrup-covered fruit, Bozidar requested the bridge to open a link to the blue ship.

Marsel tapped a panel on the wall behind the head of the conference table. A large rectangle resembling a flat-screen TV monitor began to glow, changing from an icy blue to a deep indigo. A rotating icon flashed. The image of the blue captain appeared.

Bozidar bowed. "I am the agent of Edna of Earth. You may have questions regarding the miracles that have recently occurred on *Cold Fire*. I would be happy to answer those questions. The queen's daughter has graciously agreed to join me. We invite you to meet with us here, now."

The blue captain raised an aquamarine-toned hand. A sky-blue crew member, jumping at every squawk the captain made, tapped on a console.

Bozidar angled his head toward Susan. "Come within visual range while the captain finds her translation program."

"First of all, how do you know that's a she?" Edna took a step toward the screen but was pulled back by Scott. "Second, how do you know she's having technical troubles?"

"I can answer the second question," Susan said, smoothing her hair as she took her place next to Bozidar. "I'd recognize that look of terror when the machines misbehave on any species' face."

Bozidar stared at Susan. "The computer is not misbehaving. The blue clan is not as adventurous as the beige clan. My guess is this captain has never had need of a translation program before. She is quite young." He scowled at Edna. "I did provide you with a complete guide to distinguishing males and females, as well as color variations within each clan."

"Do I look like I do homework?"

The blue captain stuttered. "I am here. I am speaking."

"Your name?" Bozidar asked. His tone was brusque.

"I am Mila, commanding *Falling Water.*"

"I am Bozidar. This is Susan. Will you agree to negotiate with us on our ship?"

"Only you?"

Bozidar nodded. "We are the only representatives your government will require."

"You are welcome on *Falling Water.*"

"*Cold Fire* is more suitable for our alien guests. The ceilings are higher, and our translation programs are already running."

The blue captain removed her hat, a small disc-shaped headpiece with a square of azure-colored fabric hanging from the back, and placed it in front of the camera. Muffled chittering floated through the speakers. The hat appeared to fly of its own volition back to Mila's head as she tapped the console in front of her. "I will agree. My political officer will accompany me, in addition to my honor guard."

"Your political officer is welcome. The guard is not." Bozidar placed his hand on Susan's arm before she could speak. "Our guests have seen quite enough of your clan's weaponry. My queen is not impressed with their design or intended use. Nor is her daughter."

The blue captain shook, and her voice reached an octave higher as the words rushed out. "Do not forget that we captured *Cold Fire*, and boarded her."

"Yes, with the assistance of our captain. She has seen the error of her ways." Bozidar walked toward the screen. "Do not forget that while you once held our ship, your soldiers fled in terror. Shall I ask my queen to unleash her powers again?"

The captain placed her hat in front of the camera again. When she put it back on her head, her demeanor displayed defeat. "I will leave the guard. Prepare for our arrival."

Bozidar bowed. "It will be our honor to welcome you. We will provide refreshments."

Mila nodded, and the connection ended. Bozidar's chin dropped to his chest, his shoulders rounding toward each other.

"You won the first round," Edna said. "Congratulations."

"Thank you." Bozidar straightened. "We achieved our victory through bluff and bravado. The next round, as you call it, will require much more."

NINETEEN

"SO, WHAT IS IT WE'RE SERVING AT THIS NEGOTIATION?" Cecily asked. "Something that hypnotizes the other guys into doing our will?" She searched the cabinets in the kitchen and shook her head. "I don't even know what I'm looking at."

Bozidar pressed her arm with his fingertips, moving her aside. "These are packaged meals for exploration missions. Marsel has already consulted with the chef about the menu for the meeting with Mila from *Falling Water*."

"So what are we doing in the mess hall?" Cecily asked.

"Your grandmother will require a snack soon. She always does." Bozidar gathered two flat boxes wrapped in blue foil. "These contain a product similar to your ham-and-cheese sandwiches. That should appease her for a while."

"Make sure you tell her you're feeding her MREs. She loves that stuff." Cecily picked up a square container. "What's in here?"

"Emmerries?" Bozidar squeezed his eyelids shut. "What manner of animal or vegetable is that?"

Cecily giggled. "I'm sorry. MRE stands for Meals Ready to Eat. It's what soldiers carry with them." She shook her head. "It's more complicated than you want to know. Just tell me what's in this package."

Bozidar examined the label on the white paper wrapper. "Either dried fruit bars or disinfecting towelettes. The label is damaged."

"A surprise then. I'll take it in case Grandma gets bored." Cecily tucked the box under her arm and followed Bozidar back to the conference room.

Susan stared at the stars and did not turn around when Cecily and Bozidar entered. Gary and Scott whispered in a corner but broke off their conversation. Edna lounged on a couch near Susan until she saw Bozidar, and the boxes he carried.

"Splendid, you have food." She snatched one of the blue boxes and ripped open the foil wrapper. "Sandwiches. I was hoping for something else, but this will do."

Bozidar put the other box on the table and joined Susan. "You will not see them approach from this vantage point. *Falling Water* is on the other side."

"I'm not looking for the transport pod. I'm looking for Agnes."

"She Who Found Us is long dead," Bozidar said. "She could be anywhere by now."

Susan closed her eyes and snorted. "Well, wherever she is, I hope she's working on a plan. Lord knows I've got nothing." She looked at Bozidar. "I don't suppose you've got any ideas. A few bargaining points, at least."

"We're working on that," Gary said. "Scott's a pretty good negotiator. We should be able to talk some sense into these blues."

Susan felt her skin tingle. *Talking sense into an alien species, like that's going to happen.* She wasn't certain if those were her thoughts or a message from Agnes.

"What about protocol?" Edna said between bites of her sandwich. "I'm tired of getting in trouble because I don't know which fork to use."

Susan rubbed her temples. "Why bother with the rules, Mother, when you know you're going to break them anyway?" Her fingers stopped, she dropped her trembling hands.

Cecily pushed a box of sandwiches across the table. "That's a little harsh, Mom. Maybe you need something to eat?"

Susan rounded on Edna like a terrier on a rat. "In a minute. Mother, how would you like to give us outrageous lessons?"

"Seriously, Mom, your blood sugar must be at rock bottom." Cecily pushed the box closer to Susan. "And you're scaring the daylights out of me."

"We haven't been playing to our strengths,"

Susan said. "We've been trying to appease the blues to get them to negotiate with the beiges. How's that been going for us?"

Bozidar coughed. "Not badly. They have responded to reason."

"Not quickly enough." Susan intertwined her fingers. "We have to make them understand that the stakes are too high. We can't let the spoilers make all the decisions, because they're only interested in fighting."

"So tell them that." Edna pointed her sandwich at Susan. "Sit down with this blue captain, just the two of you, and tell her to lock the spoiled children in a padded room while the grown-ups fix things. If we're going to play to our strengths, your way is more likely to get us what we want."

Bozidar pressed his fingertips together. "May the gods not punish me, I agree with Edna. Allow one slight alteration. Let me join Susan. Mila will bring her political officer. I can neutralize him."

"You mean that in a good way, right?" Gary asked. "You didn't just offer to take out the competition."

"Where would I take him?" Bozidar asked. "Outside the ship would be in space, and neither of us would survive."

"I accept your offer," Susan said. "Tell Marsel to set up a buffet in here. No guards, no protocol, just the four of us trying to save the world."

* * *

Mila and the blue political officer followed Marsel into the conference room. His narration continued without pause, and his voice sounded as if he had been talking non-stop since the transport pod opened in the landing bay.

"Not knowing which sub-clan you are, I arranged for a variety of delicacies representing the entire blue culinary heritage. We decided to spice sparingly, but there are bowls of seasonings available on either end of the buffet. That is a human word, well, an English word. Or is it French? Buffet. It means the meal or the table. It is also used as a metaphor. The humans adore metaphors. I plan to make a study of them. There seem to be parallels with our use of prophecy in non-sacred contexts."

"Marsel," Susan said, "stop talking."

He bowed to her, then to the blues, and trotted from the room.

Mila pressed a round fist to her midsection and extended her arm. A gold scarf wound from her shoulders, around her arm, and fluttered from the wrist. "I acknowledge the gift of his silence. And his absence."

Susan bowed her head. "You are most welcome. Please, have some refreshments."

Mila glanced at the food on a table against the wall. She nodded at her companion, and the two selected some food from the colorful choices offered.

He carried both plates to the conference table.

Susan sat with her back to the viewing screen. "Sit wherever you like. We're going to be informal today. What we need to decide is too important to get bogged down in details of ritual and ceremony."

Mila stood, silent and still. She pointed to a spot opposite Susan, and the other blue placed her food there. He sat at one end of the table, Bozidar at the other. Mila removed her hat and put it just beyond her plate between her and Susan.

"That makes a lovely centerpiece," Susan said. "I'm very fond of blue. Your hat looks like velvet, a perfect velvet dome."

"Thank you," Mila said.

Susan drank tea and nibbled on a cracker topped with a shredded vegetable the color of cornflowers. "There are some in the beige clan who have been working to start a war with the blue clan. We think that's a silly thing to do."

"We?" Mila asked.

"My mother, Edna, and I and the rest of the human delegation. We've seen enough of wars at home, no need to go through one here. Mother is apparently the queen of the beige clan now. She's not quite sure how that happened. Your planet's traditions are still new to us."

"You find it silly to counter a deadly threat?"

"Where is the threat? From an old woman? My daughter? Me?"

Mila crushed a cookie in her fist. "Of course you.

You three are the descendants of prophecy. A beige prophecy that proclaims their supremacy over the entire planet."

"Not if no one fights. If we all find a way to get along then no one will be supreme. We'll all be equals."

"Spoken like someone who has no status." The political officer muttered, but the words were clear.

"I suppose I don't," Susan said. "At least, no status that means anything to me."

The blues trembled in their seats. Their skin tightened and turned ashy as a smoke-filled sky. Faint puffs of red smoke drifted from the political officer.

Susan leaned into the table. "I'm sorry I've offended you, but the universe is bigger than your planet. My people haven't learned that lesson yet. Your people are so much more advanced. Can't you show us how to adapt? You and the beige clan could visit Earth together. Establish a friendship between our two planets."

Bozidar twitched. "We invited Mila to discuss a temporary alliance of our ship and hers. Perhaps we should pursue that objective first?"

"Let's be bold." Susan tapped her fingers. "You're a soldier, Mila. You understand the cost of war. Do you believe this conflict with the beiges is worth it? Is the blue clan really at risk? With so much to gain, shouldn't we do all we can to cooperate?"

Mila glanced at her companion. She grabbed the hat and crushed it, leaped to her feet, rushed at the other blue and threw him to the floor. Whipping her scarf from her shoulders, she hog-tied her political officer around the ankles and wrists. "I am sorry," she said as she stuffed her hat in his mouth.

Bozidar and Susan remained motionless, frozen, as Mila returned to her seat. "There was a listening device concealed in my hat. I have disabled it. I believe it is fitting that it should be used as a gag for my officer. You are correct. This conflict is being driven by a desire for personal gain among a few leaders. Even if we win, there would be few benefits for most of the clan." She pointed at the political officer struggling on the floor. "His sub-clan would profit the most."

Bozidar pressed a hand against his chest. He inhaled, coughed, exhaled. "Should I have him moved to a holding cell, or just leave him on the floor?"

"Remove him." Mila examined Susan. "What are you offering?"

Susan bit her lower lip. *How do I sell the unknown?* "An adventure?" She turned to Bozidar. "Wasn't your trip to Earth full of unexpected events?"

Bozidar raised his eyebrows. "Unexpected? Of course. Pleasant? Rarely."

Mila chuckled. "That is the definition of adventure. It is a situation which becomes enjoyable in the retelling."

"Because you live through it," Susan said. "And that's what I'm offering, something you'll live through. You can't say the same about war."

"I am a soldier. To run from danger would be weakness."

"So is going along with an idea you know will end in disaster." Susan watched Bozidar make his way to the panel by the door and tap a command. "A good commander knows that it takes more courage to be a conciliator than to be a bully. Go with us to the beige capital. Listen to the clan elders, and report to your own council. No obligations, no threats, no bribes."

Three beige crew members entered the room. Bozidar pointed at the prisoner. They lifted him like a rolled carpet and carried him to the door. They paused long enough for the one holding the blue's feet to nod to Bozidar and Mila before exiting.

Mila waited a moment after the door closed. "Suppose I do as you ask, and I discover that you have deceived me?"

"You and your crew will have safe passage home."

"Easy to say, hard to achieve."

Bozidar returned to the table. "She speaks for our queen. I am a witness. All the necessary documents will be in place before we begin the journey."

Mila seemed to retreat within herself in silence. Susan held her breath. Bozidar clasped and unclasped his hands.

"I agree." Mila rose. "Show me where you have put my political officer. He is in your custody until his trial, but I would like to report that he is being treated as befits his rank. I will return to *Falling Water*. Send me the safe passage treaty, and then we will go."

"You don't want to take him with you?" Susan asked.

"It would be best for him to remain here." Mila offered her hand to Susan. "I believe it is an Earth custom to shake hands when concluding an agreement?"

Susan grasped the small blue hand with both of hers. "Yes. Thank you. Your common sense and kindness do you credit. I will do my best to repay your trust."

* * *

Gary raised a glass. "Here's to Susan. Congratulations, and may all your negotiations be this successful."

"I can't believe it went so smoothly. I expected to have the treaty snatched from my hand even as I was signing it." Susan removed her dinner from the oven and joined the others. The dining hall was festooned with floral garlands. Small lanterns, with bulbs resembling flickering flames, were grouped in clusters of three around the room. The scent of roses and cinnamon mingled with the aroma of the meal.

Bozidar placed his glass on the table. He scanned each one at the table, ending with Scott. When Scott averted his gaze, Bozidar said, "Let us hope the appearance matches reality."

"Are you being gloomy again?" Edna said. "You're one step closer to getting rid of us. You should be celebrating."

"I will, when you are safe on Earth, and we are safe on Schtatik. For the moment, my joy must be tempered with experience."

"He's right," Scott said. "There's still a lot that can go wrong. If we can trust the blues, or at least this Mila, we've got a chance."

"But she could be lying," Susan said.

"Could they be playing for time?" Gary asked.

"Good lord, I haven't seen a mood change this dramatic since I hit menopause." Edna held a breadstick, punctuating her words with jabs in the air. "This is a party for Susan. We can schedule a wake later if needed, but I for one intend to eat, drink and be merry."

Susan sipped her drink. The thick liquid tasted like a strawberry milkshake. "Bozidar, is there a reason you're mentioning your doubts now rather than when we signed the safe passage documents?"

"I had no alternative plans to suggest. We achieved our goal and solved the first of many problems facing us. Prudence demands a clear-eyed evaluation of the situation, however, so I mention my concerns now with everyone present."

Cecily said, "There's one thing in our favor. Mila had us lock up that other blue guy. She must want the negotiations to succeed as much as we do."

Scott smiled. "Of course she does. But it doesn't hurt to keep our eyes open."

"Do we have a fallback?" Gary asked. "If Mila has a hidden agenda, what are our options?"

Silence fell around the table, itchy and uncomfortable as an old wool blanket.

* * *

Susan wandered the hallway, opening doors and calling, "Salia?" *Why did I volunteer to find her? I get lost going from my quarters to the dining hall.* As she opened the sixth door, she caught sight of Salia padding down the hall.

"There you are. We're almost at the capital. Mila is on her way, and we hoped you would join us on the bridge."

"We are in danger," Salia said, panting. "We still have her operative in our cells."

"Yes. She said it was better to keep him here."

"Better for us, or better for her?"

"Mila is on our side." Susan frowned. "At least, she says she's on our side. Do you think she's lying?"

Salia trembled. "I just overheard a taupe crew member telling the blue that we were not to be trusted. She told him about the experiments Scott was forced to perform with the *machute* plant."

"Oh, no," Susan gasped. "We can't let Mila hear about that."

"She knows already. The communications device in her hat has been transmitting continuously. I slipped away before I was discovered to inform you."

"We have to tell the others now." Susan ran her hands along the wall. "Where is that intercom?"

Salia trotted to the wall and engaged the panel.

Bozidar's voice sounded tinny but clear. "Bridge here. Report."

"It's me, Susan. Salia says the blues know about Scott's weapons research. Mila put on an act for us. The bug was never destroyed, and a taupe conspirator told our prisoner everything."

Bozidar did not respond immediately. Susan reached for the pulsing icon on the panel, but Salia stayed her hand.

"The device is functioning properly," she said.

"There is nothing we can do at this moment," Bozidar said. "Come to the bridge at once. I will make sure the others are here."

"What will we tell Mila?" Susan asked. "We should explain that Scott was forced to help your scientists."

"We will tell Mila what we must when we know what explanations she requires."

The panel went dark. Salia tugged on Susan's elbow, leading her down the hall. They entered a transport tube and arrived at the bridge. Edna and Scott entered from the opposite side a moment later.

"Didn't I warn you about jinxing things?" Edna snarled when she saw Bozidar. "We were having such a wonderful time, and you go throwing disaster out to the universe."

Scott put his hand on Edna's shoulder. "Hush, dear. You know it isn't his fault."

"Hmph." Edna crossed her arms, glaring at no one in particular.

"How soon before Mila gets here?" Susan asked.

"She has arrived." Marsel tapped on the screen in front of him, then turned to Bozidar. "I do not hear explosions. Perhaps she will speak with us first before attacking us."

"Your optimism is welcome, if misplaced." Bozidar pointed at the viewing screen.

Falling Water hovered alongside, its hull glittering from reflected starlight. As they watched, the blackness between the stars became dotted with glowing discs. The discs changed color along a rainbow spectrum, blues warming through green to yellow. The brightness intensified, and the discs expanded. Gleaming ships materialized as each disc faded.

TWENTY

The ships rotated until all of them had their gun ports aimed at a target. Some faced *Cold Fire*, while others angled toward points in the city below. Marsel squeaked, one wailing note that caught in his vocal chords and rattled to silence.

"This is intolerable," Edna said. "How many times are these critters going to try to kill me? I'm not a cat, and even if I were my nine lives would be up by now."

Mila's image appeared on the screen. "Prepare to be boarded."

"I'm getting tired of standing in front of invading soldiers," Edna said. She marched to the screen and shook her finger at Mila. "We had a deal. The blues and the beiges were going to sit down and talk things out. Where's your honor?"

"We do not negotiate over the bodies of our dead." Mila's blue skin glistened.

"Who's dead?" Edna whirled on Bozidar. "You didn't kill anyone, did you?"

"No, nor did I give orders to have anyone killed."

"You executed my protocol officer," Mila said.

"We most certainly did not," Susan said. "Even though we discovered he was spying on us." She turned to Salia. "He was alive when you left, right?"

"Correct." She bowed to Mila. "He was speaking with your taupe allies. They would have no reason to harm him."

Edna threw up her hands. "Don't tell me he's going to kill himself to get this war started."

Bozidar was already tapping the communications screen when Scott ordered, "Secure the brig. Send your best doctor on the double."

"I'm going too," Susan said. "Tell Cecily to meet me at the brig with Agnes' silver ring."

She ran from the bridge, followed by Salia. A beige soldier waited for the transport tube.

"Move." Susan pushed it out of the way. "Forgive me," she said as she pulled Salia into the tube.

Susan paced the entire ride muttering hurry, hurry, hurry for the few seconds it took to arrive. When the doors opened, she raced down the corridor.

"Please, wait for me." Salia hopped like a kangaroo and panted like a St. Bernard in the desert.

"Make your legs grow," Susan said, increasing her pace.

"It is difficult for me to transform under stress."

Susan whirled on the little beige critter. "Do it. Now." She grabbed Salia's hand and squeezed it.

Salia skidded on her heels. She stumbled as her legs stretched and unsettled her center of gravity. She braced herself against the ceiling with her arms. Her legs snapped back as if they were bungee cords. She regained her equilibrium on the third bounce. Her legs stabilized at half again as long as they had been before.

"How did you do that?" Salia gasped. "How did you make me transform?"

"Don't know, don't care. Let's get to the brig before someone dies."

Cecily reached the entrance to the prison cells as Susan and Salia arrived. "You're taller," Cecily said. "How did you manage that?"

"Your mother assisted. I do not know how."

"Neither do I," Susan said. "Give me the ring." She slid the ring on her finger as the hatch to the brig opened.

Salia chittered to the doctor who stepped aside and bowed. Susan marched toward a group of beige guards circled in front of a cell. They parted as the kinetic energy from Susan's footsteps radiated along the floor. The blue protocol officer lay sprawled on a bench at the back of the cell.

Susan knelt by the body. She moved her fingers

along his wrist. "Cecily, where would I find a pulse?"

Cecily wiggled through the crowd and crouched by her mother. "I'm not sure. Marsel taught me how to use the medical equipment on humans, not Schtatikians. Is he breathing?"

"I don't know. Where are their noses?"

Use the ring.

Susan heard the whisper in her mind. She breathed on the ruby and polished it on her sleeve. She pointed the stone at the blue creature. The ring grew warm on her finger. The heat spread throughout her body. She placed her palms on the protocol officer's shoulders.

His skin rippled. A glow spread around him, as if his skin covered scores of tiny tea lights. The light enveloped Susan. The scent of roses and fresh bread filled the room. The blue creature curled into a ball and rolled onto its footpads.

Susan pressed her hands together, fingers rubbing the silver band of her ring. "Are you well? Do you need anything?"

He bowed to her. "Your forgiveness. You saved me when we intended to do you harm."

"Tell Mila," Susan said. "I'll forgive anything once we stop this war."

"Have you also saved the captain of this ship?"

Susan recoiled. "Cecily, is she in the cells or her quarters?"

"I don't know," Cecily said as she slapped the communications pad. "Bozidar, check on the captain."

"I did so as your mother left the bridge." Bozidar's voice sounded smug even through the crackling of the intercom. "It seemed a wise precaution, and was. The guards prevented the captain from poisoning herself."

"Bring me to her," Salia said. "The taupes fear shame above all else. I was born to use that fear for a worthy purpose."

"It worked with the councilor," Cecily said. "It's worth a shot now."

"Wait," Susan said. She pushed herself to her knees. Panting, she staggered to her feet.

"Mom, are you okay?"

"This healing business isn't as easy as it looks." She wobbled to the communications panel. "I'll be fine. Bozidar, bring the captain to the bridge. We'll show Mila her plan has failed."

* * *

Susan entered the bridge along with the blue protocol officer. Salia followed at their heels. Her legs were normal length again, and she trotted to keep pace.

"Excellent," Bozidar said. He turned to the view screen. "As you can see, your officer is unharmed."

A hint of green smoke curled around Mila's body, and her eyestalks withdrew into her head. She sputtered and shivered. "Explain. Explain!"

The blue shrank next to Susan and held her

hand. "I followed orders. She has my loyalty because she rescued me from the whisperings of death."

"How?"

Salia stepped to Susan's side, taking her other hand. "The Descendants of She Who Found Us are wise and powerful."

At that moment guards pushed the captain of *Cold Fire* toward the view screen. She snarled at Salia, and green smoke poured from every inch of her body.

Salia released Susan's hand and extended her legs. She grew taller than Susan, and her body expanded until her scarf scarcely covered her shoulders. She marched toward the captain and stopped inches from her. Staring down upon the captain's eyestalks, she said, "Your schemes have brought harm to our clan. Your failure has brought shame to all taupes. You are not fit for command."

Without waiting for a reply, she faced the viewing screen. "Nor, for that matter, are you, Mila of *Falling Water.* Your plot would have mired the entire planet in pain and destruction for generations. Your name will become a curse throughout the clans."

"Who are you?" Mila demanded.

"I am Salia. A prophecy from the blue clan foretold my coming as the unworthy one who would point the way to salvation. Our salvation is not on a path but through a person. There she is!"

Salia whirled and pointed at Susan.

Susan smiled, a weak upturn of her lips that fled before fully forming. She reached her free hand to

Cecily. "My clan is here." Holding on to Cecily, Susan whispered, "Blue guy, step back." When he retreated, she reached her other hand to Edna.

Edna squeezed Susan's hand as she strutted to the screen. "Hey there, you old blue meanie, remember me? I'll bet I'm your worst nightmare, and I'll sure make your life miserable unless you surrender. No conditions, no hedging your bets. I'm not even going to offer you safe passage. You do anything we don't like, I'll let Salia rip you to shreds."

"Don't argue," Cecily said. "The prophecy is from your own clan."

Susan and Cecily joined Edna. "We are waiting for your answer," Susan said. She glanced at the taupe captain. "Yours too."

Bozidar motioned to the guards. "Her silence is answer enough. Take her to the brig, then tell her co-conspirators to join her. *Cold Fire* is in the hands of patriots, not traitors."

Mila nodded. "My other ships will return to blue clan territory."

The screen switched to the exterior monitors. One by one, the blue ships left as they had arrived in a glowing disc of energy.

* * *

Susan, Cecily, and Edna stood on the balcony of the beige clan's palace watching Schtatik's twin moons, hazy in the mid-day sky. Scott and Gary sat in the adjoining room with Marsel. They took notes as he read from scrolls. Bozidar picked up a glass of cold, ruby liquid and joined the women.

"You were splendid today, Descendants of She Who Saved Us." He raised his glass. "I believe this is the appropriate gesture for a toast."

"Yes, it is," Susan said. She glanced in the other room. "Where is Salia? She deserves much of the credit."

"She is resting. Transformation takes a significant amount of energy, especially for those not adept at the procedure." Bozidar gazed at the city below him. "I have always loved this view of the capital. I never thought I would see it again."

"Neither did I," Edna said. "I'm surprised that I'm happy to see it. Of course, I'm happy to see anything. It means I'm still alive."

"Has a nice ring to it, that word. *Alive.*" Cecily stretched and yawned. "Salia has the right idea. I'm going to take a nap." She froze. "I have time for a nap, right, Bozidar? It seems whenever things are looking up you come in with bad news."

"I have no information to share, good or bad."

Cecily grinned. "Awesome. I'm off for a nap."

Edna leaned back on the guardrail and studied Susan. Her lips twisted and she scowled. "I've got a question."

"Really?" Susan asked. "It looks more like you've got a sour lemon drop in your mouth."

"I'm serious. How did you save that blue critter?

And get Salia to shoot up taller than you?"

Susan folded her arms and dropped her chin to her chest. When she raised her head, she sighed. "I wish I knew. It would make it a lot easier to pull these magic tricks out on cue instead of waiting for a crisis. I heard Agnes tell me to use the ring for healing. I don't know how I helped Salia. She usually crumbles when I yell at her."

"You actually shouted at that poor critter?" Edna chuckled. "My bad-mood attitude survives in the next generation after all."

"I didn't really scold her. More like told her to put on her big girl pants." Susan glanced at Bozidar. "Another Earth expression. Don't try to figure it out."

"Your words were irrelevant," Bozidar said. "On our planet, leaders inspire."

"Ours do too. At least, that's what their ads claim," Edna said. "And I guess it's true. I'm usually inspired to grab a couple of beers after listening to them."

"I do not mean politicians." Bozidar took a deep breath. "The perfume of my city is inspiring. It encourages me to continue working for peace. The heroism of Salia, once a traitor but now an ally, inspires me to trust even the blues. That is leadership. It is the quality of making those around you do more than they could ever imagine possible, without thought of reward."

"That's my daughter," Edna said. "Everyone in

town knows if you want to get something done, put Susan Morgan in charge of the committee."

"And they know I can't refuse a request for help." Susan twisted Agnes' ring around her finger. "I think there's more to it. I can feel the power in this ring. I'm starting to rely on it the way Marsel relies on his prophecies."

Bozidar held out his hand. "May I examine the stone?" He held the ring to the light, tilting it to catch different reflections of sky and sun. "Our engineers, like yours, learned to exploit minerals for energy and profit. This stone, however, is made from a mineral that is difficult to manipulate. There are some who claim it holds magical powers, or unleashes magical powers in those who possess it. That explanation has never made sense to me." He returned the ring to Susan.

"Oh, there's magic in that ring," Edna said. "Just staying hidden in my jewelry box proves that. I know I never saw it before, or I'd be wearing it now. It waited until the right person came along to use it. That's magic in my book."

"For once I agree with you, Mother," Susan said. "Healing people? Bringing the blue officer back from the dead? He wasn't alive when we got there, but he's walking and talking now. No human has that kind of power." She snapped her mouth closed as Marsel shrieked in the other room.

"What's got into him now?" Edna rolled her eyes. "You have to take those scrolls away, Bozidar, before he drives us all nuts."

Marsel bounded onto the balcony. "I solved the riddles!" He bounced in place, and the scroll in his hands rattled like dice.

Bozidar pressed down Marsel's shoulders until he stopped bouncing. "I am pleased for your achievement. Which riddles did you solve?"

"All of them." Marsel twirled around the balcony like a child, waving the scroll in the breeze. "I know why the original explorers went to Earth, I know why Agnes and Pala created such a strong bond, and I know what awaits us when we put our differences aside. The prophecies all point in the same direction. We are linked with the humans, Bozidar my cousin, our future with theirs. Oh, the stars we will see, the planets we will explore, the songs they will sing of us!"

"Let's draw straws to see who gets to deck him," Edna said.

"Oh, thank you," Marsel cooed. "I love your songs of decking halls with flowers and garlands. There are some lovely flowers in the courtyard below. They smell so sweet."

"Later, Marsel," Susan said as she guided him back into other the room. "Tell us more about your discovery."

Marsel scampered to the table and grabbed at Gary and Scott. "You know what I found. Tell them, tell them, and we can all rejoice."

Gary settled against the pillows on the sofa and

motioned to Scott. "Be my guest. You seem to understand most of what he says. I'm lucky if I can get one word in five."

Scott grimaced as he picked up his notepad. "Apparently there are many stories about finding other planets, other races, and exploring the universe together. Pala, the captain of the ship that crashed on Earth when Agnes was a child, may have been following those stories when she set out. The key to all the stories is cooperation. Making friends with strangers, learning which ones to trust. Pala and Agnes made a profound connection."

"Their trust in each other surpassed the boundaries of time and space, life and death." Marsel danced around the room.

"Yes, something like that," Edna said. "Bozidar, can we tether him to something? Nail his foot to the floor?"

"I will constrain him," Bozidar said.

Scott cleared his throat. "As I said, Pala and Agnes made a profound connection, which seems to have been passed down Agnes' line."

"The ring augments that connection," Susan said. "At least, I think it does. Maybe because it's made from materials from both planets."

"That would be consistent with Marsel's conclusions." Scott consulted his notes. "He is convinced there is a golden age coming. Exploration, discovery, peace. It all depends, however, on learning to cooperate."

Bozidar dragged Marsel back to the group. "Who is required to cooperate with whom? The various clans on Schtatik? The clans and humans? What about humans learning to cooperate with each other."

"That is why we need the magical powers of the Descendants of She Who Found Us," Marsel said. "We have all the artifacts. The ring. The quilt holding the remains of the brave captain Pala. The embroidery that Agnes made on the quilt. The embroidery that Susan started here. There is more than enough to convince the blue and beige clans to stop fighting."

"And do what?" Susan asked.

"That is obvious," Marsel said. "Together the clans will launch a magnificent expedition to Earth. Once there, we will join forces and create a scientific armada to explore the universe."

Susan stared at Marsel, her jaw slowly dropping. She pushed it closed. "Marsel, sweetie, do the prophecies say how we're supposed to accomplish this?"

"Oh, yeah," Gary said. "They're just like any other prophecies. Step one is getting your butt kicked, step three is everyone happy, and step two is where the miracle occurs."

TWENTY-ONE

"YES, A MIRACLE OCCURS, AND IT WILL BE GLORIOUS."
Marsel tapped his feet on the floor as he squirmed in
Bozidar's arms.

"That's nice, Marsel." Susan took the scroll. She
ran her finger along the writing. "You'll have to teach
me how to read these. If we're going to be part of a
miracle, I'd like to know what I'm supposed to do. In
the meantime, Edna and I have to prepare for the
negotiations between the blue and beige clans. We'll
need Bozidar to help us. Scott and Gary as well.
Would you mind going to the library to continue your
studies?"

Marsel stopped dancing and reached for the
scroll. He clutched it against his body, bowed, and
skipped from the room.

"You couldn't have done that before?" Edna
asked.

"The sweet voice is like the command voice," Susan said. "It's more effective if you use it sparingly. Besides, we gleaned useful information from him. It might help the cause."

"Convince both sides there is more profit in cooperation than war?" Scott asked. "Yes, that qualifies as a miracle."

Bozidar wiped his hands as if dusting off Marsel's exuberance. "Perhaps. Let me review the biographical data on the negotiators, their aides, and any others consulted by the panel. There may be something in their backgrounds we can exploit."

"Would it help to have all the artifacts in one place?" Gary asked. "That's what Marsel called them."

"An excellent suggestion," Bozidar said. "We should use any weapon at our disposal."

"Including the *machute* research?" Scott asked. He leaned against the back of his chair, arms folded, his eyes focused on Bozidar.

Bozidar dropped his gaze. He curled his fingers into a tight ball, then released them knuckle by knuckle.

"My country had the same reaction to sharing weapons research," Scott said. "We wanted to be the only ones who could take out anyone we didn't like. As you can imagine, it didn't go over well with our allies."

Susan felt the air around her vibrate before she saw the shimmer that announced Agnes' arrival. "I know what you're going to say," Susan spoke aloud.

"Please tell me you're having a vision," Edna said.

"I will be as soon as you stop distracting me." Susan closed her eyes and waited for Agnes to whisper in her mind. She heard a snort instead.

Do I really need to tell you what to do? Negotiation takes sacrifice. You can't get to 'yes' without giving up as much as you get.

Susan chuckled as she opened her eyes. "We can't threaten the blues. When we reveal the work you've done to counteract *machute* poisoning, and we will reveal it, it will be as an act of good faith."

"You're giving up a pretty big bargaining chip," Scott said.

"Then our job is to make sure it buys the peace." Susan settled on the couch. "I'm used to working with people who want the same thing but aren't on the same page yet. It's easier to bring people together if the one who appears to have all the toys gives most of them away."

"I'm used to working with people who want to shoot me," Scott said. "Different skill set."

"We can use both," Gary said. He pointed at Bozidar. "You said it yourself. We can use all the weapons we can get. Skills are weapons."

"We're going to need a bigger buffet table." Edna stood beside Scott's chair and put her hand on his shoulder. "Did you ever work on those fake parties to pull in gang members?"

"We live in the suburbs, dear," Scott said. "The low-crime suburbs. Still, I understand your meaning. We start off with a celebration of some kind, lots of food and whatever intoxicants are appropriate. Break the ice."

"It worked on Earth," Susan said. "The ice cream party."

"That's exactly what I had in mind." Edna rubbed her palms together as she advanced on Bozidar. "You told us which ice cream flavors most closely resembled the sacred *stotlet*. It brought those renegade taupes to Susan's shop and turned them into allies. Let's try it again, but on a bigger scale."

"I could help with staging," Gary said. "We could base the look of the room on how the taupes arranged the things we brought with us when we were held in the castle."

Bozidar nodded. "A credible plan. My people have different color skins, but our rituals are similar. We respond to the same visual cues for reverence. We are awed by grandeur in the same ways." He took Edna's hands in his. "An excellent suggestion, your majesty. Thank you."

Edna's mouth sagged open. She uttered a strangled string of syllables. "You're welcome."

Susan smiled. "Now, if only we can get the blues and beiges to be equally as speechless. And agreeable."

* * *

The celebration took a day to plan and a week to arrange. The entire capital threw itself into the work. All the inhabitants had seen the blue warships materialize over their heads only to depart without firing a shot. Wherever Edna appeared, crowds would stop their labors and bow. When Cecily and Susan joined her, the crowds prostrated themselves on the ground.

Marsel spent hours with the religious leaders of the beige clan, explaining his interpretation of prophecy. He struggled with the chief advisor to the elders until Bozidar sat in on the discussions, accompanied by their top military leaders. The taupe priests assented to Marsel's logic after a private lunch with the taupe captain of *Cold Fire*.

The day before the blue delegation was scheduled to arrive, Edna, Susan, and Cecily toured the capital. They rode in a hovercraft similar to the ones used by Edna's taupe captors at the pink castle in the mountains but much larger. The vines that created the uprights were as thick as palm trees. Armed guards rode on the tops.

"I'm going to miss this when we get back home," Cecily said.

"Not me," Edna said. "I've done the beauty queen 'elbow, elbow, wrist, wrist' wave for too long." She demonstrated, turning her wrist and moving her elbow back and forth. "Even switching arms isn't helping anymore, but if I stop waving they'll think I'm ticked off with them and go punish themselves." She smiled at the crowds. As she turned away, the smile became a wince. "And my cheeks hurt. I'm telling you, there will be serious repercussions to all this forced cheerfulness."

"You're supposed to be serene," Cecily said.

"That frightened the crowds more than her not waving." Susan nodded as a Schtatikian tossed a bouquet at the hovercraft. The flower bundle was captured by a tendril from the vines. The tendril twisted toward Susan and presented the bouquet. "I never expected you to like the paparazzi life."

"It isn't the attention," Cecily said. She took the flowers from Susan, smelled them, and passed them to her mother. "I like the pageantry. I've taken gobs of notes for my next film."

"At least someone is having fun," Edna said. She sniffed the flowers and sneezed. "Right now, all I want is a quiet corner in a quiet room, a pan of double-fudge brownies, and unlimited access to Netflix."

Susan patted her mother's arm. "Is the non-stop adoration boring you, Mother?"

"Yes." Edna waved the bouquet, causing it to shed half of the flowers. "I've been on my feet for days. No one is listening to me. They're just cheering. And I haven't had a snack for hours."

"We've been riding through the streets for precisely twenty-five minutes. There's a box of goodies tucked in the corner, which I will bring out in five minutes. We'll be at the riverbank then, and the crowds will be smaller. We're listening to you, but if you continue to whine we'll stop." Susan smiled. "Happy now?"

Edna snorted and turned back to the crowd. "Five minutes, not a second more. I don't care if the critters see me eating."

Cecily opened the box. "Here, Grandma. You always used to sneak me a cookie when I was a kid. Now I'm returning the favor. But keep on waving. You know how important it is to have the entire clan united for the negotiations with the blues. Right now they'll do whatever we ask because we kept the warships from attacking."

"I know. I was there when Bozidar suggested we make ourselves as visible as possible."

"Be grateful he didn't want us to receive visitors," Cecily said. "Marsel wanted us to meet every living being in the city, including the more sentient pets. Can you imagine shaking all those hands? Or paws?"

Edna flexed her fingers and rotated her wrist. "You win. But I'm going to be grumpy tonight, so don't you dare try to improve my mood."

"Poor Scott," Cecily whispered to Susan as she faced the crowds from another side of the craft.

"I heard that," Edna said.

The hovercraft soared above the heads of the cheering crowd and floated over the river. The golden water reflected pale green clouds in the lilac sky. Willow-like trees grew along the banks. They reached their branches out when the tendrils from the craft's uprights fluttered in the breeze as if in greeting.

Susan distributed snacks to both humans and Schtatikians. She placed the guards' food on a leaf. A tendril from the upright curled around each cookie, creating a bowl, which it lifted to the guards at the tops of the vine tower.

"Hurry and eat," Susan told Cecily and Edna. "We're going to be floating by those apartment complexes soon." She pointed to a cluster of buildings on the far side of the river.

Each building was a monolith festooned with ivy and trailing roses. Balconies ringed each story. Each balcony was an individual garden with potted plants, vines encircling the railings, and espaliered trees on either side of every door and window.

The balconies appeared devoid of Schtatikians until the hovercraft cleared the midpoint of the river. Then eyestalks popped up like full-blown dandelions. The eyestalks rose, and as the heads of the creatures cleared the railings the air was filled with shrieks, cheers, and whistles.

Edna covered her ears. "Who knew those critters could make so much noise, with such variety?"

"Smile, Grandma. They've been waiting all morning to see us." Cecily stood on her tiptoes and waved at the crowds. She wobbled and lurched, grabbing at the railing.

"Careful, sweetie," Susan said. "Our reputation is sunk if you fall on your fanny."

"I'm getting tired of being graceful," Edna said.

"Get over it, Mother. You're supposed to be a goddess-like figure. All-powerful beings don't list to starboard while they're walking down the street. Or standing in a flying basket for everyone to see." Susan lifted her hand in the classic beauty queen wave.

The wind picked up behind them, increasing their speed. The craft adjusted like a sailboat in choppy waters. They resumed their course, flying along the waterfront buildings, then bobbing around the upper floors of buildings inland.

"Do Schtatikians get suntans?" Edna asked. "Or sunburns?"

Susan frowned. "I've never thought about it. Why do you ask?"

Edna pointed to a balcony below them as they floated past. "The critters down there don't seem to be beiges."

Cecily leaned over the basket. "You're right. One is much darker, and one is kind of red. And the ones on that balcony over there could be green."

Susan pulled both of them back. She arched an eyebrow at them, stretched herself to her full height, and waved at the creatures as they passed. "Don't be so obvious."

"They're not going to shoot us," Edna said. "Bozidar said we would be safe."

"We don't know what the guards will think." Susan glanced upward. "I don't want them sending security forces to track down anyone just because we looked at them too intently."

"I wonder if they're from other clans," Cecily said in a low voice. "We've focused on the conflict between the blues and the beiges, but I remember Bozidar saying the rest of the clans had issues too."

* * *

The sun rose over the city, sending light in gentle waves into every corner. Morning flowers bloomed, bathing the streets in fragrance. Dragonfly-like creatures swooped from bush to vine to tree, their wings adding a cheery buzz to the sounds of the city awakening.

Marsel trotted down the hall of the guest quarters in the palace, knocking on each door. "Get up, get up. Today is our great day, the day of our triumph, the day of peace." He spoke in a chant, his voice following a rhythm almost, but not quite, Gregorian.

Susan stumbled out of her room and grabbed Marsel's hand. "You do know we have little boxes in our rooms that chime? We call them alarm clocks. According to mine, we have another hour to sleep."

"But how can you? This is a special day." Marsel rocked from one footpad to the other. "Do you sleep late on Christmas?"

"There are presents and chocolates on Christmas," she said. "Do you have presents and chocolates for me?"

He stopped his rolling bounce. "Not yet, but I

will." He propelled himself down the corridor in something resembling a canter.

Scott slipped out of his room, closing the door behind him. "What did Marsel want at this hour?"

"He's too excited to sleep."

"He'll be sleeping forever if your mother wakes up cranky." He pulled his robe tighter.

"Mother can sleep through the finale to the 1812 Overture if she chooses. She can also hear a candy wrapper opening even in the deepest REM sleep." Susan rubbed her eyes. "On the other hand, now that I'm up it is unlikely I'll get back to sleep. I don't want to wake Gary any more than you want to wake Edna."

"Bozidar is probably up," Scott said. "Perhaps we can discuss any last minute details for the agenda."

As Susan nodded, she noticed a shadow on the wall near the stairway. "That might be him now."

Bozidar trudged into view, head down, brown curls drooping. He wore a velvet jacket the color of polished pine. His boots resembled soft calfskin, and his linen pant legs were tucked into the rolled boot tops. He raised his head, revealing a frilled yellow collar on a silky, butternut shirt.

"Did Marsel wake you up?" Susan asked.

"Of course." Bozidar's voice was quiet, his tone disgruntled. "I should have posted a guard at his door with orders to keep him inside until breakfast."

"Never mind." Susan appraised Bozidar's clothes. "Why aren't you wearing a robe?"

"The elders thought it would offend the blues if I were to appear in a Schtatikian garment while I am still trapped in human form. They decided this would be more appropriate." His head drooped again. "My opinion of the outfit was not considered."

"Oh, no, you look … " Susan's voice trailed.

"Fine," Scott said. "You look fine. Besides, there is a long-standing tradition of men feeling like fools in formal clothes."

"I am not a man. I merely look like one." Bozidar shrugged. "It does not matter. The blue delegation will not notice me." He pointed to Susan. "You will be the center of attention, with your mother and daughter."

Susan shuddered. "Scott suggested we review the arrangements for today. As long as we're up, we should use the time well."

"There is nothing which requires our attention," Bozidar said. "Any efforts on our part now would only muddle the waters, as you say."

"Muddy," Scott said. "Muddy the waters. But I take your point. Perhaps we could get some breakfast?"

"The staff will not have arrived," Bozidar said. "However, we could try to find something to eat without creating a disturbance."

Susan put her hand to her lips. "Oh, dear."

"What?" Scott asked.

"Marsel went to find presents and chocolates for me."

Scott shook his head. "So much for not creating a disturbance. Dare I ask why you sent him on that particular errand?"

"He said today was better than Christmas, and I disagreed." Susan's glanced from Bozidar to Scott. "Don't look like that. I was only half awake."

"Bozidar, where do you suggest we look for Marsel?" Scott asked.

"The kitchen first. That is where he would go for chocolate. If he is not there, we can at least make hot beverages for ourselves while we consider other options."

The kitchen was quiet and gleaming. Brass trays filled with food and covered with a clear, shiny wrapping were stacked on multi-level rolling carts arranged in columns like so many tanks waiting for battle. Carafes and pitchers stood on long tables against one wall. Woks and pots and pans waited on the cooking surface. Knives of various metals and crystals hung on a rack next to them.

"We shouldn't touch anything," Susan said.

Marsel tottered into the room from another entrance. He carried a satchel on his back. "You are here," he said in a puzzled tone. "Were you concerned I would not return?"

"No, not at all," Susan said. "You're as good as your word, so I knew you would come back." She leaned toward Scott. "I'm babbling, aren't I?"

He squeezed her arm. "Yes. You need coffee. We're all suffering from a lack of coffee."

"That is my gift," Marsel said.

"Coffee?" Susan asked. "How? We didn't pack any."

Marsel pulled a red metal canister from his satchel. "My studies of human culture showed me how dependent you are on stimulants. Coffee seemed the least hazardous. I synthesized it from its chemical description."

He gave the canister to Susan. "The head chef agreed to make a container of the brew. I intended to offer it to you at breakfast." He opened a small cabinet, retrieved a pitcher, and placed it in a warming device. He took two cups from another cabinet and filled them with the steaming brown liquid.

Susan took one of the cups, cradled it in her hands, and inhaled. "I've missed this. It smells like real coffee, Marsel."

"Splendid," he said, searching a drawer. "Forgive me, Descendant of She Who Found Us, but I am unable to offer you chocolates at this time. I thought there was a supply here, but it is missing or relocated."

She sipped gingerly. Her eyes sparkled and she gulped half the contents of the cup. "Don't worry. This is perfect."

"I agree," Scott said after his first sip. "But I would like something to eat."

"Follow me," Marsel said. "The chef agreed to leave us food. Truly, I expected all of you to be awake long before now."

"So you took the liberty of arranging a breakfast we could make at our convenience?" Bozidar smiled. "For once, I approve of your initiative."

Marsel glowed, and his shining skin looked as if it were warmed by candlelight. He bowed at the waist, his eyestalks nearly touching the ground. "I am honored, and grateful." He examined his own feet. "Look at me now. I am glowing so much that I could be mistaken for a yellow."

Susan straightened. "That reminds me of something, Bozidar. While the three of us were touring the city, Cecily thought she saw someone from the brown clan. And the red. And maybe the green."

"That is unlikely," Bozidar said. "The crowds were quite dense. The light must have deceived her."

"I thought of that, but Edna saw them first, and she has an excellent eye for color. And they weren't in the crowds on the streets. They were on the balconies. Easier to see."

Bozidar paced. "Members of other clans rarely travel to the capital. They must be here to monitor our negotiations."

"How would they even know about it?" Scott set his cup on a counter. "Are they a threat?"

Bozidar shook his head. "Unknown."

TWENTY-TWO

Susan closed her eyes and sighed. "I hate the word *unknown.*"

Scott frowned. "So do I. Alert your security forces, Bozidar. We can't afford to let other clans disrupt the negotiations."

Marsel straightened, holding his arms to the light. "This color is lovely. It is strange to think that other clans are worthy of our admiration." He gasped. "My thoughts are not worthy of notice, much less admiration."

"It's okay, dear." Susan patted the top of his head. "We all have a little prejudice. We have to resist, and the first step is acknowledging the problem." She stopped patting his head, but her finger tapped against an eyestalk. When it wrapped itself around her wrist, she said, "Sorry, I had a thought. Bozidar, by all means, inform security of what we've seen, but let's consider being bold. The whole planet knows about the conflict between the blues and the beiges. Why not let the whole planet know how it's going to be solved?"

"Broadcast the negotiations?" Scott said. "I like it. We add another level of pressure on the clan leaders, demonstrate that we are not a threat, and show everyone all the artifacts. Unfiltered information."

Bozidar's eyebrows knit together as his forehead and nose wrinkled. "I am not fond of giving more information than I receive. However, conventional diplomacy has failed." He paced along the wall next to a communications panel. "First, I will report the possibility of agents in the capital." He tapped the panel and relayed Susan's information about seeing members of other clans to the palace guard.

"Are you certain about broadcasting everything?" Susan whispered to Scott. "I didn't think to bring in cameras."

Scott raised an eyebrow. "Were you expecting to issue press releases, or hold news conferences at the end of the day?"

"Call me old-fashioned." Susan lowered her voice when Bozidar scowled at her. "I like newspapers."

"How last century of you." Scott pulled Susan to another part of the room as Bozidar scowled at them both. "We don't need to solve the communications problem, my dear. The Schtatikians have their own technology."

Susan opened her mouth and snapped it shut again. "Of course they do. And I can stop micromanaging any time now, right?"

Scott chuckled as he nodded. "It isn't easy to transition from supreme leader to head of the committee."

"Don't let Edna hear you," Susan said. "She thinks of herself as the supreme leader. No matter where she is, or what anyone else is doing, she is always in charge."

"I've noticed." Scott nodded toward Bozidar. "Looks like he finished his report."

Bozidar joined them. "We are not accustomed to broadcasting official meetings. My own clan leaders will object strenuously. I imagine the blues will also object."

"Then we need to persuade them," Susan said.

Bozidar nodded. "It will not be a trivial task." He pressed his lips together. "I believe our best hope for success is Edna."

"I agree," Scott said. "And I'm just as pained and surprised as you are about it."

"Can we make such a huge change this late in the day?" Susan asked.

"Yes," Bozidar said, "if Edna commands it."

* * *

Four musicians playing a fanfare that might have been written for bagpipes had it been composed on Earth marched into the meeting room. The musicians played what looked like long copper-colored tubes, which wiggled over their heads.

Schtatikians lined the walls, blue on one side, beige on the other. A blue and beige plaid rug separated the two groups. Susan and Cecily stood near the door with Edna while Scott and Gary were on the dais at the opposite end of the room. Bozidar hovered at the side of the dais, shoving Marsel behind him each time the excited creature jiggled forward.

"Why does my theme song sound like someone is strangling goats?" Edna muttered to Susan.

"It sounds regal to them." Susan adjusted Edna's gold-fringed shawl. "It's forty feet to the dais. You can manage that in twenty seconds. Another few seconds to sit down and the music stops."

"I can make it in ten seconds if I put my mind to it," Edna said.

"Think royal, not race track." Susan gave her a gentle shove. "That's your cue."

Edna jerked forward, followed by her musicians, then by Susan and Cecily. Her pace increased with each step. The musicians played louder but did not speed up the music or their marching. Susan and Cecily prodded the two in front of them, who trod on the foot pads of the two ahead of them. By the time Edna reached the dais, she was power walking. The musicians struggled to keep in time, and Susan and

Cecily bit back the giggles.

"Enough with the screeching already," Edna said, whirling about and plopping on the throne. She leaned back. "Thanks for coming. We've got a busy day scheduled." She pointed at the crowd. "But not for you. Take a breather this morning, go out and see the sights, take a nap, whatever. While you're out, we're going to wire this room for sound and video so we can broadcast the whole shooting match."

The delegates, blue and beige alike, stood in perfect silence along the edges of the room. Nary an eyestalk twitched.

Bozidar moved to the front of the dais. "Honored delegates, the deepest desire of us all is an end to mistrust between the clans. The Descendants of She Who Found Us have in their wisdom decided that all of our cousins of different colors will know what we discuss in this room. With true and complete information comes true and complete trust." He bowed to the delegates, turned, and bowed to Edna. As he walked back to Marsel, he motioned the musicians to play.

The four beige creatures lifted their coppery tubes. One played a note. Another played a different and not entirely harmonious note. The other two began a lilting jig and retreated down the carpet.

The delegates followed. Those closest to side entrances slipped out there. The room emptied, and the bleating faded.

"Not the most elegant dismissal, my dear," Scott

said as he leaned around the throne and kissed Edna on the head.

"It got the job done," she said. "And stopped the music. Now bring in those techie critters."

"They are already at work," Bozidar said. "We should be ready to broadcast early this afternoon."

Gary hopped off the dais. "Bozidar, has security said anything about the spies from the other clans?"

"The morning status report did not mention the spies." Bozidar removed a communications device from his pocket. "Nor does the latest update."

"I wouldn't worry," Scott said. "News about the broadcast will spread quickly. Since the other clans won't have to infiltrate the proceedings to find out what's going on, it should reduce the risk."

"That assumes their intention is disruption, not destruction." Bozidar studied his device, a slim, glossy black square. He glanced at Scott and Susan. "Assassination is as much a tradition on Schtatik as it is on Earth."

"You're not helping, space boy." Edna scowled. "Although a bullet to the brain might be less painful than listening to more of that music."

Marsel crept out of his corner. "May I join the festivities now?"

Cecily took his hand and guided him up the steps to the dais. "It's not really a happy time, Marsel. Save the dancing until the negotiations are over."

"If they do not start well, they will not end well." Marsel scuffed the linen-like carpet.

"Do you think we've ruined things?" Susan said. Marsel squeaked. "I would never entertain such a blasphemous thought. I am only trying to smooth the way. What was done was necessary, but not elegant, as the Consort Scott himself noted."

Scott cleared his throat. "Yes, well, shaking the delegates up a little might work to our advantage."

"Unless they explode like soda cans," Cecily said.

Bozidar returned the black square to his pocket. "I agree with Scott, and with Marsel. We have demonstrated that this negotiation is entirely new. Breaking the rules of etiquette gives us an opportunity to find a real solution to the conflict, if we can reassure the delegates that they are finding a way out of chaos, not falling into it." He counted on his fingers. "There are thirty members of each delegation. Ten of them hold high status. Of that group, only three are known by sight even within their own clan."

"Three from each clan, you mean?" Susan asked. "That would be a total of six delegates we have to influence?"

"Not influence, charm." Bozidar stared at Edna.

Edna glared back. "I don't do charm."

"You can smile and shake hands," Cecily said. "Or smile and accept their bows."

"I had something more complicated in mind." Bozidar motioned for Cecily to join him. "If we begin the session with you, your mother, and grandmother personally greeting the most well-known delegates, we tell those watching that the entire galaxy recognizes their worth and by extension the value of all Schtatik."

Cecily nodded. "Like an endorsement. The delegates get a power boost, and they owe us a favor."

"Space boy," Edna said with pride in her voice, "I believe you've learned our human ways."

* * *

When the technical crews finished their work, blue and beige delegates clustered in the meeting room. Their eyestalks arched and swooped to note each camera and microphone positioned on walls, windows, and freestanding poles. They drifted into small groups, circling to avoid each other and the cameras.

The room had been redecorated as well as prepared for the broadcast. The carpet was gone, as was the dais. Seven round tables that could accommodate eight or ten delegates each were clustered at one end of the room. The other end was open, with benches lining the walls.

Bozidar entered and stood in the middle of the cleared space, head high and shoulders square. He carried a long metal staff topped with an intricate carving of spheres within a cage. He pounded the staff three times on the floor. "Honored delegates, the Descendants of She Who Found Us thank you for your patience, your kindness, and your wisdom."

As he moved aside, Edna, Susan, and Cecily entered. When Susan and Cecily were positioned on either side of her, Edna clapped her hands.

Bozidar cleared his throat and spoke a name. A blue delegate at the far end of the room hid behind a comrade. He stumbled forward when his friend pushed him and said, "I am the one."

Bozidar smiled and bowed. "Please approach and let our queen afford you the honors that are yours by right."

The blue delegate moved as if walking through a swamp. His long tunic swished against the floor. Flashes of blue metallic thread on the tunic's panels glinted as he passed under the chandeliers.

"This is going to take all day," Edna said. She closed the gap between herself and the blue creature, grasped his hand, and pulled him toward Susan and Cecily. "Come meet the girls. Bozidar, pick up the pace."

"As you wish." Bozidar bowed deeply and made a small flourish with his hand in Edna's direction. He called four more names, blue and beige delegates.

Each delegate came forward with more confidence than the first. Each was pulled into the growing circle by Edna. Susan shook their hands, Cecily hugged them.

Bozidar said, "Asura, leader of the turquoise subclan, leader of the blue delegation."

A tiny and delicate Schtatikian separated herself from a group of blues. She seemed to glide across the floor. A sky-blue fringed shawl covered her shoulders. Her tunic was heavily embroidered with motifs that looked like bird wings, all in shades of blue from the deepest indigo to the lightest azure. Teal and turquoise beads glittered along the hem and on her hat. Her pace slowed as she approached Edna.

"Honey, it is too late in the afternoon to stand on ceremony." Edna reached down and grabbed both of Asura's hands. "If you haven't met your beige counterpart, now is the time."

Asura's eyestalks stiffened like steel rods. Her pupils dilated. She sank to the floor, her tunic folding around her like a blooming rose.

"Mother, what did you do?" Susan said as she knelt by Asura. She patted the blue creature's arm above the hand.

"Mom, that doesn't work the same way it does on humans," Cecily said. She massaged Asura's temples.

Asura shivered as she regained consciousness. "I have lived to see prophecy fulfilled."

"I heard that," Marsel shouted as he dashed through the crowds. He pushed Susan away only to freeze as he watched her roll to her side. "Please, please forgive me."

Susan propped herself on her elbow. "Is this the miracle we need, Marsel? If it is, I'll forgive you just about anything."

Marsel nodded, bowed, and knelt next to Asura. "Blue cousin, speak. Tell me the gods have favored you with wisdom as they have me."

She rolled to her feet, pulling Marsel upright with her. "Your face is known to me. I have seen you in my dreams. And her." Pointing at Edna, she took a step closer, holding tight to Marsel's arm. "I thought she foretold the end of all I love. A beige queen from another planet, assisting our rivals. What else could we believe? But when she drew me into her presence, I remembered a prophecy from my childhood. It promised an end to conflict and a time of joy for all the clans."

She raised her arms and chanted while circling Edna, Susan, and Cecily. The other blue delegates joined her, both in marching about the humans and in chanting.

Marsel bounced and jiggled. "Do you see? Do you hear? The miracle is upon us, and the whole planet will experience it."

Edna put her fingers in her ears. "What is it with these critters and cacophony?"

* * *

The session changed from a negotiation to a celebration. Asura continued chanting. She began to dance, taking the hands of other blues until the entire blue delegation joined with her. They formed a long, sinuous line that wove around the room. As it worked its way back to Susan, she offered her hand to Asura, who pulled her into the line behind her.

"Looks like we can join too," Edna said as she wiggled between two blues.

"Just remember, Grandma," Cecily said while finding a place, "it's not a conga line."

"It could be," Edna said, but she kept pace with the others.

Scott and Gary found Bozidar and pulled him to the wall. "How long is the dancing going to last?" Scott asked.

"Hours perhaps," Bozidar said. He watched the line sway in time to the chant. "It is actually a good sign. The blues use dance as a form of communication. They are exceptionally good, better than most clans."

"What are they saying?" Gary asked.

Bozidar studied the snaking line. "If I read the steps correctly, Asura is leading them in the reconciliation dance. They are a proud clan, so it is not a dance they use often."

"Then we've won," Gary said. "We stopped the war before it started."

"Don't say that out loud," Scott said. He watched Edna attempt to mimic the steps, only to lapse into a two-step and skip. "We don't want to jinx anything."

Marsel wriggled through the line and scampered to Bozidar. "May we join them? The Descendants of She Who Found Us are dancing. It would mean so much for our cousins to dance as well."

Bozidar raised an eyebrow. He glanced at Scott. "I would appreciate your thoughts."

"Shared celebrations are important on Earth," Scott said.

"You wanted the lead delegates from both clans to share a meeting with Edna," Gary said. "Wasn't this the result you had in mind? We just jumped from step one to step forty-two."

Bozidar nodded. He took Marsel's hand and led him to Asura. She slowed her pace. When she stopped, the room grew still. Bozidar joined Marsel and Asura's hands. He bowed and stepped back.

Marsel gripped Asura's hand with both of his. "I have read the prophecies, and also rejoice to see them fulfilled."

"Then join us," Asura said. She slid her arm through his. "I will teach you."

Marsel bowed. "I am honored."

Asura tapped her right footpad, then her left. She took two steps forward, one step back, and began the sequence again starting with her left footpad. Marsel followed, swaying and humming.

"That is good," Asura said. "Now for the chant."

She warbled a string of syllables. Marsel repeated them, not always in perfect pitch. She repeated the verse, and his performance improved.

Marsel said, "The song is sad, but not mournful."

"It is a song of hope as well as loss," Asura said. "There is joy in discovering new truth, and relief in letting go of old hurts."

Marsel's eyestalks quivered. "Such beauty in your words, in your song." He faced the crowd. "My cousins, we can learn new ways. We can create a better future. Blend your voices with our friends the blues."

The beige delegates, who had inched to the sides of the room and plastered themselves against the walls, shuddered as if a cold wind roared through the space. Bozidar grabbed the lead delegate by the shoulder and marched him to the line. Two blues made a space between them, and Bozidar pushed the beige into the opening.

Another delegate took the hand of a comrade. Together, with caution, they approached the now moving line. As the blues passed, spaces opened for the beiges.

Other beige delegates approached the line, singly and in groups. Spaces opened, and even the clumsiest and least tuneful of them blended into the celebration.

Susan felt a vibration in the air around her. She slipped from the line and found a spot against the wall. She closed her eyes and waited for Agnes to speak. Instead, the crazy quilt and her ring appeared in her mind. She whispered, "Do you want me to bring the artifacts here?"

Yes, she heard. The voice sounded altered as if it were two tracks played a heartbeat out of sync. *Pala and I both agree the time is here.*

Susan motioned for Gary to join her. "Agnes

wants me to bring the quilt and the ring," she said. "Pala too."

"How do you know Pala wants it?" Gary asked.

"I heard her voice, and Agnes confirmed."

Gary took her arm and hurried her into the hall. "That's good enough for me. Scott just reminded me that this is only the opening for the negotiations. We don't have a signed treaty yet."

Edna leaned out of the line enough to shout to Cecily, "Where's your mother going?"

"Not a clue."

Edna waved at Scott and Bozidar. As they approached, she said, "Susan and Gary left. Any idea why?"

"No, but I will discover the reason," Bozidar said. "Scott, perhaps you will take Susan's place in the line?"

"With pleasure." Scott waltzed in place until Edna passed, then slid between two blues.

Bozidar side-stepped the dancers, finding open spaces as if he were crossing a fast-running river on stepping stones. He reached the door and inhaled deeply. He moved one foot forward but immediately stepped back. He raised his hands above his head and turned to the dancers. Walking behind him were three Schtatikians: one brown, one green, one red. All three carried weapons.

TWENTY-THREE

BOZIDAR STOOD IN FRONT OF THE SNAKING LINE OF dancers with his hands raised. His lips compressed, his left eye twitched, and an anemic puff of green smoke slid from his ears. "Honored guests, allow me to present armed representatives from the brown, green, and red clans."

He moved toward the dais, each step slow and deliberate. The armed critters followed, the green one pointing a weapon at Bozidar's back. The other two aimed their weapons at the crowd. Bozidar climbed the steps and turned to face the crowd.

Multicolored smoke swirled around Marsel's head. "Cousins, please. This is a moment for rejoicing."

"Too late, Marsel," Bozidar said. "They are here. We should keep silent, and listen."

Edna stepped forward, hands on hips. Then she

followed Bozidar's gaze to the recording devices positioned around the room. She inclined her head toward the dais. Turning to Marsel and Asura, she said, "My dears, Bozidar is, as usual, quite correct. Let's *all* hear what our new friends have to say."

She settled on the floor. Scott and Cecily glanced at each other. They sank to the floor and crossed their legs. One by one, blue and beige Schtatikians sat, crouched, or knelt where they were. All eyes and eyestalks focused on the green, brown, and red critters on the dais.

The green one prodded Bozidar with his weapon and hissed a question.

"I believe they are waiting for you to speak," Bozidar said to Edna.

Edna raised her hand. "Repeat the question, please."

"He asked what you are doing."

"Getting comfortable." Edna stretched her legs in front of her. "But that won't last long. I'm too old to spend much time on floors."

The green hissed another question. Bozidar turned in place, put his hand on the barrel of the weapon, and pushed it aside. The green backed up to his companions.

"Our queen is quite capable of answering questions herself. The translation devices are activated." Bozidar crossed his arms. "It would be more efficient."

Green smoke puffed from the red creature's ears.

"You dare to mock our traditions? Truly, you have spent too much time with strangers. She is not one of us. She can never be a queen over the clans."

"That's what I said, but they wouldn't listen." Edna pushed herself to her feet. "For the record, I'm only queen of the beiges. The rest of you can strong-arm anyone you like into the job." She stamped her feet. "Hang on, let me get the blood flowing, and I'll join you."

Marsel leaped to her side. "I shall accompany you, my queen."

"Oh, hell no," Edna said. "You stay right where you are." She glared at the crowd. "That goes for everyone. Just stay put."

Bozidar bowed as Edna wheezed up the steps to the dais. He offered his arm and walked her to the throne. The green and brown creatures let them pass while the red stood still. Edna extended her hand and turned the red by the shoulder, knocking off the creature's scarlet-sequined scarf.

"Sorry about that," Edna said as she caught the scarf before it hit the floor. She rubbed her thumb against the glittering embellishments. "These sequins are cool. They're soft, pliable. Usually, I cut my fingers to ribbons on them."

The red lowered her weapon and snatched the end of the scarf. "My clan mastered the art of creating shine without sharpness generations ago."

"Bully for you," Edna said, settling herself on the throne. "I just said I liked them. I didn't expect you to divulge state secrets about them." She motioned to Bozidar. "Pull up a chair and get comfortable."

The green creature gasped. "Do not mock us, human."

Edna leaned her elbow on the carved wooden arm and rested her chin on her palm. "I'm not mocking anyone. You wanted our attention, you've got it. Speak your piece. Unless you want chairs too. Is that it? Been on your feet a while?"

Bozidar bent toward Edna. "I believe they would be happier if you showed at least a glimmer of fear. They do have weapons."

"My panic button is worn out. Since I've been on your planet I've been kidnapped, shot at, elected to be the scapegoat for a fight I don't understand. There's not enough chocolate in the universe to make up for that. If I were a drinking woman, I'd be looking for a bar about now." She raised an eyebrow and glared at the other three. "So are you going to stand there and pout, or get on with the raid? You did have a plan, didn't you? A speech? Some reason for being here?"

"We have pledged our lives to stop the takeover of our world by humans and traitors." The red wrapped her scarf around her shoulders. Her eyestalks stood at attention.

Edna rubbed her forehead. "Worst raid ever. In the first place, the only humans who know about you are in this room."

"That is not an entirely accurate statement," Bozidar said.

"Shut it, space boy," Edna said, jabbing him with her finger. "In the second place, the blues and beiges are … were … too busy with their own squabbles to take over a tool shed, much less an entire planet."

"Lies," the red said. "Clever lies to distract the other clans."

"No, it is true," Marsel said. He jumped to his feet and grabbed Asura's hand. Pulling her along, he trotted to the steps. "We are in the presence of miracles. The blue clan and the beige clan have seen prophecy fulfilled. All that remains for a golden future is for all clans to co-exist in harmony."

"Under your domination!" The red pointed her weapon at Marsel.

"What part of 'co-exist in harmony' do you not understand?" Edna said. "No one wants to dominate anyone else."

"It is true," Asura said. "I myself taught our beige cousins the reconciliation dance. Become our friends, and dance with us."

"We have no reason to believe a blue," the red said.

"So what?" Edna pushed herself from the velvet cushion, stepped toward the red, and swatted aside her weapon. "So they've lied to you in the past. Or your leaders told you they lied to you. Big deal. Trust their actions if you don't trust their words. I told you we don't want to control anyone. The only life I want to run is my own. You don't want to play with me, say so and find something else to do."

The little spies huddled together, weapons pointing to the floor. Edna advanced on them. She stopped in front of the brown and threw her arms around them all. They shrieked like boiling teakettles. The brown fell to its knees, panting.

"That's called a group hug," Edna said. "Some of my people use it to show friendship."

Bozidar helped the brown to its feet. "The queen assured us she intended to be charming today. The terror she has inspired is entirely accidental."

Edna scratched the red spy between the eyestalks. "We're just getting to know each other, right little buddy? Give them a chance to look around, and they'll see for themselves this isn't a war council. We were getting the party started when they dropped by, so let's boogie."

Cecily jumped to her feet. "Absolutely. Asura, will you please start the dance again?"

While Marsel and Asura returned to their places at the head of the line, Edna pulled the spies toward her again. "I may not have mentioned, but this whole exchange has been broadcast around the planet. You might want to call home for instructions."

Bozidar nodded as he ushered the green creature to the dance floor. "She is telling the truth. At this point, all of the clans have seen your actions. And heard your screams."

Susan entered the room, carrying her embroidery and other artifacts. Gary followed with the quilt. They slid along the side, backs pressed to the wall.

"What's happening?" Susan whispered.

"No one is bleeding. That's a good sign," Gary said. "Tell me that's a good sign."

Susan squared her shoulders. "I'm going to take a page from my mother's playbook. Damn the torpedoes and full speed ahead."

She marched across the room. Dancers separated as she approached, closing ranks as she passed. When she reached the dais, she held out the artifacts to Edna. "Agnes wanted us to bring these here, Mother. Show them to your new friends now that they've put their weapons on the floor."

Edna cackled. "Don't you want to ask what I've done?"

Susan scanned the trembling Schtatikians, then Bozidar. "They're still breathing, and Bozidar isn't surrounded by green smoke. No harm, no foul."

"Now you're getting the hang of things." Edna took the sewing box, the embroidered square, and the ring. "Bozidar, where's the table for the artifacts? And where's the food? If the crowd isn't hungry now, they will be soon."

Bozidar removed the ring from the stack. "If I knew how to use this, I am not sure who I would annihilate first, the elders for electing Edna queen, or Edna for bringing me to the edge of despair, or myself."

"Space boy, we're winning," Edna said. "Enjoy yourself."

He shook his head. "My queen, I have spent a

lifetime in service to my clan, and I know the danger of enjoying oneself. Knowing that has helped me survive the forces of history and politics."

"And now you've survived a force of nature," Susan said. "Mother, when we get back to Earth—and for the first time since I landed here I believe we will return intact—we're going to have a long talk. And I intend to do most of the talking."

"Anything you say, my darling daughter."

The red retrieved a buzzing communications device from the pocket of her scarlet tunic. She tapped a whirling icon. The sound of shouting spilled around her. She tapped the icon again. "You spoke truthfully. My commander has instructions for me."

Despite pressing her lips together, a smile spread across Susan's face. "Broadcasting the meeting worked. Perhaps we should leave all three of them to take calls?"

Bozidar nodded. "Follow me." He motioned to attendants as he led the women to a table at the end of the room. Gary threaded his way around the dance line and met them there with the quilt.

"What's the plan?" Gary asked. "If it were up to me, I'd let them dance. The brown guy is already in line, and it looks like the green will join soon."

Bozidar pointed to nearby tables as the attendants returned with ice cream, cupcakes, and Schtatikian delicacies. "I agree. When the scent of *stotlet* permeates the room, the dancing will most likely stop. We can present our proposal then."

Susan stroked the quilt. "No."

She caught Cecily's attention, pointed at Marsel, then strode to the head of the line and blocked its advance. Cecily took the hands of those beside her in line and stopped dancing, as did Scott. Susan nodded and cleared her throat.

"Honored guests." She stopped, hands at her side, and waited for the room to become quiet. "We have a story to tell you, one we want the whole planet to hear." She took the quilt from Gary. "When my mother's grandmother was a child, some of your people visited my planet. It was a tragic journey. Most of your people did not survive, but some returned home because the captain was brave and resourceful. Her name was Pala. She is with you today."

Susan pulled back the edge of the quilt. The air around her shimmered, and the foundation beneath the embroidered patches glowed. She heard a voice whisper *thanks* as the spirit of Agnes as a young girl appeared before her, holding Pala's hand.

Marsel and Asura swooned.

"Hey, I can see them," Edna said.

"Everyone can see them, my queen," Bozidar said. He motioned for the staff to continue setting out food. "Cecily, would you and Scott be so kind as to attend our stricken comrades?" He took the quilt from Susan and whispered, "Will we be hearing from the dead as well as seeing them?"

"I have no idea," Susan said. She smiled at the crowd. "My, um, great-grandmother and your captain

… well, their spirits … have led us, uh, here." She grabbed Edna's hand. "Us. Say, something, Mother."

"I got nothing." Edna patted Susan's arm. "But you're doing great, kiddo. Just give that new-found backbone of yours a minute to settle into place."

"You are so not helpful," Susan said. She motioned to Cecily. "My daughter, my mother, and I are privileged to return your captain to you, both her remains and her spirit."

Cecily scrambled to her feet and made her way to Susan. "Tell them about the ice cream, Mom."

"Good idea," Susan whispered as she put her arm around Cecily. "As we have come to know the people of Schtatik, we have seen similarities in our culture. What you call *stotlet*, we call ice cream. Let us begin a long and beneficial friendship as we share this delicacy in sight of the whole planet."

The red spy walked to the center of the room, each step as deliberate as if she were navigating a broken field salted with mines. "My elders welcome your proposal." She bowed, looking as if she were made of glass and would shatter with any sudden movement. As she straightened, the ghosts of Agnes and Pala floated toward her. They also bowed, a graceful and fluid motion, then vanished. The red spy paled to a delicate pink and collapsed on the floor.

Susan sighed. "So, how about that *stotlet*?"

Marsel propped himself upright while Scott assisted Asura. "When an age of miracles presents itself, the proper response is acceptance. Come, my blue cousin, let us lead the way in this new ritual."

They helped each other to their feet. As Scott moved to attend the red spy, Asura scanned the room. "Dear cousins from other clans, I invite you to join us." She lifted her arms and began to dance toward the red.

Scott lifted the groggy but conscious red to her feet. Asura and Marsel supported her as they danced toward the green. The brown began his own dance, skipping toward the group and dragging blues along with him.

The two groups converged on the green, and the dance line reformed with Asura and Marsel in front, flanking the three spies. Blues and beiges joined ranks behind them, and they inched their way to the food tables doing something that resembled the bunny hop.

Gary beckoned Scott, and they joined Susan, Edna, and Cecily. "We have to tell them about the *machute* research."

Scott nodded. "And the sooner, the better."

"I have an idea," Susan said. She took the silver and ruby ring from the tray of artifacts and slipped it on her finger. *I need you now*, she thought. *I have to show them that we are stronger together.* She felt Agnes' presence. Rubbing the ruby, she smiled at the Schtatikians. "There is one more gift we bring you. There have been exceptional healers among you. Pala was one. Her ability was so strong it survived her death, and found its way back to the universe." She held her hand above her head, displaying the ring. "With a stone from Schtatik and metal from Earth, I have been able to channel Pala's healing power."

She turned to Scott. "This man helped study a way to heal your people from the deadly *machute* plant. The plant has no effect on humans. Quite by accident, we discovered Earth has a similar substance, chenille. Once, we used it as a weapon. There were some on Schtatik who wanted to use it again, against their own people."

Asura gasped. The ice cream she was about to spoon into her mouth fell back in the bowl. She whirled to face Marsel. "Is this true?"

Marsel's eyestalks drooped. "Cousin, my shame is boundless. Members of my clan did this horrible thing. They took the consort of the queen and forced him to labor for them, as humans have no reaction to machute."

"Well, that's a lie," Edna muttered. "Some of us get a sour stomach just looking at the stuff."

"Hush, Mother." Susan knelt before Asura. "What was intended for harm can be turned into good, if we work together." *This would be a good time to appear, Agnes.*

Asura trembled and stared at her bowl. She clutched it to her chest. "Since I was a podling, I have been warned against trusting other clans, to say nothing of off-worlders." Her eyestalks rotated toward the spies, who also clutched their bowls as if they were life preservers. "I came expecting to hear lies. Instead, I saw prophecy come to life and joined a beige in the dance of reconciliation. These came to kill us, and yet I welcomed them. Twice I have trusted and twice have been deceived."

"Not deceived," Susan said. "Life just got in the way. We have a saying for it on Earth, no good deed goes unpunished."

Asura twirled the spoon in her fingers.

Edna fidgeted. "We've got some other sayings. Want to hear my favorite?"

Cecily's eyes widened. "Grandma, be nice."

Edna winked. "I was only going to say my favorite saying is third time's the charm."

"I understand the individual words," Asura said. "The combined meaning eludes me."

"It means give us another chance," Edna said. "Give prophecy another chance. Give the age of miracles another chance."

Asura rocked from one footpad to the other. She hummed to herself as her rocking turned into a two-step. After the second round of her tune, she danced into Marsel. "Forgive me."

Marsel bowed. "If it would bring peace to our planet, you could tread on my footpads every day."

Almost as if the spoon had its own mind, Asura plunged it into the ice cream and shoved it into her mouth. "Present your charm, and I will forgive."

"Splendid," Agnes said as she and Pala reappeared, looking less like spirits and more like a living being.

TWENTY-FOUR

Cecily pointed. "I hear her. Mom, can you hear Agnes?"

"Yes, dear." After she steadied Asura, Susan approached the two spirits. "I believe everyone can hear her now. Do you have any wisdom for us?"

Agnes' spirit morphed from her childhood self to that of an old woman. "You don't get off that easy. There's a lot of hard work ahead of you, all of you."

Pala put a hand on Agnes' arm. "What my companion means to say is that we will answer your questions, but all decisions must be your own."

Asura placed her ice cream on the floor, bowed, and stepped forward. "Blessed be all the gods. Tell us, please, how you are here?"

"There are wonders in the universe waiting to be found," Pala said.

"That's a fancy way of saying we don't have a clue." Agnes stretched her arms. "It feels good but not like I'm really back from the dead. I've got a feeling this is just a stop on the road."

"The road to where?" Susan asked.

"Damned if I know."

Marsel toddled forward. His eyestalks quivered. Even as he bowed, one eye remained focused on Pala. "Prophecy … miracles … wonder." He toppled over.

"Courage, cousin," Asura said as she knelt by his side. She massaged the top of his head. "All is as it should be. All that we have experienced, all that we have suffered, all that we have feared, was necessary to bring us to this moment."

Pala bowed. "You speak with wisdom, blue one. May such clarity always attend you."

Susan beckoned Edna and Cecily to join her. "Agnes, you asked for us all to be here with the quilt. What do you want us to do?"

"You did it. Bringing the quilt to Schtatik was the only way our spirits could be released." Agnes reached toward Bozidar, who gave her the quilt. "Now we can go on to wherever it is we're supposed to go."

"And where is that?" Bozidar asked.

"It is an adventure, that is all we know," Pala said. "The universe has been whispering to me since the quilt was made."

"Took me a while to hear that part," Agnes said. "Pala kept telling me something wonderful was going to happen. Do you have any idea how long eternity seems when you're waiting for a new beginning?"

"But what are *we* supposed to do?" Susan asked. "The whole planet is waiting for an answer."

"Get off your butts and solve your problems," Agnes said. "That's all we're ever supposed to do. Now, if you'll excuse me, I have a universe to explore."

"Will we ever see you again?" Cecily asked.

"If you travel far enough." Pala bowed, and she and Agnes faded away.

"As revelations go, that was disappointing," Scott said.

"Ya think?" Edna crossed her arms and scowled. "Does that mean I'm still queen?"

"I believe so," Bozidar said. "Would you like to give an order? It will probably be ignored, but you are entitled to make the attempt."

"I think I liked it better when you were afraid of me," Edna said. "However, I do have a suggestion. Agnes and Pala worked together, and look what they got in return."

"One encased between layers of embroidered velvet and the other considered a lunatic?" Cecily asked.

"The chance to explore space." Susan smiled. "Even if they did have to die first."

"These days, dying isn't a prerequisite," Edna said. "We made it off Earth. Okay, on an alien spaceship, but still."

"Your planet does not possess the technology to travel beyond your own moon," Bozidar said. "Travel on a Schtakian ship was your only option."

"That's true." Edna pointed to Susan's ring. "But we do have something of value. Silver. Look at what Susan can do with your ruby set in our metal. Even your own people can't heal with the stone. What if we could negotiate a trade deal? Our silver for your ships?"

Scott raised his finger. "We can also trade our immunity to your *machute* plant. A joint research project would greatly benefit your people."

Asura picked up her ice cream and joined the conversation. "Cooperation between the clans was considered improbable until today. If beiges, blues, reds, greens, and browns can dance together, eat *stotlet* together, why should it be impossible for us to work with humans?"

Scott stroked his chin as he studied Edna. He beckoned Bozidar and Gary to follow him a short distance from the crowd. "Gentlemen," he said in a low, soft voice. "I adore Edna, but I do understand she is an acquired taste. So is Marsel. Do you think we could convince the clans to embark on joint exploration missions with Earth if they saw it as an opportunity to employ some of their more interesting citizens?"

Gary dropped his gaze to the floor. When he raised his head, his expression was neutral, but his eyes were sparkling. "Good heavens, man, you aren't suggesting we send Edna out as a representative of Earth? There's no counting the number of wars she could start just by saying hello."

Bozidar shuddered. "The thought alarms me as well. However, there is some merit in the suggestion. Marsel has proven to be an asset after all. I, for one, would relish the thought of him continuing his career in a far-off galaxy. With a sufficiently large crew, his influence could be mitigated, or they will leave him on a convenient planet somewhere. Either solution is acceptable." He retrieved his communication device and tapped a series of icons. "I have presented your suggestion to the beige council of elders and also to my counterpart in the blue clan. If they agree it has merit, they may use it to hold a meeting of all the clans."

"When was the last time that happened?" Scott asked.

"Not in living memory."

Cecily joined the men, carrying ice cream. As she distributed the bowls, she said, "What are you plotting now?"

"The fate of those who have made my life insufferable," Bozidar said.

"Oh, please," Cecily said, rolling her eyes. "You were sent to Earth to kill my mother, and you kidnapped me. If anyone's fate is up for debate, it's yours. And anyway, it looks like we're winning."

They scanned the room, watching one creature after another choose a flavor of *stotlet*, bow before

Edna and Susan with reverence, then attack the food like starving rats. Some returned for another bowl and added a cupcake or piece of chocolate to their plates.

Susan started at the sound of communications devices chirping. She looked around until she found Bozidar. She beckoned to him. "Will this be the elders from the other clans?" she asked as he joined her.

Bozidar shrugged and reached for his own device as it buzzed with an imperious tone. He read the message and smiled. "We have permission to proceed."

"Proceed with what?" Susan asked.

"With everything. Peace with the blues, cooperation with the other clans, an alliance with humans, research, and a mission to the stars."

Asura squeaked, leaped three times, and began a new dance. "The gods are kind and generous. They have shown the leaders of the blue clan how glorious the future will be." She twirled around Marsel. "You and I will not only see prophecy fulfilled, we will enable prophecy to be fulfilled."

Bozidar whispered to Susan, "I believe the other clans will cooperate."

Susan shook her head. "I don't want to jinx anything, but why is everything working out so well?"

"I took the liberty of suggesting any joint ventures with your people would be much more successful if they included clan members of the caliber of Marsel and Asura." Bozidar smiled at the dancing couple. "Perhaps your leaders will also see the wisdom of an occupation for their excess population of lunatics."

* * *

Susan watched the blues and beiges dance. She sat cross-legged on the dais, her hand-sewing kit and embroidered squares spread in front of her. Her sketchbook lay open to a page of trees and vines she had drawn while still in the pink castle. A plate of cupcakes and chocolates sat next to a bowl that still retained a few drops of melted *stotlet*.

The green spy slipped out of line and approached the dais. He bowed to Susan. "Honored one, what will you say to the combined council of elders about the actions of my co-conspirators? And me?"

Susan tilted her head. "There isn't much I need to say. The entire planet saw you enter the room with your weapons aimed at Bozidar. Gary and I must have missed you by seconds."

The green trembled. "No one was harmed. We are cooperating."

"Yes." Susan regarded the creature. "I won't ask for any punishment if that's what you want to know. Nor will my mother, and she speaks for the beige clan."

"My own people may not be so forgiving. My red and brown cousins also fear the wrath of their clans."

"What can I do about that?" Susan leaned forward. "I'm going to have my hands full with the repercussions back on Earth."

"Take us with you." He crept to the edge of the dais, eyestalks-to-nose with Susan. "We would be loyal, and quiet, and we do not eat much." One eyestalk wandered in the direction of the empty bowl.

Susan swallowed a chuckle. "Quiet is good. I'm not sure how much influence I have on crew selection, but I'll put in a good word for the three of you. Now, get more *stotlet* if you like, and come back to sit with me. You can help me with my project." She held up her hand. "Wait. Before you go, please tell me your name."

"Firan." He spun about on the edge of one footpad and cantered to the tables.

"Are you making new friends, Mom?" Cecily picked up an embroidered square.

"I hope so. It would be nice not to worry about someone shooting at us for once." She retrieved a pencil and flipped to a blank page in her sketchbook. "He asked me to take him and his co-conspirators with us."

"Back to Earth?"

Susan smiled. "I suspect he doesn't care where we go as long as he doesn't have to stay here."

"Do you think their clans will abandon them?" Cecily asked. She snatched a chocolate. "You're not going to eat all of these, right?"

"Go ahead. There are more. And yes, I do think the poor little guys will be made scapegoats." She closed her sketchbook. "I told Firan he could help me with my project. Maybe they all could. Marsel said embroidery is their poetry. I could ask all the clans to give me a representative to create an embroidered record of the planet's flora and fauna. It could be a new legend for them and a source book for me."

"Mom, they came to kill us."

"Well, so did Bozidar," Susan said, leaning forward and observing the celebration. "That worked out okay. This will too."

"Is that another message from Agnes, or your own intuition?"

"My own." Susan turned to Cecily, a sly grin playing on her lips. "You got a problem with that?"

* * *

Susan sat on the dais surrounded by determined Schtatikians. The creatures clutched squares of fabric and needles threaded with multicolored woven strands resembling fine silk ribbon. They stitched in a rhythm that made their fingers seem like tiny dancers swirling across a stage.

Bozidar wandered between them, observing a tree outlined in pink on a blue square, flowers in shades of yellow on a green square, lines of Schtatikian poetry built one stitch upon another. He nodded, smiled, patted a shoulder.

"They're doing amazing work," Cecily said as she stepped carefully around the creatures to join Bozidar. "Mom will have her project finished in no time."

"This is only the beginning," Bozidar said. "There will be many more joint embroidered projects. Remember, for us these stitches are poetry. They tell our stories the way your Vikings would recite the sagas. As long as we share a destiny, we will have tapestries and quilts to make together."

"So you think we do have a destiny?"

Bozidar cocked his head toward Marsel. "He thinks we do. He always thought we did. Once he latched onto the prophecies, he never wavered. Who am I to stand in the way of such faith?"

Susan rolled to her feet and sidestepped her way to Cecily. "What are you two plotting now?"

"The time for plots is over," Bozidar said. "Now that the clans have agreed to send an expedition to Earth, all the leaders are anxious to see how many of their problem citizens they can send along."

Cecily crossed her arms. "I still have doubts about bringing the spies with us. How do you know you can trust them, Mom?"

Bozidar held up his hand. "If I may answer for you. We can trust them because they are grateful. Firan may have asked to go to Earth to escape punishment, but traditionalists from all the clans were impressed that a human asked for representatives from the brown, red, and green clans, the ones that once gave our planet its rulers. The propaganda value is immense. Firan and his co-conspirators now have titles and position. Their families will benefit, not least because their embarrassing relatives will be far away for a significant amount of time."

"Do the clans understand that no one on Earth will understand the symbolism?" Cecily asked. "Even if they did, they wouldn't care. They'll be too busy panicking about the spaceship. We'll be lucky if they don't shoot us out of the sky before we land."

Bozidar's eyebrows shot up. "Surely we will not be landing in public view? I assumed we would make a discreet overture to a few well-placed humans. We should not be in a hurry to reveal ourselves."

Susan shook her head. "I disagree. I think the best approach is shock and awe." She took Bozidar by the elbow and led him toward the buffet tables. "Humans are unpredictable, but give them enough time and they'll usually leap to the wrong conclusions, the wrong course of action, and absolutely the wrong alliances. No, we land in broad daylight for the whole world to see."

"Yes, because that works so well in science fiction movies." Edna joined them, and swallowed the last bit of a cupcake. "Space boy, what do you suggest?"

Bozidar crossed his arms. "Is this a trick? You never ask for my opinion."

"No trick." Edna licked frosting from her fingers. "By some miracle, we're getting off this planet in one piece. I want to arrive home in one piece too."

He nodded. "We need to approach one, at most two people. Someone trustworthy. A person with influence would be useful, but more important is an individual without a stake in the outcome. Someone with nothing to gain except perhaps the honor of having served humanity."

Susan paced by the table, snatching a chocolate each time she passed the tray. "I don't know anyone who fits that description." She gobbled the candies in one bite.

"Of course you do," Edna said. "All of your quilting buddies are trustworthy. They just don't have any influence."

Susan stopped in mid-stride. She pointed at Edna. "You know someone with influence. Betty Busby."

"In the art quilt world, maybe," Edna said. "That's not going to get us an interview on the morning news, not even on the local station."

"There may be a way," Susan said. She nodded, almost to herself.

"Can I help?" Cecily said as she joined the group.

Susan did not answer immediately. Then she shook her head as if to clear cobwebs from her brain. "Yes. We'll need everyone helping. Let me work out a few more details." She took the tray of chocolates and left the room.

Cecily followed Susan, but Edna stopped her. "I've seen that look before," Edna said. "The first time was when she set her sights on your father, and later when she got the idea to open a quilt shop."

"But those were good decisions, Grandma."

"Exactly. If we don't distract her, she'll come up with an idea to get us home safe." Edna leaned closer. "And I bet it will be a doozy."

* * *

The celebration echoed down the hall. Susan took no notice. She ate one chocolate then another without noticing the flavor. She frowned and leaned against the wall.

The air before her shimmered. *Don't eat the whole tray without tasting them* she heard in her head. *Marsel will be so disappointed.*

"Agnes?"

"Pala." The ghost of the Schtatikian captain appeared. "I know how hard he worked to recreate your favorites."

"He did work hard, didn't he?" Susan chose another chocolate and savored it. "Where is Agnes? I thought you two were off to see the universe now that your spirits are free."

"Soon. I wanted you to have one last gift. Going back to your planet will take courage, patience, and resilience. There will be many competing voices giving you advice, and expecting you to follow it. I cannot help you choose, but I can help you look inside yourself when you question your path. Where is the ring?"

Susan held out her hand. Both the ruby stone

and Pala began to glow. Pala reached out and touched the stone.

"It's warm," Susan said. "Both the stone and the setting. It feels the same as when I used it to heal."

Pala nodded. "You and the ring become more powerful each time you use it for good. The healers among my people bond with the stones. They respond to our energy and help us to focus and direct that power."

"Is that how you were able to transform your people?"

"And communicate with Agnes. Now I share that gift with you. In turn, you will share it with your daughter. One day she will have a ring of her own." Pala's image faded.

"How?" Susan clutched the tray to her chest as she scanned the hall for shreds of Pala's spirit. "Is there another ring in Agnes' jewelry collection?"

Bring stones back with you. Marsel will know which ones.

The words echoed in Susan's head, bringing a sense of peace. She loosened her grip on the tray, stretching and flexing her fingers. She popped another chocolate into her mouth, letting the flavors explode on her tongue as the candy melted.

"Okay," she said aloud, "time to get to work." She looked at the tray's rapidly dwindling collection. "But first, I'm going to need more chocolate."

TWENTY-FIVE

Susan folded her hands at her stomach. "I know my plan is sketchy at the moment, but I believe it will succeed." She paced in front of the small, silent group in her quarters. "Humans don't know they aren't alone in the universe. I can't predict how they will react when we show up. There's bound to be some risk."

Salia raised her hand. "That is an understatement. When my companions and I were stranded on your planet, we were seen at various times. The reaction usually involved screams. Occasionally throwing things at us. We learned that if they did not run, we should."

Bozidar, Scott, Gary, and Cecily voiced objections, talking over each other. Marsel and Salia quivered closer together on the couch.

Edna finished eating her sandwich, took a sip of

a lemonade-like drink, put her fingers in her mouth and whistled at freight-train decibel levels. "So it's not perfect. Get over it." She nibbled on a cookie. "You don't have a better idea or you would have said so. And, by the way, who actually stopped the war? Who's been coached by the ghosts of ancestors past? Who managed to organize and conduct a wedding without my being there and lived to tell the tale?" She pointed at Susan. "That's the person, in case you didn't pick up on the clues."

Bozidar pressed his lips together, and a wisp of green smoke slid from his ears.

Cecily rolled her eyes and sighed. "Of course, you're right, Grandma, but even Mom admits there are gaping holes. We're supposed to alert every quilter we know to get the word out through social media that we're coming back with creatures who look like big, rubbery pillows with arms and legs and something resembling a head. But it's okay because we're all going to be great friends. How is that going to stop every government on Earth from launching missiles at us?"

"What if we don't bring the big ship out right away?" Gary asked. He motioned to Bozidar. "You guys shielded the landing pod. No one could see it until it was in our back yard. Why don't we come down in a pod and leave the ship parked behind the moon?"

Bozidar tapped the table. "Technically, there are no issues. Strategically, how do we establish our presence with such a small delegation? The landing pods only hold a few people."

"Flash mob," Cecily said. "We're going to be in touch with friends anyway, right? So we can coordinate a landing and have people there, waiting."

"Where would we land?" Scott asked.

"It has to be San Francisco." Edna dusted crumbs from her hands. "Someplace open. The Presidio?"

"Closer downtown. We need a bigger audience," Cecily said.

"How about United Nations Plaza? Well, near there. Maybe in front of the Asian Art Museum?"

"Wouldn't it be safer to land in front of City Hall?" Gary asked. "It's a bigger space."

"With more people." Susan tugged on a strand of hair. "Unless we de-cloaked before we landed. Give everyone a chance to move out of the way. Could we do that, Bozidar?"

"Yes." He tilted his head and stared at the ceiling. "Yes, we could do that. We could also send down three or four landing pods. Flying in close formation is a specialty of the blues."

"More people and a better show. I like it." Edna smiled.

"The authorities will descend on us like wolves on caribou," Scott said. "Just because they can't send out missiles doesn't mean there won't be a lot of firepower."

"I know," Susan said. "I'm open to suggestions."

No one spoke. One after another, every pair of eyes focused on some fascinating piece of lint on the floor.

Susan clapped her hands. "Then we're agreed. We're going to mobilize people power, hope for the best, and adjust our actions based on new information. Let's go break the good news to the clans."

* * *

The council of clan elders filed out of the meeting room. They were quiet for the most part, confining themselves to the occasional squeak or whistle.

"That could have gone better." Susan waved away the remaining traces of green smoke.

"On the contrary," Bozidar said. "While the immediate response was not encouraging, they did agree to our plan."

"The immediate response was a roomful of green smoke," Edna said. "My lungs will look like a leafy forest for months."

"Marsel can fix that," Cecily said. "Bozidar is right. The elders came around. They even suggested ways we can get a message to Earth before we leave Schtatik. That will give us at least an extra week."

"Then let's use the time efficiently." Susan picked up a pad of paper and a pen. She ran down the list on the pad and checked off an item. "Cecily, I'll need you to make a video with Schtatikians' embroidering squares. I also want a record of all the squares we've finished. Maybe add some of the plants we used for inspiration."

"Mom, I'm the filmmaker in the family. Let me handle this." Cecily tugged on Bozidar's sleeve. "I could use your help putting a technical team together."

"Bozidar already has a lot on his to-do list." Susan glanced up from her list. "You'll probably need an assistant. Maybe two. Scott, you'll need to go over the flash mob idea from every angle. The last thing we want is someone getting hurt, or killed."

"It may happen anyway," Scott said.

Susan bit her lower lip. "We can't allow that. Figure something out."

"Honey, be fair," Gary said. "Even in the movies, where everything is under control, actors and stunt men get hurt." He put his arm around Susan. "But that does give me an idea. I know some people who may know someone on the city council. We could tip them off that something is going to happen. Maybe that will be enough to keep the police from panicking."

Scott nodded. "I should have thought of that. There are people on the San Francisco police force who will listen to me. Gary, let's discuss how to approach our contacts."

Edna cackled. "I can see the press release now. Aliens coming to a park near you. Be the first to greet visitors from another world. Tee shirts and commemorative tote bags available at bargain prices."

"Why not?" Susan made a note on her pad. "Tee shirts would be perfect. We could send a picture of you and Marsel to Louise at the quilt shop, have her print up enough for everyone who can be there when we land. When you come out of the landing pod, everyone will recognize you. They'll think it's some kind of publicity stunt."

"What do you mean when I come out of the landing pod?" Edna narrowed her eyes at Susan. "You want me to go first?"

Susan crossed her arms but smiled. "Like you were going to let someone else introduce the planet to its first aliens from outer space?"

"She's got a point, Grandma," Cecily said. "You do love being the center of attention."

"Oh, I don't have a problem being the lead story on the evening news," Edna said. "I just wanted someone else to suggest it."

"You're welcome," Susan said, reviewing her list. "Now get busy. Videos, contacts, merchandise. We need action plans for everything by tomorrow morning."

Cecily patted Bozidar's hand and nodded toward the door. "Come with us, Grandma," she said in a low voice as she pushed away from the conference table.

"I think you're right," Edna said. "Time for all of us to vamoose."

Susan leaned one elbow on the table, resting her chin in her upturned palm as she made notes. She glanced up briefly when Gary said he and Scott were leaving too, but did not speak. When the room was silent and empty, she ran her finger down her list. She paused at the last task: *tell Eleanor and Olivia we're coming home.*

She closed her eyes, remembering the way her youngest daughters smiled on that last day together. She shook her head and clamped her lips together. "I don't have time to cry." *And I haven't had time to think of you. That will change when I get home.*

Her eyes sprang open as Marsel toddled through the door. "Just who I need," she said. "I want to bring something home for Olivia and Eleanor. What do your young females play with?"

"These females are your pets?" Marsel asked.

"No." Susan jerked back from the table, her chair tilting at a dangerous angle. "They're my daughters."

"You have more?" Marsel's voice squeaked.

"Yes, two more lovely little girls." She settled her chair on all its legs. "You'll meet them when we get to Earth."

Marsel rocked from footpad to footpad. "There is another prophecy. A spreading of the bloodlines like roots from the *havila* trees." He continued rocking.

"Very nice. What does it mean?"

"I do not remember. I must go to the library." He scampered out the door.

"Don't forget a present," Susan called after him. "He didn't hear me." She made a note to find gifts for the girls.

The next morning at breakfast, Cecily showed Susan the storyboards she had drawn for a video about Schtatik. "I thought I would open with the castle where Grandma was held. It's a beautiful scene. I'll segue into a montage of flowers and trees, then your embroidered squares. You can do a voice-over describing the poetry these stitches represent. We'll end with Agnes' crazy quilt, tying the two cultures together."

"That sounds wonderful," Susan said between bites of a thick, creamy dish that resembled a savory egg custard. "Do you have all the equipment you need?"

"Bozidar arranged everything. I met the crew last night. They're very excited about the project." Cecily squinted. "Do you hear shrieking?"

Marsel cantered into the room, knocking into walls and dropping small items from the three baskets he held. Two other beige attendants followed with baskets of their own. Their squeaks were a cross between a banshee wail and a fire alarm, and increased in intensity each time they retrieved something Marsel had dropped.

"I found the most splendid prophecy of all." Marsel skittered to an unsteady stop next to the table. "Your bloodline, the descendants of She Who Found Us, will bring joy to the universe for all eternity." His legs folded beneath him, the baskets fell around him, and the last of their contents bounced about on the floor.

The attendants stopped their caterwauling and came to a complete stop. They dropped to the floor, scooting their baskets beside them as they scooped up scrolls, small books, balls of yarn, scraps of fabric, and anything else they could reach.

Susan pushed her egg custard to a safe spot. "Marsel, please don't dash about. You know how it upsets the guards."

Cecily shook her head and knelt by Marsel. "Don't talk, breathe." She picked up a small feathered block that squished when she pressed on the sides. "And when you do catch your breath, tell me what this thing is."

Marsel rolled onto his back. His legs waved in the air, footpads to the ceiling. "There, that is better." As his legs dropped to the floor, his eyestalks craned toward Cecily. "That is a favorite play device from my childhood. The feathers purr when they are stroked."

"Put the toy down, Cecily," Susan said. "Tell me about this new prophecy, Marsel."

Rolling like a pill bug, Marsel attained a vertical posture. "Prophecy may not be the correct description. Aging relatives told me a story, which they said had been told to them and they wished to pass down to me. My guardians were not pleased, but I treasured the tale."

"Sounds like Grandma and Agnes," Cecily said.

She ran her fingertips along the edges of the feathered block. "What do you know? It does purr."

Susan rubbed her temples. "One peaceful morning, that's all I ask."

Cecily passed the toy to Marsel. "My sisters would love this. Did you plan to give it to them?"

Marsel held the block with both hands. "At the request of your mother. It will be my honor to present it to them."

"The prophecy." Susan continued rubbing her temples.

"I found a poem that resembles the story I remember," Marsel said. "Three podlings traveled to distant stars. They found beauty, terror, and wisdom. Eventually, they reached a place so cold and lonely that the universe itself warned them to go no further. They gathered all they had collected, all they had seen, all they had learned, and returned to their birthplace. They shared the gifts of time and space, creating the world we know. The poem ends with a promise that such a time will come again." He rolled up on his toes. "Do you not see? Your offspring will bring joy to two worlds."

Cecily said, "Eleanor and Olivia are much younger than I am. They aren't going into space anytime soon." She leaned forward. "Marsel, you don't need to find a reason in your scrolls for everything we do. Life doesn't need to be validated by prophecy. Just live it."

Susan felt the air grow warm and sweet as if she

had opened the oven to remove a tray of perfectly baked brownies. She pictured her family together. Every cell in her being told her the dream would become a reality, and then life would change again. Her lungs tightened, her heart raced, and her breathing and pulse relaxed. "You're right, Daughter. That's all we can do. Just live. And when life throws us a curve, we live through that." She picked up her bowl and finished the last of her custard. "Heaven knows I've tried to plan for every contingency. Doesn't always work. Time to take a page from your grandmother's book. Let's count on bluff, or whatever it is she does. It works for her, and it will work for us."

"Mom?"

Susan stood. "I've delayed our return to make sure I've thought of everything. But I can't think of everything. No one can." She moved to the door in three strides. "Come along. It's time we got home. Your sisters are waiting for us."

* * *

Susan held her arms tight against her sides as she passed anti-grav sleds loaded with supplies for the trip to Earth. She sidestepped the control stations and tiptoed over power cables as she kept to a specific path from the entrance of the loading bay to the shuttles. She avoided eye contact with anything resembling a computer panel.

"Splendid, you have arrived." Bozidar tapped a command on his black box. He gave instructions to the workers around him and watched them set about their tasks before turning his attention to Susan. "I do not hear a collision alarm. This is a good sign."

"I may be trusting that the universe wants us to get home, but that doesn't mean I trust these machines," she said. "If I don't touch anything, maybe they won't malfunction."

"We can always hope." He guided her to a quiet corner of the staging area. "One does wonder, however, why you are here at all."

"A form of therapy. If the shuttles get loaded properly, and take off properly, I can convince myself that the rest of the trip will also go properly."

Bozidar blinked twice. He cleared his throat. "My research suggests your behavior indicates the onset of madness."

"Oh, we are so past onset. Before this is over, I'm going to be crazy as a loon." She rubbed her temples. "Don't worry. It will all work out."

He blinked again and nodded. "The reference to birds is mystifying, but I have been instructed to agree with you. I do not understand how my assent will guarantee the success of the mission, but I will follow orders."

"Good man." Susan scanned the cavernous bay. "Is this the last supply run?"

"Yes. Scott is already on board. Cecily and Gary are finishing the video and will join us in the waiting area for our shuttle. Edna is in the dining hall."

"Where is Marsel?" Susan asked.

"In his library."

"His library? I thought that was already on the ship."

Bozidar inhaled. "His private collection of scrolls is in his quarters. I was speaking of the palace library."

"I don't understand." Susan's hands fluttered as if they wanted to carry on the conversation by themselves. She clamped her arms by her sides. "We told him we didn't need more prophecy."

"He disagreed. He said there could never be enough prophecy. In the last two days he has ransacked every shelf of the library. The attendants are staging a hunger strike until he leaves."

Susan closed her eyes. "Lucky for them we take off today."

Bozidar leaned toward her and whispered. "Would it be too much to ask to leave Marsel behind?"

"And let the librarians starve to death? That would be cruel."

He dropped his gaze to his shoes. "Yes, I suppose it would be. Although, the loss could be considered acceptable." He shook his head. "No, you are correct."

Susan linked her arm through his. "We'll go together. It may take the both of us to carry the scrolls he wants."

He sighed and led her from the hanger along the

emptiest wall. They skirted the last of the machinery and exited to a quiet corridor. "I will not be sorry to leave, even with Marsel. The healers say they are no closer to finding a way to restore my true form than when I arrived."

"You mean you'll have to look human for the rest of your life?" Susan released his arm. "That doesn't seem fair."

"Fairness appears to be a concept which the gods redefine on a regular basis." He examined the screen of his communication device. "We will be cleared for departure on schedule. Edna is on her way to the waiting area. It only remains for us to bring Marsel, willing or not, as he chooses."

"Then we'd best get a move on." *And hope that today the gods define fairness in our favor.*

TWENTY-SIX

Susan replayed Salia's farewell on the viewscreen in her quarters. "I vowed to protect you and your husband. While my duties on the council of elders prevent me from returning to your home planet, I will not forget my promise. My quest now is to strengthen the bonds between our worlds, to wipe away even the memory of the evil I planned when I joined the taupe expedition to invade Earth."

Susan flicked the screen, and the vista of space danced in front of her. Starlight blended into streams of colors, some swirling as they hit the bow wave from the *Cold Stream* and its stitch runner engines. She tapped the screen again, and a star map appeared, complete with an arrow showing where Susan was in the universe and how long until she arrived at the far side of Earth's moon.

"Oh, what I would have paid for an app like this when Cecily was young." Susan heard the door opening and footsteps.

"It's called GPS tracking, Mom," Cecily said, joining Susan at the console. "The girls probably have it on their phones."

"That might explain why they rarely ask if we're there yet."

Cecily snorted. "You don't throw them in the car and take off as much as you did when I was their age."

Susan held up her hand. "We're approaching old argument territory. If it makes you feel better, the next time I plan a boring road trip I'll take Olivia and Eleanor and let you zip around in outer space. Do you have a progress report for me?"

"We're as ready as we'll ever be," Cecily said. "Quilt ladies really know how to network. The squares you and the Schtatikians embroidered have been featured on more social media than I knew existed. All the local guilds came up with quilt challenges on what first contact with an alien species would be like. Studio Art Quilt Associates picked it up as well and ran with it. I have a hundred firm commitments for the landing with another eighty maybes."

Susan blinked. "You're telling me there could be almost two hundred people waiting for us at Civic Center?"

"Yeah. Why? Were you expecting more?"

"I thought we'd be lucky to get thirty." Susan turned the monitor off. "This is terrifying."

"That's usually the definition of an adventure," Edna said as she entered. "Any breakfast left?"

Susan waved at bowls on the table. "Help yourself."

"You should have a hearty breakfast too," Edna said. "Big day coming up."

Susan covered her face with her hands. "Don't remind me. Why did we think this was a good idea?"

Edna cackled as she drew close to Cecily. "She was like this the night you were born. Your father didn't know whether to laugh or insist the doctor drug her."

Cecily patted Susan's arm. "Mom, relax. This is going to be brilliant. Your name will go down in history." As Susan groaned, Cecily added, "In a good way, Mom, in a good way."

A bell sounded, and Bozidar's voice came through the speaker. "All those assigned to the landing, please report to the appropriate pod."

"That means us," Edna said. "Time to make a little history."

* * *

"Fog," Bozidar said, and a relieved smile flashed across his face.

"What about fog?" Susan asked. She carried the crazy quilt and her sewing box. The noise in the docking bay made her head ache.

"That is better than darkness. Your people take pains to see in the dark. They give up in the fog. Our landing should attract little attention."

"Even if the rest of the city is socked in, Civic Center will be clear. And crowded with people we invited to welcome us home."

Bozidar frowned, but his gaze followed Marsel trotting around a cart piled with small cases. "Marsel, you had strict instructions not to bring anything. The humans are bringing all the artifacts necessary."

Marsel grasped the smallest case and clutched it. "These are gifts. Susan herself gave me the idea." His eyestalks quivered, and he rocked on his footpads.

Bozidar glared at Susan. "Have we not discussed many times the danger of giving Marsel ideas?"

"I swear, I didn't say a thing." She bit her lower lip. "No, I take that back. I asked him what Schtatikian children play with. For my younger daughters. He brought me a little cube. With feathers. It purrs when you pet it."

"I am familiar with the playthings of a podling." He shook his head. "At this moment, our options are you persuading Marsel to leave his gifts behind or me killing him."

"I'll talk to him." Susan smoothed her tunic, straightened her posture and headed for Marsel.

"You are bringing gifts for your family. Should we not bring gifts for those we hope to add to our family?" Marsel opened the case, revealing a jumble of bright colors and shiny surfaces. "Will these not appeal to your friends? We need their goodwill and influence, so your people will accept us."

Susan shut the lid and placed the case on the cart. "You are kind and wise, Marsel, but the gifts should come later. I'll have them put in a safe place until they're needed. Do you know which landing pod you'll be in? We're leaving any minute now."

Marsel bowed and scampered away. Susan beckoned to a work crew and told them to take the cases away. Edna approached as they rolled the cart out of the docking bay.

"Bozidar tells me San Francisco is socked in," Edna said. "The fog is going to ruin everything."

Susan closed her eyes. "Mother, with their technology they could land in a blizzard without blinking an eye. And as I told him, Civic Center is in a fog-free zone."

"Who's worried about a landing? It's the light, child. We're going to be all over the news, and the video is going to be dreary beyond belief. We'll look awful." Edna cocked her head, one eyebrow raised and a sly twinkle in her eyes.

Susan stared at her mother. She inhaled. "Mother." A smile flickered on her lips, and she giggled. The giggle turned into a snort, then a laugh that filled the entire bay.

Edna hooked her arm through Susan's. "Good, you're laughing. Now, how about we get on the ship?"

Cecily waited for them in the staging area. She held Marsel's hand. He trembled. Puffs of smoke in various colors spurted from his ears and drifted around his head and torso making him appear to be crying a rainbow.

"Marsel, the gifts must stay here for now," Susan said. "Please don't make a fuss."

Cecily leaned toward Susan and whispered, "Bozidar yelled at him."

"Everyone yells at him. What makes this time different?" Edna said.

"I have been banished," Marsel said between hiccups.

Cecily patted him between his eyestalks. "It will all work out. Trust me." She dropped her voice again. "Bozidar ordered him off the landing pod. Something about contraband. I was standing right there, and Marsel looked so sad."

"So you said you'd be responsible for him," Edna said. "And he's coming with us."

"Sort of. Yeah, exactly that." Cecily pulled Marsel closer to her as if he were a stray puppy. "He'd be crushed if we left him behind. Besides, I think it would be cool to have him in the video. I've got an idea about framing some shots over Grandma's shoulder."

Edna pouted. "I thought I was the star."

"I'm certain Cecily plans lots of close-ups for you, Mother." Susan crossed her arms and narrowed her eyes at Marsel. "Young ... beige one, we had an agreement. Bozidar had every right to be angry."

"I know." Marsel uttered a series of clicks and buzzes.

"That's what they sound like when they're crying," Cecily said.

Susan inhaled. A rough and growly noise rattled around in her throat.

"And that's what Mom sounds like when she's deciding whether to smack you or hug you," Cecily said to Marsel.

Edna grabbed Susan's arm and Marsel's hand. As she dragged them both to the stairway, she said, "Enough, already. Cecily, you're in charge of critter control. Marsel, don't do anything unless Cecily says it's okay." She released them both and climbed two steps toward the hatch. She turned around on the stair. "This is our moment of triumph. We are going to have fun. That's an order."

Susan watched Edna trudging up the stairs. "You heard the queen. Everyone get in, sit down, shut up, and hang on."

* * *

"Hatches locked. Cargo secured. Crew strapped in. Ready for launch." The pilot's voice sounded as cold and metallic as the interior of the landing pod.

Susan adjusted her safety harness as the pilot waited for permission to proceed. "This pod is much different than the one we used when we came here."

Cecily fiddled with her camera. "Uh-huh. *Cold*

Fire is a warship. We get a lot more bells and whistles."

"It's still just a glorified tin can," Edna snarled. "I don't like these straps. I feel like I'm in an onion bag."

"Would you prefer Marsel on the loose?" Cecily panned from Susan to Edna. As she waited for Edna to finish making faces, she shifted in her seat to get a clear shot of Marsel.

He wiggled in his straps, getting a hand tangled. One eyestalk swooped down to investigate and was also caught on the webbing.

"Do I have time to free him?" Susan asked the pilot.

"If you are quick. The other two pods will depart before us." She chirped into her headset. "Your spouse requests the pleasure of speaking with you. Should I put him through on the main viewscreen?"

"Yes, please," Susan said as she slipped from her seat and untangled Marsel. "Now sit still. I won't be able to help you again until we land." She glanced over her shoulder at the viewscreen when she heard Gary's voice.

"We're first in the queue, honey. Everything is fine. Well, Bozidar is calm, so I'm guessing everything is fine. Oh, Bozidar told me the critters are wearing translator patches so we'll be able to communicate with them on Earth. They're the size of a small bandage. The Schtatikian scientists were thrilled to get a chance to test their new invention."

"Good, great. I didn't even think about the communication problems," Susan said as she adjusted her safety harness. "I guess the universe does provide. Anyway, aside from Marsel unleashing his inner toddler, we're good to go here. See you in a bit."

Gary smiled and the screen went blank. The pilot said, "There is a request from the consort." She tapped the console, and the screen glowed a light blue. Scott's face appeared. He did not smile, but his voice was cheerful.

"Hello, everyone. Resting comfortably, are we?"

"Who's this we, peasant?" Edna cackled.

"Is that any way to talk to the queen's consort?"

"It is when you're the queen." Edna blew a kiss to the screen. "I'm looking forward to a blue sky again."

"No such luck, my love," Scott said. "The fog is so thick they're talking about visibility in inches. Civic Center is in the sunnier part of the city, but it will still be cold and gray." He winked, and again the screen went blank.

"Prepare for departure." The pilot pushed glowing icons on the control panel.

Susan closed her eyes. "Don't film me now, Cecily."

"Of course I will, Mom. Every award-winning film has a snoring sequence."

"Hush." Susan opened one eye. "Just for that, you're in charge of keeping Marsel quiet during the trip." She settled back in her seat and concentrated on deep breathing.

The pod engines hummed, and the craft lifted.

Susan felt herself floating straight up. She inhaled and felt herself tilting a few degrees. She fought a growing sense of dread.

What are you afraid of? she heard in her head.

She opened her eyes. Agnes appeared before her, looking as she did in family portraits taken when Edna was a child. "Right now, I'm afraid of everything." She hoped she was speaking only to Agnes.

"Well, that's probably healthy. You are taking a big step." Agnes leaped across the pod. "So am I, stepping into the great unknown. And yet, here I am."

"To help me?"

"To show you you're never entirely alone. Your friends are heading for San Francisco. Your family is around you, human and Schtatikian. It's going to work out just fine, in the end."

"Yes, well, it's getting to the end that has me worried." Susan glanced around the pod, which appeared to be frozen in time. "A lot of people can get hurt very quickly."

"If they do, help them." Agnes pointed to the ruby ring on Susan's hand. "That's why you wore the ring, isn't it?"

Susan gazed at her hand, wondering when she put on the ring. Cecily's voice tickled inside her ear.

"Mom? Did you hear me? We're about to land." Cecily gave Susan's shoulder a tiny poke. "Are you asleep?"

"No." Susan rubbed her eyes. "Where's my sewing box?"

Cecily picked it up. "Right here. It fell off your lap."

"She thought you were asleep," Edna said. "I said you weren't twitching enough. Or snoring."

Susan rummaged through the box. Maybe I was dreaming, she thought, as she slipped the ring on her finger. Doesn't matter. Peering at Cecily, she said, "Shouldn't you be buckled up for the landing?"

"Yes," the pilot said. "We materialize in fifteen seconds."

The engines hummed again, and the craft settled with a tiny thump. The lights dimmed.

"We are now visible." The pilot tapped the console, releasing Marsel, then again to open the hatch.

Edna leaped to her feet, smoothed her hair, and stood at the exit. "Are you getting it all?"

Cecily stood behind her, filming over her shoulder. "Every bit. This is so cool."

Susan stood, watching and listening. A cool breeze drifted inside, and riding along was the sound of cheering. Little by little the retracting hatch revealed balloons, banners, and placards. Susan took a step forward and saw hats and hoods.

When the platform and stairs locked into place, Edna opened her arms wide and stepped out. "Hello, San Francisco. It's good to be back."

Cecily followed her, camera panning the crowd. "Not too fast, Grandma. Let everyone get a good look."

"I think I know how to be the center of attention, dear." Edna paused on each step, sometimes posing like a beauty queen, sometimes bowing her head to the crowd.

Susan grabbed Marsel's hand. "Stay behind me. We'll wait for Gary, Scott, and Bozidar to get in place. Edna will let us know when we can go out." She crept to the edge of the open hatch, keeping out of sight. She scanned the square and saw the other two craft beyond the trees around the plaza. City Hall looked bleak under the overcast sky, as did the Federal Building.

Edna descended halfway down the stairs and stopped. She raised one hand, motioning for the crowd to quiet. As she did, Louise and Kyle threaded their way to the pod. With a microphone in her hand, Louise bounded up to join Edna. Both she and Kyle wore tee shirts with Edna and Marsel's picture on the front.

"It's been a long time, Edna, but we're all here to welcome you back. Aren't we, ladies?" Louise waved her hands at the crowd to cheer again. "Tell us, what is it like out there?" She handed the microphone to Edna.

"Cold!" Edna held the microphone close to her lips. "I was looking forward to some California sunshine, but I guess you didn't want us to get overheated." She waited for the giggles to die down. "The pictures we sent can hardly begin to show all the wonders we saw on Schtatik."

Louise took the microphone back. "Well, I can hardly wait to show you the quilts those pictures inspired. I've seen some of them, and they are amazing. Am I right, ladies?" As she motioned to the women at the base of the stairway, they lifted a dozen quilts high in the air.

Cecily leaned out to film them. "Bring the quilts up here, so everyone can see." She backed up, followed by Edna and Louise.

As the women with quilts climbed the stairs, Susan crept out of the pod and called to Cecily. "I feel like I've tuned in during the middle of a movie. What's going on? Where's the speech we worked on?"

"Change of plans." Cecily scurried to the platform. "I thought it would be best to treat this like performance art. All the quilt ladies know what's going on, but anyone else will be too confused to be scared."

"Are you sure? What about when Scott and I come out with what are clearly aliens?"

Cecily checked the progress of the women up the stairs. "Don't panic. Everyone will think it's part of the show."

"For how long?" Susan gripped the hatch opening. "Eventually they'll figure it out. That's the whole point, to let people know we're not alone in the universe."

"Relax, Mom, it will all be fine."

Cecily edged around Louise, who arranged the

women holding quilts. As they raised their arms, displaying the quilts to the crowd, Edna said, "These are fabulous! The colors, the designs. I am so impressed. Tell me, Louise, will they be exhibited anytime soon?"

"Absolutely," Louise said. She pointed to Kyle. "My son and his friends are handing out flyers to the location of five quilt stores in the East Bay. These quilts and many more will be on display for the next month. In addition, there is a complete photo gallery on the web. The link is on the flyer."

Susan took Marsel by the shoulders and peered down on his eyestalks. "You stay right here, understand? I'm going to hide behind one of the quilts and take a look around. Don't make a move until I come back for you." She stepped out again and glanced at the other pods.

Gary and Bozidar stood just outside their craft. The platform had extended, but the stairs had yet to unfold. Scott stood in the open hatch of his landing pod although its platform and stairway were in place.

So far, so good, Susan thought, no one has noticed them. She squinted to read the writing on the banners and placards. Most held variations on *welcome back*. Some had pictures of quilts, others pictures from Schtatik. She edged past the quilts, watching the people below. She recognized several faces. Some of those she did not know seemed to be tourists. Others were clearly on their way to someplace else. She noticed some in uniform and from their relaxed posture deduced they were friends of Scott.

A flicker in the corner of her eye brought her attention to Scott's pod. He directed Schtakian guards from the pod to the square. Susan saw the people closest to the craft glance up, then back to the quilts. After a heartbeat, she saw each one turn as if they were links in a chain unrolling in slow motion. Like dancers in a chorus line, she saw one arm after another raise, pointing at the beige critters. Before she heard a sound, she knew that screams were working their way up from the toes of dozens of people, and in mere moments the crowd would become a mob.

TWENTY-SEVEN

Susan dashed inside the landing pod and grabbed Marsel. "Do as I say, and don't ask questions."

He shook, and tiny wisps of pink smoke fluttered around his shoulders. "I will obey."

Susan pulled him out to the platform. "When we step in front of the quilts, start puffing smoke in as many colors as you can manage. Leap up and down, run around in circles, sing songs, do whatever you want as long as you attract attention."

"I thought you did not want me to attract attention."

"That's coming close to a question." Susan took his hand and dragged him in front of the quilts. "Do as I told you."

Marsel rocked on his footpads, brilliant streams of multi-colored smoke cascading from his ears. He rolled up as if he were standing on tiptoes, causing the platform to shake and shimmy.

Edna's mouth fell open. Susan pulled her aside.

"Mom, Scott sent the guards down the stairway. Look over there." She pointed to the line of beige critters standing on the stairway. "Someone's going to start screaming any second now."

"Leave it to me." Edna put one hand on Marsel's head and grabbed the microphone with the other. "Louise, look what we brought home with us. Marsel here is a one-critter color machine. Show the folks what you can do, little buddy."

Marsel's eyestalks wobbled like coils. He chittered a string of sounds that almost sounded like human speech. He leaped up and down as if his legs had become pogo sticks.

"Isn't that marvelous?" Edna waved her hands at the crowd, encouraging applause. "Start clapping," she hissed at Louise.

Louise raised her hands above her head and applauded vigorously. Kyle tucked his flyers under his arm and clapped too, nodding at those around him to join in.

Susan watched Scott lean toward the two beige guards nearest him. They bowed, nudged the ones on the step below, and began to sing. The movement and music rippled down the stairway.

The activity on the landing pod stairways became more festive, and the crowd responded with cheers and applause. Even those who first reacted with fear appeared relaxed. Some pointed and waved. Some filmed the scene on their cell phones.

Cecily sidled up to Susan. "Quick thinking, Mom."

"Save the praise until it's over," Susan said. "Gary still has to send the assassins down."

"Don't call them assassins," Edna whispered. "You'll jinx everything."

"Here they come," Cecily said.

She aimed her camera at Gary's pod. Bozidar was already halfway to the ground, followed by Tolar, the brown. Gary and the red and green spies, Vima and Firan, stood on the platform. Vima took a step down. Firan tugged on Gary's sleeve, pointing to something near Scott's pod.

Susan scanned the crowd and saw two men wearing camouflage jackets push toward the stairway. They watched the dancing guards. One took off his blue baseball cap, releasing a mass of graying, wispy hair. He inched closer and tossed the hat on top of the guard's eyestalks.

The guard wobbled. The guards around it wiggled. The stairway shimmied, and most of the guards tipped over and rolled as if a jar of butterscotch sticks had fallen. The rest wrapped themselves around the railing, eyestalks whipping and footpads flailing.

"Oh, dear," Susan said as she watched Tolar push past Bozidar and leap into the crowd.

His legs extended to giraffe length. As he grew, he snatched a scarf from one woman and a shawl from another. He soon attained a height that allowed him to step over most people, and he headed straight for the men in camouflage. They wriggled past a couple of downed beige guards but were stopped by people in the crowd.

Tolar held the shawl in one hand and the scarf in the other. He bellowed, the crowd retreated, and he flicked the garments upward. They snapped like whips and swirled around the men like living duct tape.

The men screamed as they were violently swaddled. The hatless one's knees buckled. He brought his buddy down as he fell. Their heads hit the pavement with a thunk that echoed throughout the square.

"Stay here," Susan said to Edna. "Keep everyone calm."

"How?" Edna said. "I'm better at sarcasm than comfort."

"Keep them laughing." Susan hurried down the stairs.

The crowd parted as she approached, opening a path to the injured men. She heard Edna rambling on, half telling a story and half throwing one-liners. The crowd listened to Edna, and most people barely noticed her by the time she reached the injured men. She knelt beside them, rubbing her ring. The stone glowed, and the metal warmed. Energy ran through her fingers. She placed one hand on each man.

An iridescent circle of light spread from Susan's

hands to the injured men. It surrounded them, glowing stronger around their heads. The light intensified and Susan heard small crackling sounds, as if hundreds of pixies were snapping their fingers.

"I'm an EMT. Let me help," a young woman said. She checked both men. "Pulse is within normal range for both. Breathing seems to be regular."

"What about the cuts on their heads?" Susan asked.

"I don't see any cuts. Even the blood on the skin is disappearing." The EMT bit her lower lip. "This isn't performance art, is it?"

Susan paused. "Not exactly."

Scott joined Susan. He held Tolar by the arm. "I'm a police officer. Retired." His voice was low, firm, and authoritative. "Please listen carefully and stay calm. Yes, these are aliens from another planet. No, we are not under attack."

The EMT indicated the unconscious pair.

"They assaulted one of my crew first," Scott said. "This being here came to their defense, as any of you would." Scott made eye contact with each person listening. "As you can see, my associate is healing those two numbskulls. She is using a combination of Earth and alien technology to do it. The aliens have much to share with us, but we need to present them to the world in a safe way."

The EMT nodded. "Just so you know, some people ran when these guys fell, and I called for an ambulance."

"So we can expect intervention at any moment." Scott tapped Susan's shoulder. "Are you almost finished?"

Susan felt the ring grow hot. She heard her patients inhale and saw them open their eyes. "They're going to be fine, Scott, and so are we," she said. She focused on the EMT. "Will you help us?"

The young woman nodded. "What do you need?"

"Take charge of the people around you." Susan glanced at the anxious faces watching her. "You folks are part of history. Make it a good day." She stood and took Tolar's hand. "Tell me why you attacked them."

"As the consort said, these creatures assaulted a brave soldier. He did nothing to them. He did not even retaliate although it was his right." Tolar's eyestalks drooped. "Was I wrong to come to his aid?"

She patted his head. "Of course not. There were bound to be complications." Her eyes widened. "Scott, I didn't even ask about the beiges. Are they alright?"

"Yes, I believe so." Scott scanned the beige soldiers, who had reformed their lines on the stairway. "They aren't showing any injuries."

Tolar said, "They would not. They have their duties."

"Then I'd better check," Susan said. She climbed the steps, gently touching each soldier. When she reached the third step, one of the critters trembled as her fingertips brushed him. Susan pressed the ring against his arm.

The creature bowed. "I am grateful, Descendant of She Who Found Us, Daughter of Our Queen. I am unworthy of your notice."

"Don't be silly. Everyone deserves to be noticed." She continued checking the soldiers, healing bruises and cuts as she went. When she reached the platform, Gary waved to her. He shouted, but she couldn't hear him above Edna's monologue and the crowd's laughter. She pointed to the red and green critters on either side of him and motioned for him to descend to the plaza with them.

Gary nodded and led his charges down the stairs. He worked his way through groups of people, introducing Vima and Firan. The critters stuck to his side as if velcroed to him but extended their hands and bowed.

Susan caught the end of one of Edna's stories about Schtatik. She chuckled as she scanned the crowd. She saw Cecily motioning to Louise, who scurried across the plaza. As Susan watched her progress, two groups of official-looking people approached from different sides of the plaza. Louise's path put her on an intercept course with three gray-suited men in sunglasses.

Susan shouted to Scott, "Three men in suits are approaching from the federal building. Louise is on to them. Two men and a woman are coming from the direction of city hall. Who do you want to handle?"

"The suits. Look after Tolar." Scott surveyed the crowd and marched after Louise.

Susan hurried down and grabbed Tolar. "Do as I tell you. Everything will be fine." Everything will be fine because it has to be, she told herself as she dragged the brown Schtatikian behind her.

Susan heard a siren in the distance. She quickened her pace. "Coming through. Lady on a mission. Coming through."

"Honored one, I am afraid," Tolar said. "You claim I have not caused difficulties, but your actions indicate otherwise. Am I being taken for punishment?"

She did not slow down. "No, you won't be punished. We are in a bit of a mess, but we always were. I'll explain later."

Two men and a woman with ID badges stood in a small clear space. Susan waved at them and curled her mouth into what she hoped was a smile rather than a grimace. "Hi, do you folks work for the city?" she asked. When they nodded, she shoved Tolar in front of her and said, "Splendid. How do I apply for sanctuary status? Not for me, for my friend. He's an undocumented alien."

The trio stared at Tolar, mouths agape. The woman tapped her chin to shut her mouth, swallowed, and said, "This isn't some new reality TV show, is it? You can be charged for wasting city services."

"I am absolutely serious." Susan joined Tolar's

hand and the woman's. "This is a living creature from the planet Schtatik. San Francisco has the honor of welcoming our first interplanetary visitors." Susan craned her neck as Scott and Louise tried to stop the federal agents from advancing. "Look, I hate to be pushy, but there are federal agents about to arrest someone for something, and that siren is an ambulance. Which isn't needed, by the way."

"That is true," Tolar said. "The Descendant of She Who Found Us has healed my people and yours."

"Jesus, Mary, and Joseph." One of the men jumped back. "It talks."

"They all talk. One talks to excess, and if you're very unfortunate I'll introduce you to him. We're running out of time. My friends have kept the crowd entertained, but that's going to fall apart if you don't help us." Susan clasped her hands together at her chest.

The trio exchanged glances. "Right," the woman said as she watched Scott, Louise, and the agents over Susan's shoulder. "I've had dealings with those guys. Let me speak with them." She gave Tolar back to Susan. "You two stay here."

Susan watched the trio walk away with determined strides. "You did very well, Tolar." She squeezed his hand.

"Should we not assist in some way?" Tolar asked.

"No. Now we wait, and hope for a miracle." She inhaled. *I can't watch. Where's Gary? What's my mother doing?*

The sound of laughter rippled through the plaza. Edna clapped her hands above her head, encouraging the audience to join her. Susan knew that Edna was speaking but could not process the words.

Tolar tugged on her arm. "Your consort approaches. He beckons. He calls. Do you wish me to remove him from your presence?"

Susan shook her head. "Gary is here?"

"Yes," Gary said, side-stepping a teenager with a skateboard. "I've been shouting at you. Couldn't you hear me?"

"I couldn't hear myself think. If I could think. City officials and federal agents are here. We planned for this, but now that it's happening I have a bad feeling about the result."

"Should we hustle our friends into the pods?"

She glanced at Tolar, still tugging on her elbow and pointing to Vima and Firan, struggling to reach them. Her ring tingled, and her sense of dread drained away as Edna's cackle exploded in her ears. "Momentary stage fright." She squared her shoulders. "We need to clear the plaza."

Scott and his beige soldiers joined them by the time Susan and her entourage reached the stairway where Edna continued to entertain. "Time for phase two?" he asked.

"I've still got a few butterflies in my stomach, but I'm ready," Susan said.

Tolar shook. "When did you ingest the insects? Are they a hazard? Shall I assist you in purging?"

Gary rubbed his chin. "I really have to work on that idiom dictionary." He shuffled Tolar next to Vima and Firan. "Thank you for your offer, but she is in no danger. You three are going to obey Scott's orders now, okay? My duties as consort require me to accompany my wife now."

The three ex-assassins bowed. "We hear and will obey."

Gary ushered Susan up the steps. As they passed a woman holding a quilt, they sent her down to the plaza with instructions to help with crowd control. When they reached the platform, Edna finished her last story and handed the microphone to Susan.

"Who said I never give up the spotlight," she whispered as she moved to the open hatch with Marsel.

"Thank you, Mother." Susan squeezed her hand. She turned to face the crowd. "Hello, everyone. Most of you know me, but for those who don't my name is Susan and I'm a quilter."

She paused, and the crowd shouted, "Hi, Susan."

Cecily moved closer, "Seriously, Mom?"

"Just keep filming, child," she said out of the corner of her mouth. She smiled and waved. "Folks, we've had a wonderful time, and we're so grateful you all came out to welcome us home. But everything must come to an end, and so must this celebration. Make sure you post all those pictures and videos, and tell everyone you know about the quilt exhibits. And don't forget, we want to see more quilts inspired by this historic event. Be safe on the road, and good night!"

She turned off the microphone and retreated to the back of the platform. Cecily took one more pan across the plaza and finished with close-ups of Susan, Edna, and Marsel.

"Now what?" Edna asked.

"We wait for whichever officials win the argument to arrest us," Susan said. "Are people leaving? I really don't want to be led away in handcuffs in front of an audience."

Cecily glanced over her shoulder. "Yes. The quilt ladies can clear a space as fast as they can fill it." She looked closer. "I think the gray suits won. They're on their way."

Marsel wriggled to the railing. "They do not look friendly."

"No, dear, I don't imagine they do." Susan motioned to Cecily. "You'd better lock your camera in the landing pod."

"Let me get one shot of the feds," Cecily said. She snapped the photo as she scurried through the open hatch.

Marsel fidgeted, and small puffs of pink smoke wafted around his head. "I am confused. Are not all these people your friends? You sent invitations."

Gary took Marsel by the shoulders and peered into his eyestalks. "We sent invitations to make sure you guys wouldn't get shot on sight. You're safe enough, but you have to promise to be quiet, okay?

The men who are coming probably won't know what to do with us. Things could get a little tense. Just remember, calm people live."

"But I am not a people." The smoke changed from pink to red and came thicker and faster. "This is most distressing." He craned one eyestalk toward Susan. "On my planet, we present a small token to unwelcome guests."

"Why?" Susan asked.

"To encourage them to leave." Marsel fidgeted until Gary released him. He toddled to Susan. "If the token is pleasing, they leave happy. I am particularly adept at providing pleasing tokens."

"Somehow, that doesn't surprise me," Susan said. "But that's not what we do here. In fact, it's against the law to offer tokens to government agents. It's called a bribe."

Marsel watched the men in gray suits climb the steps. "If you had allowed me to bring the gifts, I would have found something appropriate under your laws."

"Marsel, dear, you don't even know what our laws are."

The first federal agent reached the platform and held out his identification. "We'd like to have a word with you."

Marsel stretched his eyestalks to the man's outstretched hand, then snapped them backward as he hid behind Susan. "You should have let me bring the gifts."

TWENTY-EIGHT

SUSAN, EDNA, SCOTT, AND GARY SAT IN THE efficiently furnished conference room. Marsel bounced around the edges, patting chairs and walls.

"This is splendid," Marsel said. "I did not know your people were capable of such reserve in decorations."

"I thought you critters preferred glitz," Edna said. "Everything I saw on your planet was ornamented to the hilt."

Marsel stroked the side of a steel filing cabinet. "We appreciate that which shines, but I find myself drawn to these simple lines and the sparse embellishment in this room. I find it comforting." He spun around on his footpads. "Do you not also find the atmosphere in this room soothing?"

Scott said, "This isn't the welcome we'd hoped for."

Susan reached out her hand to Marsel. "Come stand next to me."

He trudged to Susan's side, his eyestalks drooping. "I must do what I am told again."

"Yes, dear," Susan said. "It would be best for you to keep still as much as possible."

"Why did you keep me by your side if you did not intend for me to help explain our presence?" he said. "Our soldiers returned to their landing pod, as did the assassins. Even Bozidar and Cecily stayed behind."

"Trust me," Edna said, "if I could have shoved you back in the pod you'd be there now." She stretched. "Do you think they got away?"

Gary nodded. "Between the cloud cover and their stealth technology, I don't think anyone could track them. They should be somewhere on the edge of the stratosphere by now."

"Hush, I hear voices," Susan said. Edna snorted, and Susan scowled at her. "In the hall. I hear voices in the hall. Someone is coming."

"I didn't say anything," Edna said, smiling.

The door opened and two gray-suited men entered. One carried a light green file folder. They sat at the table and made eye contact with Scott, Susan, and Gary. They avoided looking directly at Marsel and Edna.

"I'm Agent Flores," the one with the file folder said. "This is Agent Johanssen." He addressed Scott. "Perhaps you can tell us what you and your friends were doing at Civic Center Plaza today."

"Don't ask him," Edna said. "This was my party. You talk to me."

Flores and Johanssen exchanged a glance. Johanssen cleared his throat. "According to the city, there were no permits issued for an event."

"So? If San Francisco wants to give me a citation, let them." Edna shifted in her chair. "Ask the question that's really on your mind."

Marsel slid from Susan's grasp. He rolled to the front edge of his footpad and craned his eyestalks toward the agents. "I know the question. You want to know about me, do you not?"

"Good god," Flores said, jerking straight. "How do you make it talk?"

"They do not make me talk," Marsel said. He shrank into himself. "In fact, they asked me not to talk. Specifically, the Descendant of She Who Found Us, the one who is the daughter of our queen, requested that I keep still." He bowed to Susan. "Forgive me. I thought we were playing a game. We have a festival of empathy. We choose teams to determine what is in the mind of the honored guest. The team that wins is … perhaps I should save this story for another time."

Susan rubbed her face. "Yes, dear, another time." She drummed her fingers on the table. "Our little friend is an alien." She stared at the agents.

"An alien." Flores flipped through the papers in the folder. "These are dangerous times. How do we know you aren't terrorists? You're lucky no one was hurt with this stunt."

"Oh, but someone was," Marsel said. He puffed royal blue smoke. "The Descendant of She Who Found Us is a healer. We are ever so proud."

"What do you mean someone was hurt? Who? Where is the victim?" Johanssen asked.

"Susan healed him," Edna said. She swatted at Marsel. "We told you to keep still, so zip it."

"There were two," Marsel said as he ducked behind Susan. "I saw it all. Tolar was there."

"Who is Tolar?" Flores asked. His voice squeaked.

"Another alien," Susan said. She sighed. "Actually, I requested asylum for him, so perhaps you will be receiving a report from the city about that too."

Flores motioned to Johanssen, who left the room. "By the time he gets back, I expect some straight answers from you."

Scott crossed his arms. "We can tell you, but you won't believe us."

Edna leaned across the table, a gleam in her eyes. "Here's the deal, friend. You've got yourself a first contact situation. Real, live space creatures. Dropped in your lap." She rested her chin on her palm. "Your move."

"Mother, please," Susan said. "Agent Flores, I can understand your suspicions. There are thousands of people in the area with the technical expertise to create robotic creatures and large-scale special effects."

Gary coughed. "Sweetheart, you're not helping."

Susan closed her eyes. "Let me get to the point." She inhaled, opened her eyes and said, "We are authorized by the joint governments of the planet Schtatik to negotiate peace, trade, and exploration agreements with the governments of Earth. We chose this place to land for its historical significance, being the place where the United Nations charter was signed. Please inform the Secretary-General of the UN, and the President of the United States, that we await their response."

Flores blinked. "Excuse me." He exited the room. As he closed the door, he shouted down the hall, "I need a psych evaluation team. Now."

Scott compressed his lips. "That went well, don't you think?"

"But you gave him what he requested." Marsel inched closer to Susan. "The idiom he used indicated he wanted the truth. You told him the truth. Why is he displeased?"

"He doesn't want to believe us," Gary said.

Marsel shivered. "He refuses to accept the evidence before him?"

"That's a more complicated question than you might expect," Susan said. "And to be honest, I don't have the energy to explain it to you now. Ask Cecily, when you see her again."

"Will I see her again?" Marsel asked.

Gary looked at his watch. "Be patient. They have to get back to the ship, and we need to wait for the video from today's landing to go viral."

Marsel tugged on Susan's sleeve. "I recognize all the words he used, but I do not understand what he means."

Susan patted his head. "He means we're going to be in this room for a while."

* * *

The door to the conference room creaked open. Agents Flores and Johanssen entered, followed by two young men carrying coffee, and a middle-aged woman in a dark green suit. The agents sat at the table, the young men distributed the coffee, and the woman stood at the end of the table near Susan.

"I understand you've requested asylum in San Francisco," she said.

"For the representatives of Schtatik," Susan said. "I didn't want them apprehended before they could present their credentials."

The woman in the green suit nodded. "Sensible." She extended her hand. "I'm Alexandra Harris. I'm from the State Department. We don't have an alien planet desk, you understand, so there isn't a protocol to follow. We're charting new territory here."

"Could we start with some food?" Edna asked. "It's been way too long since my last meal, and I'm much more pleasant on a full stomach."

"That's true of all of us," Alexandra said. "Will donuts do?"

One of the young men said, "We can be back with a couple dozen in fifteen minutes."

"Fine with me," Edna said. "You say there's no protocol to follow, but we've been here for hours. Plenty of time to get instructions from someone."

"You are correct." Alexandra pulled a cell phone from her jacket pocket. "Let me show you what your landing has created." She handed the phone to Susan.

Susan swiped the screen and watched a video of Edna emerging from the landing pod. She put the phone on the table so Edna could see it.

"I look good," Edna said. "Can you turn up the volume?"

"Mother, please," Susan said. She returned the phone to Alexandra. "I assume there are more videos?"

"Hundreds. Social media is going crazy," Alexandra said. She swiped to another entry. "This one broke the internet."

Susan took the phone and watched a few seconds of her healing the drunken tourists. "Yes, I thought that one would get some attention."

"Especially after a reporter tracked the gentlemen in question and interviewed them. They're rather embarrassed by their behavior and wished to extend their apologies." Alexandra shook her head. "Amazing, really, considering the circumstances. That sort usually threatens a lawsuit. But in response to the events of the day, the President has expressed an interest in meeting with your representatives."

"The events of the day," Scott said. "Our landing was one event. What else happened?"

"A spaceship calling itself *Cold Fire* is parked overhead."

Susan stole a look at Gary before she focused on Alexandra. "Doing what?"

"Streaming more video." Alexandra swiped the screen.

Edna moved Susan aside. "This is Cecily's footage? Oh, it's wonderful."

"The message that accompanied it is also causing a sensation," Alexandra said.

Susan groaned and put her head in her hands. "This isn't the way it was supposed to go." She looked up, eyes wide. "It wasn't a threat?"

"No, but there were consequences mentioned if we didn't open negotiations."

"Consequences?" Gary asked. He leaned toward Susan. "Honest, honey, I didn't mention anything about consequences."

"What are you talking about?" Susan asked.

Gary tapped the table. "Okay, we kept you out of the loop on this one. Bozidar and I—"

"You and I and Bozidar," Scott interrupted.

"I wasn't going to incriminate you," Gary said. "Okay, the three of us thought that if—"

"When," Scott said.

"When things started going off script, we should

retreat. So we agreed to get the Schtatikians back on the ships and take off. We figured the worst that would happen to us is we'd get arrested, but who knows what would happen to the critters?"

"A successful tactic," Alexandra said. "As was the use of social media."

The young men returned with three pink boxes. The scent of sugar and hot oil filled the room. Edna reached for a box and positioned it right in front of her.

"Smells great," she said. She took a bite from a chocolate-frosted cake donut with rainbow sprinkles. "Tastes even better. So who sent the message, and what did it say?"

Alexandra said, "It was signed by His Excellency, Diplomatic Envoy Bozidar. He suggested that since the delegation arrived in peace and was received with open arms, the governments of Earth had nothing to fear from Schtatik, but a great deal to fear from a population that would be deprived of contact with a new world."

Edna paused in mid-chew. She swallowed and cackled. "Well, the title is a little pretentious, but my space boy got the sentiment right. Listen, Ms. Harris, this genie isn't going back in the bottle. We let a lot of people know we were coming so there wouldn't be another Roswell incident."

"There never was a Roswell incident," Alexandra said. "We've never been contacted by aliens before."

"We weren't taking any chances," Edna said.

"You've been contacted now and everyone knows. The only thing you have to decide is how big a party are you going to throw to celebrate."

"It isn't that simple," Agent Flores said.

"Actually, it is." Scott rose. "Or it could be. I've been in your line of work all my life, protecting people, so I know your concerns. Uncertainty can breed chaos. We don't want that, nor do the Schtatikians."

"Trust me on that," Edna said. "We've just spent the last few weeks dealing with a bunch of knuckleheaded Chicken Littles. They don't want conflict."

"What do they want?" Alexandra asked.

"To see prophecy fulfilled," Marsel said.

"Hush, you," Edna hissed. "Don't mind him. He's always going on about prophecies. Sometimes it works to our advantage, so we let him babble."

Marsel rocked from one footpad to the other. "The prophecies are braiding together in exquisite patterns. The resolution will be glorious." Pink smoke puffed around his head. "And I do not babble."

"Never mind, dear," Susan said.

"But I do mind," Marsel said as the smoke ring around him grew. "She should not dismiss the prophecies."

"Let her have another donut," Susan whispered. "She'll be less cranky." She put her arm around Marsel as one would comfort and control a child.

"I heard that," Edna said between bites.

"Good. Eat faster." Susan smiled at Alexandra. "To answer your question, the Schtatikians are much like us. They have art, beautiful cities, thriving and diverse cultures. They are also explorers. In fact, they came to San Francisco before. My great-grandmother found them. A few years ago, they returned and found my family. Now they would like to share their technology and explore the galaxy with us."

"And what do they want in exchange?"

Susan paused, looking toward the ceiling. "Our perspective, for one thing. We showed them the value of considering different points of view before taking action."

"What do they really want?" Alexandra arched an eyebrow.

"Well, they would welcome as much silver as we can spare." Susan removed her ring and held it out for Alexandra. "With their stones and our metal, their healers could cure almost anything."

"So can my daughter," Edna said. "She's got a special gift for healing."

"Can you teach others how to use this?" Alexandra examined the ring and returned it.

"I'd be willing to try." Susan turned to Scott. "You saw something of their science and technology. Tell her what we could gain."

Scott folded his hands on the table. "They have impressive medical research facilities. They also have instant translation devices. We're using one now, which is why you can understand Marsel here. Add to that the chance to reach the stars now, and I'd say we're getting a pretty good bargain. They are asking for silver, yes, but in exchange for something of far greater value."

"What are their other requirements?" Agent Johanssen asked. "I'm still waiting for the catch."

Scott leaned back in his chair. "Edna and Susan brought them here. Edna and Susan head up the negotiations team."

"They have no standing with any government on the planet," Alexandra said. "They also have no experience."

Gary snorted. "You'd be surprised. They single-handedly averted war on Schtatik."

"As the prophecies foretold," Marsel said, keeping his voice low.

Johanssen scowled at Marsel but spoke to Gary. "He's not part of the negotiation team, is he?"

"No." Scott, Edna, and Gary spoke simultaneously. Gary inclined his head toward Marsel. "He is on long-term assignment here, however."

"Another catch?" Alexandra asked.

"Another catch," Susan said. "He's also my responsibility, not yours."

Marsel said, "Your planet has visionaries and dreamers. The council of elders wished to show you how we utilize such gifted beings."

"Off-shore them," Scott said under his breath.

Alexandra's phone beeped. She swiped the screen. "*Cold Fire* is sending another message." Her face grew pale. "Your comrades are tired of waiting. They're presenting their demands directly to the public."

"More tweeting?" Edna asked.

"Not exactly. Let's go outside."

Alexandra and the agents led the group to the sidewalk. Drivers stopped their cars and stood in the middle of the street. People clumped in groups, pointing to the sky.

Susan looked up. The early evening sky was already dark because of cloud cover, but she could see streams of colored light coalescing into patterns. "Can we go to the plaza? I can't see much from here."

The group threaded its way around the block, dodging pedestrians filming the sky with cell phones. A gentle wind tugged at them as if drawing them forward. As they turned the corner, the streets around the plaza were also gridlocked as drivers and passengers emptied from their cars.

Susan stopped in the middle of the street. Gary put his arm around her and said, "Cross my heart, I never told them to do anything like this."

"I believe you," she said. "This has Cecily's fingerprints all over it."

They gazed at the changing light show above them. A sheet of neon blue light undulated across the sky. Spots of crimson grew in a random pattern only to explode and reassemble into a LeMoyne Star. The diamonds separated, elongated, and transformed into peace symbols. They faded, replaced by wiggly yellow lines. The lines curled and straightened, inching closer to each other. As they touched, they swirled into a huge dove with flapping wings. A glittering olive branch appeared in the dove's beak.

The dove faded, as did the blue background. The olive branch remained, stretching across the charcoal gray clouds. As it grew, branches spooled out. They curved, and birthed new branches. When the entire sky was covered with glittering green stems, white roses blossomed from the ends.

The green stems sparkled and winked out. The roses collapsed on themselves until they were perfectly round. As they turned themselves into circles, they rearranged into a grid six across and seven down.

Susan snorted. "Forty-two. The ultimate answer."

"What?" Gary tapped his forehead. "Right. *The Hitchhikers Guide To The Galaxy.*"

"I told you it was important to read that book."

Orange diagonal lines snapped into place between the circles, which shrank until they looked like polka dots. The grid expanded. One of the polka dots at the bottom of the array turned blue. In the opposite corner, another dot turned pinky-purple. A tiny turquoise speck flew away from that dot. As it made its way to the blue dot, the orange lines folded in front of it like a fan. When the speck reached the blue dot, it morphed into a spaceship shape. The orange lines snapped back into place.

"She's telling the people how we got here,"

Susan said. "And that we come in peace."

"Do you think they'll understand?" Gary asked.

The array exploded into gold and violet shooting stars. As the last star faded, a huge smiley face appeared and winked.

As the crowd began to applaud, Susan said, "Looks like they do."

TWENTY-NINE

ALEXANDRA HARRIS TAPPED SUSAN'S SHOULDER while listening to her cell phone. She nodded and said, "Yes, yes, and yes." She pocketed the phone. "On behalf of the President of the United States, welcome back to Earth."

"Does that mean we're free?" Susan asked.

"Not really. But you aren't under arrest." Alexandra guided Susan and Gary back to where Edna, Scott, and Marsel stood. "Off the record, I expect you'll get your freedom, and anything else you want."

"We're not asking for much," Susan said.

Edna rolled her eyes so vigorously her head made a full circuit. "No, of course not, Daughter. We're only asking for a complete shift in the way people understand the universe and an entirely new definition of the word alien."

"The human race has made paradigm shifts before," Susan said.

"Not without bloodshed, and not overnight." Edna turned to Alexandra. "I'm cold and hungry."

"I can take you back to the Federal Building. We'll find a more comfortable room, bring in some food, and see about landing the rest of the delegation."

* * *

Susan paced the length of the conference room, followed by Marsel. She laced and unlaced her fingers, and jumped at every sound in the hall.

"Please decrease your velocity," Marsel said. "My stride length is barely half of yours."

"I'm sorry, Marsel, but all of a sudden I'm a nervous wreck." She paced even faster.

"Understandable. This room is far less comforting than the other." Marsel stepped aside and waited for Susan to pass him on her return. "All these soft chairs. The leather. And the smell of processed animal flesh from the food trays. I find it disconcerting. Perhaps if I sang the prophecy cycle to you we would both find comfort?"

"Thank you, no," Gary said as he guided Susan to a couch. "Everything will be fine when Cecily gets here." He brought Susan a cup of hot coffee. "You haven't eaten properly, and the reality of what we've done is hitting you. Tell me I'm not right."

She closed her eyes, sipped, and relaxed against the back of the couch. "No, you're spot on." She opened her eyes and grinned. "That's one of the reasons I married you."

Edna snapped around. "That reminds me. Now that we're back home, I've got a bone to pick with you two. What do you mean getting married without me? We had big plans for that wedding."

"We know," Susan said. "It wasn't that wedding. It was my wedding. Mine and Gary's."

Scott handed Edna a sandwich. "Leave the kids alone, Edna. You finally learned how to work together despite everything. Don't ruin it now by slipping back into old habits."

"I just wanted to contribute," Edna said. "I want to make sure someone remembers me."

Marsel leaped to her side and knelt. "My queen, you will be remembered forever. No one on Earth or Schtatik will forget your name. I will take it upon myself to write the stories of your accomplishments and sing them until the stars grow cold."

"Now see what you've done." Susan chuckled. "It's no less than you deserve."

Marsel rolled to his footpads, multi-colored smoke pouring from his ears. "Oh, the Descendants of She Who Found Us deserve so much more. I will write all of your stories. They will build a new library in our capital city to hold the scrolls. They will build a new performance platform to hear the story cycles. It will be magnificent." He twirled around and hummed.

"Oh, my," Edna said. "That may be more attention than I want."

"Too late, Mother," Susan said. She cocked her head. "Wait. Do you hear someone in the hall?"

The door to the conference room opened, and Cecily entered. She ran to the couch and threw herself in Susan's arms. "We did it, Mom. Everyone is safe, there's no war, and we're going to negotiate the first interplanetary treaty in Earth's history."

"Do not expect the discussions to be easy or quick," Bozidar said as he entered. He greeted everyone with a nod of his head and sat in a chair.

Alexandra Harris followed him. "Given the late hour, we've arranged hotel rooms for you. Tomorrow will be very busy. The president is en route already, as are delegations from … well, just about everyone will want a photo op with you."

Susan groaned. "All I want to do is pick up my two youngest girls and be a family again."

"We can arrange that if you wish."

"Thank you. I can't imagine what they must be going through seeing all this on television."

Cecily smiled. "Don't worry, Mom, I texted them from the ship. I told them you couldn't talk, but everyone was fine, and we'd all be together soon." She handed Alexandra her phone. "The contact information is right there, Ms. Harris. They'll be ready tomorrow morning."

"You called them?" Susan hugged Cecily.

"Texted. It wasn't the first thing I thought of, but it was at least the second or third," Cecily said. "I sent them the video of you sleeping in the landing pod." She looked her mother in the eyes. "Don't even think of calling them now. They'll be in bed. I miss them too, but not when they're cranky from lack of sleep."

"She's right," Edna said. "They need sleep more than you need to see them. They're going to be caught up just as much as we are. Cameras, reporters, all of it."

"We all could use sleep," Scott said. "Clean clothes wouldn't hurt."

"Oh, we brought all the luggage," Cecily said. "Even the gifts for Olivia and Eleanor."

Bozidar ground his teeth. "If all humans are as attached to things as you, I foresee significant difficulties in joint space expeditions. Even our largest landing pod struggled with the weight of your possessions."

"I guess I have to leave my shoe collection when I head out again," Cecily said.

"What do you mean again?" Susan asked.

Cecily glanced at Bozidar. "The elders want me to film the first Earth-Schtatik exploration mission."

"They asked you to go, or you argued them into submission?" Susan stared at Bozidar, her green eyes as cold as the Pacific Ocean in winter. "Did you know about this?"

"Yes, of course," Bozidar said. "I am always

aware of potential disasters. In this case, however, I supported Cecily's case to the council. You must admit that adequate documentation and publicity have worked to our advantage."

Marsel toddled to Cecily. "May I go with you, Descendant of She Who Found Us Twice Removed? You have said before that I am a talisman. Is that not a stone of good fortune?"

Edna said, "I've heard you called a lot of things, little guy, but never a talisman."

Cecily shrugged. "I may have called him a good luck charm. He was sad, and I wanted to cheer him up."

"His prophecies sure came in handy," Gary said. "But I should tell you, Bozidar has already been informed no one on *Cold Fire* will let him back on the ship."

"That is correct," Bozidar said. "Also, the joint councils of elders would consider it a great courtesy if, as part of any treaty, Marsel is attached to Earth. We are not concerned with the position."

"Either he goes with me, or he stays with you," Cecily said to Susan.

"What about Kyle?" Susan asked. "You two have some unfinished business."

"I've been in touch with him. He's ready to go on the first ship out."

Susan jerked. "Does Louise know about this?"

"By now, probably."

Susan's skin tingled as if she had a fever. *The next*

words out of your mouth better be the right ones. Don't slip into old habits. She couldn't tell if the words came from her better self, or were a message from Agnes. "We just got home. I'm not ready to lose you."

"Mom, I'm not leaving tomorrow." Cecily rolled her eyes, but her voice was gentle.

Scott said, "Regardless of how quickly Schtatik may be able to outfit an expedition, I am reasonably certain it will take our government months to get on board."

"I should hope so," Cecily said. "I've got weeks of work ahead of me with my documentary."

Susan shook her head. "No, that's already been broadcast."

"Some raw footage has been released," Cecily said. "I've got a lot more. I'll need to edit it after I write the story framing it. Gary can explain it to you later." She laughed. "Anyway, I want to enjoy coming home as a hero, and I want to see my sisters and my friends. Then there's your wedding to celebrate."

"Oh, no, Cecily, not you too," Gary said. "Couldn't we just have a big welcome home party?"

Susan's skin stopped tingling, and her nerves stopped jangling. The icy sensation in the pit of her stomach gave way to a sense of calm that spread throughout her body. "I'll make you a deal." She pointed at Edna. "I'll make you both a deal. Cecily lives at home while she's editing and preparing for her next big adventure. Edna gets to throw the gaudiest party of her life, but it isn't all about Gary and me. I get a chance for a normal family life again, at least for a little while. Agreed?"

"What about me?" Marsel asked.

Susan turned to Gary. "Eleanor and Olivia have always wanted a pet."

He grimaced. "At least he's housebroken."

Alexandra cleared her throat. "We still have unfinished business." She waited until all eyes were on her, and Marsel finished puffing little balls of colored smoke. "As I said, the president is en route. That doesn't mean everyone is ready to give your delegation the keys to the city. There have been incidents, not only here but around the world."

"How bad?" Scott leaned forward in his chair. He clasped his hands and rested his elbows on his knees.

Alexandra said, "It could have been worse. The mayors of most of the larger cities called for curfews and had the police force on the streets within a couple of hours of the news of your arrival. Some of the governors called out the National Guard. Congress called a special session. Everyone is busily showing that we're all on top of the situation, no need to panic, yada yada yada."

Scott nodded. "How many have been injured?"

"Less than a thousand. And no deaths." Alexandra checked her phone. "A lot of looting. Some drunken yahoos in the smaller towns tore through fields in their SUVs. I don't see any new reports, so maybe things are calming down."

"Where is the worst damage?" Gary asked.

"The Great Plains states. I was surprised there weren't more riots in the South until I heard one radio host say this is what you'd expect of California, and the aliens wouldn't dare invade Biloxi." Alexandra laughed. "Believe it or not, there is a convention of alien abductees in San Francisco now. They've actually been helping to keep a lid on things."

Susan raised an eyebrow. "How?"

"Well," Alexandra drawled as she settled into a chair, "they're claiming that since these aliens are out in the open where everyone can see them, we don't have to worry. The bad aliens come in secret."

Edna cackled. "And people are buying that?"

"It's too early to say, but the more air time these abductees get, the better. From what I can see, public panic goes way down every time one of them is interviewed."

Marsel inched away from Cecily. His eyestalks quivered. "I can see."

"That's nice, sweetie," Susan said. "Cecily, take care of him."

Cecily knelt beside him. "Marsel, come stand by me." She took his hand and immediately released it. "Mom, he's ice cold."

Bozidar rose from his chair. "There is no puffing smoke." He came to Marsel's side in two strides and grasped one of his eyestalks. "This is not his normal state."

Marsel's eyestalk slid from Bozidar's hand. He

rocked from one beige footpad to the other. "I can see. I can see."

"What do you see?" Susan asked. *Agnes, whatever you're doing, stop.*

"Agnes has no part in this," Marsel whispered. "This vision belongs to me alone."

Alexandra leaned toward Scott. "Does he usually do this?"

"No," Scott said. "His specialty is prophecy."

Edna and Susan joined Cecily, making a circle around Marsel. They watched him rocking. Susan held her hands out as if to steady the little creature.

"I don't think he's going to fall, Mom," Cecily said.

Marsel stopped rocking. "I will not fall. We will not fall. We will meet new friends, so many new friends."

Edna snorted. "What the heck is that supposed to mean?" She shot a glare in Bozidar's direction. "He's one of yours, space boy, so what's going on here?"

Alexandra glanced from Marsel to Bozidar. "What do you mean the alien is one of his?"

"I am also from the planet Schtatik," Bozidar said, not taking his eyes off Marsel. "It is a long and distressing story."

"Can others of your species disguise themselves as humans?" Alexandra asked in a clipped tone.

"After my experience, no one would want to," Bozidar said.

Scott said, "The aliens can change shape, but not easily. Bozidar is the only one who looks human, which is why he was sent as the planetary ambassador. It is a courtesy to us."

Marsel began to chant, warbling a string of melodic chirps and squeals. After three sharp bleats that sounded like a goat had inhaled helium, he turned his eyestalks to Edna. "My queen, I have been given a vision for our success. But first, I must ask forgiveness."

"What did you do now?" Edna crossed her arms. "And how much trouble will it cause?"

"I left the gifts on the ship although I knew the gods wished me to bring them. Now we need one."

Susan leaned forward and whispered, "Now, sweetie, remember what I told you about bribes."

"The gift is not for her." Marsel patted Susan's cheeks. "You have had visions and trusted them. Trust my vision."

Let the little guy speak. You'll thank me later. Susan chuckled at Agnes' advice. Aloud, she said, "Okay, Marsel, I'll trust you. What did you see?"

He rose up on the front edge of his footpad. "I saw a human. A woman. She stood in front of me and bowed as she accepted a tapestry. I know the exact one, and where I packed it. When she receives the gift, we will be accepted. Our mission will succeed."

Edna pushed herself off the floor with a grunt. "Terrific. Any clue who she is? It's a big world, you know."

Marsel stamped his footpad. "The vision will provide!"

Cecily stifled a laugh. "Take that, your majesty."

"Quiet, child," Susan said. She glared at her mother. "You too." Her voice softened. "Marsel, did you see anything else? Something that might tell us what we should do next?"

Marsel's eyestalks turned to the ceiling. After a moment, he said, "In my vision, we are on *Cold Fire*. You are there. Cecily is as well, and she is transmitting the meeting to your planet. I give the woman the tapestry. She thanks me, and tells the people of Earth how happy she is to have such fine new allies. The translator tells me she is speaking English, but that it is not her first language. There are pennants on the wall. One is the same as that one." He pointed to the American flag in the corner.

"Describe the other one," Susan said.

"It was divided into three bands." Marsel pressed his hands together. "The top band was black. The middle was red. The bottom was a deep yellow. Do you recognize it?"

"I'll bet he means gold, Mom," Cecily said. "He's talking about the German flag."

Alexandra tapped her phone as she approached Marsel. She showed him the screen. "Is this the woman in your vision?"

Marsel's eyestalks bent over the screen. One scanned up and down while the other went side to side. "Yes, I believe it is. She was not wearing the same clothing, but I believe it is her."

"That is the German chancellor," Alexandra said, showing the phone to Susan. "She's the most powerful woman in Europe, and the most respected person in the world. If she's on your side, the rest of the world will follow."

THRITY

Edna poked Marsel. "Did you see her phone number? The vision isn't much help if we can't get in touch with her."

"I do not know how we made contact. I only know that we will." Marsel wriggled between Edna and Susan. He toddled to Alexandra and took her hand. "And I know that you will help."

Susan said, "Marsel." She stopped and studied Alexandra's face. "He's right. You will help us. I know it. What I don't know is why." She rolled to her feet. "Now that I think of it, you've been helping us all along. Why?"

Alexandra put her other hand on top of Marsel's. She compressed her lips, then blew out a deep breath. "When I was a child, my family went to the desert. Joshua Tree. I crept out of the tent after everyone was asleep so I could look at the stars. They were so beautiful. One star was particularly bright. It got bigger and brighter as I watched. Then it left the sky and landed in front of me."

She dropped Marsel's hand and leaned back in her chair. "A being emerged from the light. I asked if it was an angel. It said no, but it understood that word and would be my angel if I liked. It beckoned for me to follow into the light."

She focused on Susan. "You understand that I've never told anyone else about that night. Until this very moment, I convinced myself it was only a dream."

Scott cleared his throat. "Now you know it wasn't."

"And it scares me," Alexandra said.

Susan smiled. "Why? Did the alien harm you?"

"No."

"Are you unnerved that other planets have sentient life?"

Alexandra hesitated. "Not really. I mean, I am, but only because I don't know anything about those species."

"Here's your chance to learn," Susan said. "They're offering humanity a chance to visit other planets with them."

Alexandra nodded. "I may be able to set up a meeting. I met a member of the chancellor's staff recently."

"Let me guess," Edna said. "He was at the alien abductee conference. Along with you."

* * *

The cool night air gave Susan a jolt of energy as if she had drained three cups of coffee topped by a handful of chocolate-covered espresso beans. She checked over her shoulder for the second time. "Are you sure this is a secure location?"

"As secure as your backyard," Alexandra said. "If a landing pod could get in and out of there without being seen, it can get in and out of the parking lot of the recycling yard."

"Mom, we've been over this." Cecily waved at the open water beyond them. "Those are the docks in Oakland. No one will be watching us from there, and no one is around to see us here."

Marsel said, "Trust the vision, Descendant of She Who Found Us."

"I would say I'm about at my limit of trust," Susan muttered, "but that hasn't mattered before."

"And it won't matter now, Mom," Cecily said. Her voice was kind. "There's always another battle to fight. That's what Scott says."

"This one will be glorious," Marsel said. "Listen, I hear the approaching pod."

A small whoosh preceded a thump, and the landing pod materialized a few yards from the group. Once the stairway had locked in place, the hatch opened.

"Time to go," Susan said. "This is one of the automated pods, isn't it?"

"Yes," Marsel said. "Once we are strapped in, the pod will take us to the ship."

Alexandra led the way but hesitated at the foot of the stairway. "This is real. We're going into space." She turned to Susan. "I don't know if I'm excited or terrified."

"Both would be appropriate, but save it until we get to the ship," Susan said.

Cecily maneuvered between them, Marsel in tow. "Mom's right. The ride on the pod is a cross between a subway ride and an enclosed ski lift."

"We should use the time to meditate," Marsel said, following Cecily toward the hatch. "Visions are gifts, and gifts should be appreciated."

The four climbed up and into the pod. A dim yellow light, no stronger than a bathroom night light, shone in the interior until the hatch closed behind them. The light brightened to the level of a trendy cafe as the humans settled onto benches and secured their seat belts. Marsel sat on a stool in the center of the pod. Clearly designed for Schtakians, the upholstery molded against his skin like plastic wrap.

"I shall meditate now," Marsel said, folding his eyestalks against his body.

"Do you mind if we talk?" Susan whispered.

"Not at all," he whispered back.

"Thank you." Susan leaned toward Alexandra. "Tell me again how we're getting in touch with the chancellor?"

"I sent her a message on her private email

already," Alexandra said. "When we're on the ship, we'll send a landing craft to fetch her. Marsel will present her with the tapestry from his vision, and we'll broadcast the ceremony planet wide."

"I still can't believe she agreed to this," Cecily said.

"Agreed to it?" Alexandra chuckled softly. "It was her idea. She has her own family story about aliens from outer space. When I told her about Marsel's vision she was ready to commandeer a plane to San Francisco immediately. It was all I could do to convince her our way would let her see the aliens sooner."

"And she'd be on a spaceship," Cecily said.

"That too."

Susan said, "Bozidar received assurances the crew of *Cold Fire* is willing to show the chancellor every courtesy." She closed her eyes and held her breath. "It does seem things are going our way, doesn't it?"

Cecily patted her arm. "Just be grateful, Mom, and enjoy it."

The lights dimmed a bit, and the air warmed. Marsel whispered, "Yes, let us meditate on gratitude."

Silence bound the travelers until the pod docked with *Cold Fire*. Susan popped up from her seat first and waited for the hatch to open.

Marsel peeled himself from his seat and stood by her. "Allow me, Descendant of She Who Found Us. I have finally been shown my purpose. All will be well."

Susan watched as Marsel marched onto the platform, chittering orders to three waiting creatures. They bowed and scurried off in different directions. Marsel descended the stairway, dispensing orders to other crew members who approached. As he reached the last step, he turned. "Follow me, please. We have much to do."

Cecily eased past her mother. "You heard him. Come on." She hurried to Marsel, giggling as she went.

"I take it this isn't his usual behavior," Alexandra said.

"Nope," Susan said. "But he seems to have a plan. Maybe he is our good luck charm, after all."

As Marsel predicted, the arrangements went smoothly. The chancellor was brought aboard and given a tour. *Cold Fire*'s crew tolerated both the humans and Marsel's leadership with grace. They even decorated the conference room to Marsel's specifications without complaint.

While Marsel supervised the arrangements for the ceremony, Susan, Cecily, Alexandra, and the chancellor chatted in the corner of the conference room. Alexandra checked her phone at intervals.

"Is everything okay?" Susan asked.

"I want to make sure I can monitor the response to the broadcast," Alexandra said. "Is that all set?"

"Yes," Cecily said. "Bozidar set up all the right feeds and connections when we made our getaway from Civic Center."

Squares of orange and red flashed along the upper part of the walls, and a light fragrance of cinnamon swirled through the room. The beige crew members bowed one last time to Marsel and took positions around the edge of the room.

"It is time," Marsel said. He held the tapestry with both hands. "Please take your places where we practiced, and wait until the squares change color."

The women positioned themselves in the center of the room with Susan and Cecily on either side of the chancellor. The orange and red squares ceased flashing and turned green.

Marsel said, "People of Earth, you know now that you have friends in faraway places."

As he spoke, Susan felt the air around her tingle before she saw the familiar shimmer that preceded her visions. She heard Agnes' voice in her head. *This is good. Enjoy the moment. Trust that there will be more good moments, no matter how scary the lead up to them might be.* Susan blinked and saw in her mind Eleanor, Olivia, Gary, and herself, at home, happy. She blinked again and realized Marsel was at the end of his speech.

The chancellor stepped forward to receive the tapestry. "Thank you," she said. "I will speak in English for the benefit of the Americans who have brought these people to us in friendship. The history of Earth is filled with painful stories of the damage a more advanced civilization can cause. We are grateful this first encounter with another species will be different. I urge all the governments, and all the people, to welcome our new allies and rejoice in the wonders that we will discover."

The green square faded to match the color of the wall. Marsel led the chancellor to the table where she unrolled the tapestry. He pointed to different areas of the piece, explaining the embroidery and trying to condense thousands of years of Schtatikian history into a few sentences. The chancellor smiled and nodded, although Susan thought her eyes were starting to glaze over.

Alexandra watched Marsel lecture for a moment. She turned away and checked her phone. "I think that went well. The immediate reactions I'm seeing are all positive."

"You have no idea," Cecily said. "When Marsel gets going, he can be terrifyingly energetic. I've never seen him so controlled."

"Like he said, he finally knows his purpose." Susan crossed her fingers. "Let's hope our lucky streak continues when we get back home."

* * *

The gold dome of San Francisco's city hall glistened in the sunshine. Hundreds of cameras snapped frames as the mayor, the governor, and the president approached the podium. Hundreds of cell phones waved above the heads of the crowd in the plaza.

Susan smoothed her beige tunic and adjusted her

taupe scarf before the line of dignitaries reached her. She shook hands with each one, glad when they moved on to Cecily, Gary, Bozidar, Scott, and Edna.

"You look wonderful, Mom," Cecily whispered. "Bozidar said you are more elegant than any of the elders."

"I just wish you and your grandmother had worn something similar."

Cecily glanced at Edna, who wiggled her fingers in a tiny wave. "I think Grandma was tired of robes. We both thought simple business suits would be best."

"You're probably right." Susan motioned to their chairs. "Time for speeches now."

The mayor presented Edna with keys to the city and extended honorary citizenship to all the Schtatikians. Bozidar accepted the document. Firan, Vima, Tolar, Marsel, and all the beige soldiers chittered or squealed in their own clan's version of a cheer. Eleanor and Olivia, standing on either side of the alien critters, indicated when they should be quiet and sit down.

The governor spoke on the value of social media and Silicon Valley's vital contribution to the new era now dawning. Susan pretended to listen, keeping her eyes open by studying the faces of the journalists in the front row. Most of them focused on their recording devices, but once or twice Susan caught the eye of an equally bored and equally trapped reporter.

The president thanked Bozidar for becoming the

first off-world ambassador, Edna and Scott for agreeing to be part of the team that would choose the American ambassador to Schtatik, and everyone else on the dais for some small service to truth and democracy. Susan resisted the temptation to hold her eyelids open with her fingers.

Bozidar spoke next, welcoming Earth into an alliance that would take humanity to the stars. Susan fought a giggle as she remembered the earlier versions of this speech, fueled by exhaustion and exasperation at Marsel's new-found leadership. Her suppressed giggle turned into a gasp as she heard Bozidar introduce Marsel.

All the journalists paid attention now, letting their recording devices do the jobs for which they had been designed. The crowd inhaled as one, and an eager silence settled over the plaza as Marsel approached the microphone.

"My friends," he began, "for I do indeed consider you all friends, thank you so very, very much for embracing your new future. The prophecies of my people all point to a time of exploration, vision, and reward with those who are strangers and yet not. We thought it referred to an alliance of clans that had previously been at odds. Now we know that prophecy pointed to you. Luck and wisdom have brought us to the beginning of a great adventure. I rejoice to live in such a marvelous, wondrous time. Now, my friends, I invite you to join us in celebrating all the future holds, both at the reception which will begin shortly, and throughout the city in private homes and public houses."

He clapped his hands twice and began a chant. The rest of the beige clan joined in the chant. The crowd applauded and cheered, and the more musical tried singing along. Marsel waved his hands as if conducting a choir and brought the chant to a conclusion. A hungry-looking mayor invited all those who held tickets to the reception to make their way there, and all those who didn't to make their way to their own celebrations elsewhere.

Susan sought out Bozidar at the reception. He stood apart from both humans and Schtatikians, far from the buffet tables.

"I'm glad you agreed to become the ambassador, but I'm surprised you didn't choose the UN post," she said.

He shook his head. "I have endured competing voices long enough. Listening to speeches from representatives of all your nations would be far too stressful. I would never be able to return to my natural form, even if our scientists perfect the procedure."

"I'm so sorry. It must be dreadful to look in the mirror and not recognize yourself."

He leaned toward her. "That is not the worst part. I find that I *do* recognize myself, which gives me nightmares."

"Being human isn't all that bad, space boy," Edna said. She carried two plates full of food, one for sweets and one for savories.

"Being human was never my aspiration. It does appear, however, to be my fate. The gods must be very angry with me. Still."

Susan patted his arm. "Perhaps Agnes and Pala will find one of those gods of yours on their travels. I know they'll put in a good word."

Bozidar snorted, bowed, and wandered toward the food.

"You're starting to sound like me, daughter," Edna said. She put her plates on a side table and began to nibble. "Probably a good thing, because you'll be the only Descendant of She Who Found Them around here soon enough."

"What do you mean?" Susan helped herself to a brie-stuffed celery stalk.

"When the president asked us to be part of the team vetting the new diplomatic staff for Schtatik, I thought we would write up a few notes and be done. Turns out we're going to Washington, DC, for a few weeks. There's a new Department of Alien Affairs in the works. Already have someone lined up for Secretary. Really gung ho. Wouldn't be surprised if he had a batty grandmother too." She munched on a cookie. "Wasn't that a hoot about the German chancellor? Her grandmother saw aliens and was called crazy, just like Agnes."

"Alexandra was right, though," Susan said, dabbing her lips with a napkin. "Once Marsel presented her with the tapestry, everything fell into place. The UN, the Vatican, China, India. With so much of the world begging for an alliance, the anti-alien factions faded away."

"Almost faded away," Edna said. "There will still be some pushback. That's why Scott and I will be in DC for a while. We'll be testifying before Congress first. Anyway, Scott suggested that since we would be on the other side of the country, we might as well take advantage of it."

"So you'll be traveling? What do you plan to see?"

"Everything. Or at least as much as we can in whatever free time we get. We'll get a car and start driving. We might even include Canada."

Susan shivered. "I'll miss you."

Edna swallowed and said, "Good. That will make it easier for me to ask you to look after the house. We'll be renting it."

"Everyone is leaving," Susan whispered, more to herself than to Edna.

"Horse hockey. You've got Gary, and three kids now with Marsel."

Susan shook her head. "Change in plan for him too."

"They're not letting him go on the expedition?" Edna gasped.

"Cecily convinced the elders on Schtatik, and the crew of *Cold Fire*, that Marsel could be an asset. Since his vision really saved the mission here, how could they refuse to let him go?"

Edna grinned. "That girl will make a wonderful mother. Who knows, by the time Cecily and Kyle get back you might be a grandma."

"Mother!"

Edna cackled. "Don't tell me you haven't noticed how they are. Wouldn't surprise me a bit if they got married in space. Elopement runs in the family."

Susan scanned the guests until she saw Cecily, Kyle, and Gary talking by the chocolate fondue fountain. Cecily slipped her hand through Kyle's arm. Even from across the room, Susan could see the joy in Cecily's face.

"You're probably right. Do you think Louise knows?" Susan asked.

"Are you kidding? She's the one who suggested that the going away party should double as a wedding shower."

"That may be pushing it," Susan said.

Edna closed one eye and looked to the ceiling. "Possibly. How about an everyone-but-you-knows-you're-getting-married party?"

"Sounds like the same thing to me, but go ahead. You're going to do what you want anyhow." Susan put her arm around Edna's shoulders. "And it will work out fabulously, just as it always does."

"Things have worked out well, haven't they? Even the government is cooperating. I've never seen Congress act so quickly. That treaty with Schtatik will be ratified in less time than it takes to order lunch."

Susan grinned a small sly smile.

Edna studied her face, put down her food and took one step back. "What did you do?"

The sly smile spread, and Susan's eyes twinkled. "I sent every senator and representative a text."

"No! You?"

"Cecily helped." Susan leaned toward Edna and lowered her voice. "I told them that if anyone had a notion to stall on the negotiations, or worse yet, think about a war, the only way to protect yourself from a Schtatikian soldier is a chenille suit of armor."

Edna chucked, "Oh, I can see the press photos already. No one will want that."

Susan nodded. "Exactly. Which is why they made the right choice after I gave them The Chenille Ultimatum."

Glossary

Terms:

blobbling - A Schtatikian child.

havila - A tree from Marsel's prophecy regarding Olivia and Eleanor.

machete - A deadly poisonous plant on Schtatik; contact with chenille has the same effect on Schtatikians.

podling - A Schtatikian sibling.

stotlet - A ceremonial food resembling ice cream.

turgan - A scooter with anti-grav capability; looks like a guillotine with a living rail of ivy that has a symbiotic relationship with the energy collector/blade.

Aliens:

beige clan - One of the largest, with a subclan of taupes. The beige clan has traditionally had female leaders.

blue clan - Also one of the largest clans. They are contentious, especially with the beiges.

brown, green, and red clans - Small, but important. In ancient times, these clans provided the consort to the planetary queen.

About the Authors

Ann Anastasio and Lani Longshore are writers, fiber artists, and entertainers.

Ann plays viola in two orchestras. She is a docent at the historic Santa Fe, New Mexico, hotel La Fonda and the Museum of International Folk Art in Santa Fe, because she loves to learn and share that information. As well as being a museum junkie, she is also an art quilter, and the co-producer of Art Quilt Santa Fe, an annual art quilt retreat. For more information go to: www.artquiltsantafe.com.

Lani Longshore writes a weekly blog at www.lanilongshore.wordpress.com. She has been published in *Eve's Requiem: Tales of Women, Mystery, and Horror*, and in the anthologies of the California Writers Club Tri-Valley Branch.

Together, Ann and Lani entertain quilt guilds as Broken Dishes Repertory Theatre. Their musical comedy productions celebrate quilts and the women who make them.